Dry Tinder

———

Dry Tinder

JANICE C. THOMPSON

ISBN (PAPERBACK) 979-8-218-19976-0
ISBN (HARDCOVER) 979-8-218-19977-7
ISBN (DIGITAL) 979-8-218-21692-4

For Allen, Jeremy and Xander: three
men in my life—father, husband, son—
who never stopped believing that I could
write this story.

*The dry tinder of inequality was everywhere,
just waiting to be set on fire.*
> **Gloria Steinem,** My Life on the Road

*Rumors are like lightning on summer tinder,
producing flames that dance in flickering brilliance
from person to person, sometimes flaring in great
conflagrations of exaggeration before finally
extinguishing themselves in the cold waters of fact.*
> **Stephen Leigh,** Speaking Stones

*In this view, the witch trials weren't an
anomaly; like dry tinder to a carelessly lit
match, the conflagration that followed should
not be a surprise.*
> **Dry Tinder,** from the Appendix

Disputed boundary between Topsfield and Salem Village, 1670-1692

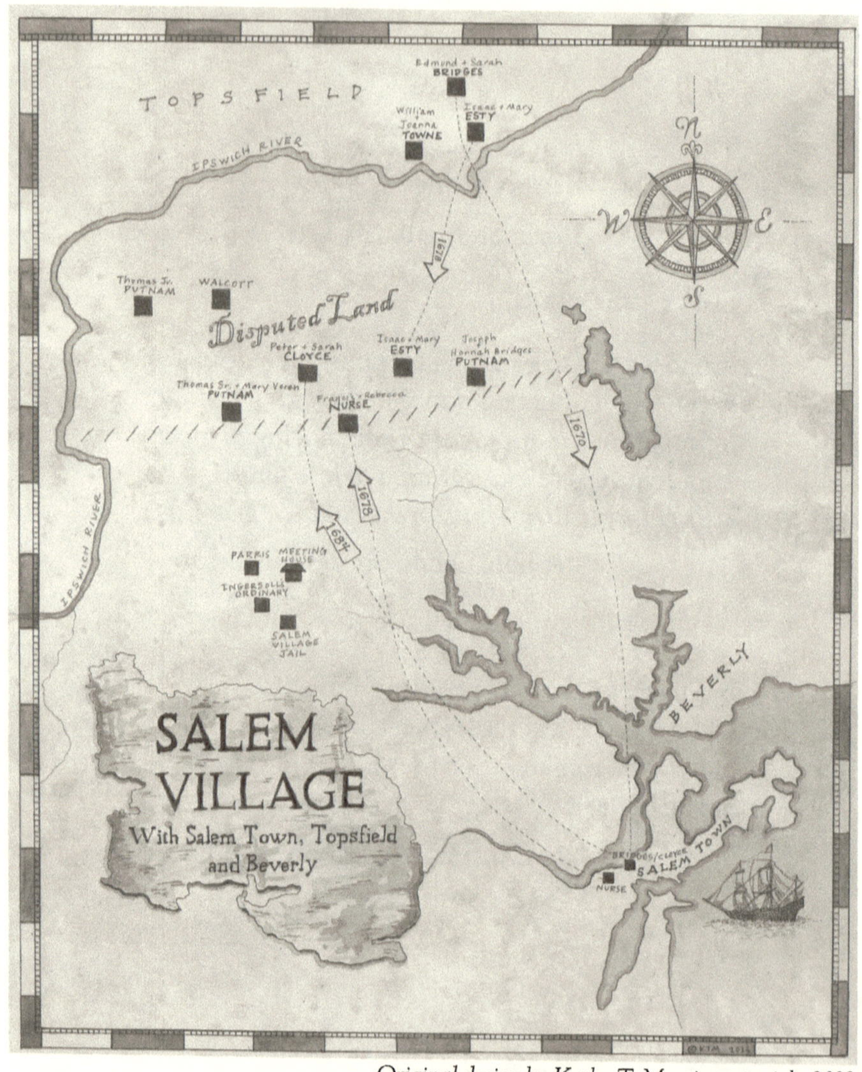

Original design by Kathy T. Martin, copyright 2023

This map is not 100% historically accurate. The locations of some of the actual homes have been simplified for narrative purposes.

Prologue

Salem Town Jail
August 1692

Hands over ears, eyes shut tight.

Was it happening now?

Or, like Rebecca before her, was Mary already dead? Was this the moment the jailer pushed away the rough wooden platform Mary stood on, her tiny body almost too light for the noose to kill her?

Was it happening now?

When they took Rebecca from the jail last month, Sarah had clung to Mary, the horror reflected in each others' eyes. Kind, gentle Rebecca. Seventy-two years, near to a saint, always giving. Sarah's second mother. Dead.

Now Sarah was truly alone. With no beloved fingers to clutch, Sarah's hands pushed hard against her eyes.

Still, the image came.

Mary's tiny body, swinging above a crowd of jeering faces.

Was it happening now?

A ragged boulder of grief choked her. The grime collected in the crevices of her aging body, so many weeks gone without a single washing, meant nothing. Nor did the stench that arose from her skin, or that of the fifty other prisoners crowded alongside her on the dirt floor of the jail.

Right now, all she could fathom was the image of her sister, dangling from a tree.

CHAPTER ONE
1670

Topsfield, Salem Village, Salem Town
Massachusetts Bay Colony
Twenty-two years before the first witch trial

The walk from Sarah's homestead to her sister Mary's wasn't a long one, and the path along the Ipswich River was clear. Sarah welcomed the opportunity to put baby Hannah in a linen sling across her back and get out of the house. Edmund was getting on her nerves with his constant complaining, and besides, it was a lovely spring day in the colony. An excellent time to visit with her sisters, to put aside the constant chores for a few hours. It was always a good distraction, spending time with Mary and Rebecca.

Sarah stopped to adjust one of the makeshift straps of Hannah's sling – the baby had already fallen asleep, her little head dropping – thump! – against her mother's back. She would be out for a long time, jostled gently by Sarah's strong body as she walked down the lane. Sarah took advantage of the quiet by sitting for a moment to rest on a long, sloping slab of granite that pocked the entire surface of the Essex County farms, the bane of the colonists' attempts to tame the land. She loved the feeling of the warming spring sun on her face, and the breeze that came up from the river.

Looking around furtively and seeing no one, Sarah quickly tugged on the string of her white cap and pulled it off her head. She yanked off the thin leather thong that bound her hair into a tight bun. She sighed and closed her eyes, running her fingers through her unruly locks, letting the breeze cool the thin sheen of sweat that seemed always to build up on her scalp under the uncomfortable cap.

She could do things like this when no one was looking, but otherwise there would be hell to pay. The church's tithingmen seemed to be everywhere, watching out for ungodly behavior on the part of the congregation. The elect. The chosen ones.

Sarah huffed aloud, thinking of it.

Rebecca and Mary never complained about anything, not like she herself did.

Why couldn't she be more like her sisters?

Rebecca was old enough to be her mother, Mary almost so. Perhaps they were so similar – and so different from Sarah – because they were old enough to remember their lives back in Great Yarmouth, before they sailed with their parents William and Joanna to the colony in 1635. Maybe they could recall how difficult it was to practice their religion back in England, having to hide from the papists and worship quietly in neighbors' homes. When you have to fight for something you tend to value the thing in a deep way.

Sarah, on the other hand, was born in the Massachusetts Bay Colony, a full twenty two years younger than her oldest sister. She never knew what it was like to have to smuggle a beloved Geneva Bible into a neighbor's home for worship because it was illegal to read anything but the dreaded King James version. Sarah's parents, William and Joanna, risked everything by sailing to the new world, along with so many other thousands of English people. They put all of their hopes in their new home, a place that signified freedom: freedom to live out in the open, to worship God in the way they chose, to maybe even get ahead in ways they couldn't have in England. Perhaps Sarah was born with that newness in her veins, full of promise and wide fields and the chance to create a different model for living.

Regardless of the reason, Sarah would always be Young Sarah to her parents and sisters, no matter that she was now a wife and mother in her own right, almost twenty-eight years old. And don't youngest children tend to be unruly and questioning?

Sarah wiped her brow, loving the feel of the breeze in her hair. Baby Hannah began to snore lightly in her sling. Wasn't it good to be outdoors on a day like today?

A loud crack broke Sarah's idyll, a thunderous noise sounding like a shot from Edmund's musket. Now alert, she gazed over the gently flowing waters of the river to see two young people – two men, probably not yet twenty years old – next to a tall pine tree that was falling to the ground. One man had an ax slung over his shoulder as he watched the tree hit the ground with a crash, its pine branches shaking with the blow. That part of the river was quite narrow but still Sarah couldn't hear what the two were saying.

That's not good, Sarah thought. She knew the acres that bordered the Ipswich River to the south had been in dispute for over thirty years now, a long time before William and Joanna Towne moved to Topsfield with their three daughters. Salem Village farmers who lived near the region to the south and the Topsfield men who tilled the land to the north of the river had been in front of the General Court since 1639, both arguing that the acres belonged to the Village on the one hand and Topsfield on the other.

Her father William used to tell Sarah all about it, bouncing her on his knee when she was a child, eager to hear about the conundrum. She was always interested in the town's goings-on, even though Mary and Rebecca never wanted to hear anything about the dramas, big or small. William himself had been heavily embroiled in this particular dispute, serving as one of the Topsfield contingent before the court. "The Court granted the lands to Salem Village at first, but then the magistrates, in their intelligence, reversed their decision, and since 1650 they have never wavered in their view of it. Those acres belong to us."

Joanna would try to shush William. Sarah's mother never backed down from a fight with her husband, as long as it was behind closed doors. "Be silent, please, husband," she would caution. "Little girls don't need to hear about such things."

But Sarah was whip smart and always wanted to hear more.

William had kept vigilant about the issue, especially when Sarah's sister Mary married Isaac Esty and purchased land south of the river. Isaac was a smart man, too, and even though he did not yet have the resources to tame his new acres, he knew that a farm that spread from the north to the south, over the river, would be a profitable one in the future.

But William had died the year before, leaving the Towne family bereft. And since then no one was really watching what was happening to the south. Even Sarah's brother-in-law Isaac was too busy with his Topsfield acres to make sure his new property in Salem Village was protected.

Even though Sarah had never met the Putnams – William's rivals on the side of Salem Village – she knew in her heart that the people she was seeing across the river were from that family. She felt a pang of dread in her heart. They were cutting down trees on Isaac's land.

Without thinking, Sarah jumped to her feet, waking Hannah, who started immediately to wail.

"You!" she screamed above the noise of the babbling river, shaking her fist in the air. "You!"

The men stopped in their tracks, looking at her from where they stood, shading their eyes with their hands so they could see her. Even from this distance Sarah could see that they were frowning.

"I see you!" Sarah cried. "You, I tell you, are breaking the law!"

The two threw down their axes and walked toward her in a way that made her feel relieved that there was a river dividing them. She stood her ground, though, even as Hannah cried, unhappy to be awoken so abruptly. Sarah, too, approached the river's edge.

"I am not sure who you are," one of the men, a few years older than the other, said gruffly, his words easily heard now that they were closer. "But you'd be better off not meddling in our business and paying more attention to your own state of undress."

Suddenly Sarah realized that her cap was still off, now lying back in the twigs near the rock she had been sitting on, and that her hair was unkempt and flying free.

"Jezebel!" the other man cried out. "Are you not a daughter of God? Shame, shame!"

Every ounce of Sarah's being urged her to argue, anger flooding her body, thinking of her dear father and what he would say in such a situation. "We will never back down, young Sarah." William's words flitted through her memory.

But she also knew the danger that came to women who flouted the church's laws. And modesty was certainly at the top of the list, especially when it came to women. Her mother Joanna had taught her well, too, along with her father. "Do what you will in your own home," Joanna would tell her. "You see how your father and I disagree about things. But never, ever challenge a man when you are in public."

Clenching her fists, Sarah spun on one foot, kneeling to pick up her cap and pulling Hannah from her sling. She hugged Hannah to her chest while she ran – quickly – from the scene.

~~~

"Come in, come in!" Mary cried as Sarah knocked on the heavy door to the Esty homestead, but frowned as soon as she spied her sister's countenance. "What has happened?"
~~~

Sarah handed Hannah to Rebecca, who was sitting in a rocking chair in the corner of the room. The baby had settled since her mother had just nursed her once she got out of sight of those terrible people across the river. Sarah sat heavily on one of the benches at the large table in the middle of the hall. It was only then that she let out a long, drawn out sigh of relief, although her heart still beat furiously. Rebecca cooed to Hannah, tickling her little cheek, but her eyes were on her youngest sister. Something was obviously wrong.

"Just let me sit for a moment," Sarah said, taking the tankard of ale that Mary handed to her. She needed to settle down. "I am most bothered."

Mary and Rebecca knew not to push her. Sarah would often get flustered about this thing or that, and it was best to leave her to it. The woman always calmed down eventually. She hadn't changed since she was a young girl, stomping her foot when she didn't like something.

After several minutes – and several quaffs of the ale – Sarah spoke. "Those people – almost children, they were – across the river. They were cutting down Isaac's trees, Mary! It was truly a travesty!"

"What people, sister?" Rebecca asked, not wanting to get up off her seat now that Hannah was starting to doze once more, her face nestled against Rebecca's bodice. "Why are you so aggrieved?"

"They must have been Putnams, although I have never spied them before," Sarah answered. "And when I called out to them to stop, they came after me, accusing me of undress!"

"Undress?" Mary asked, her eyes widening. She sat next to Sarah at the table and took one of her hands in her own. "What kind of undress were you in?"

Sarah felt like pulling her hand away from her sister's grip, annoyed as she was at Mary's question. It was just typical, her thinking that Sarah had done something wrong. "I was in no such state!" she cried out, sounding even to herself like a petulant child. "I had taken off my cap to catch the spring breeze, is all."

"Wait, wait," Rebecca said, her voice, as always, steady and calm. "Start from the beginning, if you will."

Sarah sighed again. "I was taking a short rest on my way here, and enjoying the spring sunshine and the breeze off the river. To my knowledge I was alone, but for Hannah here. I realize that our hair is not to be seen in public, but I was not in public. I was in God's own sanctuary, doing no one any harm."

"Sanctuary?" Mary asked. "But I thought you said you were outdoors."

"I was," Sarah replied, her impatience growing." God communes with us in all realms, not only within the meetinghouse walls."

She caught her sisters eyeing each other, wary.

"As I said, I was doing no harm, when I spied these two young people cutting down a towering pine tree on Isaac's lands. Anger filled me entirely, as I thought of our dear father, and how hard he worked to protect those acres. Now that he has gone to God, it seems that these people are taking advantage of the void he left in all of our lives. And for them to come after me! It's just atrocious!"

Sarah's last word hung in the air in the room. She knew she was disturbing the peaceful surroundings of Mary's home, and started to feel a bit guilty for it, as she knew Rebecca had traveled the long journey from Salem Town to make this visit. And Rebecca, close to fifty years old, was not as young and spry as she used to be. Sarah put her head in her hands, leaning her elbows on the rough hewn boards of the table.

"One of them must have been Thomas Putnam Jr.," Mary said, patting Sarah's shoulder in a motherly way. "His father is aging and yet newly married, and Isaac tells me that he is not as involved with the farm as he used to be. Perhaps his son Thomas Jr. is taking over for him."

"And you are not angry that he is taking Isaac's property?" Sarah asked, exasperated.

"What's a tree or two in God's wide universe?" Mary asked. "As long as they do not take too much."

Sarah rolled her eyes.

"But young Sarah," Rebecca warned. "You must be more careful with your appearance. You might have thought you were alone, but you obviously were not. We cannot afford to anger anyone these days, not here in Topsfield nor in Salem Village. Not with papa newly dead and mother getting more and more obstreperous every day."

Sarah pouted, walking across the wide pine boards, pretending to check on Hannah who was sleeping soundly in Rebecca's arms. She doubted her sisters ever had a single urge to doff their caps on a sunny afternoon, obedient as they were. She was always more like her mother Joanna, who was as stubborn as Sarah was. But even Joanna handled life in the colony better, restricting her complaints to closed doors, always pious in public.

By now, though, Sarah had learned that getting angry at her sisters did no good. They would never see through Sarah's eyes, never feel overly constrained. She stood, sighing in resignation.

"What is mother doing now?" she asked, sitting back at the table and taking another sip of ale.

"It's her obsession with the minister issue," Mary answered. "And John Gould."

At Gould's name, Sarah's ears perked up and she felt a frisson of anxiety buzz through her. Gould.

"Don't you worry your head about it, young Sarah," Rebecca said quickly, sending a look of warning to Mary. But Mary seemed to be ignorant of the message, and continued on.

"I know you have your own troubles with Goodman Gould, Sarah," said Mary. Indeed that man was the subject of far too many arguments between Sarah and her husband. Would his specter arise here, too, during what she wished would be an enjoyable afternoon with her sisters?

"I don't know why mother is so involved with church matters," Rebecca said, hoping to change the subject. "Perhaps it is the loss of dear papa."

"Mother has always been a good Christian," Sarah said, shaking off her thoughts of John Gould. "But she was never interested in goings-on at the meetinghouse," Sarah commented. "You might be right, Rebecca. She grieves papa."

"I grieve, too," said Rebecca. "But it's frowned upon, you know that. We should not grieve any one of the chosen going to his maker."

At that moment Sarah wished Rebecca would just be silent.

"But what of this minister issue?" asked Sarah.

"She has true respect for Reverend Gilbert," Mary answered.

"And so?"

"So the town is fractious. You know that some do not share mother's feelings."

Sarah glowered. "The poor man is our first ordained minister. Mother is right to stand by him."

"Aye, tis true, but still I worry so about her, especially when

John Gould is trying to get rid of Mr. Gilbert," said Mary. "She is drawing suspicious glances from the villagers. It may be dangerous, going up against a man as powerful as Goodman Gould. Especially now that papa is gone."

Well, then, Sarah thought. I suppose I cannot escape this conversation about the dreaded John Gould.

For years she had no reason to give the man a second thought. She knew that her father, William Towne, was a close friend to Zaccheus Gould, John's father who, like William, had recently passed away. Even though the Townes had moved north after Topsfield had been founded by Zaccheus and a handful of other colonists several years before the family's arrival, William had quickly become involved with the affairs of the town. William and Zaccheus had both been on the team to fight against the Salem Village farmers for ownership of the disputed acres south of the Ipswich River, even though Zaccheus was related to the Putnams in some way that Sarah couldn't recall. The elder Gould would often visit the Towne homestead when Sarah was still a girl, along with his wife Phebe, who always seemed to Sarah to be a pleasant woman. Sarah wished that her son John was equally congenial as his mother was. Alas, John was a mean, nasty creature who was the bane of Sarah's husband Edmund's existence.

"Mother is merely standing up for what she believes is right," Sarah now interjected. "There is no reason why John Gould and his friends should want the minister ousted. The poor man has done nothing wrong."

"May we talk about easier things?" Rebecca pleaded, moving sleeping Hannah from one shoulder to the other.

Dear Rebecca. Always focusing on the good.

Once again Sarah wished she could be like her sisters. Then again, would life seem dull to be so certain of God's love, to never question what the minister has to say? She missed Rebecca terribly, ever since she moved with her husband Francis to Salem Town so many years ago, when Sarah was still a child. She could remember that day, when Rebecca was so young and smiling, happy to wed Francis, a tender sprig of lily-of-the-valley tucked into her bodice. Sarah was just four years old and no one told her that Rebecca would be leaving the house, leaving the bed she shared with Sarah and Mary up in the loft above the hall. She believed that Francis would merely join the Towne family at their Topsfield farm and life would go on as it always had. But joy turned to hounding grief when the new couple rode off in Francis' cart after Rebecca hugged each of her sisters, the scent of lavender wafting from her always-immaculate clothes. Sarah was disconsolate, running after the rickety cart that rumbled down the muddy spring path, her dear sister's back getting smaller and smaller by the minute. The child Sarah screamed Rebecca's name, hoping against hope that the cart would turn around and it would all be a joke.

Because Rebecca had been as much a mother to young Sarah as Joanna had. A desperate fear of the dark hounded Sarah as she realized she would not be able to sleep without Rebecca's warm arms encircling her from behind as they hunkered down in the straw-filled ticking, Mary on the other side, the two older girls singing softly into Sarah's ear.

But Francis Nurse was a traymaker and had to move to Salem Town if he were to support Rebecca and his new family. There were many more people in the town and the homes were built close to each other, housing the men who worked the massive ships in the harbor and the shopkeepers who plied their wares along Front and Federal Streets. That was over twenty years ago, but the three Towne sisters remained close, taking every opportunity to visit each other once all three were married. There were some times when months would go by without Sarah seeing Rebecca – Mary was easier as she and Isaac had stayed in Topsfield – but still the bond stayed strong.

Now Sarah worked hard to put away her worries about John Gould, her mother and the minister troubles, to respect Rebecca's request to keep the conversation simple during this particular visit. It was the least she could do. Rebecca had a difficult life, even though Sarah had not ever heard her complain, not once. The Nurses were happy together but were not financially comfortable, even with Francis' steady income from his business. They never moved up from the small house they rented near the Salem Town wharves, and the rooms quickly filled with one child after the next. The Nurse sons and daughters were now grown themselves and were spread all over the colony, a few in Boston, one venturing west toward Sudbury, some staying in town. It had only been recently that Rebecca had the time to venture north for regular visits with her sisters and parents.

The rest of the afternoon was spent helping Mary snap the peas that had just come to ripeness in the kitchen garden outside the door to the back room of their comfortable saltbox house, and to prepare a venison stew over the fire. It was rare that visits did not involve some sort of chore to be done together; there was always work to be done on the farm. Once Hannah woke up from her deep slumber in Rebecca's lap – Sarah was again reminded of the countless naps that she had herself experienced in those same arms – she played quietly on the floor, chewing on a pea pod and making up stories for two cast-off doll babies that one of Mary's daughters had left when she herself went to her marriage. Hannah was always a good-natured child, if not a bit stubborn when things didn't go her way. Like mother like daughter, Sarah thought.

Once the supper hour approached, Sarah took up her baby and bid her sisters good-bye. Rebecca was spending the night at the Esty farm, as she did not like driving the horse and cart back to the Town in the dark. Despite the angst she felt early in the visit, Sarah was content as she walked the two miles back to her home, Hannah once again securely fastened to her back. She was glad that the two Putnams were nowhere to be seen as she walked the path along the river. Perhaps Mary was right, that if they took down just a few trees no one would suffer for it. If Mary herself wasn't worried, why should Sarah be?

Her good mood didn't last, though, once she entered the door to her home. Edmund was sitting at the table in the middle of the hall, a sheaf of wrinkled papers in front of him. Sarah could see that there were numbers written all along the sides of several of them, and Edmund was holding his head in his hands. She loved this man desperately and had ever since she noticed him when he first walked into services at the meetinghouse almost ten years ago. But he was also the source of great anxiety, as he never seemed content with his lot in life, always wanting to do something bigger, more lucrative. Sarah too had an adventurous heart but was also happy to live her life on a successful farm, near family.

"What is it, husband?" Sarah asked, putting Hannah down on the floor and eyeing the cauldron on its crane in the fireplace. Had she saved enough of last night's chowder to feed them tonight? After the long visit with her sisters she did not feel like starting something from scratch.

Edmund banged the top of the table with his fist, making a racket loud enough for Hannah to whimper. "It will not do," he growled. "This debt to Gould, it is killing me."

Gould again, Sarah thought. Would he never be completely gone from her life?

"You must pay him, husband," Sarah said to Edmund, picking up Hannah, who started to fret when she heard her father's consternation. "Goodman Gould will not stop now that your debt to him rises over one hundred pounds. And not now that my own mother challenged him about the minister trouble. You do well to remember this."

Edmund stared at his wife, incredulous.

"My Sarah, I will pay him the original fee, which is no more than fifty pounds. The fact that he increased his own price after the fact should be no matter to the court. And you know that God forbids usury."

"That may be," Sarah retorted. "Yet Gould has the law on his side. Tis nothing you can rightly ignore."

Edmund poured himself some ale and sat heavily at the table, gazing into the pewter cup in front of him. "It has come to this, has it?" he asked. "Let him come, I say. Let him show his sinful exploitation to the court. I assure you, he will not succeed."

Sarah let out an exasperated sigh. Such animosities seemed to be a regular occurrence in their Topsfield community, which Sarah had always thought was ridiculous, as they were all supposedly a family – a true community of saints – in the face of God. Yet now, with her mother getting embroiled in minister politics and her husband about to be sued, it seemed more dangerous than foolish. She wished Edmund would take things more seriously. What would become of them if Goodman Gould had his way?

~~~

All Sarah wanted was to take care of her small family, to help Edmund in the fields and at his blacksmith shop, to love her sisters and God and her mother. When she was harvesting vegetables from her kitchen garden or nursing Hannah or feeding the animals in the barn or doing any one of the countless chores about the farm, she felt happy. The anger and anxiety and questioning hounded her only when she lifted her head from her daily routine and noticed what was going on around her, when the larger world came
~~~

into stark relief in her mind. Like the Putnams encroaching on her family's lands. Like her mother's making trouble for herself. Like Edmund's money woes and John Gould's part in it.

She didn't want to go to the meeting house to hear Gould's testimony, or to discover what the magistrates had to say about it. But wives always supported their husbands in the colony, especially in public. Harsh words between couples could be punished by a stint in the stocks that stood, warning, in front of the meetinghouse. And so she went with Edmund to his trial.

Rebecca rode up from Salem Town once more to be with her, and Mary sat with them, leaving the younger children with the older ones. The three women grasped hands as they usually did when they were together, and Rebecca put her arm around Sarah's shoulders, exuding warmth and encouragement through her touch. When the proceedings began, Sarah put her head on Rebecca's shoulder, and Rebecca whispered "shh shh shh" into her ear, just like she used to when Sarah was a young child.

The magistrates listened seriously to Goodman Gould's accounting of Edmund's debts and how long they had accrued. Sarah watched her husband from across the room where the women sat, and his face grew darker and darker as the testimony went on. When he was called to the front of the room in front of the three men in dark robes and caps, he seemed almost to jump up and down in his angst.

"What is your response to these accusations, Goodman Bridges?" one of them asked.

"My response is from God," Edmund answered. "Is it not true that His son Jesus Christ rid the temple of the sinful money changers? We must follow His example and do the same here."

The three magistrates looked at each other in amused surprise. "Is it your meaning that Goodman Gould is a money changer?"

"Aye, tis certain," Edmund replied, standing his ground. "Tis true that my purchase was of his iron. Yet he is today claiming to be paid much more than that price."

The magistrates put their heads together, murmuring.

"We applaud your reasoning," the middle magistrate said, nodding his head. "Yet it was agreed between you that the iron would be paid for within a span of two months. Instead of following this order, you purchased more iron, in truth you made several purchases of Goodman Gould, who seems this day to be a reasonable and godly man."

"Godly!" Edmund cried. "He enjoys his wealth. He enjoys influence over our congregation. Tis not the same thing."

Sarah was impressed with her husband's thoughtful rationale. She felt her frustration with him melt away once more into devotion. Surely the court would understand what was really at play here: the unjust treatment of one man by another. The magistrates were ruled by God's word, and God would never forsake Sarah's family. In that she was sure. She relaxed within the embrace of her sisters.

Yet her original fears eventually did come true: after Edmund's testimony, the magistrates ruled that he need pay Gould the full one hundred pounds that very day. Her heart sank as she saw Edmund's body seem to deflate. Fear shot through her, making her fingers tingle and her breath come short. Rebecca patted her back. Mary rubbed her arm. They could say nothing to help.

Sarah knew they did not have a hundred pounds.

And there was her husband, in front of the magistrates, reporting the same fact, asking for mercy. Yet no mercy was granted. He was given two other options: give over the deed to their entire farm, or go to jail.

He looked across the room at Sarah and their eyes locked in mutual helplessness. She tried to reach out to him, but the constable took Edmund out of the room, and suddenly there was just an empty space where he had just stood.

Sarah collapsed into her sisters' arms and wept. "What do I do now?" she cried out through her tears. "What of Hannah? What of the farm?" Although this outcome was what she feared, she had still hoped that Edmund would be forgiven and he would be coming home with her. Now he would be going to jail and her own mother was in decline. What would she do if she hadn't her sisters at her side? She let herself be led out of the meeting house and onto Rebecca's cart.

"God will provide, dear Sarah," Rebecca reassured her, climbing in beside her with nimbleness that belied her fifty years. "God always provides if we just believe in Him."

~~~

Six months later, the Topsfield congregation was sitting through another of Mr. Gilbert's sermons one Sunday morning. The entire extended Towne family -- except Rebecca and Francis and their children and grandchildren, who still attended the Salem Town church -- were present, and all sat in hard pine benches
~~~

with heads dutifully bowed. Men and women on separate sides
of the meeting house, they took up various seats behind the first
rows, where more wealthy families like the Goulds resided for services. As always, the children and servants crowded the benches
up in the balcony above. This mid-fall day was colder than usual,
but no one yet brought the buckets of hot coals that warmed their
feet in the wintertime. Today many shivered underneath warm
cloaks and blankets.

Sarah Bridges had to work hard to pay attention to the minister, who spoke from the high dais in the front of the room, the
simply-carved sounding board above him helping to amplify his
words. She was not the only one in the congregation who noticed
that Mr. Gilbert was slurring some of his words, but none would
dare snicker about it in the meeting house that served that morning
as the house of God.

Since Hannah was still a baby, she stayed with Sarah on one
of the cold benches on the first floor, not up in the balcony with
the older children. The child cuddled up against her mother's side,
trying to draw warmth from the embrace. It had not been an easy
six months for the both of them, what with Edmund still sitting in
the Salem Town jail, none of them knowing when or if he would be
released.

Many hours later after the service was completed, Sarah
clutched her mother's arm as they came to the road that led to the
parsonage. Joanna had been invited by Reverend Gilbert to partake
in the noon meal at his home, and she was excited to be on her
way, but Sarah was holding her back.

"Mother, please do listen to me," Sarah implored her mother,
grabbing her by the hand while holding Hannah in her other arm.
"Do not vex your companions this afternoon. You have been most
obstreperous of late. People are saying that this is unbecoming of
a Christian woman, a member of the elect no less. I fear its consequences."

Joanna looked up into Sarah's blue eyes. The old woman had
shrunk several inches over the years, and Sarah was struck by her
likeness to a withered crone. "Young Sarah, do not worry yourself
over me. I am old and unimportant in the village. My behavior will
not be minded nor remembered beyond this day."

Sarah, not at all placated but understanding that her words
would have no effect, saw her mother off up the hill to the parson-

age on the other side. Hannah pulled at her sleeve, demanding to be fed, so Sarah's focus was diverted. Yet her worry continued. She knew that the Goulds had also been invited to supper, and she did not trust that her mother would keep her disdain for them to herself. Sarah was glad that she had not been invited; she tried hard to keep her composure in front of the man who ruined her life while they were in the meeting house together, but Sarah knew she would not be able to keep her mouth closed in such a social gathering. She feared the same of her mother.

Why Mr. Gilbert invited these two to dine together was a mystery to Sarah. He must know that Gould was working against him -- rumor had it in the town that he was trying to get the current minister ousted so that he could bring in someone more to his liking. It could be that the minister wanted to help Gould and her mother to mend fences, or perhaps to try to gain his affection. But Sarah had to admit, the man seemed more hapless than strategic.

After services were completed for the morning and back at the parsonage, the hall was chilly, as the fire that Mrs. Gilbert had built to cook breakfast had died down to a dangerously low level during the long hours of her husband's sermon. She quickly tended to it as soon as she and her husband's guests arrived at the house, their cheeks pink with cold. Luckily the coals had not yet darkened to black so no one had to trot off to bring back live ones from the next farmhouse over.

The parsonage was a simple structure, with much less decoration and space than Joanna or any of the Goulds enjoyed in their own homes. They all ducked their heads under the lintel of the front door and were initially reluctant to give up their warm woolen cloaks. But Mr. Gilbert was in a jovial mood, happy for the company, and went about taking his guests' wraps and storing them up in the loft so they could all sit together at the table. Mrs. Gilbert soon passed around strong cider in pewter cups which warmed everyone's bellies and hands. Joanna, the eldest in the group, was led to a chair next to Mr. Gilbert's at the head of the table, the only two chairs amid a series of hard benches for the others. Everyone seemed to be on their best behavior. Mr. Gilbert bade his other guests sit as his wife stirred the beans over the fire, sweet with the smell of the syrup from the many maple trees that dotted the landscape outside. John Gould eyed the minister's cup, which was not steaming as the rest of theirs were, and in his glance Joanna could tell that he suspected that a harder drink than cider was swirling around inside.

There were six at the table that afternoon: the Gilberts, Joanna, John Gould and his wife Sarah, and Mary Redington, John Gould's sister. Joanna looked about, wishing that there were more guests present; being the only Towne against three Goulds was a trial that no old woman should have to bear. She worried at the minister's motives for bringing them together. Even she knew that she should behave, despite her protestations to Sarah, but she didn't know if she could hold her tongue if Gould started off with his complaints against Sarah's husband, or the goings on at the church, or -- God forbid it -- berating the dear minister himself.

Once the meal was started Joanna realized that there was no ulterior motive for the gathering, as Mr. Gilbert seemed unaware of any subtle anxiety in his home and the Goulds, despite their surreptitious annoyed glances her way, remained outwardly friendly. After the beans and bread were consumed, Mr. Gilbert made a show of smiling beatifically at his guests, standing at the head of the table and retrieving a silver cup from atop the mantelpiece.

"My brethren," he announced, looking around the room. "I thank you for joining my wife and me on this beautiful day that God hath made through his infinite mercy and grace. As a show of fellowship I pass this cup amongst us, and we shall drink of it together."

The minister's guests were awed at the cup that Mr. Gilbert held in front of them. It was of shining silver, not pewter or wood as all of their own drinking vessels were made. Though all of them had visited the Gilberts at one time or another throughout the years, none of them had spied such a treasure within the parsonage. As Mrs. Gilbert poured a generous portion of wine into the cup, her husband was pleased with the looks of amazement about his table.

The cup was first passed to Joanna as she was the eldest in the room. She sipped the wine with a small motion, tasting the sweetness on her tongue and yearning for more. Yet even she decided it best to be decorous this one time. The rest of the guests seemed satisfied with her behavior, although Mrs. Gould sniffed ever so slightly, just enough that her husband and sister-in-law received her small message of distaste.

"It is a wonderful example of God's great beneficence, this cup," Joanna said. "And we count ourselves most lucky to partake of it with you, Mr. Gilbert. Thank ye. Thank ye, most assuredly."

She passed the shining cup to Mr. Gilbert, who was obviously taken with her words, and most grateful.

He took the cup from her and took a most heavy gulp from it, enjoying how the warmth of the drink suffused his whole being. As he finished and put the cup back down on the table, he expected to see smiling faces of people joining in his contentment and camaraderie.

But he was disappointed.

The Goulds and Mary Reddington stared at him in disbelief. Momentarily surprised, Mr. Gilbert looked down at the inside of the cup. He had inadvertently emptied it in his excitement and joy.

"What a goodly drink, Mr. Gilbert!" Joanna cried, noticing the horror of the guests at his gaffe. "We are much graced with such a hale and hearty host!"

Smiling weakly, Mr. Gilbert bade his wife pour more wine before the cup was passed to Goodman Gould to his left. Mrs. Gilbert scurried away to quickly fill the cup once more. Her husband passed it to Gould, and bade him drink.

John Gould took a deep breath, knowing it would be remiss to chide the minister at such a gathering, and on a Sunday no less. But he was unhappy, as he had been for a long time before this. He believed in the importance of sobriety and decorum in a minister, and this was just one more instance of Mr. Gilbert's devilish behavior in public. Yet calling him on it in the hospitality of the parsonage would be equally disturbing.

The cup was passed from guest to guest, with dainty sips being taken by the rest, and nods of polite thanks made. Joanna carefully watched her neighbors' demeanor, and without warning felt very tired. A shiver ran through her, as if a cold hand was dragging itself down her spine. Her resolve to stand by Mr. Gilbert was unwaning, yet she suddenly found it exhausting to be so contrary against the powerful Goulds. Was it age that was bothering her? It had certainly been difficult to be without William, who had been such a close partner to her for so many years. Without his genial reminders to calm herself, her edges seemed sharper, her opinions more intransigent. Why was it she who often had to say what others were thinking? Why weren't her neighbors braver, more willing to tell the truth?

The meal was quickly finished and goodbyes were said without more conversation. It was time to get back to the meeting house for the second part of the Sunday services. After she wrapped her cloak around herself, Joanna held back from the other departing guests, not wanting to hear their disparagements of her and her loyalty to Mr. Gilbert.

"Dear Mrs. Gilbert," she said. "May I take another cup of cider before I leave? The weather turns cold and my old bones creak with pain when the damp comes in."

Mrs. Gilbert, who rarely said anything, silently went to fetch the cider for Joanna. Mr. Gilbert was still in good spirits, regardless of the black looks he had received from his congregants. Joanna supposed that the alcohol he had imbibed throughout the morning and afternoon had an easing effect on his mood.

"I am grateful, Goody Towne, for your presence today," he said, placing his hand on her stooped shoulder. "Sit a moment more while you enjoy your cider."

"Thank ye for your kind invitation," Joanna said, grateful to put off her walk back to the meeting house for now. She took the warm cup from Mrs. Gilbert, drank from it, and asked, "I have always supported your ministry here in Topsfield, sir, ye know that?"

"Aye, I do," Mr. Gilbert said, joining her at the table. "And I am also aware that not all congregants are of your mind, Goody Towne. Tis true, I see what their eyes say. Tis no matter. I continue to speak the word of the Lord."

Joanna eyed him over the rim of the cup, her eyes narrowing. "Tis good that you do," she said, but was shaking her head. "But I fear no good will come of this trouble. I fear it most awesomely."

~~~

Joanna's trepidation was founded. The Goulds proved unwilling to let go of what they deemed as sinful behavior on the part of the minister. Even as the farmers were hard at work bringing in their crops, gossip flew from homestead to homestead: about Mr. Gilbert's over-imbibing, and about Goody Towne's support of him. Indeed the next time the Boston magistrates came to Topsfield, John Gould formally accused the minister of drinking too much. All of the guests were summoned to testify to what they saw that Sunday afternoon. As Joanna sat in the meeting house with her daughters Sarah and Mary close by, she was dismayed to hear that the Goulds not only spoke of the silver cup at supper, but of Mr. Gilbert's
~~~

supposedly intemperate behavior during church services. They reported his forgetting the blessing, being late to the meeting house, and slurring of words. Joanna clutched the hands of her daughters, outraged at the injustice she was seeing right before her eyes.

Sarah whispered into her mother's ear: "Be peaceful, Mother. How would father have admonished you at this moment? You need to be careful, speaking out against this family of all families."

Sarah saw her sister nodding, having overheard her words. She also saw her same worry reflected back in her sister's eyes.

Yet when Joanna was called to testify, she uttered not a word to defame Mr. Gilbert. She spoke of the generous spread that he and his wife provided for their guests, and of the beautiful silver cup.

"I was at dinner at Mr. Gilbert's table that sacrament day," she said, "and sat next to him on his right hand, and though some report that he drank too much of the sacrament wine; then, that his eyes grew dim and that he sank down in his chair. Yet I believe he is wronged, for that I sat next to him, and saw no such matter."

An audible gasp could be heard throughout the room.

But Joanna's testimony held little weight in comparison to the views of the powerful Goulds. In the end the court chastised Mr. Gilbert and bade him leave Topsfield. When Joanna heard the verdict, she slumped in her seat with such sadness that her daughters had to hold her up on either side of her, lest she fall to the floor.

"I beg you, mother," Mary whispered as the rest of the participants filed past them to the bright outdoors. "Please leave this be. It is of little concern to us. You are but a widow, and an aged one at that. You know that you cannot fight the court. Nor can you fight against such families as the Goulds."

"Nay?" Joanna cried, her eyes flashing. "Then why do your husbands continue this land feud with the Putnams of Salem Village? Should they also bow down to wealthy, powerful clans as they?"

"That is different," Sarah replied.

"Aye," Mary agreed, sighing. "They are men."

Once the meeting house was cleared, Mary and Sarah pulled their tired mother up off her seat and made their way out the door. They were chagrined to see that most of the participants in the hearing were milling about the yard, their heads together, whispering. Sarah was filled with a fierce pang of loyalty to her mother, and squeezed her hand harder, bidding her, without words, to rise up with head held high. And with that resolve, the three women wove through the crowd, although the looks they received were fierce.

"Witch," they all heard someone hiss. "Goody Towne is a witch."

~~~

When Sarah put baby Hannah to her breast to feed her, she shivered as the merciless cold of the room assaulted her bare skin. She quickly drew the baby to her and covered both of them with her woolen cloak. It was December and the hall of the Bridges homestead was colder than usual. With Edmund in jail and Sarah trying to care for Hannah as well as keep up with the farm chores, there was none but Mary's Isaac to cut wood for them this winter. And dear Isaac, so generous and kind, was getting worn out, Sarah could tell. With seven mouths to feed and supporting his own family, the man certainly had his hands full. And he was still having to deal with the Salem Village Putnams who continued to insist that part of Isaac's lands actually belonged to them.

The dire worry that had overwhelmed Sarah as she watched her husband hauled off to jail six months before hadn't abated since that terrible day. She had visited Edmund several times over the weeks, desperate to know that he was well, and they both had managed to maintain the facade that their respective lots were satisfactory -- yet grim. Edmund told his wife that he believed it was only a matter of time before he would be set free, although he never gave a reason for expecting as much. The debt was still outstanding and John Gould was not backing down.

Sarah knew that the extended Towne family would never let her or her children go hungry or homeless, and for that she was most grateful. Still she couldn't let go of the stark fear that kept her awake at night, especially in the last week, as Mary brought her word of yet another Indian massacre up north, in the District of Maine. As Sarah lay in the bed that used to hold her husband along with the baby, she missed Edmund's strong arms around her. Mary and Rebecca used to complain of her tossing and turning in their shared bed when they were girls, and when she first married she had worried that her nighttime habits would disturb her new husband as well. Yet from the first night they shared together, when Edmund had fallen into blissful sleep with her in his arms, her nocturnal stirring ceased for good. She felt safe with him, and even when they were worried over some issue or other -- the ongoing debate with Gould, or the random accusation by a tithingman that
~~~

a member of the Bridges family had somehow strayed from God's stern dictates, or trouble with their cow's milk production -- she slept soundly.

But recently, even as baby Hannah slumbered peacefully next to her, Sarah felt cold and alone. Life in the colonies was never easy, but without Edmund it seemed impossible. Worry. There was always worry. Her father was gone and her mother had somehow given up after the Gilbert debacle. The entire congregation seemed to have turned away from Joanna, even though in her younger days she had been considered a member of the elect, and a strong believer in God. With Mr. Gilbert gone and no minister in the pulpit, Joanna had taken to her bed, unwilling to engage with anyone. This was a blessing in disguise, as her absence from the meeting house and the cessation of her engaging with any one Topsfield resident probably saved her from any further public utterances of witchcraft. With Edmund in jail, and the continuing boundary disputes along the Ipswich River, Sarah didn't think she could handle any more attacks on her family. And she knew accusations of witchcraft could mean death, as practicing evil magic was a capital crime in the colony.

Sarah drew her strength from Joanna, even after she married, as she drew her strength from her sisters. But with Joanna taking to her bed, Sarah felt less secure with every step she took. It was like the ground beneath her was shifting and she was in danger of losing her balance.

Of course she couldn't show her fear or weakness to Hannah, nor even to her sisters or brothers-in-law. Just a few days ago Sarah found Mary eyeing her closely, uncertainty written all over her face. "Young Sarah," her sister had said. "You walk about with seeming strength and confidence. Yet I suspect that you suffer without your dear husband. I do worry for you. Perhaps it is time to consider moving in with Isaac and me?"

But Sarah had dismissed this suggestion, and her sister's worry. She carried on.

Her frustration was at a high pitch on a Tuesday morning, when it was bitterly cold outside and Hannah was fretting more than usual. Sarah was trying to mend Edmund's old shirts, but had to keep getting up from the chair in front of the fire to rock Hannah in her basket on the floor.

It was then that the door crashed open and none but Edmund himself walked into the house, shaking off the snow that had

collected on the shoulders of his cloak. Sarah jumped in fear that
quickly transformed to utter joy as she looked up at her husband,
shocked into silence.

Edmund laughed his hearty laugh. "What, is this a fitting welcome for a man who has been away from his family for so long?" he
kidded. "What silence awaits me? Tis truly a shameful sight!"

At that, the momentary spell was broken and Sarah ran to
Edmund, embracing him and kissing him at the same time. Hannah
started crying at the tumult, and Sarah broke away to lift the baby
into the wonderful moment.

"Edmund, Edmund! What has brought you to us?"

"Tis God's blessed grace, my dear one," her husband responded, sitting heavily at the table. "Now bring me some ale, if
you would, and I mean to give thanks to the Lord and His good
providence."

Sarah ran to the cask in the corner of the hall, the one that
Isaac had repaired just the week before, and dipped a wooden cup
into the liquid inside, sloshing several spoonsful over the side in
her excitement. Edmund drank a long measure and patted his belly.
Sarah noticed that his pants hung loose on him.

"Now bring me nourishment," he ordered in good humor.
"For the provisions in the Salem Town jail have been sorely lacking
and I have a grave hunger."

It was only then that Sarah came down to earth enough to
notice the reek that emitted from her husband's clothing. His hair
was lank and she feared the onslaught of lice. Suddenly her strong
desire to wrap him in her arms was usurped by her duty to keep the
house clean.

"Go now first, Edmund," she instructed, pointing to the door.
"Get to the barn and a barrel of clean water and lye. You carry the
stench of jail on ye, and I must have a godly household before such
infestation carries into these walls!"

Sarah, her heart still racing, picked up Hannah and hugged
her tightly. "Sure tis your father, bonny baby," she cooed into the
child's soft ear. "Sure tis good days ahead."

Although the larder was depleted by that time of year, especially since Edmund left, Sarah prepared a feast for her husband's
homecoming and asked no more questions. Instead she regaled
him with small stories of what had transpired at the farm since his

departure. The candles on the table and the fire roared with life, as Sarah no longer worried so that the logs would soon be depleted. Edmund bounced Hannah on his knee until she giggled uncontrollably. As Sarah watched her small family about the table, with faces glowing and happiness in great abundance, she felt the ghostly hands that had constricted her chest in worry slowly release their grip. Edmund was home. All would be well.

But trouble returned in a very short time. The family feast was over, stories told and laughter laughed, and Hannah was put down in her basket next to the bed in the corner of the hall. Sarah climbed into the quilts that now felt warm and inviting rather than cold and lonely, eager to embrace her husband in welcome. His newly clean body felt strong and secure, albeit thinner, as he joined her in the darkness. She kissed his face and he pulled her to him as she sighed in great relief.

"You are here," she whispered to him. "My thanks to God is truly great."

"Aye, as is mine," he said, and she could sense the smile in his words.

"Yet you must now tell me the story of your release," she admonished, pulling the bottom of his ear as she was wont to do in jest. "Goodman Gould did forgive your debt? Perhaps we were wrong about his intentions toward this family."

She hugged him tighter to her, but a shiver of cold ice shot through her as she felt his body pull away ever so slightly, his arms relaxing almost imperceptibly. She waited for him to speak, yet he did not. She waited several moments more, her reward a muffled groan rather than a happy response.

"Husband," she said, more a statement than a question.

His silence continued. The cold she felt turned to ice in her bones. She sat up, unable to make out his face in the shadowless dark.

"Husband," she said again. "Do speak, I beg of you."

He sat, too, although she still could not see him.

"Please, Sarah," he finally said. "Have a glad heart at my return."

"I am most happy, and relieved too," she retorted, her words constricted in her throat. "That is not to be debated. I must know, though. What is our predicament now?"

She noticed that he did not embrace her. All of the happiness that she had felt earlier in the evening dissolved, and a sense of dread, returned in full stead.

"Tis not such a burden, wife," Edmund said. "Yet there is indeed a price to my release."

This time it was Sarah who remained quiet, bracing herself for what would come next.

"I have lost the farm."

His words seemed to hang in the cold dark between them, as sharp and biting as the icicles that hung from the eaves of the house outside. Sarah had no words with which to respond. She tried to speak, but she choked instead. Coughs overtook her, until Edmund patted her on her back to calm her. The fit seemed to last forever as she struggled for breath. The ghostly hands of fear that had her chest in their grip for so many months moved back to her throat, dry and cruel.

"My dear Sarah," Edmund pleaded. "I beg of you. Please. It brings me great pain to see you so distressed. Please believe me, we will not be lost. While the sale of the farm will complete my debt, it will also provide enough for us to start a new life. I have plans for us. God will provide."

"Plans, Edmund?" she asked, words finally coming to her, each one feeling like a blade in her throat. She did not scream. Instead she spoke with a simmering anger that scared her husband more than diatribes. "Always plans. Always something better that is awaiting you around the corner. Where do these plans leave us? It does occur to me that they are bringing ruin with them."

"Shh," Edmund said, pushing her cap off her head, running his hands through her loose and unruly hair. "I do assure you. All will be well in our new home."

"New home?" Sarah was not to be placated. "Where is this new home? I do hope it will be here in Topsfield."

"Nay," Edmund answered, and the excitement in his tone was hard to miss. Always looking for the next adventure. Sarah clenched her hands under the sheets so that she wouldn't reach out to try to strangle him. "Tis in Salem Town, right near the wharves. I met a man in jail who wanted to travel further west into the colony, into the wilderness. He told me he would sell me his little ordinary right on Front Street. He says it does a nice business, but he's sick of life in the city. I thought you would be happy; it is not three blocks from Rebecca and Francis' home."

The noose-like grip that overtook her throat released enough to let loose a great wave of anger. All of the trials she had endured over the past months, the meager rations she had fed Hannah, the work that overtook her so that she felt she could fall to the ground in fatigue, the shame she felt in relying on her sisters for sustenance, all came flooding back to her. And for what? Why must her husband be so stubborn? Why must he always be more concerned with his ambition than with the well-being of his own family? Why could he not have been satisfied with the fate that the Lord had given them? She wanted to scream in frustration.

"Salem Town!" Sarah finally raised her voice, not even noticing whether she would wake Hannah. "Salem Town! That is a full five miles' ride from here, a good half day! Aye, Rebecca and Francis and the children are there, to be sure. Yet what of my ailing mother? And Mary and Isaac? What of our congregation, the saints with whom we have prayed and suffered and praised the Good Lord together? What of our life, Edmund? What of that? And who are we to run a drinking establishment? Do either of us have experience doing anything like that? I think not!"

Edmund put his large, solid hand on her arm, and somehow it felt more like a punishing weight than a comfort. It was the sure sign of his ownership of the family, and by extension, her. His hand was certainty, it was the futility of changing her fate. It was God saying to her:

You have no choice.

Wives have no choice but to follow their husbands.

Sarah grunted, pulled the blankets away from Edmund, turned and dropped into the straw-filled mattress, her back to him. The way she had missed him for so many months, the open love she had felt for him since they were married, all of those good feelings just fell away, dissolving into the night.

She wished for the comforting arms of her sisters, not her husband's. She closed her eyes tightly and prayed to God that she was a young child again, before all of these problems, when she would fall asleep in her parents' loft nestled warmly between Rebecca's and Mary's bodies, the two older girls humming their favorite hymns to Sarah, whom they treated as if she were their own little doll. The aroma of that evening's meal still wafting gently upwards from the hall below – Joanna was an excellent cook – and the sound of the pops and crackles of the fire in the hearth.

She made those golden-colored memories chase away the punishing anxiety that Edmund inflicted on her.

"Whither thou goest," she whispered, echoing Rebecca's oft-quoted Bible verse, drifting off into troubled sleep."I will go, too."

Salem Town and Salem Village
Massachusetts Bay Colony
Fourteen years before the first witch trial

By now – eight years after she and her family made the move south from Topsfield to Salem Town – Sarah was used to the clamor of the drinking men in the hall of their small home on Front Street. She usually heard it from the back kitchen, where she tried to keep up with the constant orders for sweet cakes and stews that filled the customers' bellies and staved off drunkenness. When she and Edmund first opened their drinking establishment in the front of their new rented home, the noise bothered her. She was used to the peace and broad vistas of their Topsfield farm so many miles inland, and by contrast Salem Town and its harbor felt dirty, crowded, and most of all very loud. The houses were built close together, and the bustle of the ships in the harbor and the nearby wharves never stopped. The streets were filled with people speaking all different languages, having docked there from countries around the world.

Sarah did not enjoy sweating over the fire while also making sure that Hannah, now close to nine years old and becoming as stubborn as her mother was, stayed out of danger in the streets. At first when they moved she could not help showing her hostility at her husband's brashness. And as the years wore on, her sharp rage ripened into a dull bitterness for being thrust into this situation. Her resentment only grew as she watched Edmund acclimate himself to their new environment with such ease and happiness. They were almost penniless after renting the tumble-down house so close to the harbor, but Edmund took to the town with excitement, meeting men with ambitions similar to his: men who were bent on rising from farmer to the ranks of wealthy merchants whose warehouses were stuffed to the walls with wine from Spain, sugar from Barbados, and all sorts of goods they received in payment for their exports. The metallic smell of money was in the fetid air that came off huge hulking ships on the harbor, and Edmund was hooked, even though at the time they were barely scraping by.

Sarah missed her family terribly, especially in the years since Joanna finally died, feeble and spent, never able to come back to her strong-willed self after being rejected by the congregation in Topsfield. In a way Sarah had been relieved when they found her mother's lifeless body in her bed: it was a blessing that Joanna's suffering ended. And it had frightened all three Towne sisters, how the Topsfield congregation had shunned their mother on the few times she mustered the energy to get to church. Ever since the Reverend Gilbert affair, the whispers of witch persisted. If Joanna had been more interested in engaging with the community, the accusations might have grown from rumor to a court case, and that was the last thing any of them wanted.

But Joanna's death did come hard to Sarah, although she felt she had already lost her mother back when she moved out of Topsfield. Of course Mary remained there with Isaac and her children, and she seemed so far away. Sarah's only solace was the fact that Rebecca lived so close to her new home. Rebecca was a godsend, especially in the early years when the Bridges moved south.

It was Rebecca who had urged her young sister to accept her new life, reminding Sarah that the move was God's will, and a wife's duty was to be the husband's support, especially in times of struggle.

"Oh, Rebecca, you are too good," Sarah had responded to her sister's admonishments those many years ago during her first years in Salem Town, sitting hard on a rickety stool at the table. Hannah was at the wharves watching the arrival of a ship that had been to sea for the last year and a half, waving her arms in welcome along with a whole row of lads, not seeming to notice that she was the only girl in the group. Sarah had no idea where Edmund was. She felt her family was scattered to the winds, and she had no control over it.

She had glared at Rebecca, who was looking more and more like Joanna every day, especially now that she had a full head of white hair that creeped down her shoulder under her cap. "It's easy for you, sister, to be godly. It always has been. I have more trouble than you."

Rebecca smiled. Whenever she did that, it was difficult not to smile as well. A radiance came from her deep blue eyes and her face was filled with peace and an openness that sometimes made

Sarah want to wrap her arms around her sister in protection. Sarah's frustration started to drain from her body, and she put her face into her hands.

"May the good Lord in heaven help me," she muttered. "I am most unsatisfied."

Rebecca put her warm, worn hand on her sister's arm, still smiling beatifically. "I know your heart, young Sarah. God has bestowed upon you a soul more curious than the rest of us. It is our dear mother living through you. But remember when you were but a young child, you always welcomed change and new adventures. Can you not regard this new life as one of those new things?"

"I am trying, believe me," Sarah admitted, rising up to sit. "It is my husband's propensity for deal-making and advancing in the mercantile world that most worries me. It was this attitude that lost us our farm."

"Aye, I notice this in Edmund, and so too does my dear Francis."

"'Tis true that Edmund has begun to apply his considerable talents to practicing law, and he draws clients from these Salem Town men," Sarah countered, trying to convince herself that his new source of income might be more steady than blacksmithing had been. "Perhaps that will settle him."

Her sister had been right: Sarah had always enjoyed new challenges. And through the ensuing years it eventually felt a relief to work in the busy town, to sometimes lose herself, to not be so worried about the prying eyes of the Topsfield congregation. After what those people had done to her mother, she was glad to be rid of them. She and Edmund and Hannah attended the Salem Town church, and there were so many congregants there that they could avoid frequent contact with Mr. Higginson, the stern reverend. The minister acted as if he were a one-man army against the rising sin of places like Salem Town and Boston. Indeed just the week before, the minister spent several hours warning his flock of the danger of moving away from their faith and turning their faces toward gluttony, adultery, drinking overmuch and flaunting the Sabbath. He spoke of the famous church leader Increase Mather from Boston, and how he and a group of high-ranking ministers were meeting to write a formal epistle against such excesses. "Our Lord God said in Isaiah 59 verse 21:" he cried out to the congregation, "'And I will make this my covenant with them, saith the Lord. My Spirit that is upon thee, and my words, which I have put in thy mouth, shall not depart out of thy mouth, nor out of the mouth of thy seed, nor out of the mouth of the seed of thy seed, saith the Lord, from henceforth even forever.'!" Reverend Higginson pointed his bony finger at each of the congregants. "The Lord himself is telling us we need to keep the faith of our fathers, those brave men who left their homes in England to create a new Jerusalem for all of us on these savage shores!" Higginsons' shouted words made some of his flock feel that he was looking into the darkness of their own souls. "Ye merchants, ye shipbuilders, ye tavern keepers! You are all moving away from these truths! Woe be to you!"

The men? Sarah thought at the time. Didn't women travel on those ships as well?

This woeful message was becoming more and more frequent in Mr. Higginson's sermons, as he and his fellow conservative ministers were growing increasingly worried that with each new generation, the people of the colony were moving further away from God. Fewer younger people were professing their position among the Lord's elect, so they could not become voting members of the church. Sarah knew that the Salem Town church was filled with many who were not members, and did not see a problem with that. These people were as devout and prayerful as their neighbors who enjoyed full membership in the congregation. But Higginson and Boston ministers like Mr. Increase Mather believed that this was a sign that God was turning away from the colony, and they were sore afraid. Without the Lord's blessing, the people were in danger of all sorts of evil in the wilderness, all brought to them by the Devil himself. The wars with the Indians that had just ended were another sign of God's wrath. Those battles had claimed hundreds of lives, not only on the frontier to the north, but also the Narragansett Bay to the south, and not one family was without a death due to the evil hands of the red devils. There had been more casualties in the Indian ranks throughout the three years' war, but it certainly wasn't an avowed victory on the part of the settlers. The colonists had lost enough lives and land to make many of the church leaders feel like they were collectively losing the battle against the Devil.

Some of the Boston ministers had come up with a solution for the ever-decreasing number of God's elect a good fifteen years before, but many men like Mr. Higginson thought it was a travesty and did not allow it in the Salem Town church. This new church rule – called the Half-Way Covenant – granted partial membership in the church to offspring of the elect. These new young members were not required to prove that God had shown them that they were his chosen, but otherwise they followed all the other church rules. And most important of all, those halfway members could baptize their children into the church.

When some New England congregations adopted the covenant, Sarah and Edmund had been in their early years of marriage still living in Topsfield, and the Reverend Perkins had approved of the new rule. The church had been a fledgling one at the time, just as Topsfield itself was, and the more lax membership restrictions helped the congregation grow. Both Sarah and her husband had already had the conversion experience many years before, so the rule didn't affect them one way or the other. But when they moved to Salem Town they were surprised to hear Mr. Higginson rail against it to such a degree. Edmund told her it was because the minister thought the entire town was a den of iniquity, what with the rising fortunes of the merchants who exported the colony's timber, fish and grain and imported wine from Spain and rum and sugar from Barbados on their great ships. These men sailed many thousands of miles and saw cultures much different from their Bible Commonwealth home. They were more interested in lining their pockets than in being righteous, and the port town was teeming with them. And shopkeepers like Edmund profited by keeping their bellies full of demon rum.

Edmund didn't mind the minister's castigations, and Sarah tried to follow her husband's lead. Before they opened the ordinary they were hardly getting by, and often Sarah had to accept baskets of food from her sister Rebecca, who could hardly afford it herself. The Bridges family had been forced out of Topsfield for unjust reasons, with Goodman Gould taking over their small farm because of Edmund's debts. When Sarah thought about the unfairness of it all, she could easily sink into a rage. How dare that pious Mr. Higginson rebuke them for eking out a living the only way they could?

~ ~ ~

Once Sarah had grown accustomed to the bustling activity of their new home, she began to feel intensely interested in eavesdropping on her customers' conversations about news that came to the wharves from the great merchant ships from England and the islands of the British West Indies. She never told anyone what she knew, not even her husband, as her knowledge of English politics would be regarded by most in the colony as unseemly and unfeminine.

Even in such an urban place as Salem Town, the goings-on back in England seemed far away. It had been eighteen years since Oliver Cromwell died and the restoration of the Stuart monarchy had been hard won by the people of England. The Massachusetts Bay Colony settlers were no more a fan of the new king, Charles II, than they had been of his father who had been beheaded by the British people decades before. But at least elder Charles had, for the most part, left the Colony to its own devices – as long as taxes were paid and the great crops of New England were sent back home. And Mr. Cromwell – the man who led British armies to dethrone Charles I and had ruled the country for years – was as much of a laissez-faire ruler as the King had been. In the meantime, the New Englanders had created their own form of government, elected governors and magistrates, divided up the land among them, and were united in allowing only the godly to worship in their church-es. Quakers, Antinomians, non-believers: they were all killed or banished in the collective efforts to maintain the righteousness of the colony.

But now that Cromwell was dead and a king installed back in England, Sarah was hearing more of the merchants at the Bridg-es' ordinary complain about the new king's incursions into the workings of the colony, and they didn't like it. They didn't like it one bit. Just the other day when Edmund was out, Mr. Hathorne himself – one of the most influential magistrates in Salem Town – came to their establishment for refreshment with his friend George Corwin, an equally respected town leader. Both Mr. Hathorne and Mr. Corwin were well-celebrated for leading their troops to victory in the three years' Indian war just ended. But that day they weren't talking of the Indians: they were ranting about the King's meddling in colony affairs.

Sarah almost tripped over herself as she served the men their cakes and ale. Rarely did men of such renown frequent the ordi-nary, and she felt unusually nervous.

"Charles thinks he can govern the colony better than we ourselves can," Mr. Hathorne was saying. "He keeps sending his commissioners to these shores, meddling in our dealings, accusing us of moving unlawfully into the Districts of Maine and New Hampshire. These interlopers know nothing of our dealings with the men of those territories, nor with the red devils."

"Aye," Mr. Corwin agreed. "It does seem hypocritical. England needs the timber from our great forests for her ships' masts. The need is constant, and it sends settlers further into the content just to feed it."

"Tis a difficulty," said Mr. Hathorne. "But worse is the King's attempts to allow Episcopalians free worship within our towns! Aye, and Quakers too!"

Mr. Corwin laughed and tipped his cup to his friend. "A lot of good those edicts do on this side of the Atlantic Sea. Every person in this colony, from Governor Bradstreet on down, ignores such idiocy."

Sarah already knew of this attempt at religious freedom on the part of the English King. She had heard Reverend Higginson rail against Charles' supposed "laws," pointing to them as just one more bit of evidence that the colony was falling into the hands of Satan himself.

At that point, the two men's voices grew quieter and they moved in closer to each other, whispering conspiratorially. Sarah chose that moment to approach their table and fill their cups once more. As she walked away, she caught enough pieces of their conversation to realize that they were discussing some investments they had just made in the merchant ship Patience. The King had tried to wrangle more money out of the colony through several navigation acts over the past ten years, dictating that New England exports be sent directly to the mother country. Because the Bridges' ordinary was located on Front Street, directly on the docks, she had heard many shipmen before these talk of how the investors worked around these acts, trading with places like Barbados and Bermuda without the King's knowledge. From what she could catch from Mr. Corwin and Mr. Hathorne, the Patience just embarked on such a clandestine voyage.

While the two men appeared confident, Sarah knew that there was much worry among the colonists about how far the King would intervene in their lives. The charter establishing the colony that John Winthrop brought with him from England back in

1630 still dictated the rules, and it gave the settlers a great deal of freedom in governing itself. Now with each passing year there was a greater and greater danger that the new King would revoke the charter, and it was making the colonists very nervous.

Sarah had sighed then, wringing her hands within the cloth of her apron. Uncertainty, doubt, worry: it seemed that her life would never be without it. If Edmund were a more settled man, interested more in his own hearth and family rather than his own ambition, Sarah would be of greater comfort. She was glad, at least, for the bonds she felt with her sisters and their families.

At that moment, Sarah was overwhelmed with the need to see her sister. Rebecca could always bring peace to her baby sister's soul.

~ ~ ~

But just three days later, Sarah was in no better mood. Indeed, as she sat at Rebecca's hearth with a cooling tankard of tea in her hands, she stared into the blazing fire, refusing to speak. Her two sisters were at each side of her, touching her arm and shoulder, Rebecca with her head bowed in prayer. Mary watched her younger sister closely, worried at how wide her eyes were, transfixed by the fire in front of her. Sarah's eyes were a light blue that seemed as deep as a pool of water, and often they hinted at a mischievous twinkle. Right now, though, they seemed clouded, lost.

"Dear, dear Sarah," Mary said, grasping at her sister's free hand and urging her to look away from the fire. "Do not turn away from us."

Rebecca's white-haired head bowed even deeper as she whispered an "amen" and looked to Sarah, too. "Aye, sister," she begged. "Tis not such bad news. God is with you, as are Edmund and your beloved daughter."

Sarah shook her head in anger and frustration. Just an hour before she was beaming, happy to discover Mary at Rebecca's home as she entered the small house, not expecting such a surprise. When Sarah lived in Topsfield it was Rebecca who had to make the trip north to see her two sisters; now Mary was the one who had to travel to visit Sarah and Rebecca. It was rare that Mary could actually get to Salem Town, as the Esty farm was like a beast who would not be sated, with all the work it required. And even though the eldest of Mary and Isaac's eight children were growing quickly toward the age of twenty and could be counted on for much help in the fields and at the hearth, her youngest were but four and five, and she was seldom without them at her side. Today, though, Sarah was delighted to have both sisters to herself, with none of their children in tow. She couldn't remember the last time such a gift was bestowed upon her, and she greeted both women with warm embraces and laughter.

The good humor was not to last, though, as Sarah quickly discovered why both Mary and Rebecca were part of the visit. Before she could even ask them for their advice about her fears for both Edmund and the perilous fate of the colony, the two older women sat her down at the fire and told her their news.

"Dear Sarah, when I heard that you were to visit, I sent word to Mary to join us," Rebecca said, handing Sarah her tea and beckoning her to the best chair in front of the hearth. "Our husbands have made some decisions for our families, and we wanted to tell you what they have deemed God's will."

Sarah's happiness turned to sudden fear, and a chill ran down her spine. She had been experiencing many such phenomena of late, and she didn't like it.

"What, sisters, what is the news?" she asked. "Your faces are riddled with fear."

"There is nothing to fear, dear child," Rebecca cooed as if a mother to a babe, although Sarah was well past thirty. "Part of our tale will benefit you, to be sure."

Mary smiled at her sister and said, "aye, Rebecca is right, as Isaac is moving our farm to Salem Village, and we will not be so far away any longer. Our home will be not five miles from your door!"

Sarah stared up at Mary, her dark eyes and thin frame, almost ethereal in her countenance.

"Why, sister!" Sarah cried. "This is indeed good news! You frightened me with your long faces and downturned eyes. I will be most grateful for such a move!"

"And I as well," Mary agreed.

"But do tell," Sarah went on. "Why such a change? You have been most contented in Topsfield, have you not?

"You well know of the ongoing struggles between the Putnams and Isaac over those acres south of the Ipswich River," Mary replied. "With our land in that area unsettled and left without the oversight that papa used to give it, you were right in your fears so many years ago: the Putnams continue to encroach. First it was a tree or two; now it has become whole swaths of land. Isaac believes that we can no longer live so far away from our own property, lest those Putnams trespass further."

"For some time the danger of that family's constant suits was lessening," added Rebecca, "as Thomas Sr. and his brothers grow old as I myself do. Francis tells me that Thomas especially has little patience for such squabbles over land, not with the new lease on life he received when he married Mary Veren."

Sarah chuckled. She and her family attended the Salem Town church, but until the farmers of Salem Village were finally able to convince the church elders to allow them to build their own meeting house several years before, the Putnams and their neighbors had to travel to the Town for Sunday services and lecture days. So Sarah saw first-hand the slightly untoward love that old Thomas had for his new young wife, and how it turned some heads in disapproval. At the same time she espied his children's disdainful looks at not only Mary Veren but their much younger half-brother Joseph, who had been born to Mary and Thomas Sr. not a year into their marriage. Joseph was a pleasant, chubby young boy, on whom their parents bestowed obvious coddling. She herself never minded the display. It reminded her of her early days with Edmund, when they were so happy, before the trials with Goodman Gould developed in earnest.

"Aye, I would understand such a thing," she agreed. "Good for him. I am glad for him."

"Yet Thomas' son, young Thomas Jr., now assumes the Putnam mantle," Rebecca interjected. "Your Isaac now has to contend with the younger one's complaints. The struggle continues."

Sarah shivered, remembering the scene, so many years ago, when she was accosted by this Thomas Jr., who called her a Jezebel across the Ipswich River.

Salem Town and Salem Village were two very different communities, even though they shared a boundary between them. The inland Village was almost as rural as Topsfield to its north, with family farms dotting the landscape, while Salem Town, right on the harbor, was almost as populous and bustling as Boston. The Estys' move south to Salem Village would draw them nearer to Sarah, and they could continue to expand their acres across the Ipswich River.

Maybe with both her sisters close by, Sarah could feel safe instead of worried that her husband was going to end up in jail again.

"So wait, Mary," said Sarah. "You will be moving to Salem Village, but what of your Topsfield farm? You and Isaac and the children have worked for years to make it thrive."

"He has given the Topsfield farm to our eldest son. You know John has been married for several years now, and with the second baby on the way, he is ready to run his own place."

"While I am cheered by this news, I wonder about the move, sister," Sarah said to Mary. "Do you really want to live so close to the Putnams? I fear it will escalate our disputes over that territory."

"It must be done," Rebecca said, with more force than Sarah was used to. "Now that both mother and papa are gone, we daughters must be sure to finish what papa started. We cannot stand by while the Putnams tame more of our acres every year. The good Lord knows that I do not wish ill will on anyone. But we also need to protect what is ours."

"Let us not talk about those dreaded Putnams," Sarah advised, shaking her head to rid herself of those young people's rageful looks so many years ago. "I do love the two of you. You are my second hearts. Let us talk about that instead."

She felt Rebecca's warm hand on her own. "And you are mine, dear sister," she said. "We are blessed to have each other. But God is the true one who helps us in times of need."

Sarah's eyes opened again and she peered into Rebecca's face. What she saw there brought back the feeling of dread that had momentarily left her. "Am I embarking on a particularly hard time of need, Rebecca? To be sure, I already have my burdens to bear. Edmund does continue to trouble me."

"Edmund is rarely satisfied with his lot in life," Mary spoke the words that they already knew. "It worries us all that he is so."

"Aye, you are right, Mary," Sarah said, folding her arms and sitting back hard in the chair in front of the fire. She had started the conversation and she wanted to finish it, disagreeable as it had become. And she knew that her sisters had not yet revealed the entirety of their news. "Edmund is troublesome. I thank God every day that neither of you are pressed to deal with similar lots."

She wondered how Rebecca or Mary would feel if they had to suffer so with their own husbands. Both Francis Nurse and Isaac

Esty were good, solid men, the salt of the earth, really. For years Sarah had watched as her sisters moved through their lives, partnered so easily with their helpmeets. They were not accustomed to being left alone late into the night while their husbands were out somewhere, trying to make some deal or other. They were not accustomed to worrying about where the next meal would come from, or whether they would be able to pay the rent. How easily they criticized Edmund. Edmund gave them plenty of reasons for that. Sarah could be satisfied with her own complaints, but when Rebecca and Mary voiced the same thoughts, Sarah's ire was stoked.

Her sisters joined Sarah once again in front of the hearth.

"I know, dear sisters," Sarah muttered, feeling more like a petulant child than she would have liked. "I know you have more to reveal to me. I am discontented; it is good that you tell me now, rather than waiting for a happy moment."

So Rebecca quietly told her sister that she and her family, too, were moving, but it was in the wrong direction: north to Salem Village, away from the Bridges. Rebecca and Francis had lived in the same small house in Salem Town since they were married over thirty years ago, and their grown, married children had been begging them for ages to move inland, where there was much more land to farm. The couple had lived simply for their entire adult lives, and Francis never made much money in his tray-making trade. But their eldest daughters had made good marriages to men who clamored for property. Their two sons-in-law – Thomas Preston and John Tarbell – had recently purchased the entire Bishop Farm in Salem Village. The farm had enough acres for the entire Nurse clan – starting with Rebecca and Francis, but also their married and unmarried children alike – to live there. Rebecca and her husband couldn't pass up the offer, and besides Rebecca longed to remain in the bosom of her dear children. She would miss Sarah terribly, but an added bonus to the move was that Mary and Isaac's new farm would be right next door up in the Village.

This was when Sarah went into her rage, staring into the flames of the fire.

She felt as if Rebecca was the single thing protecting her from madness, living in such a busy town and trying to raise Hannah with an overly ambitious husband. In the beginning of their marriage Sarah and Edmund were happy together, living simply up in

Topsfield. Sarah's rebelliousness matched her husband's, and she envisioned an easily compatible relationship much like her parents' had been. But now she didn't have time to feel her own liveliness, because she was too busy making sure Hannah was fed and the ordinary stocked and running. Her mother was no longer there to talk to, and neither was Mary, for all the time it took to travel to her. And living and working in town took Sarah away from the granite-pocked fields and tall pine stands that she loved on their old farm. Rebecca's dear smile, so close by, so like a mother, had helped Sarah to follow God's word and be satisfied with the life she lived. Just last week Mr. Higginson urged the congregation to be content with their lot, quoting Matthew in verse six: "If that is how God clothes the grass of the field, which is here today and tomorrow is thrown into the fire, will he not much more clothe you—you of little faith? So do not worry, saying, 'What shall we eat?' or 'What shall we drink?' or 'What shall we wear?' For the pagans run after all these things, and your heavenly Father knows that you need them."

But now without Rebecca, how would she get by?

~ ~ ~

Despite what it meant for Sarah's fate, Rebecca and Mary were excited to move to Salem Village – Mary from the north and Rebecca from the south. Their husbands and sons-in-law had already spent many months building their homesteads, having broken ground as soon as the snow had melted.

But they weren't necessarily greeted with the warmest welcome from all of the Salem Villagers. They expected as much. The Putnams had lived in the Village for generations, and were largely considered some of the most powerful people in the congregation. Over the years they had amassed a following of other families who, like them, had been the first to settle the area. Most of the group knew of the long-standing arguments between Salem Village and Topsfield over the disputed territory south of the Ipswich River, and even though many had never met any of the Towne sisters, they shared the Putnams' resentment for their adversaries. Mary and Rebecca and their families were often met with frowns when they entered the meeting house on a Sunday morning.

Mr. Burroughs, the current minister in Salem Village, was quick to introduce himself to the Estys and the Nurses even before they had built roofs over their heads. The newcomers found him to be a solid man of God, perhaps a bit more casual than they were used to, but honest and friendly.

As soon as their home was built, Mary and Isaac sent their younger children to spend time with their Aunt Rebecca so they could invite Mr. Burroughs to dine with them.

After the meal was served, Mr. Burroughs sat back on his chair and put his hands on his big belly. "Twas a truly satisfying meal, Goody Esty," he said. "You have provided such a bounteous feast for me, and I am most heartened to welcome you to our flock. So it is difficult for me to bring up a troublesome topic. Yet I must let you know of your neighbors' feelings toward you so that I may be an instrument of God in healing the wounds among you."

Isaac put his hand on the minister's arm and smiled openly at him. "Nay, Mr. Burroughs, do not fret. I believe I already know of your news. Our families have been at odds with the Putnams and their ilk for many years now. We have disagreed about land bounds since Mary and I married. Yet we remain in the right, as the General Court has always found in our favor."

Mary rose from the table to replenish the trencher with more fish stew from the fire's cauldron. Isaac was sounding sanguine, but she herself did not feel the same way. She was well-aware of the troubles with the Putnams, but she had hoped that when Isaac moved them south, the Salem Village contingent would finally, after so many decades, concede that the land was theirs. They were all getting older, and she felt that when age approached, such tussles would seem frivolous. But Mr. Burroughs' news dashed that hope.

"I am most relieved that you already know some of the consternation in the village," the minister was saying. "Yet there is renewed fervor, given your brother-in-law's purchase of Bishop Farm."

Demure as she was known to be, Mary had to clutch the trencher hard in order to remain silent. Rebecca? Who could possibly be angry with anything that that dear woman touched? The Nurses had purchased land toward the southern part of the disputed territory, an area that had never been part of the countless court cases, far enough away from the Ipswich River not to bother anyone. What could possibly be wrong with that?

Isaac continued to seem nonplused. He actually chuckled at the minister's words. "What of it?" he asked. "This seems beyond even old Thomas Putnam's attention."

"It wasn't old Thomas who told me of the concern. It was his son, Thomas Jr. Mind you, that entire family has little love for me, either," Mr. Burroughs said, shaking his head in sadness. "They were the ones who brought my predecessor to the Village. And when he left, they were most unhappy."

Now this, indeed, was news to both Mary and Isaac. They had noticed stern faces on the countenances of the Putnam brood at the meeting house, but that didn't seem unusual for them. Mr. Burroughs now told them the entire story. The people of Salem Village had struggled for years to separate themselves from Salem Town, not wanting to pay taxes to a church so far away from their farms. The worst problem was the long trip it took for those in the north to travel to the Salem Town church several times a week. But the magistrates and the ministers in the Town were not keen to let a whole section of their boundaries secede, as they depended on the taxes for their salaries and upkeep of the town buildings.

Nevertheless, five years ago the people of Salem Village were successful in getting approval to build their own meeting house and to establish a church. The Putnams were at the head of the contingent who fought for such freedom. They took it upon themselves to seek out a minister to lead them, and quickly found a man named James Bayley. Mr. Bayley had been young – only three years out of Harvard College – but the Putnams found him to be an appropriate minister. He was from Newbury and newly married to Mary Carr, the daughter of a wealthy merchant in Salisbury.

So Mr. Bayley had come to Salem Village with his wife and her youngest sister, Ann, who was twelve years old at the time. At first the villagers welcomed the new minister, and were pleased to begin to worship in their own neighborhood.

Soon, though, some of the villagers had started to complain about the pastor. Mr. Burroughs still couldn't figure out exactly what was the problem, despite his questioning of the anti-Bayley faction after the fact. But what he did discover was that these parishioners were unhappy that he was chosen by such a small group of people. The Putnams had many friends in the Village who agreed with the move. But other neighbors weren't comfortable with this one family dictating such important decisions as the selection of their religious leader. Their spiritual lives were much too critical to be so controlled by mere men of flesh. Their faith depended on the congregation – a group of the elect who together created a communal worshiping of God. The Putnams' recruitment of Mr. Bayley was anything but collective.

The two sides of the Bayley controversy argued with each other for years, and eventually Mr. Bayley departed, just the year before, and took his wife with him. The only one left was Mary's sister Ann, who had, throughout the entire debacle, won young Thomas Putnam Jr's heart. The two married before the Bayleys departed.

"Ach, this sounds very similar to the problems we had with our minister up in Topsfield," said Isaac. "My mother-in-law supported Mr. Gilbert but others did not. It ended badly, with Mr. Gilbert being forced to leave and Joanna Towne being castigated as a witch until her dying day."

"Why must people quibble so about our religious leaders?" Mary couldn't help but interject. "It seems most ungodly."

"Aye, tis true, but I have no answer for you," Mr. Burroughs agreed, and continued the story. "And then there was me. Some of the villagers reached out to me and inquired of my interest after Mr. Bayley departed. My wife and I had just returned to Salisbury after spending years in the Maine territory. We had heard about the fate of the cast-out minister, and we were most concerned about meeting with similar trouble. But there were no other congregations seeking a leader, not since we escaped King Philip's War up north, and my wife was duly terrified of living in the hinterlands."

"You saw firsthand the ravages of the Indians, Mr. Burroughs?" Mary asked, sitting down at the table and seeking out his eyes. She and Isaac had heard of the raids, of course; everyone had for these three years, but she had never personally met anyone who lived in a town that had been attacked. Topsfield and Salem Village had put together their own militias to ward off the bloodthirsty savages, as had all towns in the colony, but they were lucky not to have been challenged. Mary knew most of the devastation was suffered at the outposts of the colony – like the isolated towns in Maine to the north.

"Aye, we did," Mr. Burroughs replied, downcast and wringing his hands. "I do not like to talk of it, Goody Esty, forgive me. Our entire town of Falmouth was taken, and the bloody images I have of that day are near to the very depths of hell. I just thank the good Lord that in his wisdom he chose to spare my dear wife and me. But she will have nothing of going back, and insists we stay close to civilization."

Mary lowered her eyes in shame for bringing up such a disturbing subject, and said no more. The horrid skirmishes with the Indians had only just been resolved, and the people of the colony were still broken from it, with so many settlers' lives lost. It was not an easy time for the people of God, who worried that the scourge was the Lord's punishment for their collective sins. She couldn't blame Mrs. Burroughs for wanting to stay close to the village, no matter the troubles that the previous minister had suffered.

"I tried my best to begin my ministry in a most constructive fashion," Mr. Burroughs was saying. "I acknowledged the past hurts of the village and attempted to prevent future suffering by accepting a smaller wage from the congregation and gathering everyone together in prayer and days of fasting. Yet the Putnams have spoken against me almost from the day we arrived in Salem Village."

He held up his cup to Mary and she quickly arose to refill it from the ewer at the sideboard. Her heart went out to him, as he seemed to her at that moment a lost soul rather than their religious teacher. "I am most sorry for this state of affairs, dear Mr. Burroughs," Isaac said, putting his hand on the minister's arm in comfort. "I wonder at the continued animosities among the people of the Village. What are your thoughts on this? Can we not all together worship the Lord and live in peace?"

Mr. Burroughs took Isaac's two hands into his own, and bowed his head as if in prayer. "You pose a most meaningful question, Goodman Esty," he said. "I hope that despite the ill feelings God will still show me the way to bring the congregation together. But I do think that our brethren like the Putnams seek to control what happens in our village. They are most wealthy and wish to stay that way. They worried when their choice of minister failed. As do they worry at your brother-in-law's purchase of the Bishop farm."

Mary looked up once more at the mention of Rebecca's family. The food having been eaten, she cleared the table of the wooden plates and left the men to speak together, although she continued to listen closely to their conversation.

"Aye, what of that, Mr. Burroughs?" Isaac asked.

"I will tell you, but please acknowledge that I do so not out of gossip, but because I want to warn you and your family. And I do know of it because young Thomas Putnam told me himself."

"I appreciate that," Isaac said. "But was it truly Thomas Jr.

who spoke of trouble? We are well used to dealing with his father, yet Thomas does seem quite young."

"Time does move us all forward. And as I did say earlier tonight, the younger Thomas is now full grown and a husband to Ann Carr, Mr. Bayley's sister-in-law. It seems that he is taking on the family's head. That is how it seemed when he told me, not three days before, of his consternation with Goodman Nurse."

"This does not bode well, to be certain."

"The Putnams do not like when men do rise above their station."

Mary clenched her fists under her apron. The gall! The hypocrisy! Who but God chooses who is to be rewarded and who is not?

"And they believe that the Nurses gain unfairly from God's beneficence?" Isaac asked. Mary could tell that he, too, was feeling vexed.

"I believe they do," the minister replied. "I try very hard to soothe their worries so they do not spread ill will to the other church members. Alas, they have little patience with me. They know that the Nurses had little when they lived in Salem Town, and for many years. Now they wonder how it can be possible that they abide so lavishly, on such desirous acres."

"I hope you reminded them that this business is nothing to concern themselves with!" Isaac's voice was now loud and he sounded most definitely irked. "And besides, why is it wrong for the next generation to thrive in this new world, and to share their wealth with their elders? That is exactly what happened with the Nurses!" Mary stood behind Isaac and rested her hands on his shoulders, more in a sign of solidarity than to soothe him. She looked defiantly at the minister, as upset as her husband. Yet she could see that Mr. Burroughs did not share the Putnams' opinions, and he looked ashamed to have to reveal them.

"Aye, of course, brother Isaac," he said. "Yet once again I have little sway. I do apologize. I reveal this to you so that you may do the same to Goodman Nurse, and to keep watch for possible intrigue from the Putnams. I will do my best to defend your family's good standing in the church. I know you all to be most righteous folk, and beyond reproach on this matter."

~ ~ ~

As the Estys were having this troubling conversation with their minister, newlyweds Thomas Putnam Jr. and Ann Carr Putnam were dining in their large home with two others. Thomas' sister was named Deliverance, and they were quite close, sharing a mutual disdain for their younger half-brother Joseph. The siblings were just two years apart and used to spend many a night at their father Thomas Putnam Sr.'s house when they were young, watching with anger how the elderly man, acting twenty years younger than his advancing age, flirted outrageously with his new wife Mary Veren and coddled their baby Joseph. Deliverance had recently announced her engagement to Thomas Jr.'s friend and neighbor Jonathan Walcott after a year of courting under the watchful eye of their father Thomas Sr. Now Thomas Jr. sat at the head of his own table, and looked around at his guests with great satisfaction. The meal was bountiful and the fire warm in the hearth. His father had granted him one hundred and fifty acres of his own farm when he married Ann, and his first harvest was planted. He felt strong companionship with his new wife, who had already proven herself to be a most admirable servant to God and to her husband's needs. She had been happy to move from her sister's home to his when Mary Bayley left the village with her minister husband, although Thomas and the rest of the Putnams were sorry to see that family go. His father and uncles were instrumental in recruiting Mr. Bayley to Salem Village, and were quite bitter that so many parishioners had been against them. Thomas' younger sister seemed to have taken the slight in stride, yet he himself could not let go his resentment. He had grown up on the reality – set by God Himself – that the Putnam family were leaders of their community. Had not his father and his uncles for years presided over the front row of benches in the meeting house that they themselves paid for?

Deliverance began to worry about her brother's consternation over the Bayley decision, but Ann was the consolation prize as the Bayleys departed. Ann saved him. She seemed to Thomas like a wounded bird, someone to care for him but also to care for and protect. She was a nervous woman but that did not bother him, as she was such a devout churchgoer and kept a neat home. Their marriage was a welcome distraction, and Thomas' anger at his neighbors abated.

This night the young people talked animatedly with each other, the women demure and the men feeling pride of ownership

– although none would admit it, as pride was a heinous sin in the eyes of the Lord.

"Friends!" Thomas called, interrupting the various conversations around the board. "I am filled with happiness this day, to have you all join us in our home. I am struck with the joy of God's grace. Ann and I welcome you."

Sitting next to him, Ann blushed and looked down at her lap, pleased but preferring less of a demonstration from her new husband. She was new to wifehood and was still getting used to it, having been coddled by her dear father in Salisbury and then by her sister while she was young. When she lived with her parents and then with the Bayleys she had at least two house servants, and was rarely put upon to do any menial chores. She used to spend most of her day reading the Bible, obsessively seeking evidence that she was one of God's chosen. Sometimes the more she studied the more she worried, even though she sought solace in the scripture. She had been particularly intrigued with what the disciple Peter wrote: "Be alert and of sober mind. Your enemy the devil prowls around like a roaring lion looking for someone to devour. Resist him, standing firm in the faith, because you know that the family of believers throughout the world is undergoing the same kind of sufferings." The Devil was terrifying to her, and at times she could almost see him, lurking in the trees, trying to grab at her skirts as she walked down a path. Her fellow church members were frightened of the same thing, and indeed warding off the dark serpent was the subject of most of the Sunday sermons. Yet for Ann her trepidation seemed just a bit more sharp than most, and she worked extra hard to be free of sin. It kept her awake at night.

These days she and Thomas – who was drawn to her because of her piety – made use of maidservants as she always had, since he was wealthy enough. But now that she was a wife she was required to direct the goings-on of the house and hearth. A natural worrier, she fretted over these new responsibilities and mourned her sister's absence. Her mother was too far away, still up in Salisbury with her father and the rest of the Carr brood. She was most thankful that her sister-in-law Deliverance had come to her rescue, jumping on any excuse to leave the elder Putnam's homestead. The two women were about the same age and had become like close sisters almost immediately, although Deliverance was quite a bit more insouciant than Ann. Even though Deliverance was never called upon to run a household, as her father had married Mary Veren very soon after her mother had died, still her stepmother Mary had burdened her with a great deal of the chores ever since baby Joseph came along. So she well knew how to put up the harvest vegetables, spin and weave flax, manage a kitchen garden, brew beer, cook all sorts of fish and meat stews, bake bread and make quilts. And she was a good teacher to Ann, who as a result managed to appear knowledgeable enough to convince the servants of her wifely authority.

Even now, as Ann ducked in discomfiture at her husband's mention of her name, she grasped Deliverance's hand under the table, and her sister-in-law returned the squeeze. Ann was glad for her presence, the only other woman in the group. And she was glad that of late she had been able to return Deliverance's favor of help by answering her questions about married life. There were some things that Ann could not bring herself to discuss – such as what happens between a man and wife when they take to their bed at night – but in general she felt she was setting up her sister-in-law in good stead as she was about to embark upon God's calling to marry.

The two men at the table were slapping each other on the backs while the women eyed each other in admiration, responding to Thomas' welcome with good cheer of their own.

"And, to add to my happiness, I am thankful to our dear Lord above that we are finally free of that Mary Veren and her sniveling brat, Joseph," said Thomas.

For the past eight years the barely-contained animosity between the elder Putnam children and their stepmother had not abated. Neither had the favoritism shown by their father to their younger step brother Joseph, now but ten years old. Thomas Sr. was growing old. The reins of the family were slowly passing to the next generation, and Thomas Jr. especially was eager to accept them, yet he and Deliverance still resented their young stepbrother. Joseph was amiable enough, and had a comely look, often trying to climb on his brother's and sister's laps when they visited. But Thomas and Deliverance couldn't accept him for anything but an encroacher on their birthright, and would inevitably shoo the young boy away, rejecting any opportunity for affection.

"Indeed, and now we will soon be fathers in our own right, if God sees fit to bring us children," Jonathan said. "It is good that we have such fortune, even if we live in precarious times."

"Ach, my dear friend!" Thomas' tone was chastising. "Why bring up trials at such a wonderful time as we are enjoying?"

"My sincere apologies, and I do not intend to mistreat your hospitality, Thomas," Jonathan responded, taking the piece of dark brown bread that his betrothed handed to him. "But you must agree with me, there have been troubles. And troubles most likely to come."

"Oh, please do not speak of my beloved sister's departure with Mr. Bayley." Ann cried out plaintively. "It is indeed most heartbreaking for me. I do miss her so."

Thomas covered her hand with his own, and he felt the tiny bones quake with anxiety. "We shall not, my dear," he soothed, and gave Jonathan a warning glance. "We shall not."

"Nay, I am not thinking of that, although it is most distressing to be sure," Jonathan continued. "And I would die before doing anything that would hurt you, Ann. I am referring, instead, to the place that our Topsfield foes have taken in our village. Now they are members of our own church, and purchase great plots of land. Does this not worry you?"

"We have certainly battled with the Townes and the Estys and the Nurses for many years, and it is true that the borders between our farms are still not decided," Thomas agreed, not noticing that Ann's hand was tightening uncomfortably under his.

"And what of the Nurses, purchasing up some of the most productive land in the Village?" Jonathan went on.

"Aye, tis certainly a mystery," Thomas Jr. agreed. "What kind of sorcery have both of them called upon, the Nurses and the Estys, that they rise so high in rank?"

It was Deliverance who had had enough. She knew it wasn't her place, and that she should let the men continue their talk. But her dear friend Ann looked like she was about to faint, and Deliverance herself could not abide the despair that was descending on the gathering.

She stood up, pounded the table with her hand, and demanded: "That will do, my brothers. Do cast your eyes upon our dear Ann, she is as white as the linens she brought with her to this house. Jonathan, I am most sorry but you anger me and I cannot abide such talk any longer. I am taking Ann outside so that we don't have to hear such devilish worries."

Ann almost collapsed with relief, but did not rise until Thomas gave her a slight nod, giving permission for her to go. She ran away from her seat, her head bowed and hands clasped, following her much stronger sister-in-law out the door.

CHAPTER THREE

1686-1687 · Eight Years Later

Cambridge, Salem Town and Salem Village
Massachusetts Bay Colony
Five years before the first witch trial

15 June Anno Domini 1686
Town of Cambridge
Massachusetts Bay Colony

My dearest brother Richard,

I send you this missive with the fondest wishes for your good health, and the well being of your wife and children. You are all in my heart each day that the good Lord God grants me, even these six years since you departed the colony to seek your fortune back in England. I am well, as are your sisters and brother Samuel, although with advanced age we all suffer at times with physical maladies. Mary as ever aids me in my travail on this earth, and endeavors to keep a pleasant disposition, although we both remain in grief over the death of our beloved son Thomas whom God took from this life just these two months ago. Thomas was fighting for God on the side of the colony against the Indians to the south of here, and we remain most proud of him, though terribly bereft. We have lost many children as you well know, mostly before they took many breaths on this temporal plain, and Mary does mourn them still, even as we are blessed with grown grandchildren by our daughters. The Lord does heal our wounds, however, and we are blessed to know that all is according to His wise and loving plan.

News from the colony, however, is not agreeable, and it brings much suffering. With the King's recent demise in England and his son's rise to the throne, affairs in Massachusetts are thrown yet again into great disruption. Mr. Bradstreet and I have been replaced as governor and his lieutenant, although we have served in those roles these ten years past with the approval of the local magistrates and ministers. We were most aware of the troubles that Charles II posed for many years before his death, and as you are aware I

worked most avidly to protest his increasing encroachments upon
the colony. Many believe that these efforts aided in maintaining our
way of life here on these shores, and that we would ultimately be
left to serve God and tend to our business in the way we had done
for three generations.

Yet now the new king has appointed Sir Edmund Andros as
his royal governor and has taken away our colony's charter: the
very one that allowed our very existence here since 1629. We are
now a place of utmost crisis. Sir Andros, although just arrived in
Boston these six months, has already made many outlandish and
aggravating changes. He has had built a new meeting house on
the public burying grounds and has deemed its use to be enjoyed
by Anglicans: the people we were wont to dispel from our towns
because of their papist beliefs. He demands that families who have
farmed lands for five decades provide evidence of the ownership of
their acres, and some grants have been rescinded. He levies burdensome new taxes on the merchants and yeomen both, and we struggle under their weight. Not only have Mr. Bradstreet and I been
taken down, but Andros has disbanded the General Court in favor
of his own appointees.

Truly this is not the Massachusetts Bay Colony that has been
the Danforth's home since you and I sailed here with our father
and brothers and sisters when we were barely children. Now at age
66, I find it most difficult to understand such transformation, even
with God's help. Indeed, our colony's name has even been cruelly
rent from us, and now we are to live in The Dominion of New England rather than the Massachusetts Bay Colony.

Many of our ministers tell their congregations that this is a
most grievous sign that God is in fact angry with us. Brother Samuel leads his church in Roxbury with this very belief. Word spreads
through the land that our sins have brought this torture upon us.
You do know that the Danforth family has always been devout,
and I do maintain the practices that our father followed when he
was a deacon in our church back in Framlingham. Many of the
young here in the colony, alas, are moving away from the church.
There exists a great deal more drinking, fornication and taking the
Lord's name in vain than when we were children and the colony
was new. Perhaps it is true what the ministers preach. Perhaps we
are doomed.

I believe with great certainty that my beloved wife and I are

among the elect, and I praise God that our children have followed
our path. I do hope that you, too, my brother, continue to follow in
the path of the chosen. This is truly the only way to salvation, even
in the midst of these treacherous times.

I remain truly yours, brother, in blood and in faith.

Thomas Danforth

Thomas Danforth – until recently the colony's Deputy Governor – looked up from his writing table, took off his spectacles and
rubbed his tired, red eyes with one hand. His heart was heavy with
the news he had just described to his brother. The parlor in which
he sat was well-appointed with a Turkey carpet and mahogany
furniture and a fire in the hearth, but his spirit was not cheered by
the warm surroundings. Mary, his wife, had already retired to their
bedchamber and he was glad of it. Her melancholy about their
son's death in the Narragansett Bay Indian skirmishes continued
to hound her, and he didn't want his own downtrodden mood to
further sadden her.

A knock came at the door, and Thomas rose with his candle
to answer it. It was late for callers but he did not mind the interruption. Company might be a welcome distraction.

The man standing outside was his friend Samuel Sewall, the
respected judge from Boston. As the hour was advanced, Bow Street
was deserted, save for the visitor. Thomas quickly ushered him in
and took his cloak from his shoulders.

"Samuel," he said. "Do come in. I am heartened to see you,
although I wonder at your being out of doors and in Cambridge no
less at this time of the night."

The two men sat in two cushioned chairs in front of the fire
that was burning low, as it was after the dinner meal and the summer weather was warm. Samuel looked as concerned as Thomas
was feeling right before his arrival.

"Indeed the hour is late and I make great apologies for my
unannounced visit," Samuel answered. "In fact I was dining with
Mr. Mather at the College. We were discussing the troubles in the
colony."

Thomas had to restrain a quick pang of irritation as he
wondered why he was not invited to such a gathering. He had been
Treasurer of Harvard for decades now and was often at Increase

Mather's side while he – Mather – served as president. And Samuel, as one of the colony's leading judges, sat on the College's Board of Overseers, which was how he and Thomas had met many years ago. Thomas could keenly feel his advancing age, as the College's president was sixteen years his junior and his friend Samuel was younger than that. Was Thomas being shouldered out of such important discussions concerning the colony? Especially when they were happening in his own backyard, at the College where he served as Treasurer for close to forty years now? When he was first appointed to that position, neither Increase Mather nor Samuel Sewall had yet reached ten years old.

But the truth, Thomas realized, was that he was growing tired. The death of his son – his own namesake – at Narragansett weighed heavily on his heart, especially since Thomas was his only son who had lived to adulthood. Thomas and Mary lost many children in infancy, and with each, his soul was laden by yet another sadness. Those early days seemed so long ago now, and Thomas was grateful for his two daughters, Mary and Elizabeth, who had grown into fine young Christian women, making good marriages to Cambridge men.

It wasn't only his son's death, though, that grieved the elder Thomas. He had worked so diligently for so many years to guide the colony along with a small set of magistrates and ministers, and to have all of his power taken away by this Andros man was a true insult. Thomas had learned from an early age that God called upon him to lead. He was only eleven years old when he sailed with his sisters and brothers and father to the colony from their prosperous farm in a tiny village called Framlingham back in England. His mother had died years before and his father, Nicholas, a truly devout man, was being taxed more each year in order to support King Charles' wars. When word had come down that Nicholas was to be knighted, it meant that the King would require an even greater financial commitment from the family. The elder Danforth would have none of it.

So they sailed to the new world, with high hopes for a better future. They settled on a small farm in Cambridge, up the river from Boston, living in a well-appointed townhouse on the corner of Arrow and Bow Streets.

But death continued to follow the Danforths, and not two years after they arrived in Cambridge, father Nicholas died from a fever. Thomas was only seventeen, but found himself suddenly in a new role as head of the house, even at such a young age. His older sisters Anna and Elizabeth were already courting, and no doubt would marry soon. That left the three boys at home. Thomas was ready to walk in his father's shoes, having spent many hours every day trailing Nicholas, learning surveying work, attending magisterial and deacon meetings, and poring over Latin and mathematics texts in the evening. Brother Samuel had been more protected, living a more traditional life of a young boy without many responsibilities. It was a boon when the local minister came to Thomas just a week after they laid Nicholas to rest, recommending an apprenticeship for Samuel under his own guidance in the parsonage. By then Samuel had already shown a love of scripture and seemed geared toward a life in the ministry. Brother Richard, the next-to-oldest, took the first opportunity to head back home to England.

Thomas himself couldn't afford the time to matriculate at Harvard, as he was looking after his father's business interests and taking on more and more civic and church roles. When he hadn't yet grown to twenty years of age, he was appointed by the General Court to be one of three commissioners to set out land in Cambridge. As the settlement grew from its immediate borders beyond the short mile radius from the College grounds, he was called to distribute outer acres to his neighbors. Meanwhile he was amassing more land for himself, starting with farmland behind the swamp north of the town and the cow yards that surrounded it.

Since those early days, Thomas had been granted by the General Court thousands of acres in appreciation for his service to the colony. His holdings were not only in Cambridge but fifteen miles west, in a wilderness that was known as Danforth's Farms, out where his brother Samuel was working with the Reverend John Eliot to try to Christianize the red savages in the area. His brother's ministry with the Indians influenced Thomas, who adopted the same perspective about those wild men. When the General Court decided to expand its boundaries to include the District of Maine to the north and appointed Thomas as that territory's overseer, he led with a belief that the Abenaki tribes could be similarly reformed. Whereas others wanted to go immediately to war, Thomas urged the colonists toward God's love for all men, including the red ones. It didn't earn him any friends, but he was able to keep some semblance of peace for all those years. This tolerance stung him these days, as those very savages whom he worked to bring to the Lord were among those who killed his dear son just last month.

Ten years ago when Thomas was elected Lieutenant Governor under old Simon Bradstreet – twenty years his senior and one of the original founders of the Massachusetts Bay Colony – he wondered whether he could manage all of his responsibilities. Harvard, the District of Maine, his own acres, and now the entire colony's affairs – they all demanded his constant attention. But his wife Mary was a good, devout wife who took care of the home and many of the necessities of their Cambridge farm, and Thomas was a hard worker. He had been forced to be, ever since he took over the head of the family role back when he was a teenager.

But now was he being shunted aside for a younger generation?

The meeting at Harvard must have been important to bring Samuel Sewall to Cambridge away from his lavish home in Boston. But Thomas' disposition was already quite low, and he did not want to exacerbate it with a petty quarrel with his friend. He had known Samuel ever since the younger man matriculated at the College, and the two formed an immediate bond, although they were so far apart in age. Samuel was highly intelligent and had a quick wit. He also possessed a sensitive thoughtfulness that Thomas admired. He had watched the young man leave Harvard to become a magistrate with the General Court, and then a respected judge.

Thomas shook off his peevishness at being left out of the meeting with Mr. Mather, deciding to give Samuel his full attention. Although he hadn't been at the table, he was very curious about the discussion.

"Troubles in the colony?" Thomas asked. "I was just writing to my brother in England about that very thing."

"Aye, troubles to be sure. This Andros man will be the death of us," Samuel commented. "It is well known that Governor Bradstreet, while beloved by the people, has been frail for a great time now, and you have been the one leading the colony. You might have been called Lieutenant, but in fact you were the one governing our little Bible Commonwealth."

"That might have been so, Samuel, but little good did it do in the end. Andros is here and our livelihoods are at stake. There is so much fear in the colony."

"Tis true. Mr. Mather is as upset as the men of the disbanded

General Court – myself among them. He says we must rebel. That's what he divulged to me this night."

"Rebellion! This is indeed the most beneficent of news, my friend!" Thomas cried, jumping up from his seat faster than he was used to. "What does Mr. Mather suggest? Is there a plan? How may I contribute to it?"

Samuel smiled for the first time since he arrived. "Thomas, we know we can depend on your leadership. You will be a key instrument of God in our strategy. Yet our plans are nascent and there is much to discuss. There is also much at stake."

"I do agree with you," Thomas said. "I am not afraid. Not with God on our side."

~ ~ ~

The developments that Mr. Sewall and Mr. Danforth were discussing made their way steadily throughout the colony. The farmers and tradesmen were no less enamored of this Sir Andros than the Boston magistrates were, and many were ready to fight.

But Sarah Towne Bridges was no longer in a position to hear nor worry about the daily distressing news from Boston. Had it been five years before, she would have continued to secretly listen to the merchants' talk as they leaned in to complain about matters over the rough hewn tables at her Salem Town ordinary. And had it been five years before, she would have been devastated by the idea that she and the entire Towne family might soon lose everything they had worked toward for over forty years, what with this new royal governor in place.

But Sarah was already desolated, and had been that way for a long time now. She had little energy to notice that the colony was on the brink of destruction.

Today the sun rose early in the morning, as it was deep summer and the days were long. Sarah, though, was too tired to get out of her bed. Instead, she stayed in the little cot in the corner of one of her sister Rebecca's second floor bedrooms, a place where she spent most of hours of late. The room was bright and well-lit, and Sarah had a view of the walled-in kitchen garden below, and the rolling fields that spread out beyond it. She was not cheered by the sight, though, nor did Rebecca's constant ministrations on her behalf have any mitigating effect on her dolor. Not even her daughters' visits to her bedside encourage her to rejoin the life of Rebecca's and Francis' farm.

Because Edmund was gone, dead and buried. He had been now for several years. And Sarah had long since sold the little Front Street ordinary that she had grown to love over time.

Sarah and the children had been living with the Nurses in Salem Village since Edmund had left them penniless. Since that terrible time, Sarah could not find her way out of the melancholy that overtook her. Before Edmund died, they had been happy for a time. They welcomed young Alice into the world, a strong and healthy babe, and Hannah immediately took to the child as if she were her own. Sarah would smile when she saw the two together, reminded of how Mary and Rebecca would treat her the same way when she was young. All was well, and Sarah thanked God for her good fortune. True to her promise to her sisters, she found great pleasure in being a strong and loving mother to her children and a faithful wife to Edmund. Being happy was so much easier to achieve when Edmund was behaving and the money was coming in.

Yet the Bridges' contentment was short lived, as Edmund grew very sick with the fever that swept across the wharves, and died not a week later. As soon as she saw the first signs of sickness, Sarah sent her two children north to Salem Village to stay with her sister Rebecca, terribly afraid that they would catch the dreaded disease. She herself stayed hale as she ministered to Edmund, yet it did no good, and he went to the Lord very soon after.

It was a terrible blow. They had been married for close to twenty five years and Sarah loved him dearly, despite her frustrations with him. They buried him the next day, as the magistrates demanded that bodies carrying such sickness be disposed of right away.

It wasn't long after the burial that Sarah learned more devastating news from the local magistrates: despite Edmund's boasts of great wealth that was supposedly just about to be wrought from their tavern business, in fact he had died with no money.

By then Sarah knew how to run the ordinary on her own, and could probably have done so with a small loan from one of her brothers-in-law. Her daughters had grown accustomed to the hustle and bustle of Salem Town and had made friends with some of the other children roaming up and down the wharves and streets of the city. Even though it was rare, there did exist some single women leading their own businesses.

But Sarah couldn't do it. She found that she couldn't do much of anything anymore. A deep, encompassing dread seeped into her heart and she was overcome with sadness. It seemed the height of unfairness that after all she had endured with Edmund, all of the pain of seeing her sister Rebecca pack up and move away from Salem Town, the still-anguishing grief from losing her parents, and her frustration with the constant harsh edicts delivered from the pulpit of the church, she was to be dealt this new tragedy.

Her daughters looked at her with great concern in their eyes at first, and then real terror as their bellies grew more and more empty with each passing day. Sarah knew she should be a good mother and snap out of her melancholy – her children needed her – but she just couldn't seem to get out of bed.

It was Rebecca who saved her.

Since the extended Nurse family had moved out of Salem Town and purchased the Bishop Farm to the north in Salem Village, Rebecca's husband Francis had done quite well financially. The homestead itself was large, with rooms double the size of the Nurses' tiny house in the town. The farm had prospered under Francis' stewardship, as did the abutting farms of their children, who were now grown and parents in their own right. Now Rebecca and Francis lived in the two-story red-painted saltbox house by themselves, and had plenty of room for Sarah and her two daughters.

Sarah could still remember how she got there, even though the memory seemed foggy. One day about six months after Edmund died, when she hadn't heard a single word from her youngest sister, Rebecca urged Isaac to help. The couple appeared at Sarah's doorstep with a rented cart and strong sacks made out of hemp, ready to be filled with Sarah's and the childrens' belongings. The door was opened slowly by Alice, now six years old, who peered cautiously from the depths within. Rebecca gasped at the sight. Sarah had always kept her daughters clean and well-fed, making sure their golden curls were pushed neatly within their crisp white caps and their petticoats were tidy. But here was a small waif, looking like a homeless street urchin. Alice's hair was matted and dirty, her cap was nowhere to be seen, and her stained bodice and skirts hung on her.

"Alice?" Rebecca said, kneeling in front of the child, her old knees creaking with the movement. "Alice, what is happening?"

Francis pushed open the door and rushed inside, filled with worry. His nose was assaulted with the smell of sour unwashed bodies.

"Mama is ill," Alice said quietly, hugging her aunt fiercely with her little arms.

Rebecca and Alice joined Francis inside. Alice slowly pointed to the lump on the bed in the corner of the room.

"Husband, take the child outside. Find Hannah first. Get them to some food," Rebecca ordered.

At that moment Hannah climbed down the stairs above – in as bad condition as her little sister was – and she, too, embraced her aunt with such a power that Rebecca felt she might topple over onto the floor.

Once Francis took the children away, Rebecca sat at Sarah's bedside, terrified that she might find a lifeless body within the blankets.

Sarah wasn't dead, but seemed to be near that state. She was hardly breathing, and the stench that came off of her nightclothes as Rebecca pulled the quilt away was overpowering.

"Young Sarah, oh young Sarah," Rebecca cried, gently slapping her sister's cheek, beckoning her to awake. "I did not know it had grown so bad. Please, please, sister. Do revive yourself."

Sarah did open her eyes, enough to peer up at Rebecca. She hadn't eaten in days and had hardly taken any of the water that Hannah had urged upon her over the past week. The eyes that were normally a bright shining blue, often flashing with obstinance and strength, were now dulled, filmy.

"Sister?" she croaked through a throat as dry as October corn stalks. "Oh sister. I cannot go on. Truly I cannot go on."

Once Francis returned the children from the meal they took at the inn two blocks away, he rushed around the house, opening windows, welcoming the salty sea smell into the dank interior. It didn't take long for him to pack up the small home and put the Bridges' belongings on the cart while Rebecca busied herself peeling the putrid clothes off of Sarah's and her childrens' backs, filling a copper tub with water warmed over the fire, directing them to soak and rub their skin with harsh lye soap.

Rebecca had taken care of Sarah when she – Sarah – was a baby, and now she would mother her again. The now-old woman was willing to do so for the rest of her life. Sarah had always suffered so, more than her sisters had, with her curious heart and quick temper. Rebecca was unaccustomed to seeing her so weak. She would heal, Rebecca knew she would, away from Salem Town, away from memories of Edmund, safely ensconced in the bosom of the Nurses and their comfortable homestead.

And now that was five years ago. Despite all of Rebecca's ministrations - and that of daughter Hannah, who was now seventeen years old, almost a woman in her own right – Sarah would not be cheered. It was as if God had cast a cold blanket of darkness upon her soul, and she could not escape from it. She had tried her whole life to survive in the uncertainty of life in the colony, and to be a good servant of the Lord. She knew she should not resist His will, but could do nothing to change her feelings. And then she was struck with an enormous sense of guilt that she was weak and unable to get out of bed, not contributing to the work of the household, not even caring for her own children. And that she was questioning God Himself. Her punishing thoughts would not desist, and she found relief only in sleep. She could not even get out of bed to attend services on Sunday.

One afternoon after the entire household had dealt with Sarah's downturn for way too long, Hannah climbed the narrow stairs to her mother's place of escape, trying hard to keep steady the tin cup of tea that she held in her hands. It was something she did every day at the same time, greeting her mother with smiles and reports of the workings of the house and farm. The young woman always tried to forget that Sarah, while struggling to listen to her daughter with maternal attentiveness, was never heartened by the visits. Hannah had always taken comfort in her mother's strength, recognizing in her the same stubbornness that she found inside herself. Since Sarah had taken to her bed, Hannah was adamant about helping her recover. Sarah Bridges was a fighter. Hannah needed her to be so again.

Today Hannah had news for Sarah that excited her and actually made her hopeful for the future for the first time in years.

"Mother, the day is a bright one!" Hannah called out to Sarah as she entered the room, trying to not notice how the air was permeated with closeness and sour body odor. She set the delicate cup on the small table next to the bed. Sarah rolled over to face her daughter and pushed herself up to lean her back against the wall. Hannah was surprised to note the tired flesh around her mother's neck and chin, struck with the fact that Sarah was aging. Her eyes were still water-blue, but had lost the depth and sparkle that used to emanate from within. Time was running out. Hannah had to make this thing happen quickly.

"My Hannah," Sarah said, fatigue overwhelming her. "You are so kind."

The younger girl picked up the cup again and handed it to her mother, not content as she usually was to let it cool, untouched, on the table.

"Thank you, mother," she said dutifully, but with more sternness than usual. "And now will you be so kind as well and drink this tea that Rebecca has recently steeped just for you?"

"Ah, no, daughter, I am so tired," Sarah answered, smiling a sad smile and turning her face toward the wall. This was the exchange the two had had, countless times before. Hannah, however, would not be swayed from her task on this particular afternoon. She put a gentle but firm hand on her mother's shoulder, preventing her from turning away.

"Mother," Hannah said, taking on the tone that Sarah herself would employ in the past when Hannah was being stubborn. "Do take the tea. And do listen to me this day. This retreat from the life God granted you is coming to a close."

Sarah sensed that her daughter was serious, and she felt compelled to obey, taking the tea cup from her and managing a sip. Not since Edmund died had anyone questioned her actions, and Sarah knew it was because they were worried about her. Rebecca had directed everyone to allow her sister her grief, and to express only love, never frustration. It was a strategy borne out of sincere feeling, yet it had done Sarah no good in the end. It felt to her as if everything fell apart because she dared to let go of the woman she was forced to be: the one who took care of things, the one who was strong no matter what trials befell the family. And, true to her belief, her daughters were suffering. But no one pressured Sarah to do anything else but sink into her own sorrow. So that was exactly what she had done.

But here was her own young Hannah, looking so much like Sarah did when she herself was her age: earnest, wanting, questioning. Strong. Not willing to brook silliness.

"Tis fine tea," Sarah said quietly, casting her eyes down into the tawny liquid.

"Aye, tis," Hannah answered, quite pleased yet somewhat surprised that her mother was responding to her. "As is the news I bring you, mother. God is once again smiling upon us."

"Oh aye?" Sarah asked, feeling bitterness overtake her like bile. "I do fear any good news, as I fear that whatever God brings us He shall snatch away with great speed. That is what He is wont to do. But do tell, my daughter. What is this news?"

Hannah smiled and snuggled closer to her mother, very much like she used to when she was a child. "Francis has received word just last night that the Lord has sent you a most welcome helper. You do remember Peter Cloyce, who lost his wife just last year? A member of the Salem Village church, with several grown children?"

Sarah had to close her eyes to think of the person Hannah was speaking of. Her mind felt foggy and old, having turned off its workings these past years. She had not attended services since arriving at Rebecca's farm, but was familiar with most of the Salem Village residents from her many visits to her sisters' lands before tragedy struck her family. It was a small community and all the neighbors knew each other well. After some searching, Sarah could place Goodman Cloyce in her mind. He was a good man, kept a reasonably prosperous farm, and was well-loved by his children, some of whom had given him grandchildren by then. But he had never made a vivid impression on her.

"Aye, I do remember him," Sarah answered, setting down her cup at the bedstead table, hoping that Hannah wouldn't notice that she hadn't drunk much of it. "He has lived in the Village for a long time now."

"His parents moved here very early, and he has been a faithful member of our congregation for many years. He is an able, righteous man. Here is Francis' news, my dear mother: Goodman Cloyce wishes to marry you."

Sarah could not repress an acrid, loud laugh, which sounded for all the world like a witch's cackle. Once the laugh started, Sarah could not stop herself. Hannah looked annoyed, crossing her arms and waiting for the fit to pass. Her mother was incorrigible. This might take more time than she had originally expected.

Once the laughter abated, she wiped her eyes and looked at her daughter. Sarah's graying hair, always unruly, escaped the strictures of her cap and fell into her face. Pushing the straying wisps away, Sarah said "Marry me? Wherefore would he want such a thing? With an old, sad widow as myself? I have lost all of my beauty, whatever there was of it in the first place. And I grow troublesome, just as my own mother did."

Hannah stood up and started pacing the room. "Oh mother, you do exasperate me," she said, crossing her arms. "You know that second and third marriages happen this way all the time in the colony. Goodman Cloyce needs a mate as you yourself do. He has been made aware of your situation, and both Francis and Rebecca have spoken highly about you to him. The match has been dictated by God in heaven. Would you turn your back on Him?"

Now it was time for Sarah to get upset. "Turn my back on God?" she cried. "He has already done so to me. How can you so easily say that this outrageous idea comes from Him? He has already deserted me."

Hannah stared at her mother, suddenly afraid for her. "Mother!" she cried. "You should not say such things! The Devil will be sure to take you!"

"The Devil has already taken me," Sarah snapped. "I have lost all."

Hannah dropped down to sit next to her mother once more. So this was to be her fate, after her short sixteen years on this earth? To lose Sarah to the devil's wretchedness, leaving herself motherless? No, Hannah decided. No. It will not do.

She shook Sarah by the shoulders and made the older woman look at her. "You have <u>not</u> lost all, mother," she scolded, great anger in her voice. "You have me, and my sister as well. You have your own sisters, and their growing wealth. We need you. You need to stop this. Now."

Sarah was shocked by her daughter's vehemence. When had this precious young girl grown to be an almost-woman, so masterful over her own body and soul? When had her childish stubbornness bloomed into such adult authority?

When had Hannah become so much like Sarah herself?

Sarah bowed her head in guilt and shame for her behavior. Tears welled from her blue eyes and spilled down her cheeks and onto the linen of her shift. She clasped her daughter's hands, silently begging for forgiveness. As she felt Hannah squeeze her hands in response, Sarah's tears became like a flood, and she started to howl. A low, quiet moan, not enough to arouse the rest of the family downstairs.

The two held each other, rocking back and forth, just like

Sarah used to do when Hannah was fretful as a baby.

They stayed like that for a good while, long enough for the sun to sink beneath the trees, casting the room in dusk.

Something was opening up inside of Sarah, and the relief flooded her entire being. Her anger at Edmund, at the animosities among people of the colony, at God Himself – she had vowed she would not allow anything to hurt her ever again. She would shut her eyes and sleep away the rest of her life. But that felt wrong, too, and she knew it deeply in her heart. Sarah Bridges, without a voice? Without fighting against injustice? Who was that woman? She knew she couldn't just stop. Not with her daughters needing her and her extended family continuing to deal with the constant castigation of the likes of the Putnams.

As Sarah's outpouring ebbed, Hannah dried her eyes with the edge of the light woolen sheet that covered her on the bed.

"So it seems that daughter has become mother," Sarah said quietly, low enough that Hannah had to strain to hear her. Sarah looked up at Hannah, and Hannah was relieved to see that her beautiful blue eyes seemed clear and shining, shed of the clouds of melancholy that had plagued them for months.

"Aye, perhaps," Hannah said. "Yet I do not relish the permanent switching of the roles."

Sarah's mouth twitched in a tiny smile. "I understand you," she said. "But please, before you give me back my position, grant me the favor of your advice. What am I to do about this Goodman Cloyce situation?'

Hannah returned her mother's smile and clasped her to her breast. "That is easy, mother. Follow God's lead. Go to your new husband."

~ ~ ~

Not three miles from where Hannah and Sarah were talking, another woman was providing comfort to a loved one. Ann Putnam and her sister-in-law Deliverance were sitting together, spinning wool with their spindles, alone in the Putnam farmhouse for a rare moment. Ann's four children were out in the fields, the eldest boy helping his father in digging weeds out of the rows between corn stalks, now almost ready for harvesting.

The girls' mothers were grateful to have the children out from under their feet. Especially Ann Sr., who was close to despondent, even while she worked. After serving her husband Thomas as his loyal wife for these eight years past, the young woman's righteous suffering and general ill health had not abated. Her husband continued to command the village politics, and Ann was grateful for it. She truly loved her husband. Still, life in Salem Village never stopped being dangerous and terrifying. Every single day Ann lived in fear of the Devil himself coming to her, with all his wily ways. She knew all about that. She read her bible. Why, even Eve, God's second beloved creation, had given into the temptation of the serpent.

Ann thanked God every day for her sister-in-law Deliverance, whose friendship with her deepened and grew. Sometimes her fellowship helped Ann's fear and fragility, as Deliverance continued to protect her dear sister-in-law in any way she could.

Now Deliverance heard Ann sigh every few minutes, and as she glanced over at her, Ann's fingers clasped the raw wool much too tightly. She would start the spindle spinning, only to make a big tangle out of the whole thing, and then have to start all over again. Deliverance could feel her frustration buzzing in the air, so much that she broke the silence by stopping Ann by putting a hand on her arm.

"Sister," she said gently. "Let us rest from our task. You seem distraught."

Ann uncharacteristically threw the entire spindle and wool to the ground and covered her eyes with her hands, bending over to cry. "I cannot help it, although I pray to God every hour for help. But it is so difficult to deal with this horrible situation with those Estys."

Deliverance already knew what Ann was talking about. The generations-old disputes about the boundaries of the farms south of the Ipswich River were still being debated, only now many of the Topsfield men had moved to Salem Village. And Isaac Esty came out ahead every time. Just last Sunday, Ann had pinched Deliverance while they sat side-by-side during the morning service, drawing her attention to Isaac's wife Mary, who sat several pews behind. At the time, Deliverance looked at Mary Esty and thought nothing untoward about her demeanor. Goody Esty had had her head bowed, listening fervently to Mr. Burroughs' words. But after the service Ann whispered to Deliverance, "Did you not see her wicked look to me? She was gloating over my misfortune. Her and her sister Rebecca Nurse both. Oh, they are wicked women."

Deliverance did not answer, not wishing to stir Ann into

more of a frenzy. Today, too, she tried to divert the conversation to happier things.

"But my dear," Deliverance said, calmly. "Do not fret so about your neighbors. God has granted you many gifts. You have four healthy children. You are most rewarded among women. Certainly you are when compared to me, as God has only granted me with one."

It was only then that Ann seemed to pull herself out of her preoccupation with her own plight. She did feel grateful for her progeny, and was sorry that her sister-in-law had lost three babies since the arrival of their first child, Mary, at the beginning of her marriage to John Walcott. Ann shook herself out of her pacing, and dropped to the floor at Deliverance's feet, putting her head onto her sister-in-law's lap. Deliverance patted Ann's cap and put her other arm around her shoulder.

"I am most mournful for your losses, my dear, dear sister," Ann said. "You do right to remind me of God's great gifts."

Deliverance, never one to sink into melancholy, remained amiable. "God's gifts are abundant," she agreed. "And you and I should also praise God that our first daughters are such close friends. As I watch Ann Jr. and Mary play together, they remind me of our own kinship. Would that you and I had met at such a young age! The two will be sure to be companions for many years."

Ann smiled for the first time that afternoon. "Aye, tis true," she agreed. "When those two girls want something, they will be sure to get it."

"God bless them, to be sure," Deliverance said, smiling to herself when she thought of their daughters, holding hands, running through the fields, conspiring in some corner. "They will make a most strong force between them for many years to come."

~ ~ ~

The circle of the year turned once again toward the autumn, and the heavy harvesting work began in the Salem Village fields and farms. One evening at the Nurse homestead, the supper dishes had been cleared and Rebecca and Sarah were sitting in front of the fireplace, mending winter clothes that had been eaten by moths during the summer months in storage. Francis was in the barn tending to the horses and Sarah's daughters were at the table, struggling with their Bible readings, lit only by a single candle in a pewter holder. Sarah had followed young Hannah's instructions and had joined the daily routines of the household, to the great relief of everyone else who lived there. It took several weeks for her to regain her strength, after being bedridden and taking very little nourishment for so long. Still her waistcoat hung on her bones, regardless of how tightly she pulled the stays. She had always been a thin woman, but now Rebecca had to coax her sister every day to eat just a little more stew or porridge. The older woman knew of her niece's deal with Sarah, and was thankful for it. Now she just needed to help bring color to her sister's sallow cheeks and fatten her up a bit before Sarah took the next step: going to church services and seeing Peter Cloyce.

The room was quiet and warm, the heavy activities of the day ended, and now the family could enjoy a bit of silence among them. On occasion Hannah would scold her sister Alice when she fell behind in her reading or stopped paying attention, but otherwise the house was quiet. The loud knock at the door made them all jump in their seats.

Rebecca started to rise from her chair, but Sarah motioned for her to stay. It was easier for Sarah to move about, as Rebecca in her advanced age suffered from pain in her joints and in her lower back, especially as the weather grew colder. But by the time Sarah crossed the floor, the door opened from the outside, and Francis walked in, Mr. Burroughs behind him.

"Look, Rebecca," Francis announced. "Look who I found at our doorstep this night. It is dear Mr. Burroughs!"

Now Rebecca did rise, pushing herself up on the arms of the chair, and took the cloaks of both her husband and the minister. "Do come in, Mr. Burroughs. It is a joy to welcome you to our home."

Rebecca flushed with happiness to receive such a visitor, as she always enjoyed discussing scripture with the minister. But she saw that tonight he did not wear his usual friendly countenance. In fact he looked quite grim.

Sarah pulled two more chairs close to the fireplace and bade Hannah to bring them cups of warm cider so that they could ward off the chill that seeped into the room when the two men entered.

"I thank you, Goody Nurse, and I do beg your forgiveness for my late visit," Mr. Burroughs said, taking the seat that Francis offered him and rubbing his chapped red hands together.

"God's servant is always welcome here, no matter the hour," Rebecca replied with a smile. "Yet I do wonder at what brings such sadness to your face, Mr. Burroughs. What is the matter?"

The minister accepted the warm cider and drank of it as if he had not had any sustenance in quite some time. Sarah watched as the old man bowed his head in what looked like despair. Since she arrived in Salem Town she had neglected to attend church services, but in the meantime Rebecca had told her about Mr. Burroughs, whom she respected a great deal. Since Mary and Isaac Esty moved to the village with their family, the Putnams and the Walcotts had grown even more unhappy with them. The distressing scene that Sarah had experienced so many years ago, with the young Thomas Putnam accusing her of sin because she had let go her cap for a moment, seemed now to be a portent of worse animosities to come between the two factions. Now that the Estys lived almost next door to Thomas and Ann Putnam – rather than across the Ipswich River in Topsfield – and were carving rich farmland out of those same acres that the Putnams believed belonged to them, the Putnams could hardly contain their dislike. And there was much talk in the village about the Nurse's move from Salem Town, as the price of the Bishop Farm was well-known to be most expensive – all of four hundred pounds. Where did that poor family get the money? There was sure to be something off about the sale. The Putnams and the Walcotts never passed up the opportunity to foment distrust on the part of the Salem Village community toward the Nurses and the Estys as well. These people were civil to Sarah's brethren in public, especially during church services, and would accept their hospitality – like when Rebecca offered some healing herbs to Ann Putnam when she was about to give birth – without question. But there was always a simmering resentment lurking right below the surface, as if the Towne women had dared to grow beyond their modest station as they became well-loved members of the church.

Whenever Sarah would hear these stories, an icicle would stab her heart, remembering how angry she had been at the Putnams before she and Edmund were forced to move to Salem Town. And she couldn't forget that it was the Putnams' cousin – that John Gould – who had been the source of all of Edmund's suffering, and thus hers, too.

Mr. Burroughs had always tried to mediate such animosity

when it came to the surface, or when Rebecca or Mary asked him what they might do to ease the tensions. The sisters knew the Putnams had no love for them, but couldn't see how to improve things besides giving up the many acres that the General Court had continued to rule were theirs, and they would never do that. And now as the friendship between Mr. Burroughs and Sarah's family had grown over the past several months, he lost even more favor from the Putnams. Even though the minister had vowed to gain the brotherly love of that family, he was never successful.

These hostilities among God's chosen, Sarah thought. Why can't we all just love each other? There is enough to fear in the colony, what with the King's interference and the savage Indian threat, as well as the weather that threatens our crops and the constant lure of the Devil. Why must the Putnams persecute us so?

Her thoughts were interrupted by Mr. Burroughs. "Tis a pleasing drink, young Hannah, my gratitude to you," he was saying.

Sarah bade Hannah and Alice up to the rooms upstairs, reminding them of their prayers before bed. The adults all sat around the minister, and waited for his explanation.

"I fear that my days leading the Salem Village church are numbered," he told them, smiling wanly at his audience. "Goodman Putnam is threatening to sue me."

"What?" Francis asked, upset. "Whatever for?"

"It is about my dear wife's passing, of all things," Mr. Burroughs replied. "I am grateful for your condolences. I miss her loving presence, even though some in our congregation have accused me of being too rough with her. Ann Putnam has even told her husband and some neighbors as well that dear Mary died as a result of witchcraft that I myself cast upon her!"

Rebecca took Mr. Burroughs' hand into the two of hers, and her eyes glistened with sympathetic tears. "Nay, it is not so, we do know that," she comforted him. "I have heard of such talk but it is idle gossip, nothing to attend to, to be sure."

"Perhaps not," the minister replied. "Although the Putnams have despised me since my arrival in this village. Regardless, when my wife died I found that I could not afford the expenses for her funeral. Some of the villagers have neglected to pay their fees for my upkeep, and I was close to penniless. Old Thomas Putnam took pity on me, despite his children's complaints of me. He is very elderly and is now, in his old age, content to dote on his son Joseph and his wife as well. He has moved away from the worries of his original progeny."

"I have seen as much, and it gladdens my heart," Rebecca commented.

"Aye, me too," the minister agreed. "Old Goodman Putnam provided a loan for me to bury my dear Mary in the proper way. I was most grateful and I was certain that my benefactor knew of my deep appreciation. He told me I could repay him over a period of time. Indeed he is not the problem. Instead, his son Thomas Jr. has taken issue with the loan."

Francis made a disparaging noise and Rebecca shushed him. "Rebecca, do not deny me my dissatisfaction with Thomas Jr.," he chided her. "I do grant him the love that God demands of me, yet I cannot come to respect the man. You know that Isaac and I had to just these months past demand he desist in cutting down timber that rightly belongs to us."

"Let us listen to Mr. Burroughs' tale, dear husband," Rebecca said, lowering her eyes and bowing her head. Such piety, Sarah thought. My hallowed sister. Such tranquility in the face of such malevolence. Contrary to Rebecca, Sarah could feel anger flow through her as she listened to Mr. Burroughs' story. It was actually a relief to feel such energy, regardless of the discomfort it brought her. She could feel herself come back to life with it, after so many months of living as if in a fog, not caring about what happened to her or her loved ones.

"Thomas Jr. just this afternoon did visit me in the parsonage, and told me that his father was too sick and infirm to make such a loan to me, and that he was acting in old Goodman Putnam's stead," the minister continued. "He made me aware that he will be bringing forth a suit against me on the morrow, and that if I cannot repay him right away, then I will be put into jail."

Mr. Burroughs stood then, and started pacing the room. Dusk had turned to dark outside the bare windows, and a sliver of a moon had risen over the tops of the trees. Sarah, Rebecca and her husband were silent, shocked that such a move could be made against their own rightful minister. Mr. Burroughs had always been kind to them, a trusted friend. The Putnams – especially Thomas Jr. – could certainly hold a grudge, and seemed to have no qualms in acting upon it. This was the village's second minister in just a few years; it would be a tragedy if they were to lose this one just because church members could not get along amongst themselves. They wanted to believe that they lived in a close community of God. Why could they not be satisfied – all of them – with their leader in Christ?

Francis stood, too, and grasped Mr. Burroughs by the shoulders. "You shall not be put into the stocks," he told the older man. "In this house we have little, as do most of our neighbors. But if young Thomas Putnam makes good on his word, I will ask those who are friends to join me in collecting the monies needed to repay him his father's loan. It is an insult that you could not afford your own wife's funeral in the first place. The Village left you in that state, and the Village should be responsible for protecting you against such persecution."

The minister looked at Francis with disbelief and surprise. Both Rebecca and Sarah joined them, and nodded their approval. Finally, Sarah thought, finally she could be part of something truly positive and loving. There was too much hostility in the Village of late. Generosity must trump hatred.

"Oh, Goodman Nurse," Mr. Burroughs exclaimed. "My heart is filled with gratitude. But do you believe that other villagers will agree to join you? I am not certain as to who supports me and who does not."

"We shall see," Francis answered. "It is at times such as these that our fellow church members and neighbors will have the chance to demonstrate their piety."

"Did not Jesus himself say to us in I Timothy, 'Command those who are rich in this present world not to be arrogant nor to put their hope in wealth, which is so uncertain, but to put their hope in God, who richly provides us with everything for our enjoyment. Command them to do good, to be rich in good deeds, and to be generous and willing to share. In this way they will lay up treasure for themselves as a firm foundation for the coming age, so that they may take hold of the life that is truly life?'" Rebecca intoned, knowing each word, smiling at the minister, who was clearly relieved, as if he had just thrown off a very heavy mantle.

"You are very good people, blessed by God," Mr. Burroughs said. "I thank you with everything that I have."

~ ~ ~

It was midwinter and the snow had been falling for two days. The Nurse homestead was buried in two feet of snow, and its inhabitants did not venture outdoors, except when they had to feed the livestock in the barn, milk the cow or haul in new firewood. Francis had shoveled a narrow path between the house and the barn but had to keep digging it out as the storm continued.

The family did what they could to pass the time and to keep warm. The wood pile was still high and the women kept the fire going, even at night. But once one moved away from the hearth the room grew chill and there was ice on every window. Sarah and her sister donned a third woolen skirt over their petticoats and kept their knitted cloaks about their shoulders as they went about their routines. The children grew restless, as they were wont to do in the winter when they couldn't run outdoors, but Hannah entertained herself by toying with her much younger sister Alice. Sarah could often hear them in one of the upstairs rooms encouraging Alice to repeat tongue-twisting gliffes faster and faster, or teaching her how to play with marbles whose rolling across the floor sounded like mice's pitter pattering feet. Just a few days ago Alice came stomping down the steps, muttering "Dick drunk drink in a dish; where's the dish Dick drunk drink in?" over and over again so she could prove to Hannah that she could do it. Sarah couldn't help chuckling to herself when she heard Alice, remembering the countless times that Rebecca and Mary had teased her like that when she herself was young.

There was winter indoor work to do: spinning new cloth for spring clothes, soaking dried beans for the next day's stew, washing clothes in steaming water in the huge iron cauldron over the fire. But in the dark days the family slept longer hours than warmer times of the year, and they also spent a great deal of time together in front of the hearth, telling stories and reading the Bible. They always made the trip to the meeting house on foot, carrying the hot stones they would leave at their feet in the icy building, unless they were truly house bound by the weather. Getting out of the homestead was always a welcome diversion and a remedy against the boredom that always came with the winter. Yet as ever, Salem Village's minister problems had continued, and now they were led by yet a third man of the cloth: Deodat Lawson.

Mr. Burroughs was right when he visited the Nurses several months ago: Thomas Putnam Jr. had indeed threatened jail for the minister's unpaid loan to his father. And Francis was true to his word, collecting the funds necessary to repay the debt from about half of the congregation. Some members had shut their doors on him when he came to their houses, asking for help on behalf of Mr. Burroughs. Most of the naysayers were connected with the Putnam family in one way or another. It was harder for the others to add to the collection plate, as they were worse off than their wealthier neighbors, but they did, with kind and open hearts. The Nurses and the Estys were among the larger donors. Mr. Burroughs accepted their charity with gratitude, although he was ashamed to have to do so. When he went to pay the younger Putnam, only Ann Sr. was at home, and she would not let him into the house. Neither would she accept the worn leather bag filled with coins meant for her husband, as she told the minister that he had garnered the money through evil magic. So Mr. Burroughs left the sack on the doorstep, turned on his heel, and with whatever dignity he could muster, walked away.

But he wouldn't stay in Salem Village. He couldn't, not with so many against him. His children were grown and his wife now dead, and he himself was aging. He no longer feared the terrors of the Indians who still roamed the northern reaches of the colony, back in the District of Maine from where he came. His wife had always feared the massacres that they had seen in that territory, but he no longer cared. Two weeks later he was seen off by the Nurses, the Estys and their neighbors who supported him. Sarah was there, too. She thought the man looked very sad as he slowly rode on his rickety cart, led by a forlorn-looking horse, on the northern road.

The people of the Village weren't going to change their ways, unfortunately, and the infighting continued as none other than the Putnams invited Mr. Lawson to the pulpit without the agreement of the full congregation. While the new minister seemed godly enough, Sarah had heard her brothers-in-law complaining about him, especially the fact that he was not yet fully ordained. She was tired of the bickering, though, and did her best to stop her ears when the subject arose. If they all just ignored the situation perhaps it would go away. Why, after all, was Salem Village so troubled within itself, when other towns in the colony seemed to be fine with their own ministers?

Besides, she had much more interesting things to think about. She smiled to herself as she drew another stitch on the hem of the shift that she was sewing for Hannah. It was lovely to feel hopeful again, after so many months and years of immense sadness. Could it be that she was all of forty-five years old? How had that happened? Recently she felt much younger than that. Could she dare believe that God had finally turned His face back toward her, granting her new life? And if so, what had she done to deserve such grace? For that matter, what had she done to suffer her husband's death, and such destitution and betrayal afterward?

"Sarah, you do have a most elusive look about you this evening," Rebecca interrupted her thoughts, smiling at her with that ever-present shining warmth emanating from her dark eyes. Both women put down their needlework and examined the progress they had made in the stitches. Sarah returned Rebecca's smile, feeling almost embarrassed for feeling so content.

"Elusive, perhaps, sister," she said. "As always, my mind does fly when it is left to its own devices."

"And what does it land on, such that would draw such a secret smile to your face?"

"Oh, Rebecca, you do already know of it, do not tease me so! It is like these forty five years have not passed between us."

Rebecca laughed. "You cannot fault me for reveling in your happiness, dear Sarah," she said. "You are right. I do know from whence your smile comes. We are all so thankful to God that He has brought Peter to you."

Sarah decided to put away any reticence she might be feeling, taking advantage of the opportunity to speak her thoughts. The family had watched as she had ventured forth to the church after such a long hiatus, and as she quietly accepted the courtship of Goodman Cloyce. Yet up until this evening no one commented on it, as they were worried that any mention of the pairing might scare Sarah away from it, scaring her back into the depths of her melancholy. Even young Alice remained silent, even though she, along with Hannah, longed to see her mother married again.

"I, too, give great thanks," Sarah said, excitedly, taking her sister's hands up in hers. "I did not believe it could be so, that God would see a way to grant me a husband again. You know I am a difficult woman, Rebecca. Sometimes a stubborn one. I did not think any man besides Edmund could handle me."

"Oh, Sarah," Rebecca chided. "You are no such thing. You have your own mind and at times you speak it. As did our dear mother. In truth you are the most generous and kind woman I know. If only you could see your gifts as others do."

Sarah was used to hearing such things from Rebecca and the rest of her family, yet she did not believe them. She knew what was in her heart. It was often filled with questions and frustration at her fate. These were not the qualities of a generous and godly woman. But tonight she let go that argument so they could focus on happier subjects.

"Whatever is the truth, I feel blessed that Peter has come into my life. And that he wants to marry me so quickly. It seems the right thing to do." Sarah looked down at her lap and the white muslin that lay there. "It is different, to be sure, from when I met Edmund. Peter and I are grown, with children and grandchildren of our own. He is offering me friendship and a steady home. Companionship in the Lord. It feels so much safer."

"You and Edmund had a good life together," Rebecca reminded her. "It was sometimes tenuous, yes. And troubling. But God brings hardship so that we may show Him that we can be stalwart in His name."

Once again, as ever, Sarah had to suppress a slight feeling of annoyance at Rebecca's accurate view of her first marriage, and her expectation that Sarah could be a better person than she really was. Another woman saying the same words would probably do so out of a sense of superiority. Sarah had to remind herself that her sister was not like other women, though, and had only love in her heart. How could she fault her for that?

"That is all in the past," Sarah said, redirecting the conversation. "Peter seems like a solid, good man. You do believe that, do you not, sister?"

"Oh aye, I do," Rebecca answered. "He has been a steady member of the church for many years now, and he and his wife raised five obedient, saintly children. When his wife died and the last of his children married, he has carried on, yet I do believe he was lonely and prayed to God for a fitting help meet. God hath joined the two of you together."

"He seems of good health as well, no? He is older than I, yet keeps his own farm well-tended with little help, so I imagine he is hale."

"'Tis also true. He is a most adequate choice."

Sarah realized that she probably wouldn't have given Peter Cloyce a second look when she was young and first met Edmund

Bridges. Where Edmund was brash, Peter was levelheaded. Edmund was always taking risks, but Peter was content with the small gifts God had granted him. As a young woman, Sarah was drawn to Edmund's passion about things, but now she craved stability and safety. And the children had taken to Peter as well. Sarah knew that Hannah was relieved to give up her role as the mother of the family, and Alice was content to be jiggled on Peter's knee while he sang songs like "Benjamin Bowmaneer" to her.

It was rare in the colony for a widow or widower to live very long without remarrying. Life in the settlements was too difficult for a single adult to carry on farm labor and care for children alone. Sarah knew this. She also knew that second and third marriages were usually made out of convenience, and indeed this was what was driving Peter Cloyce to her. But she was glad that she found her intended to have a pleasant countenance and no obvious deformity or vice. When he first proposed his intention to her, it couldn't have been in a more gentle way. Sarah remembered how relieved she felt that day when they walked out together after church services for the first time.

There was no father whose permission he had to ask, so he had approached her directly, his black felt brimmed hat in his hand, looking rather sheepish. Out of the corner of her eye Sarah caught a glimpse of Hannah whispering to her Aunt Rebecca, several feet behind her, watching the scene with great cheerfulness. Sarah rolled her eyes and walked ahead at a fast pace, even though she knew that Peter wanted to talk to her. She knew it was coming; the entire family did. Still she felt quite fragile, getting accustomed to being out of bed and being in fellowship with others.

"Goody Bridges," Peter had said, catching up to her. "Tis a pleasant Sabbath, is it not?"

"To be sure it is," Sarah answered, glancing over at him and then returning her gaze ahead. "And Mr. Lawson seems to be acclimating himself to Salem Village."

"Aye, that he is. Although some still yearn for Mr. Burroughs."

Sarah felt a quick jab of discontent at the nascent conversation, preferring to stay clear of the ongoing debate amongst the villagers concerning the ever-changing ministers. She was surprised to see that Peter noticed, somehow, her perturbation, perhaps in the change in her demeanor, or some minor shift in her stance. "Although let us not talk of unpleasant things," he added quickly. "Not when the sun is so warm, although the winter is near upon us."

Sarah looked at him for a longer moment this time, while continuing her walking. That was most sensitive of him, she thought. And I hadn't had to say a word. Her heart, which had been racing, took a slower beat, and a pleasant calm came over her.

"Aye, tis more to September than early December," she agreed.

She heard him sigh in relief. It's true, she thought. He is nervous. And wanting to please her. Had Edmund ever felt such a thing? She had always known that it was a common feeling, to be frustrated with his wild plans and his gallivanting with fellow merchants in Salem Town. But it struck her now that her consternation may have also come from a deeper place, a lonely place where she was not truly understood, not really.

The insight caused her to stop walking for a moment, overwhelmed.

This pause, too, was noticed by Peter Cloyce. "May I ask you, Goody Bridges, to sit on that fallen tree for a moment or two? I do wish to enjoy this most agreeable weather."

And so they sat, and talked of small things, as they each took quick glimpses of each other throughout their intercourse. Sarah felt both the weight of her unmarried position and the lightness of possibility at the same time, and it wasn't an altogether unpleasant contrast.

"Goody Bridges, I do understand that you have already been told of my thoughts about our mutual situation," Peter said after the more casual conversation had passed and they had fallen into shared silence. "I am a good man, and I love our Lord God and follow Him in all my doings. I know that you are a righteous woman as well."

Sarah's heart constricted. A righteous woman? That was Rebecca. It was Mary too. It was even poor Joanna, who spent her last years away from most society, feeling rebuked, accused of being a witch. She did not want to disappoint this man who was clearly wanting to save her from her peril as a widow.

Once more she must have given him some signal that her mind was ill at ease, because he said again, "you are a righteous woman, Goody Bridges. You have had trials. I am aware of them, and they do echo some of my own. We are not young. I see through unclouded eyes. You are a righteous woman."

Unbidden, tears came to Sarah's eyes as he repeated what

she longed to believe about herself. He sounded so certain. Perhaps in time he could teach her to be certain as well. It was exhausting, feeling so insecure on the inside while appearing so strong to others. She yearned to be taken care of.

Impatient with herself and slightly embarrassed, she wiped away her tears and smiled at Peter. "I do thank you with my heart, Goodman Cloyce," she said. "Your words are a most welcome sound to me, like to bells or even God's own angels singing."

~ ~ ~

It was a bitterly cold day, several weeks later, when a group of darkly-clad villagers huddled together in front of Goodman Ingersoll's ordinary, hurrying as one mass from their wagons into the warmth of the house within. The ground beneath their feet was hard and solid cold, and their footsteps rang out into the frigid air around them. The stable boy stayed behind, breath emanating from his mouth as if a frosty mist rising to the slate gray sky above, tending to the horses and wagons.

Inside, Nathaniel Ingersoll welcomed the group with open arms, though he did not smile as he always did with his dear friends the Putnams. The fire in the hearth was blazing and the room was filled with the salty aroma of a venison stew bubbling in the cauldron above it. Yet even these normally satisfying signs cheered no hearts within the room, and moods were as chill as the winter day outside.

As Goodman Ingersoll's wife took the cloaks of their guests, Thomas Jr. bade all to sit around several tables that had been pushed together for their purposes. His wife Ann was so pale and disoriented that he had to half-carry her to her seat. His sister Deliverance was close by, and took both Ann's hands in hers as soon as they sat. Deliverance's husband Jonathan Walcott, the only one accepting the ale proffered by Goody Ingersoll, sank heavily into his own chair as Thomas Jr. paced the room. All was quiet except the quiet weeping that Ann had taken up once more. Goody Ingersoll flitted about the table, encouraging the ale and stew, growing more and more perturbed as each politely refused her hospitality. Her husband had to eventually shush her out of the room so as not to worry anyone.

Soon the door opened once again, the newcomers bringing a blast of arctic air with them, causing the people inside to huddle closer to each other, hoping for more wood for the fire. In walked Joseph Hutchinson, the Village man who handled many legal cases, and a friend of the Putnams. After initial pleasantries were exchanged, Thomas Jr. spoke up. "Goodman Hutchinson," he said. "Can we not hear my father's will? The time was set with no uncertainty. We should not have to wait any longer for Joseph and his mother."

Hutchinson shook his head sadly, and replied "Nay, young Thomas," which caused a small tic in the corner of Thomas' face, unpleased to be called such a diminutive moniker when he was a father of five and close to forty years old. "Your father left explicit instructions. We must wait."

Ann's weeping grew louder, and Thomas went to comfort her, scowling with frustration. His father, dead in the ground for a full month, and this was the earliest date that his young half brother and stepmother could deign to meet with them to discuss the elder's estate. Once again they seemed to be calling the shots, and he did not like it one bit. The passing of their father was difficult enough. It was to be expected – Thomas Sr. was very old and frail, and had been ailing for some time. Yet his death meant that Thomas Jr. and Deliverance would never find the love and connection they once felt with their father, so long ago, when their real mother was still alive. When Thomas Jr. heard the news that his father had died peacefully in his sleep, he was filled with an aching remorse that had not left him still.

And how his half brother Joseph and Mary Veren did preen at the funeral, sitting in the front row ahead of the rest of the family. It irked Thomas to no end. Joseph, barely twenty – half Thomas' age! – with his head bowed and tears falling down his face. As if he were the only one who had lost a dear father. Clinging to his mother as if he were still a child. And Mary herself – throughout the service she went from appearing the grieving widow to glancing haughtily around her. Thomas was certain he caught her smiling evilly at him when no one was looking. It was unacceptable, especially in the house of God. Thomas Sr. was in heaven, that much was certain. But there was little to smile about down here on earth, where sadness and grief resided.

Those gathered today chose not to pass the time in conversation, and Thomas was glad of it. The only thing on everyone's mind was Thomas Sr's estate, and how it would be divided. There was nothing to say. Not until the dreaded Mary Veren and her son arrived.

When they did, a good half hour later, their entry felt to Thomas like an invasion. Whereas the room had been silent and mournful and dark, Mary Veren clamored amidst loud outcries of apology, swooping over the inhabitants in her yellow – yellow! – woolen cloak, hugging each with dramatic flourishes. Joseph, a most handsome young man with a shock of curly black hair on his head, stood back, looking embarrassed by his mother's show. He quietly hung his own cloak on a peg next to the door but said nothing, which somehow annoyed Thomas Jr. more than did Mary's hypocritical demonstration of familial love and concern. Thomas could not muster any feelings of sorrow or fraternity with his half-brother, not even when he saw obvious pain in the younger man's face. Indeed he looked as if he might burst into tears himself: a most unbecoming thing for a grown man, especially of the Putnam name. Let him cry, Thomas thought. He has lost his lifelong champion, the father who spent all of his love on this one child, to the detriment of the rest of his offspring. What would he be now, without their father's doting? Joseph would become just another Putnam sibling, no longer lauded above the rest. The thought was enough to brighten Thomas' mournful heart.

"Let us now settle to the business that Goodman Putnam, in his infinite wisdom and steadfastness, did set us to this night, shall we?" Joseph Hutchinson invited, and room was made at the tables for the two newcomers in between the two elder Putnams.

"May we first pray for his soul, as he would have wanted it?" Thomas Jr. suggested, eager to regain his position as the new leader of his generation. He looked about the crowd, and was pleased to see everyone's attention on him, away from the gaudy woman and her son who had just joined them. Everyone nodded in agreement, and Thomas led them all in prayer.

"Dear God our most blessed redeemer, we do beseech thee this day to welcome our dear father's soul to his rightful place in heaven," Thomas intoned, his head bowed in reverence. "And we ask that you bless this gathering of your saints as we accept the gifts of his lifelong toil and devotion to you. He was the most loving of fathers and his children are grateful for his leading us in the path of righteousness. We are your humble servants and praise your name. Amen."

Everyone murmured their own "amens" and then Mr. Hutchinson began his work. He opened the parchment paper on which Thomas Sr. had signed his name many years ago, and read aloud the contents.

Several minutes later, after the will was read, Thomas Jr. jumped up from his seat and pounded his fist on the table in front of him. "This is an outrage!" he thundered. "This will not stand! My father could not have been in his right mind to give his entire estate to this Mary Veren and my half-brother!"

The rest of the group was momentarily speechless, so Thomas' words echoed in the silent room, punctuated only by the occasional snaps and hisses of the fire.

The attorney suddenly looked apologetic, now that his official duty had been discharged by reading the will. "Please allow me to tell you more about your father's wishes," he said. "We did speak of them at great length and over a period of time before he signed the document. As you know, Thomas and I have been the most devoted of friends to each other from the time of our youth, and so I can well attest that I know his heart."

Thomas Jr. huffed and crossed his arms across his chest, not caring that he looked like a petulant child to the rest of the group.

"Thomas loved all of his children equally, as God does love His own, and we are blessed for it," Goodman Hutchinson went on. "And he has watched with great pride as his elder children have grown into adults who have made much of the acres he has already granted them. He did believe that if Thomas and Deliverance continue to serve God and work hard as we are led to do, they will be happy."

Thomas Jr. started pacing the room, amazed to see Deliverance still sitting, slack-jawed in continued surprise. Why wasn't she fighting this? Why was it always he who always had to lead this tribe?

"His son Joseph, on the other hand," Hutchinson was saying. "He is still young, and unmarried, and needful of an inheritance to set him on his way. And Thomas knew how godly and devoted a mother has Mary been to their son. He wanted to provide her with the means to continue to serve in that saintly capacity."

Thomas could contain himself no longer. "My dear stepmother," he spat out the words, "is a wealthy woman in her own right already, as her long-dead first husband left her with much!"

Young Joseph spoke for the first time, looking more worried than pleased. "Brother, please," he pleaded. "I do not wish rancor among us, not at this most unhappy time. I am sure we can revisit father's intentions…"

"We will have none of that, my son," Mary Veren Putnam shut him up, looking pointedly into Joseph's eyes and placing a firm hand on his arm. "Your father has made his wishes clear. And it was with wisdom that he has done so, as he has done everything else in his life. We will accept his terms."

"Ha!" Thomas guffawed, with malice. "You will accept his terms? Of course this is what you will do. Whether it leave his first family in tattered ruins or no. What a saintly woman you are."

With that, Mary Veren Putnam stood, and quickly ushered her stunned son out of the house. Thomas glared at her, and his cold look did nothing to quell the smug smile that spread across her aging face. She met his gaze with a look of triumph which made his heart beat faster in rage. She made sure the large wooden door slammed behind her.

At that moment, Ann Putnam let out a wail that befitted a struck animal, but Thomas could do nothing to comfort his wife. He was in the midst of his own hell as he contemplated what lay ahead for them. She rose from her seat and fled the room, into the open arms of Goody Ingersoll, who had been standing behind the door to the summer kitchen, listening with intent.

"Why did you not say something, Deliverance?" Thomas demanded. "Or you, Jonathan Walcott? Do you know what this means for our family?"

Deliverance tried to embrace her brother, but Thomas shrank away in frustration. "Be calmed, Thomas," she said. "Joseph Hutchinson did say the truth. Our farms are healthy. Look to your blessings, please, brother."

"My blessings?!" Thomas cried. "Listen to my wife scream in her agony. This is a blessing? This is God punishing us. But why, sister? Why must he turn his face away from us in our hour of need?"

Jonathan Walcott put his arm around his wife and they slowly rose to leave. Both he and Deliverance knew it would do no good to argue with Thomas when he got like this. Nor would Ann accept any comfort from Deliverance. The only thing to do then was to battle the chill wind outside once more, and hope to get home without freezing.

CHAPTER FOUR
1688-1689 – One Year Later

Salem Village and Boston
Massachusetts Bay Colony
Three years before the first witch trial

Sarah Bridges – now Cloyce – was now happily ensconced in her new life in Salem Village. The transition from Rebecca's home to her new husband's was without trouble, thanks to Peter's warm welcome to not only Sarah but her children as well. Hannah and Alice took to him as a natural father, having spent too much time without one. They had more space in which to live at the Cloyce farm, as Peter had lived alone since his youngest daughter married – as her other siblings had earlier – and moved to Connecticut several years before. No longer did Sarah's family have to squeeze into the Nurses' smaller homestead – which at the outset of their stay there seemed palatial compared to the rooms they kept behind their Front Street ordinary. Soon, much to Sarah's surprise – since she was now over forty-five years old – she soon found that she was with child, and baby Hepzibah joined the fold just a few months ago. The pregnancy was troublesome, and Sarah had to take to her bed halfway through it. This time, however, being bedridden was a happy occasion, and she remained sanguine, accepting the ministrations of her eldest, Hannah. Rebecca and Mary – now grandmothers with much more leisure time – had made frequent visits and spent hours with their sister, telling stories of their childhood and remembering a more innocent time. After so many decades, the three Towne sisters had their own homes within walking distance of each other.

The Massachusetts Bay Colony continued to be in crisis, even though the Boston men had recently ousted Sir Andros from the town with no bloodshed – Andros had allowed himself to be put on a ship back to England without much trouble at all. Some say he was relieved to be done with the colony's politics. Yet the settlers were still without a new charter and seemed adrift at sea. Still, despite these troubles, Sarah was filled with gratitude to be so close to her dear sisters once again, to be married to such a good, stable man, and to have three healthy daughters.

"Three girls!" Rebecca had said, clapping her hands when she heard the news of Hepzibah's arrival. "You and Mother, just the same as ever. Perhaps your daughters will grow up to be as close to each other as we are. I pray to God's grace that it be so."

When Sarah had been in mourning and withdrawn from society back at Rebecca's home and before she married Peter, she hadn't had the opportunity to notice the ever-widening rift that was happening amongst the people of Salem Village. Now that she was fully awake and living her life again, she was painfully aware of the growing distrust between two factions of the village. The trouble stood in stark contrast to her own happiness. Rebecca had always been reticent to talk about it, as she herself harbored no real resentment toward her neighbors – although Sarah secretly rejoiced when she saw Rebecca, several years ago, actually grow angry when Deliverance Walcott's cow got loose in the Nurse farm, coming close enough to Rebecca's kitchen garden to eat the hops plants growing on the periphery. Apparently Rebecca had stormed out of her home and shooed away the beast, her harsh words drawing the attention of passersby. When she heard the story, Sarah was relieved: even her godly sister could get enraged when injustice arrived at her own doorstep. Good for her.

Sarah knew that most of the difficulties involved the ongoing controversies over what seemed like an ever-revolving slate of ministers. And the land disputes between the Village and Topsfield had gradually, over the years, shifted to boundary arguments among the Villagers themselves. Isaac Etsy continued to take the Putnams to the General Court, whose magistrates repeated their original decision: that the lands belonged to him and his sons, not the Putnams and Walcotts.

Now that Sarah was a Salem Village goodwife herself, she experienced the ministerial anxieties firsthand. Reverend Deodat Lawson had left the pulpit, as two others had before him, quickly growing tired of the infighting among his congregation. Even though the past ministers had not been successful in healing the rifts, at least they had kept in check the outright battles. The people in the church had been civil to each other in public, and made a show of serving God together with their neighbors. But now they hardly spoke to each other.

The properties of William and Joanna Towne's progeny had widened and spread across the southeast part of Salem Village like water over parched land. Mary's children had stayed behind in Topsfield, deepening the roots that their parents had planted for them, while Mary and Isaac themselves continued to farm their acres south of the Ipswich River in Salem Village. All of Rebecca's children, too, were now parents themselves, and with the arrival of each new grandchild, they purchased more acres in Salem Village, extending the reach of their original acquisition. The families found themselves in higher and higher social positions, as Rebecca's sons were named deacons and tithingmen in the congregation, and Francis continued to serve on church committees and the local militia. Over the years, the ever-revolving slate of ministers invited the Nurses, especially, to take seats further and further to the front of the meeting house during services. Life was good, and Sarah was content with what God had given her and her entire family.

Yet outside of the walls of the warm parlors of their homes, trouble simmered. Sarah and her sisters preferred to stay out of the fray, but couldn't help noticing how their success rankled some of their neighbors, especially the Putnams.

"Why?" Rebecca had asked just the other day, her voice unusually plaintive. "Why does Ann Putnam scowl at me so when I walk past her farm? We are both gospel women. I hold Christian love in my heart for her. Why must she disdain us?"

The sisters were at the table in Sarah's house, sifting through baskets of potatoes, inspecting them for rot, tossing the bad ones to the floor before filling new baskets with the healthy ones. Sarah's children Hannah and Alice would later lug the bounty to the root cellar, tucking them in for the winter.

Sarah looked carefully at a small spud, holding it close to her face, trying to decide if it should be discarded. "Rebecca, you ask the same question often," she commented. "Your pure soul has a difficult time contemplating such things as denunciation from your fellow man. But such a thing does exist. The Putnams believe that people like us should not move up in the world, yet we have."

"Aye, we have most surely been fruitful and multiplied, as God hath directed," Mary agreed, sitting back in her chair and stretching. Sarah noticed once more how both of her sisters were getting on in years and did not have the energy that they used to have.

"I have often heard the comments from Goody Putnam about how we should not be so sinful as to deny God's purpose for us. Yet is it not true what it says in the Bible? 'For you have need of endurance, so that when you have done the will of God you may receive what is promised?'" Rebecca asked again.

"Ann Putnam does make heavy use of God's will," Sarah said. "Yet I do believe that her peevishness is born from a more earthly source."

Rebecca and Mary stopped their work and looked at their sister, waiting. Sarah chuckled somewhat sadly.

"It be jealousy, pure and simple!" she answered their unspoken question. Honestly, she thought. Sometimes her sisters were so sweet and good that they seemed positively simple minded. They were both now shaking their heads in reproach.

"Nay, it cannot be," Rebecca said. "God's rewards are many. We all share in them, each according to the Lord's plan."

"And wasn't this why our dear parents took us from our homes in England, where it was almost impossible to purchase land? Should we not enjoy the fruits of their labors?" Mary asked.

"Our parents came here to worship in the way they believed," Rebecca reminded them. "It was not for worldly gain."

"It is well that you remain in that belief," Sarah said, always more cynical than her sisters. "I am certain that your lives are happier for it."

Rebecca's face was still twisted, clearly flummoxed, but Mary and Sarah wanted to shake off such talk, so they laughed together, getting back to work. Yet Sarah continued to wonder, as she had since she first realized, as a child, why it was that she was so much more skeptical than her sisters were. Perhaps not skeptical, but realistic? She was never sure. She herself had no patience with the antics of Goody Putnam, nor of her haughty eldest daughter Ann Jr. Goody Putnam acted as if her trials were the fault of Sarah and her sisters. Sarah knew that it was often easier to blame others for the fate that God has granted a person. This did not forgive it, though. At least not in Sarah's mind.

"The potatoes are done," Rebecca announced, pushing her aging body up off the stool with the help of her cane. "Let us give thanks for God's blessings."

Rebecca was a frail, gentle one, but when she dictated the end of a conversation, neither of her sisters dared argue.

~ ~ ~

"My mother gave permission for you to come with us," Ann Putnam Jr. whispered to Mercy Lewis, the Putnams' 13-year-old servant. Ann tugged on Mercy's hand, but Mercy looked uncertain.

"Tis true?" she asked, worried. "Goody Putnam told me not a half hour ago that she needs me at the hearth."

"Aye, tis, she told me so when I begged it of her," Ann answered. "Mary will meet us at the tree."

The two girls scuttled out of the Putnam homestead, blinking their eyes when they met with the shining autumn sun outside. Mercy followed her young mistress – Ann was a good four years younger than she – yet her heart was filled with both excitement and dread. Since she had come to the Putnams last year – a refugee from the Indian massacres in the District of Maine – she had learned that Goody Putnam was a stern taskmaster, and often beat Mercy for what she regarded as her shortcomings. It was much different than when she served the young Johnson family in Falmouth, in the District of Maine. That mistress was kind and Mercy had been content in their household. When the Indians attacked the settlement, most of the several hundred colonists were slaughtered, but the Johnsons had escaped, and they made sure to take Mercy with them. They went to Wells, a settlement more protected from Indian attack, but Mercy was terrified of living in the northern boundaries, so it was arranged for her to move to Salem Village and to work for the Putnams.

Young Mercy still had nightmares about the bloody night when painted-faced savages decimated Falmouth. But she did miss the relative quiet of the Johnson household, and how easy it had been to care for their small needs. In contrast, the Putnam house was difficult, and Goody Putnam constantly criticized young Mercy. The older woman's paranoia seemed to be growing by the day, especially after news of her sister's, nephews' and nieces deaths came to her from Connecticut. Mercy tried to keep low and do her job, avoiding her mistress when she could.

But her growing friendship with Goody Putnam's daughter made her burdensome life more palatable. Ann Jr. was the oldest of Thomas Putnam's children, and sometimes she didn't like the position that put her in, always being called upon to care for her younger sisters and brothers. It was exhausting. Ann saw how her parents were respected in the Village, and she knew that the Putnam family – her grandfather and his father before him – had been some of the wealthiest and most powerful farmers for generations.

Ann expected the same deference that all the Putnams garnered in the village. To be called upon to be such a subordinate in her own home was sometimes too much to bear.

When Mercy arrived the year before, Ann Jr. immediately recognized how the new servant could be of use to her. She regarded Mercy with a mix of respect – because she was older – and imperiousness – because she was a domestic. Ann and her mother would argue over which of them could give Mercy her orders.

"You are but a child of nine," Ann's mother kept reminding her. "You have many years to live before you are mistress of your own household."

But the girl pushed back, understanding already, at such a young age, how weak her mother could be. Indeed, Goody Putnam often spent whole days in her bed, clutching at the sheets, sometimes even calling to her oldest daughter to open the window, fearing that she saw the Devil lurking in the corner. Ann Jr. knew for a long time that her mother had a frail constitution, but lately her querulousness had intensified, and she seemed frightened of everything. It was pathetic, in Ann's view. But it made it easy for her to take advantage of the situation, often turning the tables so that she acted more the parent than her actual mother did.

And so Ann Jr. had no compunction in dragging Mercy away from her chores that afternoon. She ran ahead of the older girl, past the kitchen garden and up the hill behind the house. Mercy dutifully followed her, wringing her hands in worry. Ann beckoned her partner to the huge sprawling oak tree at the top of the hill, the one with a trunk so wide that they could sit in one of the hollows at its base without being spied by anyone below. The little cave was well-worn and grassless from many such meetings, with Ann's friends or by herself.

"Ann, are you about?" came a loud whisper from below. Ann and Mercy peeked around the tree to see Ann's cousin, Mary Walcott, climbing up the hill. Ann waved her to them, urging her to hurry so she would not be seen. It was the time of harvest and many of her father's hands were in the fields, easily distracted by the comings and goings of the house. But Ann wanted this meeting to be secret.

Mary, the same age as her cousin and of equally rebellious bent, dropped down to the ground, joining Ann and Mercy. Her face was flushed from the walk from her family's farm, about two miles down the road. Mary's mother Deliverance was less manipulable than Ann Sr., and it took some convincing for her to allow Mary to leave the house chores in the middle of the afternoon.

"You have finally arrived," Ann huffed. "You are late."

Mercy couldn't suppress a chuckle, which she tried to hide behind her hand. This nine-year-old girl spoke like a fully grown adult, with authority that was lacking in most children. Ann surely acted most entitled. Mercy couldn't help feeling both frustrated and awed by it.

"Let us not think of that right now. The day is fair and I am most grateful to see my good friends!" Mary commented, reaching out to take the hands of both Mercy and Ann. The three girls had formed a bond over the past year, appreciating the camaraderie that came with it. In the colony it was sometimes rare for children to have the time for friendship, what with the heavy demands that farming required. Children were expected to work, as hard as any adults did. But Ann and Mary, being of the Putnam families, had servants to do the chores. Even though their mothers, being good Christians who believed in the sin of idleness, gave them work to do, still they had more leisure time than other girls whose families were less well-off. And Mercy, well, Mercy did Ann's bidding. She felt lucky to be chosen as one of the group.

"I do agree with you, dear Mary," Ann said. "Besides, look what it is I have come to show you!"

Ann had an impish look to her face, looking around with a dramatic flair so that she could be sure of no one watching, before she moved a large stone from its place. The stone was flat and inconspicuous until she pushed it aside. Underneath she had dug a compartment in the dirt, big enough to hold the treasure she held out for the other girls to see.

It was a poppet made out of coarse muslin, roughly sewn at the edges, not like the more carefully-constructed dolls that their mothers had given them over the years. This poppet wore no clothes and had only two small black buttons for eyes. Ann held it in her upturned hands, presenting it to the others with a flourish, clearly pleased with herself.

Mercy's eyes flew wide and she put her hands up in protest. "Ann Putnam," she cried. "What do you do with such an evil thing?"

Mary, too, was shocked, too shocked to say a word.

Ann laughed.

"Oh, tis not so evil as amusing," she said, putting on a melodramatic pout. "I sewed it out of mother's scraps. A plaything, is all."

"Ann Putnam, you know that is not the truth," Mercy kept on. "When I was in Falmouth, the minister found one of those in one of the parishioners' houses and he had the goodwife in the stocks before dawn the next day. Such a crude creation is meant for witchcraft, not for frivolity!"

Mary put her hands over her ears and started rocking back and forth. She looked madly about, expecting to see the Devil himself appear before them, and knew that if that were to happen, there would be no escape. Her heart seemed to burst from her chest and she yearned to be in the safety of her mother's kitchen, doing the chores she had so gratefully escaped just an hour before.

But Ann wasn't having any of her friends' fear. She laughed again and wagged the doll in front of Mercy's face, taunting her. "So you say?" she asked. "Then whom shall we injure this day? I do also have one of my mother's silver pins in my pocket. Just a small jab to this poppet's leg. Who should have the broken leg? Perhaps Alice Cloyce, that sniveling brat who sits so superior in the church? Or her mother Sarah? My mother does tell me that there is something evil about Goody Cloyce's luck, come so far with her new husband after being laid so low after her other stupid mate up and died so early in life. Maybe we shall turn that luck around?"

Both girls jumped up and backed away from Ann, who seemed to have transformed, before their eyes, into a raving jokester, terrifying to see and hear.

Mary finally found her voice. "My good cousin," she pleaded. "Please do put away such games. Do you not know that the Devil might hear you and accept your offer? Please, pray, stop!"

Ann continued to laugh, and pretended to prick the poppet with an imaginary pin. "Ouch!" she cried with each jab. "A pox on you Cloyces! A pox on you, too, Estys, and the Nurses, too!"

She had meant the scene to be a joke, something to momentarily scare the others. She was actually surprised to see how real was her friends' terror at something so simple as a doll she had constructed in less than ten minutes. She knew what they were talking about. She, too, had heard the warnings from the pulpit and from her own parents about the danger of playing such games. But she never thought her friends would take it seriously. As soon as she saw their reaction, she felt a new energy pulse through her young body. It came over her like a flood, seeping into her blood, making her feel….powerful. Yes, powerful, that's what it was. Suddenly she wasn't a mere nine year old girl. Look what stark fear she could cause! Look how the other girls looked at her, with terror, yes, but also awe! The hearty laughter that arose in her felt almost as if it were coming from someone else. What wonderful feelings!

It didn't even matter to her that both Mercy and Mary were now running down the hill as fast as they could, away from her. Away from the poppet.

Her laughter slowly subsiding, she carefully tucked the doll back into the hole she had dug, and pulled the long flat stone over it. Yes, she thought. A most entertaining time she had had that day.

~ ~ ~

Mary Veren Putnam, an elderly woman now but still vibrant, clapped her hands in delight as her front door opened to reveal her only son Joseph. The young man, smiling broadly and doffing his cap, drew his new wife, Hannah Cloyce, into the room behind him.

"It is done!" Joseph announced. "Here is my wife, dear mother!"

Hannah, dressed in her best Sunday clothes, knelt in front of Mary and bowed in front at her feet. "Mother Putnam," she said, beaming up at the older woman, "thank you so very much for welcoming me to your family."

Mary pulled her new daughter-in-law up off her knees and embraced her. "Of course, Hannah," she said. "It is a most fitting match. And my Joseph is so happy."

Joseph, not yet twenty-one years of age, smiled broadly at the scene. Here were the two women he loved the most in the world, together as a family. His heart was brimming with pride and happiness. God had certainly granted him much.

And Hannah herself glowed with joy, going to her new husband's side and clutching his hands in her own. She never imagined that she would be wed at age eighteen, and to such a prominent young man. The last several years had been taken up with the care of her mother while Sarah wasted away in bed, despairing. Hannah never gave a moment's notice to her own life, to the Village boys around her; it was all about Sarah and the need to get her moving again.

But once Sarah did rise from her bed, Hannah found herself at a bit of a loss. The care she had taken of her mother was no longer necessary and she felt like she needed a new purpose. Her body had filled out into a woman's during Sarah's convalescence without Hannah's even noticing it. The games she would play with her younger sisters suddenly seemed silly. She took up her daily chores again, helping her Aunt Rebecca run the homestead. But boredom set in and Hannah wasn't happy even though she knew she should be, as her mother was now doing so well in her new life.

Once Sarah joined the family once again, and after Hannah and Rebecca helped her wash her frail body and air out the fetid room, she started spending time with Peter Cloyce, whom she eventually married. The Bridges girls started to attend church services regularly as they had done before Edmund died. But the Salem Village congregation was so much smaller than Reverend Higginson's in the town, and it was difficult to blend into the crowd. Hannah didn't like the nasty glances she started getting from the the Putnam families, and did her best not to engage with the likes of young Ann Putnam and her cousin Mary Walcott, except when they would start to trifle with her sister Alice, who was about the same age as they.

One day after the Sunday morning service she spied Ann Jr. and Mary taunting Alice back beyond the church yard, at the end of a stand of trees. Hannah could see that Alice was crying.

"You there," Hannah cried, running toward the little huddle. "What are you doing to my little sister?"

Ann Jr. and Mary put on a look of feigned innocence and shrugged their shoulders. "We do nothing," Ann claimed, jutting out her chin. "Alice was crying so we came over to see what was the matter."

Little Alice hiccuped and rubbed away the tears on her cheeks.

"Is this true, sister?" Hannah demanded, putting her arms around Alice's tiny shoulders.

Alice said nothing. Hannah looked at her carefully, and was chagrined to find that there was real fear in the little girl's eyes. She waited for a moment, thinking.

"You needn't worry," she finally said to Ann and Mary. "Alice is fine. You do best to leave her alone."

With that she spun around, leading Alice away from the girls, hugging her tight.

Once they were out of eyesight of Ann and Mary, Hannah stopped, kneeled down and looked into Alice's eyes. "Now tell me what was really going on," she said. "I know they were taunting you. About what?"

Alice sniffled and wiped a hand across her blue eyes. "Doesn't mama tell us we shouldn't even talk with those girls?"

"Yes, she does," Hannah agreed. "But that does not mean you have to tolerate their persecution. So you might as well tell me the truth."

Alice glanced, frightened, over her shoulder, making sure the other girls couldn't see her. "They told me when I grow up I'm going to be a witch because my grandmother and my mother before me were."

Anger spread through Hannah like a conflagration. Those young reprobates ran around the village as if they owned it, spurned on by their angry parents. It would do if someone were to put them over their knee to get a good spanking. She sighed.

"Let me give you some advice, dear one," she said to Alice. "It's better to disregard those girls. Their power will go away if we all ignored them. Believe me."

Hannah smiled at her little sister and Alice grinned shyly, grabbing Hannah's hand.

As the two walked toward the path that led to their homestead, they spied their mother Sarah ahead of them, walking slowly along with Peter Cloyce. Suddenly Hannah felt a hand on her shoulder. It was none other than Joseph Putnam, smiling broadly at her. Joseph had never said a word to her before, but she always admired his good looks and honest eyes from the meeting house loft. And she would note that Joseph would sit in the first pew on the men's side, in front of his half brother Thomas Jr.. That always made her smile.

"Young Hannah Cloyce," he said to her now, his eyes shining. "You are a force to be reckoned with, I see."

Suddenly Hannah was embarrassed. She hadn't known that anyone had observed the little scene that just occurred, and now she thought that perhaps she should have kept a more demure demeanor. Women with strong opinions were frowned upon in the colony. Her mother had taught her that.

"My sincere apologies, Goodman Putnam," she said, lowering her eyes and making a small bow. Joseph laughed out loud, his laughter booming and attractive.

"Nay, please, Hannah," he said. "There is nothing to apologize for. I do enjoy watching someone stand up for what is right. Especially when it's against young brats."

Now it was Hannah who laughed, amazed at his response. Alice stood next to her, quietly watching the scene unfold, still holding her older sister's hand. What an unusual remark from a man, and a powerful one at that. And about his own kin. It reminded her of her father Edmund, who would always show great respect for Sarah, even when she was being obstinate.

After that, both mother and daughter were being courted by two different men in the Village. Sarah was now preoccupied with her nascent relationship with Peter Cloyce, and Hannah was free to walk the village paths with Joseph Putnam without interference. He astonished her, with his intelligence and kindness and gentle respect of her. So unlike his nasty half-siblings. She fell in love quickly. So did Joseph.

Now, in front of his own mother, Joseph was reminded that the Lord's gifts were great. The passing of his beloved father Thomas Sr. just a few years ago was difficult, to be sure, and he was continually bothered by his half brother and sister trying – and failing – to wrest his riches away from him. But Hannah filled his heart with gladness and he was delighted when she agreed to marry him.

His mother Mary, now elderly herself, was frail and not able to attend the small ceremony at the meeting house. Weddings were never much of an occasion in the colony, as the members of the church frowned upon much frivolity. The Cloyce family had all attended, Sarah having recently married herself.

Now Mary Veren drew her son and her new daughter-in-law to the chairs in front of the hearth and bade her maid to bring them hot wine in silver cups. "How are you faring? Are you all hale?" Mary peppered the young people with questions. Joseph beamed at his mother, still beautiful in her old age, remembering his father's devout love for her.

"Aye, we are well. God is good, and we receive His gifts with joy," Hannah said, taking up her mother-in-law's hands in hers. "And we will stay as long as you will have us, dear mother."

Mary squeezed Hannah's hands and smiled. "I am heartened to hear it," she said. "Your old mother is becoming a lonely, decrepit woman. With Joseph's father now gone to heaven and Joseph himself spending so much time in Salem Town, I am friendless."

It was true that Joseph was in the Town more than here at home, having enough capital to hire some Village men to tend the farm. He had purchased a small house on Federal Street in Salem Town, and both he and Hannah were glad to be away from the animosity that seemed to permeate the whole of Salem Village. Joseph had parlayed his inheritance from his father into an ever-growing estate.

"I suspect that is not the truth," Joseph said, without reproach. "You still have many companions in the church. Hannah's Aunt Rebecca does still visit, does she not?"

"Aye, Rebecca and I do see each other on some occasions, much to the discomfiture of my stepchildren!" Mary agreed. "Yet both Rebecca and I do not travel easily of late, what with my bad leg and her painful back. We do get to church on Sundays and lecture days, however."

"Speaking of the church," Joseph said. "What do you think of the news that yet a fourth Salem Village minister is to be chosen?"

Hannah made an impatient sound next to him, and he patted her hand solicitously. One of the many things they had in common was a dislike of the petty squabbles about the Salem Village church. Although they were both members by dint of the Halfway Covenant – allowing membership to children of the elect – they attended the Salem Town church more than the one in the Village. But Joseph knew that his mother enjoyed a good gossip, and as always he wished to please her.

"Aye, to be sure!" Mary responded, happy to embark on one of her favorite pastimes. "It is most entertaining to watch. It is clear that word has spread through the colony that the people of Salem Village are most fractious and impossible to align along a single path. It has come to my attention that the Village is developing a reputation among the Colony as being a den of anger and disagreements. I do wonder what it is about Salem Village that makes us this way, as no other town is similar to us in our acrimony. Anyway, it has taken two years to find a replacement for Mr. Lawson."

"So they have found one?" Hannah asked, eying her husband impishly and tacitly agreeing to engage in such conversation for his sake.

"So they have," Mary said. "Yet this Mr. Parris drives a hard bargain, and has not agreed to terms as of yet."

She went on to tell the young newlyweds of the situation. Indeed it had been difficult for the Village committee to find someone who would be willing to try for a fourth time to minister to such a contentious flock. Eventually they found Mr. Samuel Parris, a man who in 1673 left Harvard before being graduated in order to use his inheritance to invest in a sugar plantation in Barbados. His venture was destroyed, however, in a killing hurricane, and since then Mr. Parris decided to return to the ministry, which he had previously studied at the college.

"My word!" Hannah exclaimed at this. "It is quite different from the histories of our past ministers, is it not?"

Mary lifted her eyes to the rafters, as if seeking guidance there. "I do agree," she said. "It does not sound like a solid foundation on which to build a unified church."

"Perhaps some business sense would be of benefit in our fragile situation," Joseph commented, almost to himself. His wife gazed at him for a moment, and then urged Mary to continue.

The congregation had appointed a number of village elders – Thomas Putnam Jr's old uncle John, Nathaniel Ingersoll, and Hannah's Uncle Francis Nurse – to negotiate a salary with Mr. Parris, but they had had little luck in building consensus between the new minister and the congregation. At least the negotiating committee combined the two factions of the village that had been on opposite sides of past controversies, and for once the Putnams seemed willing to work in collaboration with Goodman Nurse and his compatriots.

"So much has happened since we were married here! I haven't even had time to visit my mother or aunts, so I have had no idea. So for the first time in many years," Hannah commented, "the village is actually of the same mind. This is most fascinating."

"Ever more fascinating is that now the trouble seems to be between a united congregation and the minister, rather than a minister being allied with just one faction of the church," Joseph added.

"It is all silliness and bother," Mary harrumphed. "To me this Mr. Parris seems less a man of the cloth and more a mercenary."

"One cannot blame the man, mother," Joseph said. "Look at how the past three fared. And Mr. Parris, if he has a quick intellect about him, most probably knows that there is little competition for his position."

"Perhaps he <u>will</u> be the one to unite us all," Hannah said. "It is a wondrous thing to contemplate. Our happiness, dear Joseph, and the happiness of our home church."

"Would that is be so!" To this, all three drank from their cups and sat back in their chairs, contemplating the fire in the hearth before them, and praising God for their good fortune.

~ ~ ~

In the months since Sir Andros was overthrown, the ministers and magistrates in Boston worked diligently to get the colony's workings back on track. They were still without a charter, but the great Increase Mather had sailed to England to bring a set of grievances against Andros to the crown, and to negotiate a new directive. In the meantime, Deputy Governor Thomas Danforth became known as the de facto leader, as old Simon Bradstreet was growing weaker and had taken to his bed for the better part of his days and nights.

One evening in the crisp autumn, Mr. Danforth's friend Samuel Sewall urged him away from his home in Cambridge to dine with him in his townhouse on School Street in Boston. Samuel was getting worried about his friend and wanted to provide an evening of camaraderie in order to get his mind off the colony's troubles. Thomas had taken much urging to agree to the invitation, as it seemed rather frivolous at such a time, and there was a great deal of work to be done, even in the evening. There were missives to be written to Mr. Mather and his contingent in England, documents to be drawn up for the magistrates in Boston, and he still had his responsibilities as treasurer of the College. Yet in the end Samuel was successful, and a date was set.

When Thomas was drawn into the best parlor by Samuel's maid, his mind was like a wheel, reviewing over and over the details of the day, interspersed with a general sense of jagged worry about the colony's fate. It was difficult for him to turn off this constant turning of his thoughts, even when his wife Mary brought him a hot toddy and rubbed his shoulders for him when he returned home at night. Thomas felt the full weight of the colony's situation on his shoulders, and it was indeed a heavy burden.

"Thomas, Thomas!" Samuel cried out in welcome, his words shaking Thomas out of his internal agitation. "Do come in! We have opened the windows so that we may catch a breath of sea air this most agreeable evening. We are fortunate that this side of the house turns away from the noise and grime of the street. Can I get you a libation?"

Despite his dark mood, Thomas couldn't help smiling at his good friend's cheer. He saw that there was another visitor in the room, and immediately recognized young Cotton Mather, Increase Mather's son who had taken his father's place in the pulpit in Boston's North Church during Increase's sojourn to England. Mr. Mather was not yet twenty-five but had already made a name for himself in the colony, graduating early from the college where his father served as president. Thomas knew well of the young minister, as the latter had been a visiting preacher on occasion at the First Church in Cambridge, where Thomas was a member.

Mr. Mather rose out of his chair and walked across the Turkey carpet to grasp Thomas' hand. "Greetings, honorable Mr. Danforth," he said, looking Thomas full on in the face, his countenance smooth and friendly. "I do so hope you do not think our friend Mr. Sewall here was remiss by including me at your gathering."

Samuel bade the maid to fetch some good wine, and handed Thomas a plate of hard cheese, a crust of brown bread and sliced apple as they both joined the minister at the hearth. The chairs here were upholstered with good wool and quite comfortable. As Thomas sat, he noted the pain that shot through one of his knees, and marveled once more at the growing aches that permeated his aging body.

"Nay, not at all," he said to Cotton. "I am honored to be joined by such an esteemed company."

"Thomas, Thomas," Samuel said, with more excitement than was his wont. "Mr. Mather was just telling me of some most incredible accounts of the Goody Glover case. Mr. Mather, do continue. What you tell of does fill my heart with dread."

The Deputy Governor, eager to let go of the more mundane trials of running the colony, was ready to listen. Of course everyone in Boston and even beyond had heard of the witchcraft that had been discovered in the city. A man named Goodwin had reported strange happenings in his home, where his children were afflicted with terrible pains, as if they were being tortured by some invisible creature. The young girls' arms were pulled behind their backs in horrible angles, they complained of being poked with knives, at once they seemed deaf, at another they could not seem to speak. They would run about the room with their arms uplifted as if they were flying, uttering nonsensical syllables. Goodman Goodwin accused his neighbor, an old hag named Goody Glover, and she was quickly arrested. Her trial was an easy one, as she happily confessed allegiance with the Devil, and spoke of groups of women with whom she worked her evil magic. Mr. Mather himself was deeply involved in the case, observing the girls' symptoms and praying fervently for the witchcraft to stop.

Mr. Mather continued. "Twas only when the harridan was hanged in the Common for all to see that the girls' suffering ceased."

"I have not seen such afflictions before," said Samuel, bidding the maid to refill their glasses with more wine. "Although I have heard of such stories. It is of utmost importance that we remain vigilant against such evil."

"Aye, to be sure," Mr. Mather agreed. "The Devil is never too far from our ken. He sits at the ready, making his nefarious plots to steal souls away from God."

Thomas was listening intently, the fingers of both hands tented against his chin. A most devout man, he agreed with his two companions. Like Samuel he had not before witnessed himself the rough consequences of bedevilment, but he had listened to similar stories as a magistrate in the high court. To hear of it tonight did not soothe his soul as he had hoped it would. He had enough to worry about, what with the Indian wars and the lack of a charter. The colony could be on the brink of anarchy unless he and his compatriots in the government did not contain the natural anxieties of the people. Adding spectral torment and the Devil's constant threat to the chaotic mix was nothing to be cheerful about.

"How may we do such a thing, Mr. Mather?" he asked. "How do we combat the Devil's hand?"

"We must be on the look-out for his marks," Mr. Mather replied. "We must take all reports of witchcraft seriously. I, like my father, fear that with each passing decade the colony is moving further and further away from God. Blasphemy, whoredom, larceny – they are all on the rise, no matter how many jeremiads we write, no matter how many times we ministers gather to discuss the difficulty. The people need to be vigilant. That is why I intend to write of the Goodwin case."

"I have heard of such a rumor," said Samuel, regarding the younger minister with admiration. "I do hope that you will publish."

"Aye, that is my intention," Mr. Mather replied. "If the people know the symptoms of witchcraft, they will be armed with the knowledge with which to combat it. When the Goodwin children first started to exhibit signs, they were thought of by some medical men to be some physical malady. They attempted several ersatz remedies – leeching, for example – but all that did no good. It wasn't until I arrived that the true cause was detected, and a legitimate cure could be applied."

Mr. Mather looked pleased with himself as he told the story, leaning back and smiling with satisfaction. Indeed the man was known to be a self-confident one, Thomas remembered. This was an excellent characteristic for a young leader, especially in the face of increasing sin rampant in some parts of the colony. He was relieved to know that such a man was looking out for the souls of the people, while he himself was dealing with more secular matters of government.

"Woe, woe, witchcraft," he heard Samuel mutter to himself. And then more audibly to the other men: "We are most grateful to have such a warrior as yourself, Mr. Mather, to help us fight the evils of the Devil himself."

The younger men both looked to Thomas expectantly. Thomas understood, then, that this meeting was not an impromptu one. He could see that his friend Samuel had orchestrated it in order to forge a partnership among the three of them. Each of a different generation, with Thomas as elder, and each bringing his own expertise to the circle. It did not take Thomas many moments to realize that it would be a formidable friendship, all in the service of leading the colony in its devotion to God.

Thomas, never one for jocularity, smiled. And when he did, the other men did too. "Aye, Samuel, you speak the truth," Thomas said. "It is indeed a war. And one very much worth winning."

The three men drank in agreement. Nothing more needed to be said on the subject, and they went on to discuss more mundane things. The bonds were forged, and Thomas was glad of it. At this perilous time, he could use all the partners he could get.

CHAPTER FIVE
1690 – One Year Later

Essex County and Boston
Massachusetts Bay Colony
Two years before the first witch trial

It was a bitterly cold January, and the food stores of the people of Salem Village were already becoming depleted. The cold started early this season, with snow covering the fields in early November and not melting since. Samuel Parris, the new minister, wrapped his cloak tighter around him, staving off the chill as best he could, and scowled at the dwindling wood pile at his feet. The ground below was solid, with a layer of ice covering every surface. Anger filled his heart as he bent to pick up an armload of wood and walked back to the parsonage.

He slammed the door upon entry, ducking his head under the lintel as he entered the front parlor. His wife, daughter and niece were sitting at the table, close to the fire, and they jumped at the sound of the wooden door crashing into its frame. Samuel's wife Elizabeth stood and ran to her husband, helping him with his cloak, taking his hat. Her eyes were cast downward and her movements were anxious, flitting around Samuel like a bee around a hive. The minister pushed her away and stomped across the floorboards, dropping his load of wood in front of the hearth. His daughter and niece quickly returned to their Bibles, feigning more interest in their studies than they actually felt. When the minister crashed about the house like this, they knew his temper was aflame. And when this happened, nothing could assuage it. The best thing they could do was to lay low and hope they wouldn't draw his attention.

Mr. Parris dropped his tall frame heavily into the one upholstered chair in front of the hearth. "This is an accursed place, to be sure," he grunted. "How do these people think we can survive on such a paltry allowance of wood? We are certain to be frozen to death by the springtime."

Mrs. Parris brought her husband a tankard of hot cider, and tentatively rubbed his shoulders from behind him, her face drawn and worried. She knew not to argue or even respond when he was in such a foul mood.

But he wasn't about to accept her ministrations. He stood up again and started to pace the room. Looking about the place, he felt even more frustrated. What a humble abode for such a man as he, a merchant who ruled over an entire sugar plantation in Barbados not two years ago. He remembered the fine furnishings of his beautiful Carribean manor, the silver service and the Turkey carpets on the floor and the intricately carved furniture. How had it come to this? How had he sunk so low as to accept the ministry in such a tiny hamlet as Salem Village? Why had God forsaken him, taking all of his sugarcane and wiping out the entire plantation with such a deadly hurricane?

When he was first approached by the Salem Village committee, he thought he was quite shrewd in his salary negotiations. At first they sent him a group of old men: the elderly Putnam brothers, Goodman Ingersoll, John Gould, Francis Nurse. A laughable contingent, to be sure. When they made their offer, Samuel was staying with his family in Boston, and refused to answer right away. Before his father died he had taught him well in the art of negotiation, and his first rule was never to appear too eager. And indeed Samuel wasn't. He was hoping that with the connections his father had had in Boston, he might be called by another, more prosperous community. So he had put the Salem Village men on hold for a good several months. He had heard about their minister problems, and he wasn't about to be the fourth failed leader. Everyone knew that a more contentious congregation did not exist throughout the entire colony. Samuel kept hoping for a better offer.

But then the spring came and a more youthful committee was sent to Boston from the north. This time men closer to his own age urged him to join them. Samuel learned that these committee members were all third generation colonists – Thomas Putnam Jr., Francis Nurse's sons-in-law John Tarbell and Thomas Preston – and, better, that they represented both sides of the disputing factions in the village. He found these men to be more reasonable than their fathers and uncles, and they agreed with his demands for salary and firewood.

It wasn't until Samuel agreed to the post and had moved his family to the tiny parsonage in Salem Village that he discovered that the entire congregation had never voted on the offer that the committee had put forth to him. By then it was too late. No other offers were forthcoming from other towns. He had made the move, and his wife, daughter, niece and servants were already settling into their new home.

"A pox on them all," Samuel muttered, still pacing, remembering the events that brought him to this freezing day. "Some pay their fees, some do not. Some provide firewood, some do not. As if they were the ones who know God's will and can dictate what is right."

Mrs. Parris shuffled her daughter Betty and her niece Abigail Williams away from the room, sending them upstairs to the loft above. She knew that Tituba would be crouching there, feigning work, avoiding her master. Tituba would take care of the girls. They shouldn't be around Samuel when he gets like this. She scurried around the hearth, peeking into the root vegetable stew simmering over the fire, hoping that her husband's tantrum would wear itself out as it often did. He did know how to instill fear in not only his family, but in his entire flock. She didn't blame him. They had indeed come to a bad deal in Salem Village. Over the past nine months she had watched her husband as he sublimated all of his anger into a fiery passion for the word of God. She knew because he told her over and over: the problems with the Village came from the congregation's slipping away from God's grace. They valued their own positions in the Village over their humble acceptance of God's word. They were vain and unruly. He would not allow himself to assume a weakened role in leading them to a more righteous existence. They might keep their money and their firewood in abeyance, but he would prove to them that they should bend their knees to the wisdom of God.

Mrs. Parris secretly wondered at this. She had hoped that the move to Salem Village would bring them all a warm sense of community and love amongst the people. This was surely missing in their lives in Barbados. There were few chosen people there, and the climate was steamy and hot. She had hated it, as had her daughter. Samuel had always ruled the family with an iron hand, but she thought that God's calling would soothe and quiet him. And didn't the colonists leave their homeland precisely because they rejected priests who put themselves above the people? Weren't the settlers men who decried the adornments and riches that such religious leaders demanded?

Some people in the Village, she noticed, had responded well to her husband's stern and judging style. The Putnams, for example, seemed positively relieved when they heard his sermons. And she had heard Thomas Putnam Jr. thank Samuel many times, telling him that his strict interpretation of the Bible was most welcomed by the truly righteous in the congregation. There were others like him – the Walcotts, the Hutchinsons, the Goulds, the Ingersolls – who gladly provided the firewood and fees that Samuel had been promised.

But even though the committee that finalized the deal with the minister was composed of men from the opposing sides in the village, that consensus quickly fizzled as some became not so enamored of Parris' ways. The Nurses, the Estys – those families especially balked when Samuel announced that the Salem Village church would no longer follow the Half-Way covenant. The Nurse sons-in-law Thomas Preston and John Tarbell soon regretted their role in bringing the new minister to the village. They pointed out that most towns and villages in the colony were adhering to the Half-Way rule in order to make church membership more accessible to more people. Indeed many of the children in these families had already been admitted to the Salem Village church, even without professing the conversion experience. How could they go back now?

Samuel, though, was having none of it. Elizabeth didn't expect it. Her husband was a stubborn man, and with his newfound belief in God's speaking directly to him, he would not back down from his increasingly conservative viewpoints.

Above him, Betty and Abigail crouched at the top of the stairs, watching the minister fret.

"You girls come back here, will ye?" urged Tituba, one of the slaves that Mr. Parris had brought back from Barbados. Abigail shushed her by petulantly pushing the older woman away. Tituba tried to muster superiority as she looked directly into Abigail's face, but her bravado quickly disappeared when she saw such severity in the young girl's eyes. In truth, Abigail sometimes frightened Tituba, what with her hollow, empty and often angry look. It was as if the girl had visited hell and brought some of its fire back with her. Tituba tried to feel sorry for her, as she knew that she had lost her entire family in the massacres to the north before coming to live with the Parrises. Abigail would not speak of her past, but Tituba could imagine that the scenes left engraved in her soul were torturous. The Abenaki were known to brutally kill their enemies. For such a young girl to watch her own parents bludgeoned and sliced to death, it must be a most painful plight. Yet Tituba saw no sadness in Abigail's countenance. Only cutting rage.

For Abigail's part, she had no use for the slave, whose dark skin bore a strong resemblance to those butchers who had killed her family. When she first arrived in the parsonage, having been taken in by the Parrises out of pity after her terrible ordeal to the north, Abigail had been horrified to meet both Tituba and her husband John Indian. She had never before seen such dark people in a colonist's home, and it felt to her like her uncle – the religious leader of the community no less – had himself welcomed the devil into his own abode. From the very beginning Abigail avoided both servants, and did everything she could to disobey Tituba, who was called upon by Mrs. Parris to serve as a kind of nanny to the girls. When the matriarch was about, Abigail would appear docile toward the slave, almost respectful. Yet behind closed doors she would often pinch and poke Tituba, who could do nothing about the abuse.

Young Betty, on the other hand, seemed to Tituba to be as much an angel as Abigail was a demon. The child was frail and her skin was so light that it appeared translucent. She would never say a word against her parents or Tituba, and indeed was now looking afraid, torn between her cousin's directive to watch what was unfolding downstairs and her dear slave's disapproval. Although she was all of eight years old, Betty instinctively put her thumb into her mouth and started rocking back and forth, trying to soothe herself.

Abigail, seeing the fear in both her cousin and Tituba, rolled her eyes in disgust and turned her attention back to her uncle below. He was pushing away her aunt's attempts at making him comfortable – offering him a thick linsey woolsey blanket for his shoulders, bringing him more cider. His anger seemed to fill the room around him. Indeed the very fire in the hearth looked like it was cowering before his scowling face. Ever since she arrived here in Salem Village, Abigail was fascinated by the minister. She had just come from a monstrous place, lucky to have escaped from the Abenaki with her own life intact. Much as she hated it, she felt lost, as if God had turned his mercy against her. Like she had no control over what was to happen to her ever again. But here was a man who, with his thunderous words and vivid descriptions of the hell that awaits sinners, could make men and women both cower before him. Abigail loved to watch the fear on the congregation's faces when her uncle preached from the high wooden pulpit above them, the sounding board behind him amplifying his voice so that it seemed to be coming from God Himself. How dare some of these weak people defy him? How could they even think to keep their fees and their firewood to themselves, leaving the Parris family cold and hungry? Her hands clenched in fists beneath her apron. This would not do. This would not do at all.

Tituba finally succeeded in pulling young Betty away from her cousin, leaving the older girl to her eavesdropping. Once inside the little room the two cousins shared, Tituba gathered the tiny girl to her lap, and Betty rested her white capped head against the slave's chest. "I am much afraid, Tituba," Betty said, her words muffled from the thumb she still had in her mouth. "Papa's rage is formidable indeed. Are our troubles because I have sinned?"

Tituba couldn't help smiling to herself. She rarely smiled. Her life was not an easy one, and her only joy came from this young child, whom she loved as if she were her own daughter. Betty was young, hardly walking when the daunting Mr. Parris bought Tituba from a neighboring planter in Barbados back when he lived there, trying to make a fortune from his sugar plantation. Mrs. Parris, herself a rather gaunt, sometimes sickly woman, seemed overwhelmed by the need to care for both a young child and her belligerent husband. It wasn't long that Betty was coming to Tituba for comfort, even though at first the woman frightened her. Not much more than a baby, Betty hadn't spied too many people outside of the plantation house, and Tituba's brown skin and cadenced speech seemed strange. But soon Betty began to love how the slave would put emphases on odd syllables, as if she were singing rather than speaking English. And Tituba was always ready with a hug or a tankard of the sweet juice that she would press from sugarcane and coconuts.

Besides caring for Betty, though, Tituba had to endure constant lashings from Mr. Parris, who was always unhappy with her service. She would have to awaken before the sun rose and did not lay her body back down on her thin pallet until after midnight. Mrs. Parris would often keep to her own much more comfortable bed all day, sweltering in the Barbados heat and what she regarded as the savages around her. There were other slaves in the large house, but for some unknown reason it was Tituba that the master and mistress would inevitably call when they needed something.

"Tituba? Shall I confess to papa? Will that please God, and turn the villagers' hearts toward us again?" Betty's quiet voice interrupted Tituba's thoughts.

"Hush, now, child," she chided. "What sin could such a precious girl commit that would bring God's wrath down upon us?"

Betty lifted her head from Tituba's chest and looked up at her with eyes filled with fear. "Tis a terrible one, Tituba," she said. "It has brought me these vomiting fits that have overtaken me these recent days."

Tituba thought of how Betty had indeed been quite ill of late, not being able to keep down her food, no matter how bland the slave made it. Suddenly the slave was more concerned.

"Why, mistress Betty," she said. "You do believe sin is what is causing you to ail, and not merely a temporary pestilence in your belly?"

"Aye, Tituba, that is what I am telling you! I worry so. I fear hell with all of my heart and soul. Yet I do believe that is where I am bound!"

Betty started to cry, quietly enough not to disturb her parents below or her cousin just outside the door. Tituba was no longer charmed by the fleeting worries of a child, and it seemed that a trickle of very cold water was dripping down her spine, chilling her even more than the frigid air in the upstairs room.

"Tell me, child," she pleaded, shaking Betty just a tiny bit. "What is it that you did commit? You can confess to me, aye, tis fine. I will not betray the confidence you place in me."

Betty continued to cry, squeezing her eyes shut, terrified to speak. But Tituba kept shaking her and she knew that she must confess, now that she had brought up the subject. "I did take a slice of mother's brown bread from the larder, although the meal was finished," Betty whispered, ready for the hand of the Lord to smite her where she sat. Would it be painful? she wondered. Would it be quick? She tried so hard to be good, she knew she did. But she had been so hungry. She coveted the bread in her very being, even though she knew this was a sin. And since she ate of the forbidden food, every swallow had seemed like knives piercing her gullet.

As Betty clenched every muscle in her body, awaiting God's punishment to befall her, she felt Tituba relax next to her. The woman's arms went round the girl, pulling her close once again.

"Ah, Betty," she said, and Betty could hear the relief in her voice. "It be true, believe it when I say that you should not have taken the bread without your mother's permission. It was wrong, is what it was. Tis no true vile sin, though, my girl. Nothing that would warrant God's wrath. Sure to be not worryin' your poor head."

At that moment Abigail came loudly through the door, pushing the heavy wood back so it banged against the wall behind it. She looked down at the scene before her and threw her hands up in disgust. "What is this I see?" she demanded. "Crying again, Betty? Tituba, be gone. My uncle is calling for his evening meal. He shall be angry if you linger."

Betty sniffed as Tituba jumped up and left the room, eager not to engage Abigail any further. She took one quick look back at her favorite child, and gave her an encouraging smile. Betty, still traumatized, tried to smile back, but then lay back in the bed, her face toward the wall, hoping that Abigail wouldn't berate her any further.

~ ~ ~

Sarah Cloyce had made her homestead into a welcoming, warm one, and she much preferred being there with her family rather than dealing with any matters in the Village. Long gone was her fascination with colonial politics from her days on the Salem Town wharves. In the Village, winter had arrived and the upstairs rooms were often uncomfortably cold, but Sarah always made sure that the fireplaces in the lean-to kitchen and in the hall were well-stoked and cheery. Sometimes when she looked around to see her dear husband and children gathered round her, she couldn't help thanking God for her good fortune. As she aged, her sense of contentment grew, and she would like nothing better than to live out her years in the warm comfort of her husband Peter and her little family. Her sisters Mary and Rebecca continued to do well with their farms and their own families, and death had not come to any of their doors, not since Edmund died so many years ago. Despite the ongoing controversies over the new minister and land boundaries, life was good.

It was early evening and Sarah's daughters were at the kitchen board, Alice paring carrots for the evening meals and little Hepzibah at her feet, carefully picking up the scraps that fell to the floor. One of Hepzibah's favorite things was to present the hog and cattle with a bucket of slop, believing in her four-year-old mind that the animals were her best friends. Sarah smiled beatifically, seeing the lines of her departed husband Edmund in Alice's face, and those of Peter in Hepzibah's curls and sharp nose.

"Mia!" Hepzibah called as her mother approached them, using the name she had made up for Sarah when she was just beginning to talk. "It is smelly in this house!"

Alice laughed and patted her little sister on her head, letting go the paring knife for a moment. "Tis not a polite thing to say, sister!" she chided jokingly.

"Tis true, isn't it?" Hepzibah insisted. "These new candles are horrid."

The entire family had made the year's supply of candles just two weeks ago, right after Peter had butchered the old hog, using the rendered fat for tallow. The candles always were malodorous, but the new ones were particularly so, not having the benefit of releasing their pungent smell over the course of months. Even though Hepzibah was right – the candles did smell terrible - the day of the year when the family came together to make them was one of her favorites, as it was a project requiring all hands. This was the first time Hepzibah was old enough to help, scrunching up her face with concentration as she carried each stick just dipped into the barrels of wax across the room to hang to dry. The little girl hadn't really noticed the ubiquitous smell in the house until she discovered its origin.

"Aye, tis true," Sarah agreed, moving toward the huge copper pot simmering with vegetables over the hearth. "Yet they do give off such cheerfulness on such a dark afternoon as this, do they not?"

"When I went with Aunt Rebecca to Goody Putnam's house just yesterday, I did notice that they had candles made of beeswax, so sweet smelling and pleasant," Hepzibah insisted. "Why do we not make those kinds of candles, Mia?"

Sarah sighed. She knew she shouldn't have let Hepzibah accompany her sister to visit the peevish Ann Putnam. She wished Rebecca wouldn't have gone, either, but her sister insisted on bringing fresh linens to Mrs. Putnam who was fretting over her new babe, sickly in the cradle. Sarah wondered what it would take to finally convince Rebecca that such acts of mercy would make no difference, that Ann Putnam and her entire family would always carry a grudge against her.

"The Putnams are a wealthy family," Sarah told her youngest daughter. "They have the means to purchase such costly things."

"We," Alice said with her usual cheerfulness, "do not."

Hepzibah frowned but dropped the subject, carrying a handful of orange and brown scraps to the bucket across the room. Sarah was glad to be done with the conversation. She was in no mood to be compared to the Putnams, nor any of their friends. This was why she so much preferred being in the bosom of her family rather than at the meeting house or any of the small shops nearby. The ages-old rift between various factions within the village had not been at all ameliorated by the arrival of the new minister, Mr. Parris. The Putnams, Walcotts, Ingersolls and others lined up behind the minister, providing the firewood that was promised, and even going further to grant the Parrises the deed to the parsonage. The latter was never part of the initial agreement, and soon Francis Nurse and Isaac Esty and their grown sons were protesting. It didn't help that Mr. Parris had chosen a rather aggressive stance with his new congregation. At a time when most parishioners across the Massachusetts Bay Colony were moving away from the strict rules of their forefathers, Mr. Parris preached the opposite, coming down with a vengeance against sinners. He even unilaterally rescinded the Half-Way covenant when so many other congregations were embracing it, allowing children of the elect to join the church without a conversion experience.

The Putnams and their ilk couldn't have been more pleased. They always disdained the liberal leanings of the merchants who lived in Salem Town and those in the village whose farms lay along the border with the port. They wouldn't even adopt any of the new fashions coming in on the glorious ships, the bright colors of fabrics arriving from Spain and beyond. They thought most of the town's amusements to be of the devil.

So now it's because we're "citified" that the Putnams dislike us, Sarah thought. So be it. She saw no harm in the income that diversifying into town businesses brought. Her own Hannah, now nineteen and married just last year to Joseph Putnam, had sent home goods that Sarah had never been lucky enough to enjoy before: a box of tea from China – an unheard-of luxury – and last week a pair of strong shoes made in London.

Sarah remembered Hannah's visit when her daughter presented her with the wooden box tied with a piece of rope. There she was, Hannah, a grown woman now, so strong and happy. Hannah certainly deserved it. She had spent enough years caring for her mother who had come so close to death from sadness. The young wife was wearing a waistcoat of blue indigo and two overlapping skirts of fine wool, and her face was rosy with happiness.

"You should not spend so much on such luxuries, my dear," Sarah had said, hugging her new shoes to her chest. "It is enough to me that you are content. And are you, with young Joseph?"

"Aye, I am, mother," Hannah had responded. "He is a kind, godly man, and loves me so. He just invested in another ship, and I do like spending most of our time in our home in Salem Town. To be sure, life there is....peculiar."

Sarah laughed. "Peculiar? What of this?"

"Oh mother, it is such a different world from the Village," Hannah replied. "Here at home, people seem so dreary. Farming and God, that's the extent of it, to be sure."

"And what is the problem with such things?"

"I do not intend to offend, mother," Hannah was quick to assure Sarah. "I do understand that our neighbors are good people, and it is good that they are so. But in town, life is so much....faster. So many different things to see! So much diversity in the faces of the men and women who walk past me every day. It does seem to me that God would smile on such depths of experience. Does He not wish us to be happy?"

Sarah smiled now, thinking of the conversation. Hannah was always such a hopeful, sanguine child, and she was glad of it. The girl's cheerfulness was largely what brought her mother out of her darkness many years ago. And Hannah's perceptions of the difference between the town and the village were quite legitimate. Look how the distinction in character played out in the Putnam family itself. Young Joseph and Hannah, while dedicated church members, enjoyed the benefits of their more urban existence: a bright outlook, ever-increasing coffers from Joseph's diversified business interests, friends, an active social life. Sarah was glad for Hannah. On the other hand, the other Putnams, the stepsiblings who despised young Joseph, were still farming the village as their fathers and grandfathers did before them, and seemed sour and dark in contrast.

She thought again: why did Rebecca insist on trying to find friendship with that family? And why did she take Hepzibah with her on her recent trip? Sarah was content with her life. She didn't need her youngest child starting to make comparisons between their home and Ann Putnam's, especially when the Cloyce homestead would always be the inferior in that viewpoint.

Peter came through the front door, red in the face from the cold yet sweating from his work in the barn. The mare had thrown a shoe just the day before and Peter had been trying to replace it. Sarah knew that this particular mare was ill-tempered and did not accept ministrations easily.

"There they are, my good and loyal women!" Peter called out, interrupting Sarah from her thoughts. Hepzibah jumped up from the ground and wrapped her little arms around her father's waist, trying to bury her face in the dark wool of his cloak. Thank God, Sarah thought. Thank God that He granted us a child to solidify our union. And thank God that Peter has accepted her children by Edmund as his own.

"And there, too, is my good and loyal husband," Sarah answered, smiling at Peter. Both Sarah and Peter were aging, it was a fact that couldn't be denied. But she was grateful for their continued health, and the health of her dear sisters as well. It was one of God's blessings to watch one's children grow and make happy lives of their own. Both Rebecca and Mary were already grandmothers, and Sarah herself would probably become one soon. Besides poor Edmund who was taken from this life way too soon, members of the Towne family and their spouses had been most blessed to live long lives. Sarah said a quick prayer in her mind, asking for God's continued beneficence. Please, Lord, she said to herself. Please, continue to keep my family safe. Once she thought the words, a nagging pinch of worry came over her, and didn't know why. What was there to fear? Look at what she had already endured: the loss of her first husband, her parents, losing Edmund's Topsfield farm, having to move to the Town, the depressions she fell into. Surely it was to be expected that God would be smiling upon her now, rewarding her for all of her past suffering.

~ ~ ~

Ann Putnam Jr. and her maid Mercy Lewis clung to each other in fear, cowering in Ann's room under one of the upstairs dormers. Mercy put her hands over her ears. "Make it stop!" she gave out a hoarse, quiet cry. "Tis like the screams of the Devil himself!"

The wails were coming from the large room next to them,

the one with the big fireplace and a finely upholstered bed. Ann's parents' room. It was just a week ago that similar wails emitted from the room, as Ann's mother labored for almost twenty hours with the birth of baby James. It was a difficult birth and was attended by many women from the village, as was the custom. Even Rebecca Nurse, whom Mrs. Putnam never liked, came with clean linens to help, her little niece toddling along after her. Ann remembered that scene, which had not been a good one. As soon as her mother spied old Rebecca who had entered the room slowly, leaning on her gnarled cane, she bid her leave. Ann was surprised to see that her mother could be so distracted by a guest amidst such enormous physical pain. But sure enough, her mother's eyes had come into focus and seemed herself again for a moment, escaping her dire situation long enough to point her finger to the door and cry out: "Rebecca Nurse! Get out! I will have no such woman at my trying time!"

The old woman had looked surprised, her beatific smile slowly disappearing. "As you wish, Goody Putnam," she said. "Yet please do accept this gift of linen which I just now completed on my best loom. I do mean to bring you comfort, and not distress."

At that moment young Hepzibah peeked out from behind her aunt's skirts, her blue eyes wide in wonder at the scene before her. Mrs. Putnam looked like a crazed woman, her frizzy hair all askew, her shift and the sheets about her wet with sweat, her face contorted in pain. The little girl was truly frightened.

Mrs. Putnam had caught sight of Hepzibah's curious, confused gaze and narrowed her eyes at the young girl. "You," she said, gasping as another contraction took over her body. She grasped the hands of her sister-in-law Deliverance who sat next to her, trying hard to help. Deliverance herself yelped with pain from the vice-like grip of her sister's hand.

By the time the contraction passed, Rebecca had shuttled her niece out of the room, saddened at Goody Putnam's state and her rejection of her aid. Hepzibah looked up at the old woman, questioning. "Dear Hepzibah," Rebecca said, gently pushing her niece toward the stairs. "Do not fret. Goody Putnam is a woman in labor. She suffers in childbirth because it was decried by God himself, once He discovered the dire sin that Eve committed by eating the apple."

"But aunt," Hepzibah said. "Why does she hate you so?"

Rebecca smiled sadly and responded: "Rifts between our families go back generations. Yet I always do hope that one day we can move beyond such petty squabbles to love each other in Christ."

Ann Jr. remembered that day, and the set-to between her mother and Rebecca Nurse, as if it happened at some very distant time, and not just a single week ago. Once James was finally born, he was tiny and sickly, and would not thrive, no matter how much care was bestowed upon him by her mother and her Aunt Deliverance. And now, just an hour before, the baby had gone to God in heaven, too good for this cruel world.

Ann herself was more frightened of her mother's reaction than of her baby brother's death. The elder Ann started wailing as soon as Deliverance pronounced the tiny bundle gone – and she hadn't quit since. The screams were so deep and raw that they hardly seemed to come from her mother, rather from some other mysterious, dark world.

"Shush, Mercy!" she admonished her friend. "Do not speak of the Devil at such a time as this. To say his name is sometimes to call him forward. We have no need of that right now."

"I know of despair," Mercy said. "I myself am filled with it when I remember the slaughter of my family by the red savages. But this? This seems to be something altogether different."

"You know my mother has always been fragile," Ann Jr. commented. "And she is doubly bereaved with my brother's death."

Indeed, it was just three weeks ago that the Putnams had received word of the deaths of Ann's sister Mary Bayley and her three children to the burning fever. Even though it had been many years since Mary moved to Connecticut with her minister husband George Bayley, still the sisterly bonds between Mary and Ann remained ironclad. The two women wrote to each other frequently, so much it felt that the distance between them disappeared. So when Goody Putnam heard of the deaths, she almost could not function, and took to her bed immediately. Ann's father Thomas was very worried, as his wife's time was coming and he thought the news might hurt the child. Yet Goody Putnam remained morose and pale. Ann Jr. had heard her raving at her father, talking of the Devil and how he was coming for the entire Putnam family. Claiming that God had forsaken them, as He had with his loyal follower Job.

"We should do as your younger brothers and sister have done.

We should leave this place of horror until your mother has regained her sanity," Mercy suggested. The day before, sensing what was to happen with James, Thomas Putnam sent the three younger children to stay with his sister Deliverance. He told Ann to stay at the Putnam farm, suspecting that his wife would need the help of his oldest daughter.

"We cannot. Father has ordered me to remain. We must continue to witness dear mother's awesome grief."

"Woe be to us, then," Mercy said, covering her ears again. "Perhaps your mother is right. Perhaps God is smiting us."

At that, Ann's heart was filled with rage. Why should her family suffer so, when others thrived? They must be laughing at her, those girls like Hepzibah and Alice Cloyce, like the grandchildren of Rebecca Nurse and Mary Esty. Girls who looked so high and mighty as their families continued to prosper and multiply. Meanwhile her mother loses her baby, her sister, and her precious nieces and nephews all at once. Ann knew that her mother had suffered from several miscarriages over the past years as well. And the Towne women's farms thrived while her father lost his inheritance to the uncle whose name she was not allowed to mention within the Putnam household. This would not do. This would not do at all.

~ ~ ~

"For all the law is fulfilled in one word, even in this: Thou shalt love your neighbor as yourself!" Mr. Parris shouted from the raised pulpit, the cold interior of the Salem Village meeting house reverberating with his intensity. The breath of those in the balcony – the children, the servants – rose from their mouths in foggy wisps through the frigid air, and everyone in the benches wrapped their cloaks tight about them, trying in vain to ward off the bitter cold. The minister was moving into the second hour of his sermon, and many were riveted to his words.

"But if ye bite and devour one another," Mr. Parris intoned, looking piercingly into the eyes of some in his congregation, "take heed that ye not be consumed one of another."

At the front of the room, Thomas Putnam, Nathanial Ingersoll and Jonathan Walcott all nodded their heads in approval. Here the minister was, trying his best to unite the community, and people like Goodmen Nurse and Cloyce had been fighting against him from the very beginning. Truly they were the ones that the minister was chastising in his choice of verses from Galatians.

"This I say then!" Mr. Parris boomed. "Walk in the spirit, and ye shall not fulfill the lust of the flesh. For the flesh lustest against the Spirit, and the Spirit against the flesh, and these are contrary to one other: so that ye cannot do the things that ye would."

Sarah Cloyce fidgeted in her seat, even though she was nestled snugly between the warm bodies of her two sisters. What was she to make of this man, this minister? She knew that God watched his flock with a careful eye, and that they were all to fight against sin. Yet in her mind the Lord was not only stern but loving. When she heard Him speak to her, His voice was soft and kind. This was the God that came to her after she almost turned her back on Him so many years ago. This was the God that brought her Peter and lifted her up out of her misery. But Mr. Parris was invoking fear and trepidation in the congregation, calling them to love each other with words as harsh as a hammer crashing onto an iron anvil. It did not make sense. Wasn't this the time, after the Village could not unite in the support of all of the three ministers before him, to use wisdom, strength, yes, but also quiet leadership to bring them together? To hear both sides, to try to understand?

But in Sarah's opinion, Mr. Parris was only stirring up anger, fear and hate. She wished she didn't have to attend services at all, given the intense worry it brought her every time. Surely there was already enough fear to deal with in the colony. Many of the young men in the Village had been called to the north to fight against the French-backed savages who were ransacking English communities left and right. And since Andros' overthrow, the colony was without a charter from the new King and Queen back in the home country, so no one was secure in their land holdings or legal fights against one another. It was a precarious time for the Colony.

"Now the works of the flesh are manifest, which are these," the minister continued. "Adultery, fornication, uncleanness, wantonness, idolatry, witchcraft, hatred, debate, wrath, contentions, heresies, drunkenness. I warn you, as I did before, that those who live like this will NOT inherit the kingdom of God!!!"

In the loft right above the Towne sisters' heads, an icy shiver slipped down the back of Ann Putnam Jr's neck, as if the very Devil himself were touching her. She put her arms around her cousin Mary Walcott on the one side and her maid Mercy Lewis on the other, pulling them closer, as if their bodies could protect her from the Evil One. It was true, she thought. The Village was in danger of such sin that she had never before witnessed. It must be, as Mr. Parris – someone her father had complimented and held up during many conversations over the supper board in the last year – was obviously trying very hard to weed it out of the congregation. She must be vigilant in warding off the Devil, for not only her own sake but also that of her parents. Poor mother, she thought. She had been so weak since James' death that she could not even get out of bed for Sunday services. The skin of her delicate face was so white, she looked almost like a ghost. Ann was the oldest, even though she was only a girl. Wasn't there anything she could do to help change the course of destiny for her weakening family?

Down below, Rebecca Nurse looked forward to the next part of Galatians, which she knew was a stark contrast to the words of woe that the minister had chosen to present. Even as a girl she loved to read the verses that followed: "But the fruit of the Spirit is love, joy, peace, longsuffering, gentleness, goodness, faith…." Yet Mr. Parris stopped his recitation before reaching those words, calling for everyone to bow their heads in prayer. It didn't feel right, and Rebecca was filled with guilt for even having that thought. But the beauty of the Bible chapter was the contrasts it provided: God smites the wicked, but he also provides such love and care for his people. Why wasn't Mr. Parris talking about the love? She wanted to think the best of him, as she believed wholeheartedly that the congregation needed a strong leader in God. But she was beginning to understand why her dear husband Francis was joining with the village faction that refused to pay fees to support the minister.

After the prayer, Mr. Parris continued, using his own words this time. "Do ye not see, ye people of Salem Village?" he thundered. "Evil has come to our congregation. God is punishing us for the sins of the flesh that ye have committed. The savage to the north kills us. There is death among us. There is disease, pestilence, near and far. And many of you choose to turn your back on your own minister. I tell ye, turn your face back to God! Escape certain death by committing to a pure life!"

Abigail Williams' eyes blazed with excitement as she sat next to her little cousin Betty on one of the hard benches upstairs. From where she sat, she could not only see her uncle at the pulpit but the faces of the adult members in front of him. When she noticed the fear in their eyes, her whole body seemed to buzz with hot energy, despite the frigid air around her. What control he had over these people who liked to think of themselves as so high and mighty! He alone was creating real thoughts and feelings in these adults, these old people who were so superior to children. Ha! she thought. What adult escaped the settlement of Wells? Very few, least of which her own parents. But she did. She was stronger than they were. Yet God was greater than all of them. And there was her own uncle, speaking as God, rendering his congregation mute with fright. It was truly a wondrous sight to behold.

To her side, young Betty cowered, feeling sick to her stomach. She must do better, she thought. She could not, would not sin. She would be pure in her heart and do as papa told her, even when he was fierce and terrifying. She knew the Devil was real. She knew he liked to prey on little children such as herself. But she would fight him. Fight and fight and fight him.

Mr. Parris continued in his sermon for another hour and a half. As the congregation stepped out of the meeting house into the subdued winter sun, everyone – no matter if he agreed with Mr. Parris' words or not – felt a sense of unease, of tension. Of a nagging disquietude about what was to come next.

~ ~ ~

Abigail Williams tugged on her cousin Betty's hand, frustrated at the younger girl's tentative gait. The snow came up over their boots and the sky was dark with menacing clouds that augured more storms. The girls wrapped their woolen cloaks around their small bodies and Betty kept trying to push her scarf up over her face to ward off the cold.

"Betty, you are as slow as treacle," Abigail chided. "I assure you, If ye move more quickly, warmth will be your prize."

"Why must we be out of doors in such weather?" Betty whined. "I do prefer sitting on Tituba's lap in front of the fire."

Abigail rolled her eyes and continued their walk up the hill. Betty was right, it was indeed warmer inside – although some days not so much, as her uncle rationed the ever-dwindling supply of firewood so that the house was barely tolerable. But if they had to stay inside that place for another minute, Abigail felt she would scream. By now – in early March – the farmers would have already broken ground to plant early spring greens. Such a welcome sight, those lettuces popping through the barren earth, especially after the colonists had survived on salted meat and root vegetables for so many cold months. But this year the winter was holding on much too long, unwilling to give up its grip. And though Abigail loved and respected her uncle, she was growing tired of his constant complaints about their lowly circumstances. Worse, she couldn't stand watching her aunt prostrate herself to him. Abigail knew that this was the destiny for women. But she didn't have to like it.

"Just a few more steps," Abigail said to her sniveling cousin behind her. "Ann said to look for the largest tree in the forest. I believe I spy it now."

Ahead of them was a gigantic white pine, all of two hundred feet tall, the greenery on its huge branches slashing a sharp contrast with the bareness of the oaks and maples that surrounded it. Abigail could see that the trunk was already marked with the King's broad arrow, an upside down V atop a vertical line, which meant it would one day become a powerful mast on one of the royal navy vessels. It seemed an auspicious place for a group of young girls to meet in secret.

"Abigail! We be here!" Sure enough, Ann Putnam's face peered round the tree, her hand waving to beckon them to join her. Once Abigail and Betty came near, they saw that someone had dug through the snow to make a small cave at the base of the trunk's massive width, protected on two sides by the tree and on the other two with piles of displaced snow. Abigail clapped her hands in glee. "Why, Ann," she said. "It does appear to be a secret cave! Such a fitting place to hide in!"

"Hide?" Betty asked, noticing two other girls sitting, huddled together for warmth, in the corner of the manufactured grotto. "Is our purpose to hide? Abigail, you told me we were meeting friends to study the Bible together."

Betty recognized the two other girls to be Ann's cousin Mary Walcott and her maid, Mercy Lewis. These two, along with Abigail and Ann, were older than she by a good three years, and Betty felt woefully out of place, and not a little frightened.

Abigail laughed at her cousin and jumped down into the burrow. Once there she saw that Ann had dug the hole large enough for all five of them to sit cross-legged in a circle, the snow up to their shoulders behind them. It would be difficult for a passerby to see the girls gathering, as the piles of snow and the tree behind hid them almost entirely. "To be sure, we can discuss the Bible if you wish," she said. "We just want to be together in Christian love for a time."

In fact, the Bible story was a ruse, meant to gain the approval of the minister for their outing. In fact, the older girls wished to congregate without the judging eyes of adults. Two days ago, after Sunday services, Ann had whispered the invitation to Abigail as they ascended the ladder leading to the meeting house balcony. Ann and Abigail had formed a bond between them ever since Abigail had escaped the District of Maine to join the Parris household. Abigail had recognized a kindred spirit in the other girl: one of bravery and wit, with a slight mischievousness that Abigail found highly attractive. For a long time now Ann had wanted to bring the larger group of girls together, in search of some modicum of entertainment in their dreary world. To be sure, there was never any time for play during church services or afterward, and all the girls were stuck in their own abodes, tediously learning scripture and doing chores. The boredom was unbearable. Worse, children their age had no authority over their own lives, always bidden to be silent and uncomplaining. It was a desolate existence, and both Ann and Abigail sought ways to become more than almost-slaves. Even if it meant meeting in secret.

Mercy bade Betty to sit next to her, and when Betty did so, Mercy gathered her in her arms, covering her with her own cloak. Betty immediately relaxed, feeling the warmth of Mercy's body ease her troubled mind, in much the same way that Tituba would do. Perhaps if she could stay this way, it would be like disappearing. She could observe but not take part in a gathering of which she sensed her father would vociferously disapprove.

The other girls continued to giggle as all four of them sat together in the makeshift cave, holding hands and smiling, feeling the rush of excitement from being so covert, even slightly sinful. "Ann, you are surely an inventive creature, building this lovely fort for us," Mary Walcott complimented her cousin. "From now on it shall be our secret place."

"Aye, to be sure!" Ann replied. "I do feel it necessary to have a place of one's own, do you not? Even if it be a mere temporary shelter."

"Do we dare say that here, we can voice what is in our hearts, though our betters, if they were to hear, would deem it unsavory?" Abigail asked. All the girls, except Betty who continued to cower beneath Mercy's cloak, nodded their heads in agreement.

"What IS in our hearts, my friend?" Ann asked, elbowing Abigail in her side, encouraging gossip. "I expect that young Tom Proctor resides in your dreams, does he not?"

The other girls squealed in delight as Abigail reddened slightly. "Tom Proctor?" she said. "Not as much as James Bishop is in yours, Ann Putnam!"

"And Joseph Gedny is in Mercy's!" Mary called out.

"And John Hutchinson is in yours!" Mercy cried in due turn.

The girls laughed so loudly that they collapsed into one another, tickling sides, pulling off caps. To partake in such an outburst felt to Abigail like an enormous dark stone was being magically lifted from her shoulders. The other girls felt it too, so that they let go any fetters of propriety and became almost crazed with laughter. Young Betty covered her ears with her hands, thinking that her friends' paroxysms sounded dangerously close to the cackle of witches.

It took many moments for the jollity to recede, and when it did the girls breathed hard, as if a fit had overtaken them. "It feels so wondrous, does it not?" Ann asked between gasps. "To simply laugh?"

"Aye, it does that," Abigail agreed. "Life is so dark and fearful at the parsonage. Tis a trial to bear up to it."

"It must be better than what you escaped, though, is it not?" Ann asked, slyly glancing at her friend. Ever since Abigail arrived in the Village, Ann had wanted to hear the gruesome story of the massacre to the north. She had pestered Mercy to tell her as much as well. But when her mother overheard her queries, she shushed her daughter right away. "Your innocent ears are not for that kind of information, my child," Ann Sr. had admonished. "Believe you me, you do not want to hear of such things."

Now Abigail demurred, much as Mercy had. "I try not to think of that horrible day," she said, looking down in her lap. To her surprise, Mercy reached out to take her gloved hand. When the two girls looked at one another, Abigail could see tears in the servant's eyes.

"What is this, then?" Mary Walcott burst out. "Twas just a moment ago that we were laughing together. Now there be tears? What of it?"

But the connection that Abigail and Mercy were making would not be broken. Abigail knew of Mercy's background. That she had suffered as she had. Such common experience was bonding. Abigail could feel the terror arise in her as bile in her throat as she allowed herself to observe the scenes that she had kept at bay in her head for many months. She could tell that something similar was happening with Mercy, as they both squeezed each others' hands tighter.

"Do tell us," Ann urged. "Perhaps it will be as the lancing of a boil. Perhaps you will feel peace afterward."

Ann's words were soft and caring, although in reality she was more interested in hearing what her mother thought of as unmentionable. A charge went through her to think of misbehaving so.

Betty, underneath Mercy's cloak, pushed her hands even tighter over her ears. She wanted to cry "No! No!" but was too afraid to challenge Ann Putnam.

There was silence for several moments, as the other girls stared at one another. A wind came up from the west, blowing through the pine branches with a sound very much like a sigh. The cold around the huddled girls seemed even more punishing. Abigail thought of how alone and helpless she often felt. But this girl, this Mercy. She had seen it too. Those horrible images of blood and death. The ones that plagued her nightmares. The ones she wanted to escape.

"So you want to hear of such horrors?" Abigail asked, low and soft. Her voice, just a moment ago filled with laughter, was now challenging, almost daring those around her to bid her stop. "Is your curiosity really so morbid? So be it. I shall tell."

Ann smiled in triumph and dipped her head closer toward Abigail's, waiting. Mary did as well, catching her cousin's fascination as if it were a contagion. But Abigail had no interest in these girls. She stared at Mercy, who stared back, understanding passing between them, giving rise to a strange courage and determination.

"I was outside fetching some fresh apples from the orchard," Abigail intoned, still glued to Mercy's gaze. "It was a beautiful autumn afternoon, and I could smell the warm, fishy smell of the tide going out just across the meadow. I remember praising God for such a day." She paused, and clasped her hands together, tight. "I heard my sister's scream first," she continued. "At first I thought it was something else. Perhaps the mare had gone into labor earlier than we expected. But then Margaret's screams were joined by my mother's, and they echoed across the fields, bouncing off the very trees which surrounded me. My heart did freeze in my chest. I dropped the apples."

Mercy reached across and grasped Abigail's hands, still keeping eye contact with her, who seemed suddenly dull and monotone, as if the life had gone out of her.

"The next thing I knew," Abigail said, "I was at the window of our house, peering in. The first thing I could take in was the blood. Red, angry pools spread out all over my mother's clean floor. I thought, mama will be most angry for such wreckage. She is always so meticulous. But then I see the other parts. Not just blood, but other matter. Substances I have seen when my father would slaughter our pigs. Viscera. It's strangely white, did you know that?"

A thrill went through Ann and Mary, and they shivered with a mysterious mixture of horror and delight.

"There were six or seven of them, the red men," Abigail went on. "Their hair was dark and lank, and it swirled about their faces as they carried on with their butchery. Some of them brandished knives, some guns. Have you heard it said that the French gave them such weapons? My uncle did tell me that not long after I arrived here at the Village, because I was most confused when I saw such modern instruments in such savage's hands."

Abigail looked around at her friends, awaiting an answer to her question, but none was willing to break the spell of her tale by interrupting. Once Abigail realized this would be a monologue and not a conversation, she continued.

"By that time my sister and baby brother had been murdered. I knew because of the small size of the clumps of flesh and bone I spied in the corner of the room. But I was there when the knives pierced my mother's breast bone. I saw her blood spew forth onto the ground below. I heard my father's loud curse before his voice was silenced first with a blow from a red fist and then with many piercings of knives. It took two devil men to kill him. Do you know, never before had I heard such an utterance from my father before that day. He was such a pious man."

She stopped speaking as once again a gust of cold air swept down, so strong that it felt as if the gigantic tree trunk that protected them did sway and moan. Everyone shivered, imagining the tableau that Abigail was creating for them. Ann began to wish she hadn't started this in the first place. It was just too awful to behold.

"I felt frozen in place at that window, not quite understanding. But when the slaughter was complete, I saw those red men, their eyes blazing with murderous rage, look about the room. One climbed the ladder to the loft above, and I knew they were seeking others to ravage. I knew I had to flee. I knew I had to protect myself."

"Twas so with me," Mercy said, the story weaving about them, now taken on by a new girl. "I was in the house, though. When we heard them in the barn, my mother pushed me into the root cellar below, so I did not view the slaughter. I only heard it. The screams of my parents. The heavy blows. I did so wish to go to their aid, yet I found that I could not move my body. I stayed there, as if in a trance. I sensed that the evil that was being wreaked above me was seeping below to overtake me. I feared I would be the next to die."

Mercy noticed at that moment that Betty's little body that had been so tense and rigid up until then was now limp and heavy. Whether she had fainted or fallen asleep, Mercy thought it was probably best. Why were they exposing such monstrosities? But now that it had begun, no one could stop it. The words had to be said.

"Much time passed before I was able to move myself," she said. "The silence above seemed cacophonous in my ears. Where was the sound of my mother's voice? How could it be so, after such deafening clangs and bumps? I wanted desperately for light, as my mother had bade me to hide in darkness for my own safety. But now I found a candle lamp next to the bottom of the ladder, and I lit it. I do not think that ever in my life I will forget what was the very first thing I spied. Above me, through the rough boards of the floor, drops of blood were staining the surface. As if I were overtaken by some unseen being, it seemed that time slowed down, so that every tick of the clock took an eternity to pass. And as I watched, those drops of blood drew together as a wave on the ocean. As soon as the collective weight was too much, they gave way to letting go onto the sod floor at my feet. I stood, transfixed by the image in front of me, while the small drops became larger and larger. Until the blood became a veritable stream that washed over my feet. I was afeared of drowning in that very spot."

Mary and Ann gasped and clapped their hands over their mouths, but Abigail remained stoic and unmoving. There it was. The true barbarity of it all. She felt sick to her stomach, as if she would vomit.

Suddenly Ann stood, and bid her friends to join her. Surprised but craving something to break the spell of abomination that had been visited upon them, they followed Ann's lead. As Mercy stood she shook little Betty, who had indeed fallen into a stupor, her body shutting down to protect her from hearing more. "Is it over?" she whispered to Mercy, confused to see the girls standing in a circle. "Shhh," Mercy quieted her, not knowing what was to come.

"Shake your hands, like this," Ann bade, lifting her arms in front of her and shaking each, as if to ward off flying mites. "And jump up and down, like this." Ann started doing so, liking the feel of the solid earth beneath her.

"Why, tis dancing, it is not?" Mary asked, but she did as she was told. Slowly, slowly, the other girls did as well, not understanding what was happening. Betty, though, cowered further away, burrowing her body into the wall of snow behind her. She hoped if she made herself small enough, her cousin would not notice, and would not demand that she participate in whatever uncommon ritual was unfolding before her.

"A kind of dancing, yes," Ann panted with the effort, now moving side to side so that the circle started to move with her. "Tituba told me this is what her people would do around a fire in the night."

A wave of so many emotions – fear, yes, but also relief – washed over the girls as if they were being bathed in some kind of purification rite. The strangeness of it all overtook them, and they were now dancing in a circle, letting go of the horrors they had just listened to. Gradually their terror was transformed into a giddiness that overtook them. The wind suddenly picked up so that it seemed that the girls could change the very weather around them with their dancing. Ann let out a whoop! and the others once more followed her lead. Their cries reverberated to the towering trees around them as the winter sun dipped to the horizon, casting a nascent darkness onto the circle.

Betty, scandalized, dug deeper into the snow, so that the hideous racket her friends were making was muted, distant.

Eventually, the energy the girls had stirred up started to fade, and as one they fell back on the snow, holding hands and looking up at the darkening sky. Their rasping breaths rose from their mouths in pillows of white smoke, frozen in the cold air swooping down on them. No one, not even Ann, understood what they had just done. Their antics had felt natural, intuitive, coming from the core of their beings.

Abigail smiled. She felt a surge of power run through her body. She was strong. Her past would not define her, nor would she ever feel weak again. The euphoria crashing through her veins lifted her up, waging a victorious war over the helplessness that had invaded her life for so long now.

"What was that?" Mary asked, after much time had passed. The heat their dancing had created was now dispersing and she was very aware of the cold that was seeping up through the snow through her cloak.

"Shh!" Ann snarled. "Tis best not to speak."

The girls obeyed.

~ ~ ~

That very evening, twenty miles south of where the Salem Village girls performed their impromptu rite, the Indians of the District of Maine were the subject of another conversation. In Thomas Danforth's best parlor in his Cambridge townhouse, the Deputy Governor sat in front of a roaring hearth with his friends Cotton Mather and Samuel Sewall. In their hands were mugs of warm ale, brought to them by Thomas' wife Mary. Earlier in the evening the house was filled with conversation from a great many people at the evening meal. Thomas and Mary had invited their three daughters – Sarah, Mary and Elizabeth – along with their husbands to dine with the Mathers and the Sewalls. The Danforths, as hosts of the gathering, enjoyed the opportunity to bring their daughters together with Thomas' friends, who were much closer in age to the Danforth children than they were to Thomas or Mary. It had been an amusing affair, filled with discussion about the goings-on of the colony. Now the Danforth daughters had departed with their husbands, as did Mrs. Mather and Mrs. Sewall, leaving the three friends to meet in private.

"You do have a most admirable family, Thomas," Samuel was saying, raising his glass to the deputy governor. "Twas a most enjoyable evening."

Thomas, who was glad of the camaraderie, nodded in acceptance and took a long drink, as did the minister. Indeed, he was proud of his daughters, all of whom had made good marriages, giving him beautiful grandchildren along the way. Yet every time they were together as a family, Thomas' happiness as the patriarch was always tinged with a bit of sadness which only his wife Mary truly understood. It always seemed as if there was a hollow absence when the girls visited. Thomas knew it was because of the grief he and Mary still felt for the many deaths of all of their sons. Three had died in infancy, and Thomas Jr. had perished in King Philip's war. The elder Thomas had taken his namesake's passing very hard. At the time – fifteen years ago – his wife Mary had taken to her bed for several months, not able to heal from the anguish she felt from the loss of her only son. When she did arise and rejoin Thomas in their daily lives, she was transformed from a gentle, loving, quiet woman to one harboring hatred in her heart toward the Pequot tribe as well as all the Indian tribes living throughout the colony. They had murdered her sweet son and she could not find God's forgiveness in her soul for the crime.

Thomas remembered Mary's struggles tonight, as he knew his friends wanted to hear of his dealings to the north. After the colonists overthrew Governor Andros, they took over the charter for the District of Maine and were trying to make it part of Massachusetts Bay. They had voted Danforth to be the first president of the District, along with his duties as Deputy Governor of Massachusetts. Since then Thomas, now an old man close to seventy years of age, served in both roles, and had his hands full, working many hours a day. He even had to give up his post as Treasurer of Harvard because of his political obligations.

Much to his wife Mary's displeasure, Thomas had not taken a hard line against the Abenaki in Maine. Where Mary harbored hatred for the red man, Thomas fostered understanding. Many years ago his brother Samuel had introduced him to John Eliot, the minister who was doing such good work in converting many local Indians to Christianity. Thomas had seen firsthand how the savages could be taught to read the Bible, and could be brought to God. He was a devout man who only wanted to serve the Lord, whose strength and grace helped him to overcome his grief over Thomas Jr's death. His love for his enemies had become a thorn in the side of his marriage to Mary, who would not be moved. There had been many a night that Thomas had tried very hard to minister to her, repeating many times what Matthew exhorted in the New Testament: "Please, wife, do listen," he would plead. "God said, 'But I say to you, love our enemies and pray for those who persecute you.' I have never seen you to reject the word of the Lord!"

But Mary would not be moved.

Mary was not the only one, though, who looked askance at Thomas' approach to the Abenaki. He brought the tribal leaders together with the magistrates and ministers of settlements at Wells, Yarmouth and Kennebunk, urging them to negotiate a local truce, without the oversight of the kings of England and France. The colonists, especially the refugees who fled the fighting in Maine, wished only to destroy the savages, or at the least push them north to Canada where they belonged.

"Thomas? Thomas?" He was shaken from his reverie by Cotton's shaking his shoulder. Embarrassed, Thomas realized he had almost fallen asleep with his ruminations. "My friend, you seemed to be lost in thought."

Thomas shook himself awake now, and sat straighter in his chair, smoothing the front of his doublet and taking a drink from the cup he had laid on the small table next to him. "My apologies!" he said, perhaps a bit too loudly. "It is too often that I do that. I always remain fascinated by the journeys our minds take, meandering casually from one subject to the next, without one's realizing it."

Cotton smiled reassuringly. "Many times it is God's voice that takes us on such journeys."

"What path did your thoughts take tonight, Thomas?" Samuel asked, always eager to hear Thomas' opinions. He respected the older man, and their friendship had grown over the years. The two men would often sit together and speak philosophically about issues facing the colony. Samuel, now a well-respected judge himself, many times found himself pondering the importance of the work they were doing in the colony. He wished to be guided not only by God's word, but that of leaders like Thomas Danforth, a man who seemed always committed to truth and justice.

"I began thinking of my dearly departed son Thomas," the Deputy Governor admitted. "He is still so sorely missed by my wife and me, and his memory always seems closest to us when the girls are here."

Both Cotton and Samuel murmured their condolences, remembering each in his turn their own relatives whose lives had been sacrificed in the Indian wars. Thomas looked at their downturned faces and said "now, now, my friends. I did not mean to bring sadness to our fellowship. Indeed, my thoughts turned from Thomas to the Indian problem. I do still harbor hope, along with Mr. Eliot, that these people can be turned from sin and murder toward the grace of God. And I do still believe we can live in peace with them."

"I share your confidence in this outcome," Cotton said. "To be sure, God's love is vast, and powerful enough to pierce the hearts of the savages. Mr. Eliot does admirable work with them."

"Yet you must be careful, Thomas," Samuel admonished. "It is a testament to your dedication to Christ that you are able to follow His calling us to 'turn the other cheek.'"

"'But I tell you,'" Cotton interrupted, his voice booming, quoting Matthew's fifth verse in scripture. "'Do not resist an evil person. If anyone slaps you on the right cheek, turn to them the other cheek also."

"Aye, tis true," Samuel agreed. "And you, Thomas, have certainly done so after your beloved son's death. But the magistrates in Boston do not adhere to such a loving strategy."

"That is exactly where my reverie took me," Thomas said. "I am well aware of such opinions. In my life and work, however, I do try to follow God's word, rather than ride adrift on the ever-wavering waters of public opinion."

Samuel regarded his friend with a mixture of immense admiration but also worry for his reputation. "It would be so much easier to make these decisions if we had the benefit of a charter from England."

Cotton looked down at his hands with slight embarrassment. It was his own father, Increase, who remained in England, negotiating that very thing. He had been there for over a year, with no official word on his progress. Cotton himself had received several personal letters from Increase, who reported a strong belief that he would be successful. Yet the colony remained formally lawless, and the people were getting very nervous. "I do hope that my father sails home, victorious, before too much more time flies by," he admitted. "I fret for the souls of the colonists. We cannot live like this for much longer. There is much upset here."

"There, there, Cotton," Thomas tried to comfort him. "Believe in God and His carrying us through this difficult time. And you are doing much to protect our people from sin."

"Aye, just this week last I saw your text on the Goodwin witchcraft case published and sold in Joseph Brunning's shop in Exchange Street. This will go far in admonishing the colonists against that particular sin," said Samuel.

"And the synod that you hosted for our ministers in Boston just last month," Thomas added. "Surely your leadership is strong, Cotton."

"I would like to think so," the minister admitted, taking a drink from his cup and staring into the fire, which had begun to subside. "I do wish that my father will deem it true upon his arrival. But Thomas, will your peacemaking with the Abenaki be regarded as making a pact with the Devil? We do not want to give the people something else to fear."

"I believe our Christian people believe in forgiveness," Thomas said, growing a bit peeved. He had had this same conversation with Mary many times over, and each time it troubled him.

"There should be no forgiveness for the work of the Devil. We should remain constantly vigilant against his dastardly attempts to tempt us away from God," Cotton reminded Thomas. Samuel watched this exchange with interest, knowing that he was regarding a debate between two of the most intellectually advanced men in the colony.

"Agreed," Thomas admitted. "I commit myself to this vital enterprise. And I certainly stand with the King and Queen against French encroachment. Beyond this, I have seen firsthand the devastation that the Abenaki, and the Pequots before them, have showered on our settlements. The fighting needs to cease. But do ye not see that the Indians would be angered at the taking of their lands?"

"A fair question, Thomas," Samuel said, having no intention of entering the fray of this tricky deliberation.

"Perhaps so," Cotton replied, tenting his hands in front of his face in reflection. Looking up suddenly, he continued: "But Thomas, do you not own lands previously owned by the Wampanoag out to the west of Boston?"

"Aye, and I suspected it would be but a matter of time before my farms were brought into the conversation!" Thomas said. His sour mood turned more favorable when he felt on more solid ethical ground. "Yet I did insist on paying the Indians a fair price for my acres. Not all settlers do the same."

Samuel remained silent, although he knew that his friend's claim was only partially correct. He knew about Thomas' landholdings because a few years ago he – Thomas – had approached Samuel with handling the legal details around providing long-term leases to a handful of families who had agreed to farm some of Thomas' acres. Many in Massachusetts Bay knew that Mr. Danforth was one of the largest landholders in the colony, owning over 15,000 acres to the south of Sudbury. The whole area was generally known as Danforth's Farms but for several years now Thomas had been known to call it "Framlingham," to honor his hometown in Suffolk back in England. Thomas was right in saying that he paid the local tribes for some of the acres granted him by the General Court over the past several decades. Samuel believed – although he would never challenge his friend on this – that the price was well below the true value. Samuel always excused this slight in his mind by remembering the charitable way that the Deputy Governor had gone about settling his vast holdings, not that there were many colonists interested in farming such wilderness still plagued by Indian raids. Thomas never wanted to live there himself, preferring the urban comfort of Cambridge Town. But he would offer long-term leases to those who wished to move west, forgiving rents for many of them. Besides, Samuel thought, Thomas was right when he reminded Cotton that not many landowners bothered to pay the Indians anything, since there were no permanent abodes or farms anywhere on the property. If these natives were not using their land, what value could it possibly hold for them?

Cotton laughed, wishing for more cheerful subjects. When he started worrying about the souls of his parishioners, he could easily fall into a downward emotional spiral. "You are right, Mr. Danforth!" he cried. "Indeed everyone in the colony should follow your lead. We are most grateful to have you at the helm. I pray that God will continue to guide you through these troubling times."

CHAPTER SIX
1691 – One Year Later

Salem Village and Salem Town
Massachusetts Bay Colony
The year before the first witch trial

Abigail Williams put her finger over her mouth, bidding her friends below her to silence themselves. She had stepped up on a large granite slab next to one of the side windows to the meeting house and was peeking through the diamond-paned window, eavesdropping on the gathering of men inside. The huddled group of girls kept vying for a place next to Abigail, where they could observe the goings-on inside the meeting house. The only one Abigail would allow up on the stone with her was Ann Putnam. The two had become fast friends over the past year, and had taken on the role of leaders of the others. "Shush!" Abigail whispered. "You must stay where you are, lest we be discovered!"

The only girl who kept her distance was young Betty Parris, who as usual wished she could be anywhere but with these children. The group had grown over the past year, since that first strange gathering in Ann's snow cave, and now it seems they were a veritable tribe, numbering seven. First Ann had invited Elizabeth Hubbard, an older girl, about sixteen, to join the girls when they went out into the fields together, catching fish in the Ipswich river in the spring, berrying in the summer. These tasks were good excuses for the girls to get together, as they were usually called upon to stay close to home. Elizabeth had lost her parents to the pox in Boston the year before, and Dr. Griggs, the village doctor, had taken her on as a maidservant, as she was a relative of Mrs. Griggs who had taken pity on her.

As the fall came upon the village, another newcomer joined the group. Betty was as distrustful of this Mary Warren as she was the rest of them. It seemed an awful coincidence that Mary, who had just been hired by the Proctor family in Salem Village, had suffered almost the exact same fate as Mercy Lewis and Abigail Williams had, narrowly escaping death from an Indian raid to the north. Mary's father had been killed, and her mother died several weeks later, suffering from derangement and grief. To Betty, she had the same kind of hard look to her as Abigail and Mercy did, borne out of the horrors she had witnessed in her young life. At times she almost seemed like a rabid, frightened animal, afraid of loud noises and often yelling at Betty, imitating her new friend Abigail. In fact, Betty was terrified of all of these companions, and she desperately wished she could tell her mother about it. How the girls would so gleefully mock other people in the village, or sometimes play devilish games. Just a few weeks ago Abigail showed them something she said she heard from Tituba, casting an egg white into a cup, peering into it to supposedly see the face of the boy she would marry. The other girls had tittered with delight, but Abigail brought seriousness to the proceeding, frowning and making some kind of incantation that Betty knew she was making up on the spot. Her beloved Tituba would never, ever say such unintelligible words. Still, she felt sharp jabs of fear all over her body as she watched her cousin, as if someone were poking her. At the time Betty ran away, wracked with fear that the Devil was doing it. She hid in a nearby glade of trees until the play was over, and only then was she willing to rejoin the group on their way back to their homes.

Another time Abigail insisted on pretending she was none other than her own uncle, the minister Parris, telling the other girls to sit by the side of the river bank and listen to her. She started stomping over the grass in front of them, pounding her chest and calling out words from scripture, pointing at the girls, accusing them of sinning against God and herself as Reverend Parris. As usual, the girls giggled at her artifice, and clapped their hands in delight. But Abigail was having none of it, and their enjoyment angered her.

"No!" she thundered, threatening to slap Mercy, the closest girl to where Abigail stood. "You will not mock me! I am your leader, ye sinners, all! You know how the good minister can control our village! You shall act your part with accuracy. Bow down in fear! I have the power! I have the power!"

Betty thought her cousin was acting terribly demented, but her words hit the mark, and the rest of the girls dutifully obeyed. "Aye, me!" Elizabeth cried, clutching her chest in seeming agony. "Ye are most right, Mr. Parris! My husband refuses to pay his fees, and you suffer from it! Tell me what I must do to right this grievous wrong!"

"And I, too!" Mercy took Elizabeth's cue. "I am a grave sinner, refusing to go to services this week last! The day was a fair one, and I preferred to walk through the woods and listen to birdsong!"

Ann took the game one step further, and prostrated herself on the ground before Abigail, shaking and shuddering as a madwoman. "The Devil betakes me!" she cried out. "The Devil betakes me!"

It was only Betty who wasn't play-acting, covering her ears and rocking back and forth on the ground in stark fear. Occasionally she would sneak a peek at her cousin, almost expecting her to actually take on the appearance of her father. Indeed Abigail's eyes were filled with the same combination of anger and power that were ever-present in his face. Her whole body quivered with an energy she could hardly contain. Was this real or just an afternoon's diversion? Betty wondered. The line seemed woefully thin when her cousin would take on such games.

These were the things that gave Betty nightmares. It was surely wrong, how these girls were entertaining themselves. Yet they were older and made sure to let Betty know that if she tattled on them, she would be punished most wretchedly.

So now, once again Betty remained on the sidelines as the other girls vied for position to the side of the meeting house window. Abigail and Ann were watching intently the scene inside. There four men sat, huddled close together in the unheated meeting house, and Abigail was particularly interested in their conversation, which was clearly about her uncle. Isaac Etsy, Francis Nurse, John Proctor and Ann Putnam's own estranged kinsman Joseph Putnam were all, she knew, members of the village's rates committee. This was the group that determined the salary and provisions for the minister. Abigail knew that her uncle had been angry with this faction for months, as it was composed of men who were not his supporters – besides Joseph, not a Putnam was included, and Thomas didn't not consider his stepbrother a Putnam at all. Was it fair that the congregation had voted these particular men to make such important decisions? Up until then the committee had set the rates but did not require every freeman in the village to pay them, and everyone in the group had so far refused their own share. The minister had campaigned hard to get another Putnam, or a Walcott, or a Gould on the committee, but membership was chosen by the congregation, and he had but one vote.

"It is obvious to me, Francis," John Proctor was saying, "that the greater part of our community is against Mr. Parris. He does nothing to unite us."

"Tis true, my friend," Francis Nurse responded. "You do assess the situation most accurately."

"We do realize, do we not," Joseph Putnam said, "that by officially refusing to collect Mr. Parris' pay, we will be starving him out of the parsonage? Is this something of which God would approve?"

Although Joseph was younger than the rest by at least a generation, his landholdings far outnumbered most in the Village, and now he owned a home and several ships in Salem Town. As such he was regarded by many to be one of the young leaders of the community. In his few adult years he had gained the respect of his elders in the Towne families, who thought Joseph's marriage to one of their own – Hannah Bridges Putnam – was a fit one. And the young man was known to be fair and just. He spent a great deal of his time closer to the port, yet he had not turned his back on the villagers, especially when they were in such turmoil. He and Hannah would travel back and forth between village and town in their finely-appointed wagon, visiting with both their aging mothers. Hannah enjoyed these trips more than Joseph did, as his Salem Village friends were few. He did have enemies in his home village, amongst them his own half brothers in the Putnam family. Today he was glad that none of them were on of this committee.

"We have suggested to him several times that he leave on his own," said Goodman Esty. "Yet he seems committed to staying. Methinks he does not feel that he has made some mistakes in his leadership. Instead, he blames the problems on the devil."

"We are afraid enough of late. We need no more fear to be instilled in us," Goodman Nurse said, so quietly to himself that Abigail and Ann had to strain to hear him.

Ann clenched her fists in anger upon hearing this. Goodman Nurse, afraid? she thought. According to her father, he had nothing to worry about, sitting all high and mighty on his huge farm, jealously protecting acreage that wasn't even his to begin with. For many nights Ann had heard her father rail against the man, especially after Goodman Nurse had won his land boundary case against him just six months ago. Thomas Putnam had had to pay a significant fine to pay for the trees he had felled and carried away from what the General Court deemed Nurse's land, even though the Putnams had papers saying otherwise. "It's a lawless time!" Thomas had thundered, taking way too many quaffs from his cup of ale, stomping about the parlor in his thick boots. "I am called upon to pay this ridiculous fine by a court that has no recognition by the King and Queen! I suppose we can do anything we want without the colony's charter. Just make false accusations according to our own fancy, with no real oversight! A pox on this colony. A pox on this Village!"

"The minister has his supporters in the village," Goodman Esty was now reminding the rest of those gathered inside, and drew Ann's attention back to the scene in front of her. "Should we vote not to collect, people like the Putnams can choose to provide firewood for him without penalty."

At that, the three men looked at young Joseph, who put up his hand in restraint. "Do not blame me for my brother's and sister's actions, dear men. They do not confer with me, nor I with them. I have long ceased thinking that I can sway them."

Outside the window, Abigail elbowed Ann in the ribs, glaring at the younger girl. Ann elbowed her right back, shrugging her shoulders. "It is not our fault!" Ann mouthed to Abigail, not wanting to be discovered by the men inside. It was so annoying, these kinds of accusing looks that she often received. Ann knew both her mother and father hated them as well, and wished that Joseph had another surname that did not connect him with the larger Putnam family.

"So shall we put it to a vote, men?" Goodman Nurse, the eldest of the group and by such its de facto leader. "All in favor of our ceasing to collect Mr. Parris' fees?"

All four men raised their hands reluctantly, knowing that this would cause tremendous upset in the parsonage. They were all people of God, and were loathe to create strife. It was amazing to them and many of the other villagers that this was the fourth time that the community could not come together under one leader of the church. What was it about Salem Village that created such dissension?

But Mr. Parris had to be stopped. The village was torn apart by the constant reports of bloodshed in Maine, and many of its young men had been sent away to fight in those Indian battles. Many of the villagers had been forced to take in refugees fleeing the massacres, and food and space, always stretched, had to be rationed even further. While Mr. Parris could have been preaching love and friendship among the people, he chose what some thought of as pettiness, focusing more on his own sense of popularity and what he perceived as minor affronts. He even complained of the cups and plates used on the altar for communion Sundays, and was overheard to say "These are below the status of such a man as myself. Indeed, no minister in Boston would accept such paltry trinkets." And when he climbed into the pulpit on Sundays and lecture days, he boomed on about the increasing sin and depravity of the congregation, crying out that God is turning His beneficent face from them. People of the village were walking about as if barefoot on shards of glass, terrified of being punished for some unknown violation.

As the committee men stood and made their way to the door, Ann and Abigail jumped down from their spots and started running toward the woods, not wanting to be seen. Both Marys, Elizabeth, Mercy and Betty followed in the footsteps they made in the snow. They did not stop until they reached the makeshift cave that Ann had once again dug out of the snow next to the giant white pine. Since that first meeting the winter before, the girls had taken to meeting there, even in the spring when the snow melted. The huge girth of the pine's trunk was enough to hide them from passersby, as they made sure to sit together away from the path that some of the goodwives had trampled through the forest as they took the shortest routes among farms.

Ann had had to make the snow circle wider to accommodate Elizabeth and Mary. When the group welcomed the girls at different times to their meetings, each was appropriately pleased, even Elizabeth who was so much older than the rest of the girls, at an age where such play had ceased their allure. In the warmer months all of the girls were able to make more excuses to get away from their homes, but now in the winter the opportunities to gather were rare. Indeed Mary Warren had only come to the place once before the snows had come.

This afternoon in the darkening shadows Mary Warren found the camaraderie a welcome escape from the Proctor farm. She hadn't been living in the Village long enough to understand the subtext of what had just been said by the rates committee members, although Ann had told her a bit about the rivalries between her family and others in the church. Mary Warren didn't much care. When she had arrived at the Proctors' she was just relieved to be out of Maine, although her grief at losing her family was strong. Her mistress Elizabeth Proctor was not patient with Mary's occasional fits of anxiety which sent her outdoors to walk hard amongst the rows of corn and potatoes in order to feel somewhat safe again. The girl had a way of always looking down at her feet, occasionally taking furtive glances to each side, terrified that a red man might jump out of the shadows to take her away. Goody Proctor had many children and needed a lot of help from Mary, and was frustrated by her antics. The older woman was a godly person but was worn out by the never-ending work of running a large homestead. And besides, even though she had heard, like everyone else, about the strife to the north, she herself had never experienced anything like it. She couldn't understand her new maidservant. She just needed her unpaid help.

"I am ever so heartened to be here with you," Mary spoke her thoughts aloud to the rest of the girls after they had all plopped down on the ground and their raspy breaths had quieted from running so fast. "I am grateful for your friendship, and for your welcome."

"As am I," Elizabeth chimed in.

But the rest of the girls – besides Betty, who once more huddled in the corner underneath Mercy's cloak – were more interested in talking about the discussion they had just heard. After giving the newcomers perfunctory acknowledgment, Abigail said "My uncle will be sure not to like the news that will be arriving soon at his door."

"Aye, tis true," Ann agreed, pulling off her heavy woolen gloves and blowing into her hands to warm them. "And my own father will share his displeasure."

"There is much anger already in the parsonage," Abigail added. "Whoever goes against my uncle will have a great battle on his hands. He is certain to smite them. He does God's own work. Why do certain men in the village deny him? Are they not denying God at the same time?"

Abigail was filled with disdain for the likes of Joseph Putnam, Francis Nurse and Isaac Esty. She continued to be in awe of her uncle and his power to make both men and women cower in front

of him. This power must be from God Himself. She herself yearned
for such authority, although she knew that that would never be.
Not for a female, and certainly not for a young girl. She had to be
satisfied with the role she was given by Providence, although she
always sought ways to exert her independence, even in small situations. Like pinching Tituba when her uncle and aunt weren't looking. Like controlling little Betty by instilling fear into her, always
threatening to tell the Parrises of fabricated sins. Like, on occasion,
pretending to be the minister himself, setting herself up as leader of
the small band of girls, with Ann as her right hand.

"We can do nothing about it." Ann's cousin Mary Walcott
shook her head. "We are but little girls." Mary's mother Deliverance
– Thomas Putnam's sister – had told her this many times, even as
they both had to deal with her father's railing against the injustice.
"We are but women," Deliverance would say. "God has given us the
role of serving men, while in turn men do try to serve God. It is the
word of the Lord. Nothing shall change it, so do not suffer yourself
to complain of it."

"Why must that be?" Mercy Lewis now asked her friends.
"Why must some of us serve, while others benefit, even amongst
women?"

Ann saw Mary Warren nodding in agreement, and she shot
both Mary and Mercy a withering look. Ann would never make
any protest against the arrangement Mercy had with the Putnams,
and it often caused Mercy consternation. Her job was to be a
servant to Ann, which made Ann her superior – yet the two girls
remained friends. Friends should be equals, Mercy always thought.
Yet it was rarely so with Ann. In these gatherings Mercy hardly
ever spoke up, in fear of angering Ann. About this subject, though,
she was most passionate, which made her temporarily brave in her
speech. Yet Ann's glare frightened her, and she would do anything
not to raise her mistress' ire. She knew there would be much to pay
for upon their return to the Putnam farm, not the least of which
might be Ann's total ignoring of her. And this was much more than
Mercy could take.

"I do apologize for my outburst," Mercy said, bowing her
head, hoping desperately to see Ann's frown disappear. "It is just
that I share the frustration of women, that is all."

Both Elizabeth Hubbard and Mary Warren surreptitiously

took Mercy's hand, out of Ann's sight. Since Elizabeth arrived in the village, coming to live with Dr. Griggs, Mercy and she had formed a fast bond that was borne from their mutual roles as maidservants. And now Mary, another serving girl, had joined their little tribe. None of the other girls in the group knew what it was like to have to awaken before the family, in a darkened room set apart in the back of the house, freezing in the winter and scorching in the summer, only to spend the entire day taking care of other people's needs. The three girls had lost their parents, Mercy's and Mary's to the Indians and Elizabeth's to disease, so they were all alone in the world. Besides these occasional escapes to join the other girls, the lives of the serving girls were never their own. It was a difficult existence.

"Let us be done with the subject of our own torment," Abigail said, looking around at the circle of faces with a devilish look in her eye. "I have more interesting entertainment." Her cousin Betty burrowed further into Mercy's lap, and Mercy in turn wrapped her cloak more tightly around the little girl. The rest of the group clapped their hands and begged Abigail to tell them her secret. By now they were used to either Abigail or Ann suggesting all sorts of games, and even when they seemed dangerous and slightly terrifying, there was always fun to be had.

Abigail reached underneath her cloak and pulled out a bound volume, wrapped in a length of string. The girls let out a sigh of wonder in unison, although none of them recognized the book.

"What is it, Abigail?" Ann asked, reaching for the package. Abigail quickly pulled it out of Ann's reach, holding it above her head, smiling deviously. Betty peeked out from behind Mercy's protecting cloak, and couldn't stop herself from crying out: "Cousin! That is my father's book! You stole it from his very shelf!"

Abigail glared at Betty and pointed at her. "Be silent, Betty," she said with contempt. "Do go back to your hiding place, you sniveling baby."

The rest of the girls laughed, and Betty did as she was bidden, her fear of her cousin once again overcoming her consternation at the theft.

"What is the title, Abigail?" Ann asked, giving up her attempts to wrench the book from her friend. "Why do you bring it to us?"

"Gather round closer," Abigail instructed, "and I will tell you."

The girls inched toward the center of the circle, now with their crossed legs touching, instinctively grabbing each other's hands in suspense. Ann giggled. "Why, we do appear like an old hen's party, do we not?"

Abigail once again stared at the girls, each in their turn, so that Ann quickly quelled her laughter and grew serious. "Perhaps not old hens," she murmured, "but a witch's gathering!"

With that, all of her friends gasped and drew back in shock, still clutching hands – although Ann and Mary Walcott, who sat next to Abigail, let go of her, trying to move away. "Abigail Williams!" Ann chided. "Don't speak of such things. Your uncle tells us daily how such utterances can call down God's own enemy."

Mercy felt young Betty shiver underneath her cloak, so energetically that it felt almost as if the little girl were having a fit. "Shhh," Mercy whispered to Betty, not wanting to draw attention to her comforting words. "I have you. You must settle down."

It was now Abigail who was laughing, an almost maniacal cackle that scared the rest of the group. "There is little to fear if your heart is pure, you are well aware of that, Ann," she admonished. "Just bide with me awhile. Let me tell you of this book that I found in the parsonage. It arrived but two weeks ago, and my uncle did not rest at night until he was finished with it. I observed him from the top of the stair. Never before have I seen him so engrossed. And when he reached the last page he did jump from his seat and pace the room as he is wont to do, his hands behind his back, in much consternation."

Her companions relaxed a bit, once again curious, although Ann and Mary Walcott did not reach for Abigail's hands any longer.

"He called upon my aunt, who is often close by and ready to serve as a sounding board for my uncle," Abigail continued, holding the book tighter to her chest. The snow below and about them was bitter cold, but she warmed to her story. "'Elizabeth!' my uncle did cry out. 'I have but finished the good Reverend Mather's recent publication, and it proves that I am correct in remaining vigilant against sin and witchcraft in Salem Village.' My aunt, who is as mousy as her stupid daughter here, clutched her small hands to her chest and her visage did turn a ghostly shade of white. 'What, husband, what does the book say?'"

At that, Abigail paused, letting the realization sink into her friends that the book she held in her hand was the very same as the one about which she was telling the story. "Go on!" the girls urged.

"What next?"

"Well," Abigail said, drawing out her words, delighted to be the center of attention. "My uncle continued his report to Aunt Elizabeth. You do all know, I am certain, of Reverend Mather's work in England, negotiating our colony's new charter. During his absence, his son Cotton Mather – someone my uncle highly esteems and whose friendship he does yearn for – has taken over leadership of Boston's First Church. Although the good minister – the son – is still young, my uncle says he has taken on his father's leadership with skill and devotion."

"This is what is in the book?" Mary Warren asked, starting to feel slightly bored and let down after Abigail had made them think there was something illicit in the story.

"Shhh!" Ann pushed Mary Warren, who was sitting next to her, on the shoulder. "Let her speak."

Abigail glared at Mary but soon continued. "Several years ago Mr. Mather was called upon to witness and minister to a dire situation in Boston. The family was called Goodwin and four of the children were bewitched!"

Once again the girls gasped in horror. Betty's convulsions had stopped and Mercy peeked under her cloak. The child had either fainted or fallen asleep, as she had done so many times before when Abigail was up to her antics.

"Mr. Mather writes of it in this very book!" Abigail announced, holding up the book. The girls could now make out the beginning of the title etched on the front leather cover: Memorable Providences Relating to Witchcrafts. "The poor little ones were most grievously afflicted by their laundress, who did hang for her crimes."

"Oh!" was the others' response together, now imitating Abigail's sad face, almost moved to tears. "Woe be the children!" Mary Walcott cried out. "Such innocent babes!" added Elizabeth Hubbard. The girls' laments continued for several moments, echoing against the huge pine.

"Do ye not want to read of their afflictions?" Abigail asked, once the clamor had died down. "Tis terrible to do so, believe you me."

Both Marys, Ann, Mercy and Elizabeth looked at one another, their eyes wide with fascination. Ann was the first one to nod, and the rest followed suit. Abigail smiled encouragingly, opened the bound edition, and began to read.

"'About midsummer, in the year 1688,'" she intoned. "'the eldest of these Children, who is a daughter, saw cause to examine their washerwoman, upon their missing of some linen, which twas fear'd she had stolen from them. This laundress was the daughter of an ignorant and a scandalous old woman in the neighborhood; whose miserable husband before he died, had sometimes complained of her, that she was undoubtedly a witch.'"

"A witch!" Mary Walcott exclaimed.

"A witch!" Ann repeated, with equal fervency.

"Shh!" Abigail admonished. "Pray allow me to continue. 'This woman in her daughter's defense bestowed very bad language upon the girl that put her to question, immediately upon which, the poor child became variously indisposed in her health, and visited with strange fits.'"

"Do give me the book, Abigail," Ann cried, and this time was successful in wrenching the tome from her friend's hands. Before Abigail could object, Ann continued to read: "'It was not long before one of her sisters, and two of her brothers, were seized, in order one after another, with affects like those that molested her. Within a few weeks, they were all four tortured everywhere in a manner so very grievous that it would have broken a heart of stone to have seen their agonies. Skillful physicians were consulted for their help, and particularly our worthy and prudent friend Dr. Thomas Oakes, who found himself so affronted by the distempers of the children that he concluded nothing but a hellish witchcraft could be the original of these maladies. The children were tormented just in the same part of their bodies at the same time together. The variety of their tortures increased continually, and though about nine or ten at night they always had a release from their miseries, and ate and slept all night for the most part indifferently well.'"

Abigail grabbed the book back, taking advantage of Ann's difficulty in reading, as at that moment Ann took a breath in needed rest. "Yet in the daytime sometimes they would be deaf, sometimes dumb, and sometimes blind, and often, all this at once. One while their tongues would be drawn down their throats; another while they would be pulled out upon their chins, to a prodigious length.'"

"How very, very awful!" Elizabeth Hubbard interrupted. "Could it be true that the devil can do such atrocities through evil women? Could it?"

Everyone ignored her as the reading continued. "'They would have their mouths opened unto such a wideness that their jaws went out of joint. They would at times lie in a benumbed condition, and be drawn together as those that are tied neck and heels and presently be stretched out, yea, drawn backwards to such a degree that it was feared that the very skins of their bellies would have cracked. They would make most piteous out-cries, that they were cut with knives, and struck with blows that they could not bear.'"

Abigail stopped reading. "Uncle says that the strangest part of the story was that no one else could see who was hurting the girls, none but they themselves. They would shout out 'Be gone, witch! I will not sign your devil's book!' Mr. Mather would look all about the room yet see nothing. Yet the pinches and jabs were evident, as the girls would show bruises and blood on their own skins after such an attack."

"What happened to the sad children?" Mercy asked.

"Why, the witch was hanged, to be sure!" Abigail answered. "With time the symptoms diminished, thanks be to God."

"Reverend Parris warns us of witchcraft, well nigh almost every Sunday," Ann said slowly, as if remembering for the first time. "Yet not until now have I understood what it truly does look like."

"And what a scene does Mr. Mather paint for his readers! Tis truly grotesque!" Mary Warren exclaimed.

"Aye, grotesque to be sure!" Abigail agreed, rising up suddenly to her feet. "I am a poor Goodwin child! Goody Glover, do not entreat me to join with you!"

The other girls stared up at their friend, who seemed to transform before their eyes into a tortured soul. Abigail was gone and in her place was someone else, someone who was twitching and recoiling as if being attacked. Her eyes blazed as she started flapping her arms and jumping about in the snow drifts outside the circle.

Her performance was mesmerizing, and soon the girls caught her contagion, jumping up to join her. Mercy did not join the frolics, as she did not want to disturb young Betty, so quiet and limp at her side. Yet she watched in amazement, clapping her hands as if she were watching a play. The cloak-laden girls started to dance about each other, crying out against this Goody Glover, the laundress who was torturing them. Their heads jerked back and some pinned their arms behind them as if someone were pulling them with rope. It was an awesome sight, there in the darkening afternoon.

After several minutes, Abigail started to laugh maniacally, and fell to the ground on her back, breathing heavily from the effort, breaking the spell. Once again she seemed to possess herself, and other girls followed suit. They, too, collapsed onto the snow, giggling and gasping. "Oh, what fun 'tis to play such games!" Abigail exclaimed, feeling the surge of energy run through her body, vanquishing the boredom and torpor that so plagued her back at the parsonage.

"Aye, 'tis!" Ann agreed, panting from her exertions. "What a wonder is this story you bring us, Abigail. It seems to contain both fear and fascination at the same time."

"Twas a fun game, to be sure," Mary Walcott said. "Yet I do thank our gracious God that we do not suffer such horrid torments in our true lives."

"Do calm yourselves, girls," Abigail admonished. "Tis just a folly to entertain us for a moment. Yet I do command you: do not mention the reading of this book to anyone else. It must be kept a secret among us. Promise?"

"We promise," the other girls solemnly muttered in unison. They all knew that not a one of them would ever deny Abigail anything she wished.

Betty remained sleeping beneath Mercy's warm cloak, oblivious to the goings on around her.

~ ~ ~

14 December Anno Domini 1691
Town of Cambridge
Massachusetts Bay Colony

My dearest brother Richard,
It is with great joy that I received your missive yesterday. Could it be that after so many months of trying negotiations, the King and Queen have granted us our new charter? If you do write it, I must believe it. I have always had great faith in our Increase Mather and his ability to plead our case in England. Yet this in-between time without a charter has been most vexatious to us in Massachusetts Bay. The people have been nervous. We have had to levy increased taxes on the freemen to pay for the troubles in the District of Maine, and many men in the local militias have been drafted into battle. They do not go easily into such duties, without the necessary government in place to solidify our rulings.

So the new charter is truly wondrous news, and I thank you for letting us know that it is coming. I have informed Governor Bradstreet as well as the General Court, and we all have spent the evening celebrating Reverend Mather's success. There is much to be done, and I expect that it might be months before we see the details of the new charter.

As I did mention, there is some consternation here in the colony. I have attempted to broker a peace between the northern savages and our people, yet I am saddened to report that I have not been successful. York was recently taken by the Abenaki and there is little appetite among my neighbors for my peaceful approach. My own Mary has voiced her apathy toward my attempts, and it does bring some reproach to our daily lives. She remains, of course, a staunch woman of God, but she still grieves the passing of our young Thomas, and blames the Indians.

Mary frets, as does my young friend Cotton Mather, about the sinfulness of many of the colonists. This worry worries many, especially the ministers in Boston and Cambridge. They believe that many have turned their hearts and souls away from God. I do pray that this is not true. Mr. Mather's book about the Goodwin children has just been published, and while his aim was to use the case to encourage vigilance against the devil and his evil doings, I am afraid it only adds fire to the flame of fear in the colony. I stay awake late these nights, praying and reading the Bible, begging the Lord to give me strength and wisdom to best assuage these worries among our hardworking people. I only wish to serve God and adhere to justice.

Once again, my dear brother, I thank you for your welcome letter. I do hope that you and your family are well, and that one day we may meet again, on this earth or in heaven.

I remain truly yours, brother, in blood and in faith.

Thomas Danforth

CHAPTER SEVEN

January - February 1692
Salem Village

On a Sunday in mid January, the Salem Village congregation gathered in the cold meeting house, all with rocks warmed by their homestead fires, bundled, and laid in quilts at their feet in an attempt to ward off the icy air around them. It was morning and the slate clouds hung low in the sky, threatening snow. Even though attendance at services was a requirement of every church member, some of the seats in the meeting house were glaringly empty this morning. The people who did show up lowered their heads as if in prayer, although they were really trying to avoid the glances of their fellow congregants. There was little cheer about the place, neither inside nor outdoors where the winter winds swept harshly across the roughly-hewn clapboards of the meeting house.

After everyone was seated – women on the left, men on the right, children and servants in the balcony – Reverend Parris came through the heavy back door, stamping his feet on the floorboards, ridding his boots of snow and ice. As always, his face was dark and serious. As he started to walk down the center aisle toward the pulpit in the front, he took note of the empty benches on either side of him, and the people in the congregation held their breath in trepidation. Parris halted his steps for a moment, his look darkened, and the moment seemed to last for a long time. Then the minister shook his head slightly, looked up toward the pulpit, and continued to make his way. Men, women and children all breathed a sigh of relief.

The service began as it was wont to do, with the usual prayers and reading from scripture. All Sunday services in the colony lasted for three or four hours, much of it in silent prayer. These were the moments that tried young Abigail Williams and all of her friends as they sat in the balcony, particularly on frigid mornings such as this.

The girls couldn't help it if their minds wandered, or if they had
to subdue temptations to move their hands and feet, just to regain
some circulation in them.

Abigail still admired her uncle, even now as some of the villagers decided to stay home in protest of his leadership. He was a genius
in choreographing his services to garner the greatest emotional
response from his audience. His tone would start quietly, almost lull-
ing the people into a calm, comforting place where God had found
favor with them and all was good. But Abigail knew his heart – back
at the parsonage he rarely let an evening pass without railing against
the sins of the church members – and he always built up his sermons
so that the people knew that all was not right with God.

This morning Parris had chosen the nineteenth verse of
the Book of Isaiah as his text, and by the time several hours had
passed, each of his shouted words seemed like blows to many in the
meeting house. These people – the ones who were glad that Parris
was in their midst during such a sinful time – bowed their heads
in shame and fervently prayed to God to protect them from going
astray. Others – like Francis Nurse, Isaac Esty and Peter Cloyce, all
sitting toward the front of the room – tended to become frustrated
with Parris' methods, and wished they could catch glances of their
wives across the aisle, whom they knew were shaking their heads
in annoyance. The three sisters – Rebecca, Mary and Sarah – were
sitting toward the front as well, on the women's side, and they
often held hands during such sermons, keeping each other warm
but also helping to keep their irritation under wraps. That is, Mary
and Sarah shared such emotions. Sister Rebecca watched Reverend
Parris shout and pound his hand on the pulpit to drive his points
home, always keeping a beatific smile on her face. How could she
remain so accepting of such vitriol? Sarah thought. Couldn't they
do something about this Parris man? Why must they all sit there,
just putting up with being screamed at, with no recourse? Sarah
knew that her religion was usually delivered with stern admonishments against the Devil, but this was getting out of control. She had
heard that other congregations in the colony were moving away
from the old ways, more and more of them adopting the Half-Way
Covenant, but here in Salem Village they were going in the opposite direction. Sarah still didn't understand why her community
had more trouble getting along with each other than elsewhere in

the colony, and why God hadn't seen clear to actually bring them a minister who could unite them.

"Do you not see? The Lord rides on a swift cloud and is coming to Egypt!" Mr. Parris was shouting. "The idols of Egypt tremble before him, and the hearts of the Egyptians melt with fear. 'I will stir up Egyptian against Egyptian— brother will fight against brother, neighbor against neighbor, city against city, kingdom against kingdom. The Egyptians will lose heart, and I will bring their plans to nothing; they will consult the idols and the spirits of the dead, the mediums and the spiritists. I will hand the Egyptians over to the power of a cruel master, and a fierce king will over them,' declares the Lord, the Lord almighty!"

The minister read through the entire chapter, and then read it again, all twenty five verses, as if the repetition would somehow help his flock better comprehend the peril they were in. He cried of waters of the river drying up, fishermen lamenting over the lack of fish to feed their families, and all the people of Egypt losing hope. The girls in the balcony, listening above, were mesmerized. A frisson of excitement coursed through young Abigail's veins, to hear of such destruction. God could indeed cast his rage onto his people, she knew that, especially those who sin. She had seen the devastation first hand, watching the massacre of her family and village in Maine. It could happen here.

And she hoped it would. That kind of drama would at least staunch the dreadful boredom that she often felt in the parsonage. And maybe, just maybe, it would be a way for her side of the Putnam family to become powerful in the village once more.

After the sermon was finally over, the unison sigh from the churchgoers was audible to everyone. Some were relieved that Mr. Parris had finished. Some were saying a silent prayer, begging God to forgive them for whatever sin they believed they had committed over the past week.

As the congregation shuffled out of the meeting house, Abigail and her cousin Betty could see that most people seemed to want to be gone quickly. They would all be back here in several hours for the evening services, but for now it felt good to find a bit of relief in family fellowship over Sunday suppers. Samuel Parris, oblivious to the fact that none of his parishioners wished to stay and converse over his text, stomped down the high narrow steps that led from the pulpit down to the meeting house floor. Mrs. Parris dutifully took his side, and they, too, headed toward the door in the back.

Up above, Abigail waited for the adults to leave, as all Salem Village children knew was required of them, and then she and the other girls around her walked toward the ladder leading down. The noise their boots made on the solid pine floor resonated about the hall, now that the room was nearly empty. Abigail pinched Ann Jr. in her back and giggled. At first Ann grew angry, thinking she had been attacked, but when she saw it was her friend she, too, laughed and pinched her right back. Giddiness seemed to take over the small group, and they all started poking each other, squealing with delight.

Downstairs the heavy meeting house door flung open and the minister reentered the room, glaring up into the rafters. He must have heard the noise from outside – it had grown that loud – and he was livid. Such frivolity was not to be condoned in his church, especially not on Sunday, not after the serious message he had just delivered to the congregation. He needn't say anything, though, in reprimand, as the girls immediately quieted and put their heads down in reverence as soon as they saw his blazing, angry eyes. Abigail thought she saw a slight hint of satisfaction come over his face once he saw how they cowered. Just see the power of his being, she thought, by a mere look!

It wasn't until the other girls reached the bottom of the ladder that Mercy noticed Betty. The little girl was still in the seat she had occupied for the past three hours, and hadn't made a move to leave with the rest of the congregation. Her head was bowed and she was rocking back and forth, back and forth, as if in a trance. Mercy pointed at Betty, beckoning Abigail's attention. Abigail sighed with impatience and returned to her cousin, pulling her up roughly by the arm. When Betty did not come out of her state, Abigail gave her face a quick and hard slap that echoed throughout the walls of the meeting house.

"Get over your dissembling," she growled at the younger girl, pulling her toward the exit. "These constant tantrums do bore me to the very core of my being. Why must I always have to look after you?"

Even though Betty let herself be dragged away from her seat, she spoke in a slow, quiet incantation, repeating the chapter from Isaiah that her father had recited the hour before. "The officials of

Zoan have become fools, the leaders of Memphis are deceived; the cornerstones of her peoples have led Egypt astray. The Lord has poured into them a spirit of dizziness; they make Egypt stagger in all that she does, as a drunkard staggers around in his vomit. There is nothing Egypt can do— head or tail, palm branch or reed.”

The girls watched in amazement as young Betty recited the chapter perfectly. Her voice was dull, without flection, and her gaze was far off, as if she were seeing something not there.

“Betty! Do stop! Your playacting has gone far enough!” Abigail chided, her friends staying behind her and peeking around her cloak. But Betty continued, paying no attention to her cousin. “In that day the Egyptians will become weaklings,” she intoned. “They will shudder with fear at the uplifted hand that the Lord Almighty raises against them. And the land of Judah will bring terror to the Egyptians; everyone to whom Judah is mentioned will be terrified, because of what the Lord Almighty is planning against them.”

Abigail could feel Ann shudder behind her, and spin around to leave. “She does speak as if enchanted,” she said, motioning the others to follow her. “I will have none of this witchcraft.”

Abigail, although startled herself, forced herself to laugh. “Witchcraft?” she chided. “Why, she is speaking the word of God. Tis the furthest thing from witchcraft!”

~ ~ ~

The next morning dawned as cold as the day before. Tituba was the first one downstairs, her breath coming from her mouth in cloudy wisps. She pulled her shawl closer around her body and bent to stoke up the fire. She was relieved to see that the embers were still hot from the previous evening. As she bent over, she felt a sharp pain in the small of her back, which she tried hard to massage away with her fists. After two years she still wasn’t used to these bitter winters and she yearned for the hot, humid weather of her youth in Barbados.

“Sure to be a cold one,” her husband, John Indian, said, coming into the room behind her with an armful of wood. He startled her. “I feel it deep in my bones, do you not, Tituba?”

“I do,” she replied, moving away from the fire so he could put the wood in the bin beside it. “My bones be aching.”

John looked up from his work and smiled at her. “Your bones may be aching, but you are still pleasing to my eye.”

Tituba couldn't help smiling back, despite her despair. She hated living with the Parrises. She hated Mr. Parris who beat her for the slightest mishap. She tried desperately to do her chores as well as she could, but he would never be satisfied. Abigail was a wretched child who abused her when the mood struck her. The only person who made Tituba's life bearable was sweet little Betty who treated Tituba like a mother – which was understandable when her own mother, Mrs. Parris, was usually too busy trying to please her husband. And John Indian. He was kind and strong and always quick with a sweet word at exactly the right time such as the current one, when her confidence flagged. The two had met the day that the Parrises sailed from Barbados to Boston, after Mr. Parris had purchased them from different plantation owners. They had found immediate companionship borne out of a similar fate: foreign slaves taken to a strange country, forced to serve a family living in a godforsaken village whose customs still seemed unnatural to them. After a day of backbreaking work, they found solace and warmth by huddling together on their straw mattress in the corner of the lean-to kitchen. It was the one pleasure in their difficult lives.

"Be gone with ye," Tituba scolded, although the smile remained on her face. "I have work to do."

John put his hat back on and tightened the scarf around his neck, preparing himself for the bitter air without, and stepped outside into the darkness, heading for the barn. Tituba continued to tend the fire, throwing a handful of shelled walnuts into the porridge that sat in its copper pot, ready to be refreshed for the morning meal. She knew Betty loved walnuts, even though Mrs. Parris often chided Tituba for such an indulgence. Their supply of the treats was slim and needed to be carefully rationed. Everything, it seemed, needed to be rationed. Tituba remembered the days in Barbados when sweet fruits like pineapple and mango and coconut fell from the trees in an ever-flowing stream, when sugar and cocoa and coffee were plentiful and cheap, when she never had to worry about hunger, even as a plantation slave. How far she had come. Why had God forsaken her so?

By the time Mrs. Parris descended from the rooms upstairs, the sun was coming up over the stark pines outside, the kitchen and the parlor were warm, and breakfast ready to be eaten. As usual, the first thing the woman did was look about the downstairs rooms, seeking out something to criticize, almost hoping that Tituba had overlooked something. Rarely did she find anything, although at times she couldn't help fabricating some minor gaffe just so she could berate the black woman. It felt good to be the one chastising, rather than the chastised.

"We shall bake today, Tituba," Mrs. Parris announced, in a commanding tone she reserved just for the slave. Otherwise the woman was as mousy and unassuming as they come. "Mr. Parris does enjoy his biscuits."

"Right, missus," Tituba replied, bowing her head and scurrying to the other side of the room.

"It has been so cold of late, I could benefit from warm aromas. My nerves have been most agitated." Tituba knew that Mrs. Parris often talked like this, almost to herself, and it required no response. In fact, on the few occasions when Tituba tried to converse with her, she was punished for speaking out of turn.

At that moment a clattering was heard on the narrow, steep staircase leading upstairs, and Abigail and Betty came down, their white caps tight on their heads, their clothing immaculate. They dutifully curtsied to Mrs. Parris and sat at the table, ready for their porridge. Tituba noticed that for once Abigail wasn't molesting her younger cousin in some way – poking her in the ribs, making fun of one thing or the other, chiding her. Something must have happened between them to make Abigail leave Betty alone.

"You girls will leave this place this morning," Mrs. Parris announced. "Tituba and I will be baking and Mr. Parris is going to visit Goody Corey, who is ill. I need quiet for once."

Tituba saw Betty's face darken with – what? – fear? She had to quell the impulse to go to the little girl and take her in her arms. Such a frail child. On the other hand, Abigail's eyes lit up with this rare invitation from her mother. Usually she had to beg to be let out of the house. "If you wish, aunt," Abigail said dutifully, and Tituba couldn't help rolling her eyes, although she made sure she did it with her back turned to the girls so Abigail couldn't see her.

Betty felt something snap deep inside her. She couldn't go with Abigail and the other girls, not again. She had done her best to close her eyes and pray to God during these outings, trying not to engage with what was going on. Because she knew the girls were sinning. They had been dancing and playacting and sometimes her cousin seemed to take on a wholly different personality, as if she were possessed. But now it was like she had been holding tight to a tree branch for many months, trying desperately not to fall, knowing that death lay beneath her – but try as she might, she could not continue. Somehow she knew that if she went with her cousin, the Devil would surely come to her and make her sign his book – just like what Reverend Mather wrote about with those poor Goodwin children.

Suddenly Betty's mind went blank.

Tituba, Mrs. Parris and Abigail stared, motionless in alarm, as the young child started shaking in front of them. Her eyes went back in her head so that it looked like the pupils almost disappeared. Tituba was filled with a dread she hadn't felt in a very long time. The last time she witnessed such a sight was back in Barbados, when the village medicine man brought a bewitched woman to the council of elders, seeking help in shaking the devil out of her. Now Tituba screamed and ran into the corner, cowering, even while she wanted desperately to comfort poor Betty. But she didn't dare come close to such witchery. Her mother had told her, over and over, that the devil inside such a being could easily jump out and envelop anyone who touched the sufferer. "No! No! No! No!" Tituba continued to wail, covering her ears with her hands and closing her eyes tightly.

The slave's reaction made the other two even more astonished. Abigail looked from Betty to Tituba to her aunt, all bravado gone from her, looking every bit of her young eleven years. Mrs. Parris seemed glued to her spot, not being able to move. "What is happening, aunt?" Abigail cried over Tituba's screams. Betty was shaking so hard now that she fell off the bench, and now she was twitching on the floor. Her fall was enough to break the temporary spell that had come over her mother, and Mrs. Parris sprang to action. "Shut up, Tituba!" she screamed, and dropped to the floor to her daughter, collecting her into her arms, trying to hold her tightly enough to ease the shaking. Abigail followed suit, grateful for something to do. "Yes, do shut up, Tituba!" she yelled, stomped over to the corner, and slapped the woman hard across the face. The attack did no good: Tituba continued her wailing. Abigail slapped her again and again, reveling in the action, thankful to be without restraint for a time. With each slap Abigail's fear turned into fury as she remembered the bloody scene of her parents' slaughter. Back then Abigail hid away, powerless. But now she was fighting back. The swelling anger felt like a conflagration.

Once blood started gushing from the side of her mouth, Tituba finally ceased, and crumpled into the corner, covering her head with her hands.

Abigail looked over at Betty and her aunt, hoping to see gratitude in Mrs. Parris' face for what she had just managed to do. Yet the older woman was concentrating solely on her daughter, who would not stop her fit, no matter how tightly her mother held her, no matter how many words of comfort she could utter into her ear. As Abigail watched, the room seemed unnaturally quiet, with Tituba silent in the corner and Betty not making a sound. Even as the young girl continued to vibrate uncontrollably, Abigail was able to take a few breaths and calm herself. Her anger dissipated as she realized she had to figure out something to explain Betty's behavior. Because she knew that Betty had broken down somehow, and it was only a matter of time before she started telling her mother – and Reverend Parris – why she was so scared. A pox on the girl, Abigail thought. She had to go and ruin the whole thing. The games she and Ann and the others had been playing together for the past year were just in jest, but she could guarantee that the minister would not see it that way. And she couldn't be sent away. Not back to Maine. Not back to that blood and destruction. She just couldn't.

Suddenly Abigail remembered Cotton Mather's book, and the Goodwin family. Was that why Betty was acting this way? Was she copying those children's symptoms? But didn't Betty's antics start before she had found the book and read it aloud to the rest of the group? She couldn't remember. But it certainly didn't look like Betty was faking.

"Betty, Betty, Betty," Mrs. Parris was repeating. "What does befall you? What sickness overtakes you?"

Suddenly, Abigail herself started shaking. She fell to the floor, rolling from one side to the other. Even though her eyes were closed tightly shut, she could sense that her aunt's attention was diverted away from Betty. Abigail's whole body seemed to take over, as if Betty's fits were contagious. What was happening to her now? Energy flowed through her, overtaking her, keeping her from controlling her own limbs. What on earth or heaven had started here?

The front door crashed open and in stormed Reverend Parris,

at first not noticing the strange scene inside his house, pulling off his woolen scarf, doffing his heavy cap. "Husband!" Mrs. Parris screamed, and, spying what was revealed in front of him, he reeled, taking a step back and clutching a chair that stood next to the door. For a moment he was speechless as he took in the spectacle in front of him: his wife clutching his quivering daughter in her arms, Abigail rolling about the room in fits, and Tituba cowering in the corner, muttering to herself in her native language. It was as if someone had erased the quiet, pleasant tableau he expected upon his return and filled it instead with some crazed caricatures of his own family. It was truly shocking.

"Husband!" Mrs. Parris cried again, and he was spurred to action. He knelt down with his wife, taking his young child from her arms, feeling Betty's twitching and shaking that seemed to be stronger than he could imagine his frail daughter could muster. He could not assuage her. "What is this?" he demanded. "What ails these children?"

At his voice, Tituba started screaming again. Mr. Parris' gaze flew from the slave to the girls writhing on the floor and back. He jumped up, pushing Betty back to his wife's embrace, and stormed across the room. He pulled Tituba up roughly by her arm, and pushed her hard against the wall. Glaring into her eyes he growled through gritted teeth: "What..did...you...do...to them? What have you done, you woman, you she-wolf? What vile medicine have you given them to put them into such fits?"

With each word he squeezed her arm more tightly, putting the other hand across her throat, threatening to suffocate her right there. Tituba struggled against him, shaking her head back and forth. "I do nothing, sir!" she managed to gasp, trying desperately to get air into her lungs. "I do nothing! I promise!"

At that moment John Indian came into the room, hauling two large buckets of water in either hand. "John! John!" Tituba cried out. "He beat me! He like to kill me!"

John, in his amazement, dropped the buckets, which upon impact with the floor fell over, spilling water all across the wide pine boards. He ran to Tituba, clutching at the minister, trying desperately to pull him off her. Now Mr. Parris was fighting both of the Caribs, roaring in his rage, trying to continue his attack. The entire room seemed to swirl about him as if in a nightmare.

"Samuel!" Mrs. Parris cried again. "Samuel! Do stop, I beg of you. See your daughter. She is coming out of her fit."

The minister did as he was told, unused to hearing such commanding words from his meek wife, turning his head and heaving from his exertion, yet not letting go of Tituba's arm. There on the floor Betty was no longer shaking, as the water from the spilled buckets had creeped toward her and began to saturate her shift. Her father blinked his eyes, not yet certain of what he was seeing, not then nor a moment before. Her mother rocked her gently, seeing what the water had done, not wishing to protect Betty from further soaking as it had such a positive effect. The girl started whimpering as Mrs. Parris wiped the sweat from her brow with the ruffle of her sleeve. "Sweet girl," she whispered to Betty. "Sweet sweet girl."

Abigail, too, was ceasing her own fit, as calm seemed to come over the room like a slowly descending warm blanket. She stopped rolling back and forth, and curled up in a fetal position on the floor boards.

All four adults stayed where they were, seemingly unable to move, each pondering what they had just witnessed. It was as if they were unmoving puppets in some kind of monstrous play. The only sound was the spitting and crackling of the firewood in the hearth, and Mrs. Parris' whispered words of comfort into Betty's ear.

It was Mr. Parris who broke the spell, roughly releasing Tituba from his grip and pulling Betty and his wife up from the floor. Tituba fell back into a heap, covering her head with her hands, and John Indian went to her, taking her in his arms. Abigail was left to herself on the floor.

The minister sat Betty on one of the benches at the board, and bade Mrs. Parris to bring a cup of ale to help their daughter revive. Betty's face was pale and her clothes and cap were askew, but she took the cup with gratitude, swallowing most of it in one quaff. Her father put both hands on her shoulders and shook her gently, drawing her gaze to his.

"What was that, Betty?" he asked her, trying to keep his voice even although he was filled with shock. He was used to being in control, knowing what to expect, and he was intensely uncomfortable with being so ignorant about what was going on in front of his own eyes. "When I came in, you were in some sort of fit. What did trouble you so?"

But Betty shut her eyes tightly and would not answer. Her mother put her arms around her protectively and pulled her away from the minister, worried that he would punish the girl. "It did come on suddenly," Mrs. Parris answered for her daughter. "I was bidding the girls to go outside, as I wished for quiet. Young Betty went blank, and then went into a fit so horrible that I could do nothing to bring her comfort. Not a moment passed before Abigail joined her. I could not hold both girls so Abigail dropped to the floor, writhing on her back, as if some creature were attacking her. Tituba nor John Indian were of little help, as Tituba did escape to the corner of the room, seeming in terror of the fits."

Hearing her name, Tituba quickly gathered herself together and ran to the spilled buckets of water. John Indian helped her right them and, now that the water had had the effect of bringing Betty out of her fit, mop up the mess with a flax cloth. The two looked at each other with worry in their eyes and tried to leave the room.

"You go nowhere, Tituba!" Mr. Parris roared. "Nor you, John Indian. You both come here at once. You, too, Abigail. Do get up from the floor, for mercy's sake."

The three slowly did as they were told, their heads bowed, contrite. Once everyone was seated, the minister stood up and paced the floor in front of them, pulling at his beard as he went.

"You will all tell me what is happening here, or I will flog each and every one of you," he demanded. "Do ye have fevers, girls? Are ye sick at your bellies?"

Abigail and Betty, now with clear eyes but noticeably bewildered, shook their heads in unison. "I do not know, uncle," Abigail said. "Betty fell to quivering and I found myself being equally afflicted. But it has passed now."

"Did ye eat some kind of poisonous berry? Or some spoiled milk from the cow?"

"Nay, father," Betty finally squeaked, burrowing into her mother's chest to be comforted. "My health is hearty."

"Was it Tituba?" the minister kept on. "Tituba, what did you do to these children?"

"I do nothing, master!" Tituba blurted out. "I was as afeared and much astonished by the vision as you were. I tell you, I do nothing!"

Mr. Parris drew his hand back and slapped her across the

back of her head, and the slave cried out in pain. She cowered in front of him, knowing she could not escape. "Do not beat me, I beg of ye, master! I love young Betty and Abigail too, I would never do nothing to hurt these girls!"

Mrs. Parris remained silent, running her hands through Betty's hair which had escaped from her cap. Her husband threw up his hands in frustration. "There must be some reason for this," he said, almost to himself. "Yet not one of them will tell me. Perhaps it is a momentary affliction, not to be repeated. I shall pray to God on it."

With that, he stomped out of the room into the second parlor which served as his study. The others watched him go, breathing sighs of relief that there would be no more inquiry into the strangeness that had just taken hold of them.

Mrs. Parris arose abruptly, smoothing her apron and tightening her shawl about her shoulders. "Let us leave it at that," she instructed, pushing her chin up in determination. "You girls are obviously fatigued. Spend the morning in the loft if you will. Rest. Tituba, let us be on with the baking."

John Indian quickly arose and took the water buckets back outside, hurrying to refill them, glad to be away from the house. The girls, a bit unsteady on their feet, scurried up the ladder to the loft above. Once inside the room they shared, both pulled down the heavy quilts and jumped into their beds.

For once, Abigail did not torment her cousin. Rather, she turned toward the wall and closed her eyes.

Wondering.

~ ~ ~

A week passed without further disruption in the parsonage, although the nagging tension continued. The minister increased his diatribes against the villagers who refused to pay their rates and who did not contribute firewood for the family. More people were joining the group who disapproved of him, now that the rates committee officially ruled that they did not have to sustain the ministry with their financial contributions. The number of Mr. Parris' supporters was quickly diminishing, and these men – Thomas Putnam Jr., Jonathan Walcott, Joseph Hutchinson, Nathaniel Ingersoll, John Gould – frequently met with him at the parsonage to discuss what was to be done about the rift. As Abigail and Betty eavesdropped on these conversations from their perch at the top of the ladder, they heard few real solutions, only a continued litany of complaints against the injustice of it all. Whenever the names Nurse, Cloyce, Esty, or Proctor were mentioned, the men below would groan and spit in what sounded like real hatred.

Meanwhile, both Mr. and Mrs. Parris kept a closer eye on the girls, worried about another episode of the fits that still flummoxed them – yet not saying another word on the subject, not even to each other when they were alone. Tituba was both more cautious and more solicitous around the girls, especially Abigail.

One evening toward the end of January, a knock came at the door. The girls had helped Mrs. Parris and Tituba clear away the dinner meal, and were now sitting at the table with their Bibles and their Latin texts, memorizing various passages. Mr. Parris was in his study behind closed doors, and the rest of the household knew never to bother him when he was in there. Tituba dutifully went to the door and opened it.

At the stone step outside stood a stooped woman, wrapped in a ragged cloak, holding a tiny baby who was yowling in her tattered sling. The sound of the baby brought Mrs. Parris to join Tituba at the door, and the girls got up, too, peeking around the women's aprons to stare at the visitors. They had seen this hag before, although rarely at church. She was Sarah Good, the penniless woman who lived with her husband at the edge of the village. Everyone in the church knew of her, and how she was well-to-do in her youth, only to lose her inheritance many years ago. Since then she had married a poor laborer and often came begging door to door, depending on the charity of her neighbors to feed her small family. She was probably in her forties but looked two decades older than that, with a grimy face and withered fingers reaching out for a coin. Betty Parris had always been terrified of Sarah when the beggar came to their door. Indeed this evening she clung to her mother's skirts in fear. A foul odor emanated from the woman and her baby, as if the child hadn't been washed of her excrement for days.

"Good evening, Mrs. Parris," Sarah said, more of a cackle than a polite greeting. Her voice rasped with hoarseness. "I do wish ye health and happiness."

Mrs. Parris did not bid the woman inside as was the custom of the wife of a minister. Instead she pushed the girls away from her, motioning for them to return to their books. Tituba slithered away from the door in silence. "Goody Good, what are you doing out on such a winter's night? Be gone from this door!" Mrs. Parris said. Abigail looked up in wonder. It was not often that her aunt uttered an unkind word to anyone, nor did she raise her voice to another.

"Aye, will do, will do," Sarah muttered, lifting her crying baby up to Mrs. Parris. "But take pity on my poor child, won't ye? She hasn't eaten a morsel in close to a day now."

Mrs. Parris huffed and went to the hearth, reaching into a basket and picking up two bannock cakes that had been left after dinner. She wrapped them in a threadbare cloth that was so old and used that she had been about to rip it up into smaller pieces to line a quilt. Quickly she returned to the door and thrust out the small package into Sarah Good's hands. "This is all we have," she said, disdainfully. "Now be gone, or else you shall disturb my husband."

But it was too late. The minister came into the room from his study, his face dark with annoyance for having been bothered. He joined his wife at the door and bellowed to Sarah: "Sarah Good, I do not see you nor your husband at the church. Are ye so sinful as to deny God and live outside of His word?"

The beggar looked up at him and bowed her head several times. "Ye are right, reverend," she agreed. "I do urge my husband to go to services with me, but he often beats me and bids me stay. Tis surely not my fault. My neighbor Sarah Osborne advises me to go with her as well, yet often I am kept in my home as if in a jail. Perhaps you might talk with him on my behalf?"

The girls, listening back in the room, looked at each other. Abigail rolled her eyes. They knew of this Sarah Osborne as well, another unfortunate in the village and someone few church members communed with. Goody Osborne was old enough to be Sarah Good's mother, yet they seemed to have formed a friendship over the years. Sarah Osborne was no less notorious than was her friend, having kept her two son's inheritance to herself when her first husband, Thomas Prince, died two decades ago. This atrocity happened often in families, yet the villagers could not forgive her next move: to act as a wife to her hired man, much younger than herself, without the benefit of holy matrimony.

"I have tried to intervene with Goodman Good many times," Mr. Parris was saying. "It does not sway his sinful ways. And here you are, begging for your meals, with a squalling, sick baby at your breast. Do ye not see that God is punishing you?"

"Aye, aye," Sarah Good was saying, backing away from the

door, having won her prize of food. "Aye, aye," she kept repeating. Once she was several feet away from the house, she turned her back and clambered away. The minister and his wife watched her go, disgust in their eyes. Abigail quietly got up from her chair and returned to the door, curious to see this woman demeaned in front of Mr. Parris. For once shy Betty followed her cousin, eager as well to cast one more glimpse upon the strange woman at the door.

As soon as the beggar drew close to the dark that lay beyond the circle of light cast upon the snow by Mrs. Parris' lantern, she turned her head back over her shoulders and gave the Parrises a strange smile. She started muttering something under her breath, but no one at the door could hear the words.

"What say you, Goody Good?" Mr. Parris thundered. "If you have something to tell us, speak it aloud!"

But the crabbed woman merely turned her head back and made her way into the darkness beyond the light. She continued to murmur words that were inaudible to the rest. Young Betty looked up at her father, wondering what he would do next, knowing that he did not like it when he did not know what was happening. But the minister just sighed in distaste and slammed the door. "I have enough to worry about with this wretched village," he said to no one. "I have no need of a godless beggar at my door."

He glared at the rest of his family as if they were at fault, and then walked back into his study, slamming that door as well.

"Aunt," Abigail said, sullenly as if in a trance, pointing at her cousin. "Look!"

Mrs. Parris and Tituba followed Abigail's finger toward Betty, who had slunk to the floor. She was clutching at her face as if something was covering it, and as before, quivers and shakes came over her small body.

"Husband!" Mrs. Parris cried, grateful to not have to deal with this situation by herself this time. "Husband! Do return! It's Betty!"

The minister, who hadn't had time to even sit at his desk, crashed back into the room, eyes ablaze. By now Abigail had joined her cousin on the floor next to her, and both girls were writhing with new fits. "It does come upon them again!" Mr. Parris shouted. In the lean-to kitchen behind the hearth, Tituba heard his outcry, and fear coursed through her body as it had before. This time she stayed out of the room, running out the back door to try to find John Indian.

Now the girls started grunting, and their faces were white as winding sheets. Mrs. Parris started to go to them, but her husband held her back. "No," he commanded. "I want to regard them in this state."

"But they are in danger!" Mrs. Parris cried. "It is our Betty, husband!"

Still Mr. Parris held her back, wanting to merely watch so that he could better understand what was going on. The two held each other tightly, and Mrs. Parris began to cry.

While Betty rolled around on the floor, twitching, Abigail rose up to her feet and started running around the room. "Swish, swish, goes the fish!" she started chanting, waving her arms about and twirling as she went. She laughed maniacally and pulled at her hair, letting go the cap that usually held her dark tresses in check. "Uh, uh, uh, uh," she grunted, returning to her cousin and collapsing to the floor. Meanwhile Betty said nothing, just shook violently as if some horrid fever were overtaking her.

"Is it some sickness?" Mrs. Parris whispered to her husband. "Have they been taken over by some poison?"

But Mr. Parris merely shook his head, not knowing.

"Abigail!" he shouted. "Abigail, do ye hear me?"

"Ha ha ha, it is he! It is he!" Abigail cried to the air around her, not looking at her uncle.

"Betty, and you?" Mrs. Parris asked, still crying uncontrollably. "Betty, what can we do to help ye?"

Betty was unresponsive.

"The water," Mrs. Parris said to her husband. "Remember how the water stopped it?"

He looked at her, remembering, and motioned for her to go. Mrs. Parris called for Tituba but there was no answer. She went herself to the barrel in the corner of the lean-to kitchen and scooped out a tankard of water from within. Returning to the room, she threw the entire contents into the faces of her daughter and her niece.

Immediately the fits ceased. Both girls stopped their writhing and looked about the room as if they just woke up from a deep sleep. Betty started sobbing and Mr. Parris finally let his wife embrace her to her bosom. Abigail curled up into a fetal position.

"That's it," the minister proclaimed. "In the morn we shall fast and pray together for two days. God shall help us in this strange sickness."

He stomped back into his study without another word, once
again slamming the heavy door behind him.

~ ~ ~

A few days later, Dr. Griggs was summoned to the parsonage.
He arrived on a cold, bright morning, with his servant Elizabeth
Hubbard in tow. The girl followed him into the best parlor, carrying
the doctor's heavy black bag filled with all sorts of mysterious-look-
ing medical instruments and books.

Abigail hadn't found the chance to escape the house, so there
had been no secret meetings at the giant white pine for some time.
Her uncle had made all the members of the parsonage promise not
to tell anyone about the fits, and so far Abigail believed no one had.
She knew he was nervous about how it might look to the villagers.
Just the night before she had overheard the minister murmuring to
his wife in the room next to the girls', after they thought everyone
was asleep.

"The situation does continue to try my soul," Mr. Parris said.
"Our fasting and prayer did not work. The fits persevere."

Indeed after two days of staying indoors, doing nothing but
pray and read the Bible – no food was prepared, nor eaten – both
Betty and Abigail had another bout of trembling and rolling about
the floor, white in the face, strange guttural utterances emanating
from their throats. Abigail eventually calmed, but Betty did not.
Her mother managed to get her into bed, where she now lay, as if in
a trance. The shaking stopped, but now she would not respond to
questions or offers of food or drink; rather she remained with her
eyes open, yet not quite awake.

"And now our dear Betty lies in some kind of other world,"
Mrs. Parris answered her husband last night, as Abigail lay listening
to their words. "I fear she might die."

"Dr. Griggs will come tomorrow. I do hope he will keep our
affairs private. This looks very bad for me. I can guess what the congregation would think of such afflictions attacking my own home."

When the doctor arrived the next day, Abigail was pleased
to see that Elizabeth accompanied him. The girls' eyes met as Dr.
Griggs took off his cloak and accepted Mrs. Parris' offer of cider.
Elizabeth looked both worried and curious. She hadn't heard from
her friend for a good week, and Abigail and Betty had not attended
services last Sunday – and then Dr. Griggs was called to the house.

Abigail looked back at Elizabeth meaningfully, but Elizabeth did not know what she was trying to convey.

Dr. Griggs was summoned to the large table to the side of the roaring hearth, and he sat with both the Parrises. He was an old, fat man with wisps of graying hair covering his nearly bald head, and he hadn't lived in the village for very long. Regardless, he knew of the controversy surrounding Mr. Parris' leadership and was determined not to become a part of it. Indeed, he was wary of being in the parsonage at all.

"What is the trouble, Mr. Parris?" he asked, taking a long quaff of his drink. Elizabeth stood dutifully behind him, holding his bag in her hands. Abigail stood next to her, hoping that she wouldn't be directed out of the room. She noticed Tituba at the door leading back into the lean-to kitchen. The slave was clutching her apron and her face was filled with dread.

"It is my daughter Betty," the minister replied. "She lays now in her bed, not awake yet not asleep. She cannot be roused, no matter our ministrations."

Dr. Griggs frowned. "Is her body in good health?" he asked. "Has she suffered from fever, or some kind of stomach ill?"

"No, not that we are aware," Mr. Parris responded. His wife grabbed his arm, wanting desperately to speak but knowing that it would displease him. Abigail was surprised that he did not push her away. He was rarely comfortable with any show of physicality at all. It was obvious that he was distracted and worried.

As Dr. Griggs pulled at his beard in thought, Mr. Parris continued. "Both girls, Betty and my niece, Abigail, have suffered from strange fits."

"Fits?" the doctor asked, looking up in alarm.

"Aye. They come on suddenly, with no warning and without reason. They twitch and roll as if in deep pain. We cannot gain their notice while they are so afflicted."

"Is this the Abigail that you speak of?" Dr. Griggs asked, pointing to the girl.

"Aye, that is she."

With some difficulty Dr. Griggs turned to Abigail, beckoning her forward with the crook of his finger. She snuck a quick look at her friend and took a step toward the doctor.

"How many times have you been so afflicted, child?" Dr. Griggs inquired.

"It is nigh on three times."

"What do you do in these fits?"

"I do not remember."

The doctor looked puzzled. He took Abigail's hand and turned it over, feeling her pulse. He looked carefully at her hands, at her face.

When he turned her head to peer into her ears, she pulled away from him and started barking like the dog outside in the yard.

Dr. Griggs was taken aback, amazed at what he was seeing.

"Watch!" the minister cried out. "Tis happening once more!"

Abigail ran about the room as if flying, her arms waving about her. Tituba screamed and ran from the house, and Elizabeth scuttled to Mrs. Parris, terrified and seeking comfort from maternal arms. The older woman instinctively drew the maidservant to her, and Elizabeth had to stifle a cry of desperate need for her own mother, now dead and buried.

Abigail's limbs started twitching at unnatural angles, and her eyes rolled back in her head.

"Gain control of her!" Dr. Griggs bade the minister. "Keep her steady so that I may examine her!"

Mr. Parris ran after Abigail, but the girl was agile and escaped his grasp many times. Finally he was able to restrain her by approaching her from behind, taking her in a bear hug and wrapping one leg around one of hers. He was a tall man and normally would have no problem holding such a small girl, but her strength seemed superhuman and it took a great deal of effort to keep her still. He could feel her whole body shake as if some kind of current ran through her.

The doctor, unsteady from amazement, stood and moved toward the twitching girl. He felt a wariness grip him but carried on, gazing into Abigail's whitening eyes and trying to open her mouth to examine her teeth and throat. As he did so, the girl bit his hand, and he recoiled in pain. She started laughing and elbowed her uncle in the ribs so that he released her.

Suddenly, Abigail stopped, looked around the room, and asked "Where is Tituba?"

The others stood transfixed, not sure what to do.

"I say again: where is Tituba?" Abigail demanded, her voice fierce.

"Tis good, Abigail," Mrs. Parris said, uttering her first words since the doctor's arrival. The rest of them stared at the woman as she left Elizabeth and approached her niece, holding her hands up as if in surrender. "Tituba is close by. All is well. All is well."

Abigail glared at her aunt, who continued to smile at her encouragingly. She started to calm as Mrs. Parris grew near. By the time the two met in the middle of the room, Abigail allowed herself to be embraced by her aunt, collapsing into her arms. As Elizabeth and the men continued to watch in amazement, Mrs. Parris took Abigail to the large rocking chair in front of the hearth, and held her in her lap as if the girl were a mere babe. Abigail curled up against her aunt's breast, and promptly fell asleep.

"Tis a scene that I have not witnessed ever before," Dr. Griggs said, almost in a whisper. "A wondrous, terrible thing."

"What do you think it is, doctor?" Mr. Parris asked. "It comes on like that, and disappears as quickly. We are truly perplexed."

"Where is the younger child?" Dr. Griggs inquired.

"Upstairs in her room."

"Elizabeth, bring me my bag."

Elizabeth, who had been clutching the bag so tightly that her fingerprints were embedded in the worn leather, was grateful to be doing something, anything. It was truly shocking to see her new friend in such a state, yet she also remembered the times in the woods when Abigail could almost embody another being – like when she pretended to be Mr. Parris – or when she had the strange ability to whip up the others in a frenzy. What was it about this young girl that was so compelling?

Dr. Griggs, Mr. Parris and Elizabeth climbed the ladder to the upstairs rooms. Betty lay in her bed, her eyes open but seemingly unseeing. Elizabeth thought she looked peaceful, not like the whimpering, complaining little girl she was in the woods with the others. The doctor examined Betty, calling for Elizabeth to hand him different instruments from the bag: a magnifying glass, cups, a small hammer. The minister watched, clasping and unclasping his hands in worry.

Eventually the doctor rose and the three descended the stairs.

"What is your diagnosis? What ails these children? Does it call for bleeding?" Mr. Parris asked once they returned to the best parlor. Dr. Griggs shook his head, clearly concerned, looking over at Mrs. Parris, who still rocked her sleeping niece in her lap.

"I could bleed the children, yes," the doctor replied. "Although I fear it would do no good."

"How could that be? Would bloodletting not allow the bad physick to escape?"

"Aye, it would," the doctor said. "If the problem were bad physick."

"Then what is the problem, doctor?" Mr. Parris asked again, his voice rising in frustration.

Dr. Griggs looked at the minister with dread in his eyes. "It is nothing medical, I fear," he said. "No. I am dreadfully sorry, Mr. Parris. But these children are bewitched."

~ ~ ~

This time the stakes were higher. Before now, the girls' parents or custodians knew they were leaving their houses, and had given their permission – although they never knew what the girls were doing. But now it was impossible for Abigail to escape, not with Betty still catatonic in her bed and the Parrises worried that she herself would go into fits at any time. She had hoped to get a message to Elizabeth Hubbard when she visited the parsonage with Dr. Griggs, but the fits had started before she could do so. The day after the visit, Abigail slipped a note into Tituba's hand and commanded her to deliver it to Ann Putnam Jr.. Tituba had initially said no, fear in her eyes, looking over her shoulder to see if Mr. Parris was watching. But Abigail had slapped her face and told her that if she didn't, she would tell the minister that it was she – Tituba – who was bewitching the girls.

Both Mr. and Mrs. Parris were distracted, anyway. They sat at either side of Betty's bed, praying, reading the Bible, talking together about what must be done. After the doctor left with Elizabeth the day before, they were struck dumb in astonishment and fear. Mrs. Parris started to cry, even as she was rocking Abigail, and her husband paced the floor with his hands behind his back, calling out to God, asking for guidance. Witchcraft in the parsonage! What would the villagers say? Why had God forsaken him so? He had been commanding his flock to be vigilant against such sin, and now it had been borne right under his nose. Devil, where are you? Show your face so I can wrest you to the ground, vanquishing you in the name of Christ!

When Abigail awoke, even as she saw the severe consternation overtaking her aunt and uncle, she felt the warmth of Mrs. Parris' body, the safety and comfort of her arms. This was a far too rare experience for the girl. The Parrises' focus was inevitably on their own daughter, and often Abigail was treated almost as badly as Tituba. She always knew that she would never hold the same position of love and care that Betty would; not as a motherless child, not as a refugee from the Indian wars. Mrs. Parris always regarded her with suspicion. But now here she was, rocking Abigail as if she were her own child. The young girl feigned sleep, even after she was well awake. She wanted this moment to last, even though her poor aunt was soaking Abigail's cap with her tears.

So Tituba delivered Abigail's message and the next night, after all were asleep, the girl rose from her bed, donned her clothing and outer wraps, and stole away into the frigid air. She carried a small lantern lit with a single candle that did little to pierce the cold cloak of darkness that swallowed her up. On her back was a burlap sack filled with firewood she had pinched from the ever-dwindling pile near the barn, along with a flint to start a flame.

This time, Betty, still in her trance, did not join her.

As she neared the giant white pine, Abigail heard a rustling, and quickly saw that Ann had arrived before her. She was clearing away the few inches of snow that had fallen several nights before so that the secret snow cave would be clear for the others.

"Ann!" Abigail called in a whisper. "Is that you?"

"Aye, tis I," Ann said. "Greetings, my friend. Yet I wonder why we must meet in the nighttime?"

"Did you get the message to the others?" Abigail asked, ignoring her question.

"Aye, I did."

"Elizabeth too?"

"Of course. She is part of us now."

"Did Elizabeth tell you anything?"

"Nay. What would she report?"

"Ye must wait. First, help me with this fire."

The girls quickly made a tent of the wood, placing the smaller dry tinder beneath. Abigail was good with the flint and easily started a flame. The wood immediately sucked it up into its depths, bursting into a cloud of conflagration with a sharp pop. The fire lit up the girls' faces, casting shadows against the snow piles beyond. Something in Abigail's countenance prevented Ann from pressing her further. But it had taken some doing, sneaking out of the Putnam homestead. Ann knew something was afoot.

Soon the two were joined by the others: Mercy Lewis, Mary Walcott, Elizabeth Hubbard, Mary Warren. At first the newcomers were gleeful, both nervous about the secret outing and thrilled to be thwarting the rules. They took their places around the fire, giving their friends greetings and warming their hands in front of the flames. The only serious face among the newcomers belonged to Elizabeth, whose last image of Abigail was of the girl sleeping in her aunt's lap after that horrifying seizure.

"What was that which overtook you yesterday, Abigail?" Elizabeth demanded, wanting to get to the point without Abigail's games. Her voice was severe which made the other girls stop their giggling and look, curious, between Abigail and Elizabeth. Abigail was glaring at Elizabeth.

"Tis the reason I asked for you all to gather here tonight," she said.

The girls were now rapt.

"Although my uncle bids me keep quiet," Abigail noted, looking down at her hands, seemingly unwilling to divulge her secret. The other girls cried out in indignation.

"You pull us out of our warm beds on a cold night, risking beatings from our parents," Mary Walcott said, "and tease us so? What is it, Abigail? You must now tell."

Abigail smiled with a devilish look in her eye. "I will only tell if you promise not to."

A chorus of "We will not! We will not!" spilled into the night air. That pang of power spread through Abigail once again, as she noted how she could so easily gain the curiosity and attention of her friends. Just like her uncle did with his church.

"My young cousin is having fits, and now she lays in her bed as if dead!" she cried out. The other girls recoiled in unison, covering their mouths with shock.

"Young Betty?" Mercy asked, noticing how strange it was not to have the girl cowering beneath her cloak. "How so?"

The other girls peppered Abigail with their own questions. She put her hands up to quiet them.

"Let me speak!" she commanded. "It started a week ago. She was overtaken with trembles and twitches, and if my aunt did not contain her in her arms, she would have fallen to the floor!"

"Why?" Mary Warren asked. "What overtakes her?"

"Dr. Griggs says it's…..." But there Abigail stopped, and looked into each girls' eyes, two at a time.

"What?" cried the other girls, their curiosity now at its zenith.

"It's witchcraft!"

Some of the girls stifled a scream, while the others gasped in horror. It was only Elizabeth who was not surprised. She let her friends have their shock, and when Abigail was about to continue, she said: "Abigail, who else was afflicted with the fits?"

Abigail smiled at Elizabeth, who was asking exactly what she wanted her to. But she quickly made her face serious again and said, "You know who, Elizabeth. Because you spied it yourself!"

The girls turned their attention to Elizabeth. "Aye, she is right," she said slowly, staring at Abigail. "I was with Dr. Griggs when he examined Betty. He often bids me attend him while he makes his visits to the sick. His medicine bag is very heavy, but he never relieves me of it."

Mercy rolled her eyes and said: "We know your trials! We all have them! So get on with your story, Elizabeth!"

"It was Abigail herself who flew into fits as well." As she spoke the words, Elizabeth pointed her small finger at her friend, a frown upon her face.

The girls gasped again and turned to Abigail. "Tis true?" Ann asked. "Were you smitten as well?"

Abigail's eyes opened wider in fascination. "Aye, tis true," she admitted. "It was as if Betty had a contagion. I could not help myself!"

"So ye are bewitched?" Mary Warren asked, starting to stand, fear pulsing through her body. The others drew back as well, regarding their friend in a different light. She had always served as their kind of leader, but what was this she was telling them? Did the minister not call for them daily to be ever watchful against the Devil, against witchcraft?

But Abigail was shaking her head. "Nay, tis not a bewitchment, I tell you the truth," she said, convincingly. "I know not what ails Betty. Yet I do know that when she started her twitching, I fell into the same. It was as if my mind went to sleep and I could not control my movements. Twas a wondrous thing indeed!"

"But isn't that the very definition of bewitchment?" Ann demanded. Abigail ignored her.

"And what of Betty?" Elizabeth kept on. "She is not asleep, yet not awake. My uncle tells me there is nothing wrong with her physick. She is healthy and needs no bleeding."

"You know Betty was always under a frail constitution," Abigail answered, rolling her eyes. "I am sure she will awaken soon."

"What caused her distress? Did something happen?" Ann asked.

"Nay, not the first time," Abigail answered. "But the second, she fell into twitches as Goody Good left our doorstep."

"Why, my mother has always thought Goody Good a witch!" Ann cried. "Was it she who afflicted poor Betty?"

"Nay, I do not think so," Abigail answered. "Betty is merely a very frightened person. You have seen her when we do our games. She cowers under Mercy's cloak then falls asleep."

"Yet you are not a frightened person," Elizabeth commented, still eyeing Abigail with suspicion. "Why do you follow Betty's suit?"

"Again, I tell you, I do not know," Abigail insisted, growing annoyed with Elizabeth.

"I suspect that Mr. Parris is most vexed," Ann said. At the mention of his name, the girls gazed into the small fire in the center of their circle, contemplating the reality. Witchcraft breaking out in the minister's own home! After so much admonishment and warning from his very mouth!

"Aye, he is, to be sure," Abigail said. "He is calling a meeting of local ministers to discuss the matter. Men will be coming from Beverly and Salem Town as well. But in the meantime he wants to keep it from the congregation."

Suddenly a crow called loudly from the tops of the trees, and the girls all jumped in fright. "Such birds do not make such noises in the middle of the night!" Mercy Lewis cried out. "Could it be the Devil come to find us?"

Everyone screamed and huddled close together, drawing their hoods up more tightly around their necks and heads, grasping each other's hands. "Shh! Shhh!" Abigail bade them, her eyes wide with fright as well. "We must not awaken the Cloyces, who live not far from here!"

"If Betty were here, she would surely have gone into a faint by now," Mercy commented, regaining her composure yet still breathing hard from anxiety.

"That's it!" Abigail said, looking at Mercy, impressed. "Betty is afeared of the Devil. We have seen it here: she faints away when she worries that we are sinning."

"Are we sinning, Abigail?" Mary Walcott asked, looking terrified. "Dancing and playacting. It has indeed seemed shameful to me when I think on it. What if the minister were to discover us?"

"They have been childish games, that is all!" Abigail chided them, her heart pounding. "And no one will speak of them to anyone else! We did nothing evil."

Despite Abigail's admonition, she looked as worried as the rest of them. "All will be well if we do not tell," she said again. "Promise me that! Promise!"

The girls shuddered and looked at each other, questioning. Their leader had a sudden idea, and she smiled to herself when she thought of it. She knew her uncle would be angry with them if he knew of their past games, yet they could be seen as innocent, easily forgiven with proper penance and prayer. But she had seen his face when Dr. Griggs declared that witchcraft was visiting the parsonage. This was serious, and Abigail needed these girls to be silent, lest they get into real trouble. She needed to get them to do something so horrible that they hold their tongues lest they reveal something truly sinful. Something unforgivable in the eyes of the church.

"So tonight we make a sacred pact among us," she intoned, imitating the fierce timbre of the minister's oratory. She looked at each girl in turn, keeping her gaze steady, as the fire snapped and popped its burning embers into the dark air above. "We are the girls of Salem Village, and what we do together must remain secret. Do you agree?"

Each girl solemnly nodded her head, eyes wide in her head, listening to Abigail as if she were hypnotizing all of them. What was it about her that made them so easily fall into her sway? Just like when she embodied the minister when they pretended to be churchgoers at service, she seemed to easily take on another personality, one that was intriguing, compelling, alluring. Once she started doing her tricks, it felt impossible to ignore her entreaties.

Abigail stood, and motioned for the rest to follow. She grasped the hands of Ann Putnam and Mary Walcott who were beside her, and everyone else held each other's hands as well. "Close your eyes!" Abigail whispered dramatically. Once they did, she started swaying back and forth, and Ann and Mary Walcott copied her movements. The undulations spread through the circle like the fire in front of them. Gently at first, swaying like the summer breeze that rises up from the Ipswich River in July. Abigail started to hum, and then to sing. She sang the words she remembered from the lullaby Tituba would sing to Betty at night, strange and exotic in her Barbados language. The chorus came easily to her, as the lullaby was a nightly ritual between Tituba and Betty and Abigail would hear it over and over. But when she came to the end of the chorus this night, she began to make up words of her own, pretending to call up an incantation that the girls could not understand. Her body vibrated with the energy of it all, and as she started swaying more forcefully and the girls followed her movements, she felt that wonderful power that she now realized she could muster when she wished. She knew the girls were enraptured, compelled to hum along with her, feeling the energy flow through them as well.

The swaying became outright dancing as hands were released and everyone started twirling and clapping. Abigail continued her incantation and her words echoed into the silence, although she made sure she kept them quiet enough not to disturb any of the neighbors. After all, noises carried easily on these dark, snowy nights without the leaves in the trees and underground brush to absorb them.

"Shh! Shh!" she whispered to the group, quieting her own dancing, lowering it to a gentle sway once more. "Tis time to make our pact."

The girls continued to undulate back and forth, some closing their eyes, some watching Abigail with great concentration. Abigail reached under her cloak to pull out a small knife out of her pock- et. It was an implement that she used often, to cut a piece of hemp rope or to carve apples for Mrs. Parris' pies. Tonight she held up the common tool, and the iron blade flashed as the fire cast its reflec- tion upon it, making it seem that the knife was emanating its own light. The girls gasped. "What do you plan, Abigail?" Ann whis- pered, trepidation in her voice. "Shh!" Mary Walcott silenced her, preferring to let the girl direct them.

"But if we walk in the light," Abigail was saying, ignoring the interruption. "As He is in the light, we have fellowship one with another, and the blood of ourselves cleanseth us all from sin."

The girls gasped again in horror, recognizing the verse from the Gospel of John, but knowing that Abigail was paraphrasing it for her own purposes. The true verse read "the blood of Jesus

Christ," not "ourselves." This was truly blasphemy! What was happening? Yet the spell continued, and not one of them felt strong enough to break the circle.

Slowly, slowly, Abigail took a few steps so that she was facing Ann. "Do you promise with our blood that ye shall not tell?" The two girls stared at each other, gazing deeply into each set of eyes. The fire reflected off of Ann's, but because Abigail's back was to the fire, hers seemed to be a solid pool of black. It frightened Ann to her core, but she found herself nodding solemnly. Abigail grabbed her friend's hand and made a quick slash across her palm. Before the blood could start oozing in earnest, she did the same to herself. Ann closed her eyes, wincing in pain, grabbing her wrist with her unharmed hand. But Abigail would have none of it. She pressed her bleeding palm against Ann's cheek, and with her good hand drew Ann's wounded one to her other cheek. Now Ann's face was covered with both hands, and her eyes flew open in surprise. Abigail smiled at her with a comforting smile, as a mother would gaze at her child. She drew her hand away from Ann, and Ann did the same. The other girls clapped their hands over their mouths, stifling screams. Ann's face was covered with blood. "Leave it be," Abigail directed. "For now, leave it be."

Ann was left dumbfounded as Abigail stepped to the next girl: Mercy Lewis. Mercy was shaking in fright but did not move away. Abigail performed the same fabricated rite with her, this time squeezing her hand so that more blood would seep from the wound she had just inflicted on herself. As with Ann, Mercy accepted the oath as the other girls watched, mouths agape.

One by one, as if in a dream, Abigail moved from girl to girl, bleeding them, demanding allegiance. By the third girl she had to make another slash in her own palm so that more of her own blood could be used. In the end, she pierced her other palm so that she could place both on her own cheeks, the final one to take the blood oath.

She bade everyone to clasp hands once again. The crow cawed again, high in the trees, his call now seeming more alarmed than before. Everyone jumped, but no one said anything in response. Looking around at her friends, Abigail said "Tituba often tells me of strange rites she would observe in dark Barbados. Blood was often spilled, as it has been tonight. Our blood binds us together. It shall not be vanquished. Do you understand?"

Everyone nodded their heads solemnly, feeling the cold against the drying blood upon their skin. They had no choice but to agree. Not now.

Things had gone too far.

~ ~ ~

A few nights later, Ann Putnam Sr. was still in bed, leaving the supper making to her eldest daughter Ann. She rarely roused of late, still grieving for the death of her baby and those of her sister and her family in Connecticut, and railing against the loss of the Putnam fortune to her husband's half-brother Joseph. Thomas came to their bed several times a day, between his chores and his meetings with the local militia, urging her to dress and return to her household duties. It did no good. She would wail and beg God to forgive whatever sin she committed, and would not be reasoned with. So far Thomas had avoided being drafted with his men to fight the Indian wars to the north, but he was beginning to think that he could be better used there, away from his grieving wife.

Ann Jr. was given all of the tasks usually handled by her mother, and she was none too pleased by it. She did her best to try to engage her younger brother and sisters with what needed to be done: cooking, cleaning, spinning flax for linen, sewing clothes for the upcoming spring, laundering the bedclothes – the list went on. Yet it was usually she who was the only one old enough to get anything done. It was a miracle that she was able to escape the other night to join her friend Abigail and all the other girls, given that she slept more soundly than ever, dropping into her bed with exhaustion at the end of each day. If she had to listen to her mother wailing one more time, she felt like she would explode.

Since the meeting in the woods the other night, Ann was filled with wonder at what she had seen and done. Abigail had told them that neither Betty nor Abigail had been bewitched, yet Abigail herself could not explain her own fits. And then all the blood that they had spilled: it had been truly astonishing. Ann herself had fallen into a kind of trance when her friend started her incantations. Was the devil really afoot? Was Abigail a part of it? Ever since she had returned to her home, she had been filled with fear which grew every hour to the extent that she felt she could not manage it any longer, not with the burden of running the household in her mother's stead. Her head had started to throb and she often found herself tripping over some small obstacle on the floor – sometimes when nothing was there at all. When her mother slept and her fathers and siblings were out of doors, she even heard what sounded like a whisper coming from the dark corner of the kitchen, yet no one was there.

Abigail had sworn them to secrecy, but Ann couldn't hold the secret any longer. She was too frightened of the Devil and his work. It was time that her mother acted like a mother and helped her daughter, despite her overwhelming grief.

Gathering all the resolve she could muster, Ann stomped up the stairs to her parents' bedroom above, starting to cry with relief at the thought that her mother might be able to stop her worry. Yes. Her mother would rouse for her.

The bedroom was rank with the smell of unwashed linens and bed rugs: her mother had refused to change her clothes, nor would she allow her daughter to launder the bedclothes in weeks. Lately Thomas had taken to sleeping in the upholstered chair in front of the hearth to escape from it. The wooden shades were pushed across the diamond-paned windows so that the room was steeped in darkness. Ann, still crying, opened them so that the pale winter sunlight could make its way into the room. Now she could see clearly how disheveled her mother looked, her hair unwashed and stringy, her face filled with hollows that once were filled with healthy flesh. Ann Sr. covered her eyes with her hands, unused to light in the room.

"Mother, mother," Ann Jr. cried, kneeling by the side of the bed. "I need you to wake up. I need you to protect me!"

Ann Sr. peeked from behind her hands, and was surprised to see her daughter's face covered with tears. "What is this?" she asked, her throat dry from her own wails of desperation. "What plagues you?"

"You were right, mother," Ann Jr. said. "All those years when you told me to be on the watch for the devil. I spurned your words but now I see that they are true!"

Mention of the devil seemed to shock her mother out of her downward spiral, and she watched as Ann Sr's eyes suddenly cleared. "Of course they are true," she admonished, her voice cracking. "Tis the devil himself who stole my baby from me, and did the same to my sister and her children! This is why I suffer!"

"I know nothing about that part," Ann Jr. admitted. "But mother, I fear that he is doing his evil works on me as well. I need your help, mother. I need you to be awake and to help me fend him off!"

With that, the young girl started wailing herself, her tears renewed. It was enough to rouse her mother from her stupor. Ann Sr. sat up straight in the bed and grabbed her daughter's arms, shaking her. "What is this you speak of?" she demanded, terror in her eyes. "How hath the devil afflicted you?"

Ann Jr. told her the whole story, from the innocent games to her friends' fits to the frightening ritual a few nights before. Her mother hung on every word, clenching her hands so tightly that Ann knew there would be bruise marks on her arms in the morning. As Ann spoke of the blood and the fire pit, she screamed and fell into her mother's arms. She could feel the older woman's body shake in fear, and she took to shaking as well. At least now the secret was out, and her mother would help her. She knew she would.

"Oh my girl, oh my girl," Ann Sr. said, rocking her daughter in her arms. "Tis a terrifying tale you tell. I was always afraid that such atrocities would visit our village, and now, it seems, the day has come."

"Oh mother, mother!" Ann Jr. cried out. "Is my soul damned? Is there no hope?"

"Nay, child," her mother said, sternly. "We will keep watch. We shall tell your father, and bring the horror to Mr. Parris. You say your cousin Mary did partake as well. And our maid too. We will bring them with us."

"But mother," Ann Jr. said, her eyes blazing with fear. "Will Mr. Parris not punish us for playing so? Will he banish us from the congregation?"

"He will do as he must. You might have to banish the devil from your life by sitting in the stocks for a time. Yet this is necessary to cast him out!"

"But Dr. Griggs has diagnosed witchcraft, mother!" Ann Jr. screamed. "What if I and the other girls are deemed witches? The Lord sayeth, 'Suffer not a witch to live!' We shall be hanged! We shall be put to death!"

Ann Sr., seeing the hysteria rise in her daughter, let her go, raised her hand, and slapped her hard across the face. This stopped the screams of the girl, who lifted her own hand to her face which was turning red from the blow. Red from hands, red from the blood Ann could not forget. She looked up at her mother, momentarily quelled but still terrified. "You shall not be hanged," Ann Sr. told her with quiet seriousness. "The devil shall not take another of my children. I promise you, he shall not."

~ ~ ~

Though they were supposed to spend the day in prayer, both Betty and Abigail found it hard to concentrate with empty bellies that growled uncontrollably. When the local ministers visited the parsonage a few days before, the fits came on the girls again, and the men agreed with Dr. Griggs: witchcraft had come to Salem Village. They advised prayer and fasting, and since then the girls had eaten nothing but a watery broth, leaving them unbearably weak. Many times the two girls found it easier to pass the time by sleeping in their bed, warding off the freezing cold of the loft. Both Mr. and Mrs. Parris were now often out of the homestead, feigning some errand or the other, just to be away from the girls.

One morning Abigail and Betty were awoken by sounds coming from below. Betty looked up and burrowed back under the linens, but Abigail jumped out of bed, pulling the top quilt around her to combat the sudden chill of being upright. The voices from the best parlor were loud enough for her to overhear without even having to approach the top of the ladder.

Old Mary Sibley, the neighbor woman, was at the front door of the parsonage. Abigail knew that Goody Sibley and Tituba were friends, although their ages were decades apart. The old woman was a widow who lived modestly down the road from the parsonage, and had reached out to the slave with kindness when the Parrises moved to Salem Village. Goody Sibley, who was cared for by her grown son who lived with her, had time on her hands and would often appear at the parsonage when the minister was away so that she might help Tituba with her chores, or share a tankard of cider if the work wasn't too pressing. She would never appear if Tituba's master was about, and Abigail often heard the widow talk of stark fear of the stern minister.

This afternoon Goody Sibley was telling Tituba that she had heard about the goings-on at the parsonage.

"How did ye come to hear of it, Mary?" Tituba asked. "Mr. Parris say we are to keep it to ourselves."

"The news cannot be held back, not when it is of this nature," Goody Sibley responded. "Goody Putnam was told by her daughter, and she has already told her husband and Jonathan Walcott, and people in those homes have been spreading it ever since. You know that not much can be kept secret, not in Salem Village."

"Oh, oh, oh," Tituba gasped. "Mr. Parris, he will sure to be angry."

Abigail grabbed at her waistcoat in rage and fear. Ann Putnam! That girl, that person who was supposed to be her friend and sworn to secrecy, she had squawked to her mother. Now none of them were out of danger; none of them at all. Abigail heard another set of footsteps and realized that John Indian was coming to join the women. "Goody Sibley, you should be gone," he admonished. "We are not sure when master and mistress return."

"Nay, nay, not until I bring you help," the old woman said. "I have something that will prove or disprove witchcraft!"

Tituba let out a quiet scream, and Abigail could hear some scuffling. "No witchcraft, Goody Sibley, no witchcraft," John Indian said. "Tituba, she fears it."

"Aye, I see that, John Indian," the old woman said. "Tituba, arise from that chair. I believe too that tis not witchcraft. Not within Mr. Parris' own home, such a godly man he is. At least, the girls are not witches. Rather they might be bewitched by others!"

Abigail, listening upstairs, clasped her hands together and could hardly contain her interest in the conversation. Bewitched by others? If this was thought to be true, then she and her friends would be deemed innocent, no? Go on, go on! she wanted to cry out to the old woman below. How does this work?

Goody Sibley went on to tell the two slaves to make a witch cake: rye meal mixed with urine from the afflicted and baked into a round. They should feed the dog with the concoction, and if the girls are bewitched, then the dog will identify who is torturing them. Abigail shuddered with disgust, and felt sorry for Scout, the mongrel dog her uncle kept on the farm to keep foxes out of the hen house. She didn't think Tituba would take the suggestion. It sounded too far-fetched and terrible.

Yet she heard Tituba's enthusiasm in her voice when she was told of the old wives' remedy. "Have ye seen it work before?" she asked Goody Sibley. "Dogs do speak, do they?"

"I have heard tell that dogs do speak in these cases," Goody Sibley replied. "Do ye not know that animals are sometimes taken by witches as their familiars, the devil's companions in doing his evil deeds? These dumb creatures, too, can be bewitched, and black magic makes their tongues wag."

"Then bake the cake!" John Indian said. "Fetch the girls' water!"

With that, Abigail bounded back into her bed, pulling the covers over her head, simulating sleep. Betty was soundless and motionless beside her. The older girl's heart was beating fast as she squeezed her eyes shut. Maybe this could save her, she thought. Suddenly she remembered Reverend Mather's book, how the Goodwin children were not punished once they accused Goody Glover of bewitching them. This was good. This was very good.

Tituba came into the room and pulled out the copper pan beneath the girls' bed. Abigail peeked out from under the bedclothes to watch the slave carefully carrying the specimen across the room, gazing into it as if it were some magical offering.

About a half hour later the house was filled with a putrid smell coming from the bake oven at the back of the hearth. While the cake was baking, Abigail heard Tituba and John Indian tell their guest every detail of what had occurred in the parsonage, with Goody Sibley tut-tutting at intervals. Hurry, hurry! Abigail screamed at them silently. They must perform the test before her uncle returned home!

Finally, Tituba declared that the baking was finished, and Abigail heard some scuffling and muttered phrases from below. The adults left the house, and John Indian called for Scout. Abigail knew the mutt would come quickly, as he had taken to John Indian who often snuck him handsful of corn out of sight of Mr. Parris.

Abigail flew to the bedroom window, where Goody Sibley, Tituba and John Indian bent over the poor dog. She could not see whether he ate or not, she only heard words of encouragement from his observers.

"What is this I see?!" Abigail jumped back from the window when she heard her uncle roaring outside. She heard Tituba and Mary Sibley scream, and the dog whimper, escaping the scene. "We be sorry, sir, we be most sorry," John Indian pleaded as the minister pulled both women into the parsonage by the scruffs of their necks.

Now the girl moved to the top of the ladder, expecting that her uncle, in his rage, would not notice. Her eyes widened in fear as she watched the spectacle below. Mr. Parris threw the two women down on chairs and squeezed the back of their necks with each huge hand. Tituba and Goody Sibley continued to cower and beg to be let go, but the minister was having none of it.

"What was that you were trying to feed the dog?" he demanded. "The thing had a fetid smell and Scout seemed fearful. Tell me
now! What was it?"

"Goody Sibley made me do it!" Tituba cried out.

"I was trying to help ye, reverend, please believe me!" the
other woman screamed. John Indian stood behind the three, wringing his hands in worry and looking to the ground. Why was he not
being examined as well? Abigail wondered.

The minister gave Tituba a clap across the side of her head,
and she was pushed down from the blow. He stopped, though,
before he let himself attack the widow in a similar way. "By God,
old woman, you will tell me right now what was going on when I
spied you."

Abigail heard Goody Sibley describe the witch cake, and
what they hoped would result from it. She thought this would spur
her uncle to even more rage, yet after the woman told her story, he
stopped for a moment, thinking. Tituba and her friend kept lowering their heads, preparing themselves for the next barrage, but the
minister moved away from them, pulling on his beard as he often
did when deep in thought.

"But the dog did not eat of it?" he asked, his voice somewhat
more subdued.

"Nay, he did not. He turned his nose away and begged to be
set free," Goody Sibley told him.

"Tell me again. You have heard it said that such a method has
pointed to other people bewitching the afflicted?"

"Aye," the widow replied, uncertainly, peeking up at the minister, whose response clearly surprised her.

The minister paced up and down the room as Abigail had
seen him do many times when he was angry or befuddled. The
women and John Indian remained silent, averting their gaze downward, and Abigail could feel the tension in the room as if it were a
thing she could touch. She, too, held her breath, waiting for what
was to come next.

Her uncle began to look about the room, and suddenly he
saw Abigail at the top of the ladder, crouching down in her shift.
Abigail stifled a gasp, and prepared to be summoned and castigated.
Yet the minister said nothing, just stared at his niece, who could
not help staring back at him. Never before had she seen him so
unguarded and intent, and she felt mesmerized. He narrowed his

eyes, glanced over to the women, and looked back to Abigail. Feeling glued to the spot, she found herself giving him a slight nod. He returned the gesture.

The moment felt stuck in time, as everything else seemed to stop.

But then Mr. Parris shook his head as if trying to awaken from a dream, and his gruff, angry voice returned. "So tis witchcraft that you were doing, in my own home! In the home of God's representative on earth! Tis surely an abomination!"

"No, master, no!" Tituba wailed. "We be trying to protect the girls, it be the truth, I promise!"

The minister grabbed her and threw her across the room, and she fell to the ground with the force of it. Tituba looked at John Indian, pleading with her eyes, but he did not dare to come to her aid. Goody Sibley put her hands over her head, preparing herself for his next attack.

"I will have no more of this, I assure you," Mr. Parris glowered. "Be gone, Goody Sibley, but be sure to attend services on Sunday. I will have you confess to the entire congregation what you have committed here. You and Tituba both!"

The other three stayed unmoving in their places, breathing heavily.

"Be gone, I tell you! All of you!" the minister roared, and Goody Sibley, Tituba and John Indian fled the room as quickly as they could.

~ ~ ~

By the time the next Sunday came around, the entire village had heard about the witchcraft that was being committed at the parsonage. Although the early February cold continued and over a foot of snow covered the fields and houses along the Ipswich Road, attendance at services was higher than usual. The people came to the meeting house early, wrapped up in their wool cloaks and hats, some on foot, some in carriages that could hardly make it over snow-packed paths. Once inside they huddled together, whispering. Some were overcome with fear, others were skeptical. Everyone wanted to know how Mr. Parris would explain himself.

Sisters Sarah, Rebecca and Mary arrived with the rest of the parishioners, their husbands, children and grandchildren in tow. Rebecca, who took a long time to enter the building, resting heavily on her cane every few steps, sat in her usual bench as soon as she could. Her two sisters rushed to her side, clasping each hand with theirs.

"Peter tells me it is bad," Sarah whispered to the other two. "Now there are more girls afflicted."

"Eh?" Rebecca asked, tilting her head toward Sarah. "My dear, my hearing is not good, as you know. I am uncertain what you just said."

"These fits, sister," Sarah still whispered, but now directly into Rebecca's ear. "And now there is talk of a witch cake."

The sisters looked at each other knowingly. They were well aware of witch cakes, as well as a slew of other folk remedies, from the stories their mother Joanna would regale them with on a winter's night. Joanna, who was well-versed in herbal medicine and often used it to help her family and her neighbor's ailments, would ridicule the more outrageous traditions of ages past, including the use of witch cakes. She would remind her girls of the belief, all in good fun, because she knew they would get a thrill out of the disgust they would feel at the retelling. "Oh, mother, do stop!" young Sarah would beg, laughing. "Using a person's night water! In baking! Tis enough to turn my stomach!"

But now people were taking seriously the news of Goody Sibley's suggestion, and news of it spread like wildfire in the community. What were they to believe? Was it true that God had truly turned his back on Salem Village? After all, that was what Reverend Parris had been telling them for years now.

"The poor, poor girls," Rebecca said quietly, clasping her hands together as if in prayer. Sarah couldn't help feeling frustrated. This whole situation seemed ridiculous to her. While the Putnams and the Parrises tended to direct their anger toward her sisters' families and not so much her own, she was still angry when she saw the jagged looks cast toward Mary and Rebecca and their kin, when Hepzibah reported Ann Putnam Sr. casting out dear Rebecca from her home. And it wasn't only Hannah who had noticed those girls taunting dear little Alice for years now. As a young woman, Sarah had watched the older Putnam generation pass down power to the next one, with Thomas Jr. at the head once old Thomas died and gave all of his wealth to Sarah's son-in-law Joseph. Now it seemed that the third generation was gaining influence way too early, with Ann Jr. being one of the leaders of a little gang of young girls, all of whom could have benefited from a good spanking. Yet here was saintly Rebecca, praying for the wee brats.

Tension was high in the meeting house today, but all conversation stopped when Abigail walked in with her aunt and cousin. Mrs. Parris peered at her neighbors with trepidation, and pushed the girls toward the ladder that led to the balcony above. As the girls scurried off, the older woman lifted her chin and walked to the front bench, where she was met with Ann Putnam Sr. and Deliverance Walcott. Goody Putnam embraced the minister's wife, and turned haughtily away from the crowd.

Ann Putnam Jr. was already in the balcony with the rest of the girls. They beckoned Abigail to join them, and the group quickly formed themselves into a tight circle. The other village children strained their necks to hear what was being said, and Alice Cloyce even tried to join them.

"Get away, Alice!" Abigail pushed the girl away, towering over her even though they were about the same age. "You are not welcome here!"

Alice clenched her fists at her sides and glared at the girl. "Why, I am not nearly surprised," she said. "I am a righteous girl, and none such as you would welcome my innocence!"

Abigail sneered and lunged for Alice, much to the astonishment of the others. It seemed that these tales of bewitching were making everyone disdain all sense of decorum, even in the meeting house. The two started pulling at each other's hair, and Abigail's friends began to cheer them on.

The people below ceased their talking and stared at the fracas above, but none seemed to know what to do. As soon as Sarah Cloyce saw what was going on, she felt rage seething through her. She would not let any Parris or Putnam child hurt any of hers, not after the pain those families had already wrought upon her own for so many years. It was as if all of the troubles she had had to withstand – going back to when her father battled the Putnams over the Topsfield-Salem Village border lands, to when John Gould put her dear Edmund into prison, to crazy Goody Putnam's ranting against her sisters. Those memories spurred her on as she stood up from her bench, stomping one foot on the ground so it rang loudly in the hall. The noise was enough to surprise the children, who peered over the balcony to see where it came from. Sarah's face was dark with anger. She stared into Abigail's eyes, warning her away without uttering a word.

Abigail, chastened, pulled herself off Alice, who nodded to her mother below. She began to walk past the girls, but heard Ann Jr. hiss: "You had better watch yourself, Alice Cloyce. We can make you most sorry. Mark me."

Abigail was left staring down at Sarah, wondering at how just a glance from the older woman seemed to deter her.

Mary and Rebecca looked at their sister in astonishment, pulling her back down to them once the interruption was over. "How dare they attack Alice!" Sarah whispered, wringing her hands until the knuckles turned white. "Those children will stop at nothing. They need a good beating is what they need."

Rebecca put a warm hand on Sarah's arm, calming her. Mary sent another glance upwards, seeing how Abigail's gang was now huddled together again with no further hindrance. "Be glad of it, sister," she said to Sarah in a low tone. "It is good that the girls shun your daughter. Alice is protected that way."

Sarah took in Mary's words and exhaled in relief. Her sister was right. It was clear that Alice had had nothing to do with the antics being reported from the parsonage. She was glad Alice hadn't been taken in by the little band, even though she knew that the girl had cried herself to sleep at night because of the rejection. But her daughter was safe, and that's all that mattered to Sarah.

Upstairs Abigail was speaking quickly, knowing that the service would begin at any moment. "Do not fear," she instructed her friends. "I believe we will not be punished for our games."

"But I have already been beaten for it!" Mary Warren reported, rubbing her backside where John Proctor had laid into her with his belt.

"And I, too, although Ann was spared!" added Mercy Lewis.

"The minister conferred with Dr. Griggs again yesterday," Elizabeth Hubbard told them. "And the good doctor did repeat: witchcraft."

Just then the side door opened and everyone fled immediately to their seats, hoping that the minister would not see their gossiping. Heads bowed and hands clasped as if in silent prayer. Mr. Parris entered the room and climbed up to the high pulpit, along with the neighboring towns' ministers Mr. Hale and Mr. Noyes, who sat in large chairs on either side of the platform. Many in the congregation had never seen these two other men, and knew that such a deviation from normal practices meant that something serious was afoot.

They had to wait, though, to find out how the minister was to address the issue of witchcraft in the village. Mr. Parris went through the usual order of service, with a sermon that lasted over two hours and long, silent prayers. He was as vociferous as ever, condemning sin and demanding that the parishioners seek their hearts and souls for any hint of transgressions against God. By the time the third hour came around, most in the audience were thinking that perhaps all of the gossip had not been true, and that it would not be spoken of again.

But they were wrong.

After the benediction, the people started to move about, reaching for their cloaks, the burning coals in copper pots to warm their feet having cooled hours before.

"Halt!" Mr. Parris commanded. "Our fellowship is not yet finished."

At that, both the other ministers stood, flanking Mr. Parris, looking very much like archangels serving at the side of the Lord Himself. The people sat back down on their benches, and the reverends looked down on a sea of faces filled with both curiosity and apprehension.

"Goody Sibley!" Mr. Parris called. "Come to the front of the church."

The old woman gave a short cry of fear, and looked over at her son, James, with terrified eyes. James reluctantly walked over to the women's side of the church and helped his mother up off her seat, whispering to her, urging her on. Once they were at the front of the room, Mr. Parris beckoned James to go back to his seat with a contemptuous flip of his hand.

"You are here to tell this congregation what you came to the parsonage to do, two days before now," he said loudly, pointing his finger at the cowering woman. "In front of these witnesses, as well as the good reverends from Beverly and Salem Town."

"I did but wish to help with the fits of your children," the widow explained, her head bowing up and down. "Dr. Griggs deemed it witchcraft, and I have long known a way, passed down by my own mother and hers before, to cast out such troubles."

The congregation gasped, and started muttering amongst themselves.

"There shall be silence!" Mr. Parris thundered, casting serious looks out amongst the people seated in benches. Turning back to Goody Sibley, he said, "Did you not bid my slave Tituba to bake a vile witch cake, made with my poor niece and daughter's night water?"

Cries of revulsion went up to the high rafters of the meeting house. Once more Mr. Parris glared at his flock, and they quieted down.

"Aye, twas a witch cake, that be true, good reverend," the old woman attested. "And I am most sorry for it. I ask ye forgiveness, please, sir, from you and from Christ Himself."

Garnering her confession, Mr. Parris shot a look at the ministers on either side of him, and they returned his gaze, shaking their heads in consternation. "This woman," he shouted to his congregation. "This woman did come to my own home, seeking to perform countermagic on my dear girls, who are much afflicted! This is the work of the Devil, I say!"

"Dr. Griggs does say they are indeed afflicted, but with witchcraft, does he not?" Goody Sibley asked, and the minister tried hard to calm the cries of the people in the benches and the children above.

Mr. Hale took over the questioning, seeing the trouble his colleague was having. "Aye, tis witchcraft!" he announced, and the cries grew louder. "We have seen the fits firsthand, have Mr. Noyes and myself. Yet this countermagic will not be tolerated! We shall not seek the Devil to help with his very evil work! We shall only look to God in His majesty!"

"What was the purpose of this heinous ritual, Goody Sibley?" Mr. Noyes demanded. "If it were not black magic?"

"Nay, not black, I am white as the snow!" the old woman begged. "I only sought to discover who it was who was bewitching these innocent children!"

Upstairs, the cluster of the afflicted girls drew closer together, clasping hands as if they were making a tiny army of themselves. When they heard the word "innocent" they exhaled in relief on behalf of Abigail and Betty.

"The Devil, surely!" Mr. Hale answered for Goody Sibley. "Tis what Dr. Griggs told us."

"Nay, tis not true, I tell you!" the old woman cried. "There be other instigators! Tis what my mother always taught me!"

"Are you telling me that your mother was a witch?" Mr. Parris shouted, stunned into shock. "That this village has been infiltrated by evil for generations?"

Goody Sibley shook her head violently, holding up her hands as if warding off an attack. "Nay, nay, good reverend, please hear me! My mother was a godly woman who would have died rather than bring the Devil into our midst! She only knew how to deflect such evil! She knew that when victims are so afflicted and their souls are righteous, they are being attacked by witches, and are not witches themselves."

The girls on the balcony couldn't stifle their happiness, and started jumping up and down in a single movement, laughing. Everyone stared at this most incongruous response, and it seemed to the girls that they were suddenly thrown into some sort of strange spotlight, a place without secrets. Indeed for a moment it felt like the very roof was raised, and God Himself was casting His light upon them, raising them up, out of the darkness of their small, tortured, inconsequential worlds. The girls were stunned into silence, and for several drawn-out moments the entire room was silent. What was happening?

Without warning, Abigail began to bark like a dog, as she had done now several times before. The outbursts echoed across the room, bouncing off the walls opposite, sounding as loud as a thunderclap.

And soon Abigail's friends were doing the same.

The meeting house was filled with the unnatural utterances while everyone stared at the huddled group, flabbergasted.

"They are once again afflicted!" Goody Sibley cried out, and melted to the floor, covering her head with her hands. "Ask them, Mr. Parris! Ask them who afflicts them!"

The minister was as shocked as the rest: first his parsonage was attacked, and now his own church. This must surely mean going into battle. This changed everything.

"Who bewitches you?!" he bellowed, casting his eyes upon the girls, who were now shaking, their limbs moving in uncontrolled twitches.

"Twas Goody Good!" Abigail screamed, crazily looking about the room for the old hag, although as usual she was not there. "She came upon the parsonage and uttered some evil words even as my good aunt gave her and her screaming urchin a morsel to eat!"

"Goody Good! Goody Good!" the other girls aped. "Goody Good did bewitch us all!"

"And who else, child?" Mr. Parris persisted, and his eyes met with Abigail's. Just then a small woman in the back of the room threw up her hands and started to laugh, a rough, cackling laugh that rose above the din of the room. The other cries died down as one by one members of the church craned their necks to see who was making such odd noises. Perhaps another bewitched child? But no, the laughing came from another old woman from the village, Sarah Osborne, one of Sarah Good's only friends. Both women were poor and decrepit, but the congregation was more used to seeing Goody Osborne at the church. Here she was, her gray hair wiry and jutting out from under her dirty cap, her waistcoat torn at one side and her apron gray rather than white. She was short but had a huge belly, which she was clutching as she laughed and laughed, seeming unable to stop.

"Goody Osborne! How dare you mock such afflictions!" Mr. Parris called out from the pulpit above.

"Afflictions, be they?" she gasped between chuckles. "It is an entertaining sight, your entire congregation in the thrall of misbehaving children!"

Parishioners, momentarily silenced, looked quickly from the old widow to Mr. Parris to the girls leaning over the railing above.

"Goody Osborne!" came a shout from within the mass of girls. Abigail, Mary Walcott and the rest moved a step away to reveal Ann Putnam Jr., shaking and pointing her finger at the woman below. "'Tis Goody Osborne who bewitches me! She comes to me in the night, bringing my baby brother, dead in winding sheets, bidding me follow her to the Devil or she would take my life away as well!"

Ann's mother let out a piercing shriek and was held up by the minister's wife who sat next to her. Goody Putnam fainted dead away. Her husband ran to her other side, flapping his hands in front of her face in a frantic attempt to bring her air. The room erupted once more with frightened shouts.

Sarah and her two sisters were gripping each other's hands so tightly that their fingers grew numb. None could speak; they merely watched the drama unfold, their mouths agape in wonder.

John Walcott and John Gould ran from their seat in the stalls, bounding toward Goody Osborne and capturing her by the arms. The old woman continued to laugh, undeterred.

"And Tituba!" came another accusation shouted from the balcony, this time again from Abigail Williams. She screamed and screamed, pointing her finger at the slave who stood across the way. Tituba stepped back as if something had been flung at her, her eyes widening in astonishment. "Nay, nay!" she cried. "I do not! I love these children! I love my Betty!"

The girls started pulling at their hair, making the barking sounds again, some wailing, some seeming to push away unseen attackers with their hands. Tituba attempted to run down the ladder but the serving women who surrounded her stood in her way, not letting her pass, but unwilling to touch her.

"Silence! There will be silence!" Mr. Parris tried to raise his voice so that it would be heard over the cacophony, yet no one was listening to him. Men scrambled up the ladder to capture Tituba and wrestled her down to the ground floor. The entire congregation was standing now, and surrounded the two accused. The crowd roughly pushed the women out of the meeting house, screaming "Witch! Witch!" after them. The group of girls followed, adding to the taunts, twirling about, almost in a kind of ecstasy.

Not everyone followed them as they took the women to the stocks in front of Ingersoll's ordinary. The three ministers stayed behind, arguing amongst themselves while several families looked on, including Sarah Cloyce and her sisters. Goody Putnam was still fainted dead away, despite the ministrations of her husband and Mrs. Parris.

"Mr. Parris, you need to control your flock!" Mr. Hale said, pulling his colleague down from the pulpit and shoving him toward the door. "This is not how the law works, and you are well aware of that!"

"You talk of men's laws, Hale," the minister retorted. "But the Devil is at work here, do you not see? God is the only one who can help us now!"

"I agree with Mr. Hale," Reverend Noyes said. "We cannot have plain villagers carry out justice! We are already living without a charter. What chaos are you letting unloose here, man?"

"So I must hold back the accusations of the godly? I must ignore the witchcraft that has taken over Salem Village?" Mr. Parris shot back.

Mr. Hale turned his back to the minister in frustration and disgust. He gazed upon the members of the congregation who had stayed back, refusing to take part in the mania. There were Sarah and her sisters and their families, some of them children hugging each other in fear above them in the balcony. Hannah Putnam was standing still as well, and her husband Joseph rushed to her side, confused and unsure of what to do next. The Proctors were there and some other families as well. Enough to help quell the rabble outside.

"Come, good people of Salem Village," Mr. Hale bid them. "Come with me, and help me pull back the clutching hands of your neighbors. We must handle this in due time, with the courts on our side, according to the laws of the land and not the hysteria of common men!"

Mr. Parris glared at his colleague and stood back, astonished with his invitation, but the others needed no further encouragement. The younger women – Hannah Putnam and several of the Esty and Nurse children, now mothers themselves – joined the men as they followed the black-clad, diminutive minister through the street whose snowy surface had just been trampled down with hundreds of booted feet. Mr. Noyes proceeded behind them, bringing up the rear, uttering words of encouragement to the group. Sarah pulled her sisters back to stay with Goody Proctor, not wanting them to get hurt in the melee. They hurried out of the side door, making their way toward the Nurse homestead, which was the closest to the parsonage.

With their departure, the meeting house was emptied, save Mr. Parris and the huddled Putnams in the front bench. His wife looked up at him with horror. "What has befallen our village, Samuel?" she begged. "What is to be done now?"

~ ~ ~

"The ministers say tis witchcraft that is possessing these girls," Peter Cloyce said to his wife as she rocked in her chair, back and forth on its treads in quick, jerky movements. "And three village women have been accused of torturing them. It seems possible. The girls do appear to be in grave straits. They scream in terror and there are marks on their bodies where they claim the women have attacked them."

"Shh, do not waken Hepzibah, Peter," Sarah admonished, as Peter came up to his wife from behind and putting two strong hands on her shaking shoulders, stopping her rocking. "I believe none of it. The girls are counterfeit and they are seeking attention. It is only a matter of time before their true motivations are discovered."

Peter shook his head in disagreement. "Nay," he said. "That they should be allowed to scream and shout and jump about? Tis surely a dangerous thing. They have always been unbridled, spoiled."

"Remember, Peter," Sarah said. "Just the other day Francis reminded us of the atrocities that some of the girls survived in their settlements in Maine, how traumatic those must have been. He says the girls' visions are merely horrid memories that have addled these girls' brains."

Peter and Sarah did not partake of the mob that attempted to send Sarah Good, Sarah Osborne and Tituba to the stocks after last Sunday's services. That their brethren in Christ could be whipped into such a frenzy truly shocked Sarah's soul. It was as if their own neighbors were filled with the strangeness that overtook the children, like it was some sort of devilish contagion. Even Mr. Hale disagreed with what was happening, and Sarah and her family were relieved to see that his attempts at quelling the crowd were successful. He had jumped on his horse and rose up so that he was standing in his spurs, and shouted himself hoarse, finally silencing the rabble, urging lawfulness, eventually sending everyone home. Sarah thanked the Lord above that there were no injuries or – even worse – deaths.

But that didn't stop the wheels from turning. The accused women returned to their daily lives, as best they could, although Sarah felt particularly sorry for Sarah Good. The old woman walked away, bent over her squalling infant, with her craggy husband behind, insulting her, casting the worst of aspersions. And then not two days passed when Thomas Putnam, along with his friend Joseph Hutchinson, swore out a complaint against all three of the women, and Constable Herrick brought them in his cart to Goodman Ingersoll's ordinary for questioning.

Sarah went to observe, just like most of the village did. Judges Hathorne and Corwin rode up from Salem Town to oversee the proceedings. When Sarah saw them she remembered the day, so long ago now, when she overheard these great men's discussions about the political situation in the colony back at the Salem Town

ordinary she and Edmund were running. That seemed now like a
different world, a different life.

Peter was having nothing of it, and told Sarah that things
would be much different if everyone just ignored the whole thing.
"These girls, they are injured by their past trauma, it has nothing to
do with witchcraft. The contagion grows because they are allowed
to be together and one's exclamations can easily infect the others.
Please, Sarah, do not go."

But Sarah couldn't help it. She wasn't the kind of person who
could sit idly by when such drama was taking place just down the
road. She bade Alice and Hepzibah to stay at home with Peter, even
though the girls cried out to go see what was going on. Hannah was
with her husband in Salem Town and sent Sarah a message that
she did not want to be anywhere near the goings-on, but for a very
happy reason: she was expecting a child. Sarah tried to focus her
mind on that good news to keep her soul separate from the madness that seemed to be taking over her village. She longed to be a
grandmother, and a new baby always meant hope for the future.
It helped, too, to have sister Mary at her side when they went to
Ingersoll's ordinary. Rebecca's back was giving her great pain so she
just took to her bed yesterday and she could not make the trip. But
Mary and Sarah could hold tight to each other as they listened.

There were so many people who wanted to watch the examinations that the magistrates moved the proceedings to the meeting
house. People were standing between benches on the first floor as
well as the balcony above. They started with Sarah Good, and kept
hounding her with the same questions: what evil spirit do you have
familiarity with? Why do you hurt these children? Who do you
employ to do it? Over and over Goody Good and Goody Osborne
after her denied doing anything, and indeed they stood there with
their hands at their sides, hardly moving. All of the afflicted girls
squirmed and shouted and even showed the magistrates tiny bloody
pricks in their arms and legs, pointing to the accused, begging them
not to hurt them. Yet these poor women were standing there for
all to see, doing nothing. "Her specter! Her specter!" these children
cried, again and again, and their words were believed by the magistrates and most of those around them, even though the women
denied any injury. What were the villagers to make of this? The girls
were clearly in agony, yes. But how could the women be hurting
them while standing many feet away, not touching them?

It was Goody Osborne who thought to question the magistrates' rationale, and Sarah was glad for it. "I do not know that the Devil goes about in my likeness to do any hurt," she said. If she did not know if the Devil was taking her over, how then could she be guilty of it? Yet the magistrates were having none of her case, and sent her to jail, just as they had Goody Good before her.

The slave's examination was different from the other two womens', because she, unlike them, confessed to torturing the girls. The story she told made the blood in Sarah's veins turn to ice. She spoke of a dark man from Boston leading a whole group of women, including the three on trial, forming a kind of diabolical coven, helping the evil man take over the souls of Essex settlers. Even the justices were awestruck at times, hearing of dark animal familiars who flew with these witches, how their followers signed a book with their own blood, the attacks they made on the innocent girls. And when they heard Tituba describe how there were more women involved, the judges' eyes widened in horror.

But as Tituba answered the magistrates' questions, she moved her hands about in the way she had of speaking, and at one point Sarah noticed the slave's wrists. Against her black skin were bruises, all brown, red and purple. Sarah saw, too, that there were similar marks about Tituba's neck, and they looked painful and inflamed. If Rebecca were there, she would want to soak a cloth in witch hazel and lavender oil and apply them to the wound. But no one else seemed to take note of the marks. Did it not appear, though, that Tituba herself had been attacked? Why was she confessing to such horrendous acts?

The slave told of putting up a considerable resistance to the dark man, shouting her devotion and love for little Betty Parris. "How can I hurt my Betty?" Tituba recalled asking the dark man. Betty herself was in the group of girls, but she had her hands over her ears and was rocking back and forth as if in some sort of trance. Apparently Tituba eventually gave in to the devil's bidding, because he threatened to kill her otherwise. She seemed to me to be a tortured being, and Sarah was sorry for her.

So they sent the slave to jail as well.

"What is to become of them, Peter, those women?" Sarah asked Peter, now pacing the small space in front of the dwindling fire.

"Nothing can be done now, alas," Peter answered her. "Not as long as we do not yet have our colony's charter. Word from England is that the King and Queen have approved it, and Increase Mather is on his way to Massachusetts with it in his possession. But until then, we have no legal system beyond these first examinations.”

“So those poor women have to stay in jail in the meantime? I do remember my dear Edmund’s stories of that horrid place. It makes me shudder to remember. And they have sent Goody Good’s tiny infant with her. How can that be just?”

“Tis not just, Sarah,” Peter said sadly, shaking his head and now sitting heavily in the chair she just vacated. “I told you. These girls but dissemble.”

“I do not think that these women are evil, yet what has really befallen those girls? Mr. Parris says that indeed the devil can overtake unknowing victims, yet still their soul has been corrupted, and they are doomed to hell. He has warned us of the sins he has seen in all of us ever since he arrived in Salem Village. I have always discounted his harangues. Yet could he be right in this matter?”

“He is not right, I tell you again!” Peter said sternly, although the look in his eyes was helpless and worried. “People who are frightened often make terrible mistakes.”

“Tis what scares me the most, especially when my own family has been at odds with the Putnams and the Goulds for so very long. It is those people’s children who are making these accusations, and it is they who have asked the magistrates to bring the women to their examinations.”

Sarah’s mind drifted back to so many occasions when the Townes confronted the Putnams, and it brought a shiver of terror down her back, although the room was warm.

She was very, very frightened.

CHAPTER EIGHT

Salem Village
March 1692

John Gould made his way to his cousin Thomas Putnam's farm, riding atop his best Narragansett Pacer, Tug. The horse often grew restless in the barn if not ridden enough, and John wanted to take advantage of the melting snow by giving him some afternoon exercise.

The sun was setting later on in the day, and John knew he and his hands should be putting in the early spring seeds into his fields. His farm in Salem Village was much smaller and more manageable than his holdings further north in Topsfield, but he hadn't been paying much attention to either property of late. The goings-on in the Village had grabbed his focus, as they had with everyone else living in the area. John was sure to attend every examination that was held in the meeting house – although the locals were not allowed to observe the follow-up conversations that were being had between the magistrates and the accused people in the jails. Many of the accused were examined two and three times, but usually only the first was held in a public place. That was enough to draw everyone out of their homesteads to watch both the accused and the poor afflicted girls. And now grown women were showing signs of fits, which was a very bad sign. Talk everywhere was of the arrival of the devil in Salem Village, and people were running around in stark fear that he would torture them as well.

Thomas Putnam was expecting John, but as soon as he knocked on the door, Thomas came outside to join him rather than drawing him into the best parlor at the front of the house. John followed the younger man to the barn, although he was annoyed to be prevented from the hospitality of a welcoming fire and a hearty meal. He tethered Tug in the empty stall next to Thomas' three work horses, blowing into his hands to warm them. Spring was on its way and the snow was melting, but still the barn was cold.

"My apologies, cousin, for having to talk with you here rather than in the house," Thomas said, noticing John's pique. "Believe me, though, the house is not the hospitable place you are accustomed to."

"How is Ann, Thomas?" John asked. He had watched the young girl writhe in pain and scream out accusations toward several women in the meeting house – both during church services and the accused's examinations – and it troubled him to see such torment. Yet he had also seen how Ann and the rest of the girls could come out of their fits once they left the meeting house. He expected that there would be peace at home.

"She suffers so, John," Thomas responded. "The fits come and go at seeming random, but at this moment she is raving. Worse, not only is our maid Mercy equally tormented, but now my wife as well. As soon as one of them starts up, the others follow. They tell me when they are quieted that sometimes the witches are so cunning that they try to hide from their sight, and it is not until one girl spies them that the others' sight can be directed the same way."

Thomas lit the small wood stove that he sometimes used for the animals on particularly frigid winter nights, but it cast little warmth on the two men. He began to pace up and down the stalls, mindlessly patting the horses' flanks, throwing a core of an apple that he found in his pocket into the pigs' slop trench.

"Surely this torment will end soon," John said soothingly. "Once the witches are found guilty and are put to their deserved deaths."

"But more are accused every day. And they cannot be tried yet, not without the colony's charter!"

It was true, what Thomas said. The magistrates could examine possible suspects, but without the charter, no grand jury or judge could be called, so no formal trials could be conducted. The rules that governed the colony for so many decades were now defunct, and while most settlers hoped the new charter would reinstate them, others worried that they would be tossed out completely for new laws and regulations. The women who had already been examined – Goody Good, Goody Osborne, Tituba and most recently a new witch, Martha Corey – had been put in jail but the process would go no further. Thomas had hoped that their incarceration would help his family, with the women no longer tortured, but this had not been the case. No jail could contain these evil women's specters, whose ethereal forms could easily escape through iron bars to pinch and stab the afflicted. Thomas' wife told him, in between fits, that the witches would not rest until she, her daughter and maid would sign the devil's book in their own blood. The only thing that would help was to rid the colony of these evil ones. Forever.

"But the charter is imminent, is it not?" John asked. "We hear that Reverend Mather is on his way to these shores as we speak. Would that God speed him on his way!"

"To be sure," Thomas agreed. "My home has become a centerpiece for the devil's work. And my wife was suffering enough before the scourge. She scarce can handle these fits."

"Aye. Does she still mourn losing baby James?"

Thomas nodded. "She was screaming about that very thing as you arrived. She believes the death was the devil's work. It does answer some distressful questions we have had for several years now."

"What questions?" John asked, raising his eyebrows in curiosity. Thomas pulled out two rough straight-backed chairs and placed them around the wood stove, bidding his cousin to sit.

"John, you know of our misfortunes these past years. My family and I do all we can to praise God and give Him thanks for all of His gifts. The Putnams – like the Goulds, of course – have been pillars of the community. Yet again and again we have thought that the good Lord has turned His face from us. First Ann loses her inheritance, then I do as well. Her sister Mary Bayley was taken down with fever, as were all three of her dear children. Losing baby James seemed the final blow. My wife and I have prayed and fasted on many occasions, asking God what we have done to earn His wrath, yet we receive no answer. Perhaps it was not our own sin at all, but the underhanded work of these women, working as the devil's minions! Perhaps witchcraft has been at hand in Salem Village for many years, and it is just now that it is being discovered!"

John stared at Thomas in shock. He had worried about Thomas and his sister since they lost old Thomas' fortune to their half-brother Joseph. Since that news hit the family, he had offered assistance whenever he could, especially when children were born. The days when the Goulds were on the opposite side to the Putnams in the boundary disputes between Salem Village and Topsfield were a very long time passed, and John was grateful for it. He now considered himself a father figure to Thomas and Deliverance.

"Witchcraft," John repeated, dumbly. "It could be true. After all, the righteousness of your family cannot be disputed."

"Aye!" Thomas agreed, growing agitated. "Where should the

devil strike if not the parsonage first, and then my very home? Places where the virtuous live and work."

The two men grew silent, gazing into the pitiful flame behind the iron bars of the stove. Nothing was heard except the occasional whinnying of the horses and grunting of the pigs at their trench. After several minutes of deep thought, John was struck with a memory, and sat up straight.

"Perhaps you are right, Thomas," he said, his eyes now blazing. "There have been occasions of witchcraft for decades now, not only in the village, but in Topsfield, too. No one ever took it seriously enough, in my humble opinion."

"Tis true? What such occasions?"

"Why, I remember nigh on twenty years ago, when we had such minister troubles in Topsfield. My dear wife and I were much affronted by one of them, a Reverend Gilbert. You were too young to remember this, and besides, this was in those dark times when your father and I were at odds over the Topsfield line. But this erstwhile minister was most sinful, drinking overmuch and swearing too at times. You, of course, know well your neighbor Nurse, and Esty as well. Their mother was Goody Towne, and she was an unruly, stubborn woman, although the wife of a man I called my friend when he was alive. She was a friend to Gilbert, whom we did not like at all. The minister's behavior grew so troubling that I brought him to the local magistrates, complaining of drunkenness on his part. There was a particular meal at his home, where I sat with my wife and others. Among the guests was this Goody Towne. The harridan dared to dispute me in my suit against the minister, although she was not victorious. After we ousted Gilbert, whispers began in the town that she was a witch."

Thomas was listening intently to his cousin's story, wringing his hands, trying to contain the worry that coursed through him. "Whispers, eh?" he asked, wryly. "I sense you might have had a part in initiating them."

John shook him off with a wave. "I do not remember that part," he said, a half-smile on his face.

"Tis a well-known fact that witchcraft is passed on from mother to daughter," Thomas commented, and the two men looked at each other closely.

"Aye, tis true," John said. "There is a third daughter, as you well know. Goody Cloyce."

"Of course. Goody Cloyce. I know of her well. Her daughter Hannah married my supposed 'brother,' Joseph." Thomas shook his head in disgust. "It did not surprise us, that Joseph should further soil his family name by mixing with those Townes. My dear wife reports that she has received disdainful looks from all three sisters. Totally unwarranted, is this harassment."

John stood up and now he began pacing, bringing to mind the many injuries he had suffered for so many years from Joanna Towne and her children.

"It seems that the rivalry has always been in existence," he began. "William was a hard-working man and a righteous one as well. But I always mistrusted his wife, and I also had some bad dealings with her son-in-law Edmund Bridges."

"I was old enough to remember those trials," Thomas mused.

"Aye. He was a rash, impetuous young man who tormented me to no end. He refused to pay his debts to me, and there was nothing I could do to recoup my losses than to sue him for it. The magistrates, in their wisdom, ruled that Bridges needed to pay. His debt was all of 100 pounds at the time, a most significant sum! It was not my fault that he had to sell his farm in order to follow the court's order. And since then, Sarah Cloyce has looked the other way every time I see her in the village. She does bear a long grudge, that woman does."

"Your thought that witchcraft has run rampant in the colony, only not discerned by many, brings an icy fear to my bones," Thomas said, drawing closer to the fire and holding out his hands to warm them.

The two men stared at each other, stark fear in their eyes.

"Could the Townes be casting witchcraft upon our family?" John asked slowly.

He was interrupted by a sudden clamor from Tug and the other horses and the pigs as well. The animals in the barn started a racket, neighing and snorting loudly, the horses straining against their tethers. Thomas and John jumped in surprise, looking around to see what was bothering the livestock. Perhaps one of the farm hands had come in the side door, startling them? But no one was to be seen, no one beyond the two men sitting on chairs in front of a small fire.

Not wanting to explore further, they left the barn, slamming the door behind them, making their way quickly to the house.

Thomas peeked around the front door, peering cautiously into the best parlor. He felt John behind him, pushing at his back, eager to get inside. Thomas, however, wanted to check first to see what scene might be awaiting them. When he drew his uncle out to the barn a half hour ago, his wife had been splayed out on one of the chairs opposite the settle in front of the fireplace, panting and not able to speak. His daughter and Mercy Lewis had been on the second floor in Ann's room, squealing and yelling, and Thomas could hear their loud footsteps pounding on the floorboards. But now, the house was quiet, and Ann was sitting calmly on her chair, working her needlepoint. Thomas breathed a sigh of relief and drew John into the house.

When Ann looked up at them, though, her eyes were wet with spent tears and rimmed with red. When she saw that they had a visitor, she wiped at them and stood to welcome John, dropping her embroidery ring on the chair behind her.

"Uncle," she said, clasping his hand in greeting. "It is surely a balm to my soul to see you here today."

"Ann, I am so sorry to hear that you are afflicted," John said. "I pray to the Lord every day that you and your daughter be protected from the evil that has overtaken Salem Village."

Ann bowed and smiled a wan smile, bidding the men to join her by the fire. After doffing their cloaks, they joined her. Thomas gazed at his wife carefully, gauging her condition. The fits could overtake her at any moment, seemingly at random, and he was tired, not wanting to deal with them right now. Not with his heart still racing from the odd commotion he and John had just observed in the barn.

Upstairs, Ann and Mercy had calmed as well, and were curious to hear conversation drift up from the parlor below. Sweat from their fits was slowly lifting from their skin, giving them a frisson of chill underneath their shifts. Ann pulled a quilt about herself and gestured toward Mercy, nodding her head toward the door. Mercy knew enough to follow her mistress' bidding without comment. The two girls crept out of the bedroom and down the hall toward the top of the narrow, steep stairs leading to the floor below. Ann put her finger to her lips, silently bidding the other girl to remain silent as they listened to the adults talking.

"Can you tell me, if it doesn't pain you too much, Ann, how these afflictions happen?" John Gould was asking her mother. "If we knew how these witches work, we would do better to fight them."

"I understand you mean to help," Ann Sr. said. "I can talk of it now, when I am not pinched nor tormented by these women, yet often they do take my tongue when their spectres are about. Tis a terrible sight, one I do so wish more people could observe, and not just the few of us. They fly about the room, their terrible familiars on their shoulders or heads, evil cats or yellow birds. Sometimes these creatures, too, bite me and my dear Ann."

Upstairs Mercy nudged Ann, who nodded solemnly back at her.

"The pain, John, the pain is awful," Ann Sr. continued. "They bid me sign the devil's book, yet I do put them off time and again. They tell me there are more of them about in the village, and beyond too."

"This is the part that troubles me the most," John said. "It seems that we have not yet uncovered the entire community of witches. I think we cannot be truly safe until they are all discovered."

"I agree," Ann Sr. said. "Although I have only seen the spectres of the women in jail, I sense that more are to come upon me. It is only a matter of time."

"Who, though?" Thomas asked. "Who might still be about among us, wreaking her sinister havoc while we sit at our prayers, unawares?"

"I can tell you, I would not be surprised if Goody Nurse were not among them," his wife whispered. Above the two girls clasped each other's hands, excitement running through them.

"Goody Nurse!" Thomas and John exclaimed together.

"Aye, Goody Nurse herself!" Ann Sr. proclaimed, her voice becoming more shrill. "She is thought of as such a saint in the church. Yet I do tell you this: she bewitched my poor James, so that he died in my arms. She did come to me when James was still alive, she with that little brat of her sister Sarah's, trying to force her ministrations on me. I sent her away, though, as I felt in my heart a dread and fear that I did not understand at the time. I only knew that I sensed an evil in the room, and I needed her gone. And see what happened to my baby! He is gone and I am truly bereft!"

Upstairs Ann Jr. pulled Mercy away from their perch and the two girls ran back into the bedroom. "Goody Nurse," Ann Jr. whispered, her eyes wide, watching Mercy carefully. "Goody Nurse," Mercy nodded, echoing her friend's words.

~ ~ ~

The next Sunday, Mr. Parris struggled to deliver his prayers and sermon over the yelping and twitching of many young girls sitting up in the balcony, as well as one or two women on the first floor. The congregation was trying hard to feign normalcy, yet the scene was anything but normal. How could the villagers keep calm in such a bizarre environment?

The girls' noise was certainly distracting, but not enough to prevent Mr. Parris from speaking for the most part. Not until an hour had passed when young Ann Putnam stood from her bench and started screaming, pointing toward the ceiling. As one, the girls around her stood up and pointed, too. The cacophony was enough to overwhelm the minister's words, and he remained at the pulpit, mouth agape, staring at the empty place in the rafters that the girls were indicating with their hands. Below him, Goody Putnam started screaming as well, covering her ears and shaking, while Mrs. Parris tried in vain to soothe her. Several other women joined the horrible chorus of shouts.

"Goody Nurse!" Mrs. Putnam's daughter cried out from above, loudly enough to be heard above the rest. As soon as she uttered the name, the others suddenly stopped, as if shocked into silence. And indeed it was shock that swept through the room, as every parishioner stared at Ann Jr., who stood, transfixed as if captured in some kind of grotesque portrait, her eyes wide with terror and her finger pointing. Silent echoes of the screams that had just ceased seemed to bounce off the meeting house walls, and no one moved.

"Goody Nurse!" Ann Jr. proclaimed again in an awesome scream, once again looking toward the rafters. The rest of the people in the meeting house broke out in a roar, while the girls started chanting "Goody Nurse! Goody Nurse!"

"What do you see?" Mr. Parris roared above the din. "What is it?"

"Do you not see her?" Ann Jr. wailed. "She sits on the beam above, cackling with her jagged horrible teeth, sending her yellow bird to bite me!"

"I will not do it!" Abigail Williams added. "I will not sign your book, Goody Nurse!"

"The black man! The black man does whisper into her ear! Oh, she does turn to him! Oh, oh, oh!" Mary Walcott added.

Sarah Cloyce felt struck dumb at the outbursts. It took her several moments to realize that what was happening was real and not a terrible, terrible dream. She was filled with a rage that seemed to slice her insides apart. She clutched the hand of her sister Mary, who sat next to her in dumbfounded quiet.

Sarah stood up, trembling, holding onto Mary's shoulder lest she lose her balance in the face of such a travesty. "Silence!" she screamed, trying to be heard over the noise. "You do dissemble! Rebecca is not even in this room!"

Realizing she would never be heard, Sarah crumpled in her seat, bending over her knees, covering her ears and sobbing. She felt Mary's arms over her. But it wouldn't stop, the screams from the girls. From Goody Putnam and others.

It wouldn't stop.

~ ~ ~

The villagers were sent back to their homes immediately after the church service ended abruptly, the adults trying hard to soothe their children, who were shaken by the terrible outbursts in the meeting house. Church members flew out of the building, some scared out of their wits, others wanting to find some modicum of protection against the terrors that were happening inside. Sarah had sunk to her knees in front of her daughter Hepzibah, whose eyes were wet with tears. "Mia, Mia!" the girl cried. "They accuse Aunt Rebecca of witchcraft! Is she a witch? How can she be a witch?"

"Nay, nay, child," Sarah reassured her, pulling her to her chest, trying to sound calm for the child's sake. "Your aunt is no witch. You can disregard the sham you just saw. All will be well. You go home with Alice and your father. I will be by soon. Please do not fret."

But Sarah was as worried as her children were. She shook with anger as she and Mary ran down the road to their sister's farm, wanting to warn her. Neither sister spoke a word as they made their way to Rebecca, all lost in their own thoughts.

Francis opened the door to them, all smiles to see his family visiting. He, too, had stayed home from services, bringing tea and food to his sick wife. He ushered Sarah and Mary in with words of welcome, and was about to fetch them libations when he saw their downcast faces and wringing hands. Obviously something was amiss.

"Francis, I am not pleased to say this, but we come with troubling news," Sarah said. "Where is Rebecca?"

"Why, she is in her bed," Francis replied. "What is the matter?"

"Let us talk with the two of you together," Sarah suggested, and started toward the stairs. She took Francis' arm, as the older man was frail and found it difficult to move quickly. Mary followed, silent. She had yet to find anything to say in her shock.

Once inside Rebecca's and Francis' bedroom, Sarah saw that her sister was sleeping. The bed was low to the ground, held up by a latticework of hemp rope, and Rebecca was clutching a woven quilt up to her chin. Her head was covered with a nightcap, tied beneath her chin, making her look like a slumbering baby even though her face was covered with the wrinkles of age.

Mary sat gently on the bed next to Rebecca, waking her up with a light nudge on her shoulder. Rebecca's clear blue eyes opened, and at first she looked about her in confusion. When she rested her gaze on Sarah, she smiled her beautiful smile, her face infused with the light from the fire in the hearth. "What is this?" she asked, happily. "A visit from my dear sisters! God is good!"

But soon she noticed everyone's distress, and she clutched the covers more tightly, looking from one face to the next. "What is it, dear ones?" she asked. "Is someone ill?"

"Sister, we must get you out of bed and away from here," Sarah said. "The girls accuse you as a witch. It happened just now, disrupting Mr. Parris' sermon so that the service had to end. Even now the girls are in fits, as are some adults."

Sarah watched her sister as a smile crept onto her withered face once more. "Nay, sister," Rebecca said, waving her off with her hand. "These girls cannot accuse me. They are merely playing!"

"'Tis serious, Rebecca," Sarah said, coming to sit on her sister's other side. "They may be playing, but when accusations have been made in these past weeks, each one of the accused has been sent to jail."

"They will come for you," Mary said, finally finding her tongue. "We must get you out of here. You can come to my farm for now. Then we can figure out what to do next.'

Both Sarah and Mary started to pull down the covers so they could lift her feeble body from the bed, but Rebecca would have none of it. She pushed them away with surprising strength and covered herself once more. "I am innocent as the child unborn!" she cried. "Let them come for me! God will protect me, I am sure of it."

Sarah turned to Francis, appealing for his help. "Francis, have you seen how these examinations have gone, have you not?" she asked. "Why should we not expect the same to happen to Rebecca?"

"But the other women have been sinful," Francis said, weakly. "Some not even fully covenanted church members. Rebecca is something different. As she professes, she is pure. And the people of Salem Village know it!"

His voice became stronger, more confident, as he made his case. More protective. Sarah gaped at him. He was an old man by now, frail and weak, but his love for Rebecca had always been steadfast from the beginning, when Rebecca went off to marriage, leaving young Sarah behind. The two of them had always been a good match, so good at times that Sarah felt jealous and resentful, comparing their marriage to hers with Edmund. They were not complicated souls; rather they were like the salt of the earth, simple and good, living their lives together in quiet companionship, always worshiping God, always trying to help people. Suddenly Sarah felt dizzy, as if she had awoken in some kind of nightmare, where black was white and white was black. She was the youngest Towne girl, for mercy's sake. It shouldn't be up to her to lead this family to wherever they were going next. Suddenly she ached for her mother's gruff strength. What would Joanna have done in this situation?

"Do you want to take the chance, when we can take her away from this travesty?" Sarah demanded, shaking off her dysequilibrium. She had not expected Rebecca to be so contrary. Her sister had always been complacent, uncomplaining. It is only now that she decides to put up a fight? The irony hit Sarah like a stone over her head.

"God will protect me," Rebecca said with force, despite the infection that had taken over her lungs. "I will trust in Him. All will be well."

Sarah shook her head, hearing the words that she had just recently said to her own daughter. The difference was that when she uttered them, she did not believe with certainty that they were true. Rebecca, on the other hand, looked unmoved as she stared at all of them, an ethereal strength emanating from her tiny body.

Her family tried over and over to convince her to escape, but Rebecca continued to be stoic, closing her eyes and folding her hands together in prayer even as the entreaties continued.

It was no use. Rebecca was going nowhere.

~ ~ ~

"Tis happening. Just like the Goodwin children."

Cotton Mather's face was dark and troubled as he said the words. He slumped into his favorite rocking chair in the corner of the hall of the parsonage, covering his face with one hand.

"We do not yet know the full story," Samuel Sewall said, trying to be encouraging. "Thomas and I just wanted to make sure you knew what is going on in Salem Village."

Indeed both Samuel and Thomas Danforth had read the reports coming from Judges Hathorne and Corwin for several weeks now, ever since they dispatched them from the north. The General Court no longer had any real authority, not without the new charter from England, but it was still meeting on a regular basis, and both Samuel and Thomas took their seats at the table along with the rest of the magistrates. When the group received the plea from Reverend Parris to examine what he believed were witches in his congregation, Samuel and Thomas agreed with the rest that something should be done. And since then the judges had sent regular missives back to Boston, reporting on the proceedings of the Salem Village examinations. Those exams could not proceed to formal trials without a charter, so the accused women remained in jail for the time being.

Because all of this was going on in an informal way, the information hadn't made itself known to the men who regularly posted news broadsheets on trees and posts around the Boston Common. The General Court's magistrates were glad of this, since the reports were so troubling and could very easily set off an outcry among the people living in the capital. The leaders were busy enough trying to maintain peace among the merchants and the townspeople, even the militia fighting the Indians to the north. They had to levy taxes on the people of the colony to support the war, and there was much resistance. Many men said they should not have to pay when there is no government, at least not a formal one. Things were already tenuous in the Colony.

But Samuel and Thomas together decided that it was time

to let their compatriot know about the goings-on, especially given their agreement to work together against any hint of witchcraft.

"You tell me enough of the details to make me draw reasonable comparisons to the Goodwin case," the minister was now saying. "Children being tortured by invisible spirits? A set of doctors not finding any medical causes for their predicaments? Tis certain enough for me to be convinced!"

"Let us hope the afflictions remain limited," Thomas said, sitting next to the minister and putting his withered hand on the younger man's shoulder. He knew that Cotton was under enough pressure, taking over his father's congregation, having to respond to the ever-louder questions from Bostonians about why it was taking so long for Increase to get back to the Colony.

"Perhaps I should not have published the account of the Goodwin children," Cotton mused, looking up into Thomas' face, pleading. "I did it so that we can all be on the watch for the Devil's work. But perhaps it did put ideas into people's minds?"

"Nay, I do not think so," Samuel soothed, taking the other seat next to Cotton's. "I doubt such a book could find itself to such a remote place as Salem Village."

"God speed my dear father," Cotton cried, throwing up his hands in the air. "It cannot be too soon that we spy his ship in Boston Harbor!"

"I have an idea," Samuel said, snapping his fingers. "None but Judges Hathorne and Corwin have as of yet been deployed to Salem Village. But perhaps I might travel there, in a quiet and unassuming way, to witness myself what is occurring there. None but the judges would recognize me, and I could stay in the back of the meeting house. Then I can be sure of the extent of the problem, and come back here to report it to you."

"Tis an excellent idea, Samuel," Cotton replied, and Thomas nodded. Thomas, too, would like to go north to see for himself what was happening, but there was too much to do in Cambridge for the two of them to take the trip. "Do hurry. I worry so."

~ ~ ~

On March 24th, the meeting house was once more packed to the rafters with people clamoring to watch the day's examinations. The accused and the victims were not yet brought in, but the benches had begun to fill hours before. The early spring day was growing unseasonably hot, and already the room was filled with the sour odor of bodies standing too close together for too long. And all church-like propriety had been long disposed of, as the people were anxious and agitated and ready to fight God's own warfare against the sin that was invading their community.

Sarah had made sure that she and Mary arrived early so that they could claim one of the front benches. For legal proceedings such as these, the division of gender and status that dictated seating choices was no longer necessary, and the Townes wanted to be as close to the accused as possible.

Because today, Rebecca Nurse was to be examined for witchcraft.

What they had feared had indeed taken place, despite Rebecca's insistence that God would protect her. The day after her sisters urged her to escape, the local constable, George Herrick, arrived at the front door of the Nurse homestead, clutching a warrant for her arrest. Sarah and Mary were at the house with Rebecca, worried that she would be taken, wanting to be there in case she was.

It was Sarah who answered Herrick's loud knock, and when she did, she glared at him with all the hatred she could muster. "You have no business here, Goodman Herrick," she growled. "Tis only the godly who inhabit this place."

Goodman Herrick looked abashed, clutching his felted hat in his hands, bowing his head. "I merely do my job, Goody Cloyce," he said. "I am directed by the magistrates."

"And if the magistrates bid you to turn your face away from God, would you do so?" Sarah spat, trying to push the door closed in his face. But Herrick was stronger and barged in, looking about the room, seeking Rebecca. "You cannot prevent this, Goody Cloyce," he said, apologetically. "If it not be me, the magistrates will send someone else. The warrant is made."

"Who has made the accusation?"

"Thomas Putnam Jr. and Jonathan Walcott, on behalf of Ann Putnam Jr, Mary Walcott and Abigail Williams."

"A pox on their hateful heads!" Sarah cried out, as Mary and Francis came to either side of her. Mary started to cry, and Rebecca's husband could only mutter softly to himself "Oh! Oh! Oh! My Rebecca!"

So Rebecca was taken from her bed, even though she was still suffering from her chest cold and back pain. George Herrick agreed to allow her sisters to help her get dressed so at least she didn't have to suffer the indignity of being arrested in her shift. She was so weak that Mary had to hold her up while Sarah pulled up her woolen skirt around her waist. Even then, Rebecca did not show fear, although her rheumy eyes were not as clear as they usually were. Sarah, on the other hand, found it difficult to keep from screaming one moment, and sobbing another.

"Rebecca," she said. "My own dear sister. We will fight for you. All of us."

"Do not fear, young Sarah," Rebecca said quietly yet assuredly, and Sarah winced at the pet name, remembering a time when she actually was young and Rebecca took care of her as a mother would. "Tis merely a misunderstanding," Rebecca continued. "God will protect me. He knows of my innocence."

Sarah could not argue with her, for fear of instilling distress in the old woman now that she was set on this horrible path. Yet Sarah was filled with fury, to think of those little girls pointing their fingers at her sister. Why did no one take them over one's knee and give them a good beating? Why was the village so ready to believe their accusations? And why did the girls choose Rebecca, of all people? The other accusations, although questionable in their own right, at least made some kind of sense, directed as they were to women not well-regarded in the community. Sarah did wonder when Goody Corey was taken, as she was known to quote scripture to others, and was a member in good standing in the church. Before the girls cried out against Rebecca, though, Sarah hoped against hope that the trouble would never touch her family. Now she saw that her fears had been founded. She remembered again all of the arguments they had had, for many decades, with their neighbors, going back to the days when her parents were alive and their home was in Topsfield. Images came rushing back to her mind, unbidden. John Gould's trying to ruin her poor departed husband. Goody Putnam's glare across the meeting house, filled with jealousy whenever the Towne family met with any success at all with their farms. Moments like these had always troubled her, nagging at her happiness, sometimes even sending her into a deep melancholy throughout the years. Could they now be behind this surreal accusation of Rebecca, good Rebecca who treated all people with love and kindness – even the Putnams, who were now pointing fingers at her?

They all walked about as if in a dream, Rebecca slowly making her way down the steep stairs. At the bottom Francis took her hand and helped her the rest of the way, gazing into her face with a profound sadness. When Sarah watched the two, her heart broke even more. This couple had been married for close to fifty years. They had together weathered the constant threat of poverty living in Salem Town, borne and lost children, lived to see their sons and daughters married and have lives of their own, and finally found some peace when they moved to Salem Village so many years ago. And all the while, they showed devotion and caring to the other in a quiet, gentle way. Why were they being pulled apart so wretchedly?

Sarah didn't have much time to think, though, as George Herrick pulled Rebecca out of the house and toward the high-sided cart that was standing behind his two horses. As Rebecca stumbled along with the constable, her husband and sisters followed. Sarah gasped when she saw that there was another person in the cart: a tiny child, not much more than four years old, with a dirt-stained face and ragged clothing. The poor girl clutched the side of the cart, tears pouring down her face. Shaking with fear.

"Do not tell me that this child is accused as well!" Sarah thundered, wanting to run to the girl and take her in her arms. "What is happening here?"

George Herrick once again looked sheepish. "Aye, she was accused by the same girls, and the complaint was made by the same men who brought Goody Nurse to the jail."

"Is it not Dorothy, Goody Good's child?" Mary asked. "Why yes, I do recognize her!"

"Mama!" the girl whimpered. "Mama!"

"Do not fear, child," Rebecca soothed, allowing herself to be lifted onto the cart by the constable. "I am here, and I will take you to your mother."

Sarah regarded the scene with wide eyes, finding it difficult to believe that even now, her sister was providing comfort to those in need. She watched as the wretched little girl jumped into Rebecca's arms, and sobbed even harder. The older woman smoothed the child's capless head, and as Goodman Herrick drove off, she could be heard whispering a verse from Deuteronomy into Dorothy's ear: "'The Lord himself goes before you and will be with you; He will never leave you nor forsake you. Do not be afraid; do not be discouraged.'"

So now they were all waiting to see how the two judges would handle the examination of the most well-respected woman in the village on the one hand and one of the youngest on the other. As more and more villagers entered the meeting house, Sarah and Mary, along with their spouses and Francis Nurse as well, were jostled from the aisle on either side of their bench by people wanting to crowd in with them. All four, however, were steadfast, and glared hard at anyone who approached them, sending them scurrying away.

Peter kept whispering into Sarah's ear: "Remember, dear one. I know this is most troubling. Yet please, I beg of you. Hold your tongue. This is not a place where your voice will help, reasonable as it may seem to you." And Sarah did indeed stay silent before the examinations began, even though in her heart she screamed: So I am expected to remain silent while they crucify my sister? Is that what this has come to?

Sarah glared across the aisle to the bench where the wealthier women usually sat during church services. Here instead sat a huddled group of the young girls who had accused her sister and others. Beside them sat Thomas Putnam and his wife, along with Thomas' sister Deliverance and her husband Jonathan Walcott. The girls looked scared yet defiant, obviously proud to be sitting in places usually inhabited by the most powerful people in the village. Gone was the law that they be relegated to the upper rafters where they were ignored. No, now they were the center of attention, and no one would dare challenge their position, not now. Sarah wanted to spit.

Meanwhile, unbeknownst to everyone in the crowd, the great Judge Samuel Sewall slipped into the meeting house through the side door, pulling the collar of his shirt up toward his ears and covering the bottom of his face with his woolen scarf.

At the front of the room George Herrick brought in Rebecca Nurse, who looked as pale and weak as she had the day before, when she had been wrested from her home. Sarah took in a quick breath, wanting to go to her sister to comfort her. Sarah had not been able to sleep the previous night, imagining her poor sister in the cramped and dirty Salem Town jail, probably sitting amongst real criminals. How had she survived it? Was anyone there who could help her?

At their arrival, a clamor went up in the meeting house, and already the girls started pointing their fingers at Rebecca, screaming "Witch! Witch!" Reverend Hale had a difficult time saying the opening prayer above the din. Mr. Parris sat at a side table, dipping his pen into an inkwell, as he was assigned as scribe for the proceedings. In front sat Judges Corwin and Hathorne at a table on a small platform, their faces dark with seriousness, looking down at Rebecca, who appeared confused and forlorn.

"What do you say?" Judge Hathorne started, pointing to the group of girls sitting on the bench across from the Townes. "Have you seen this woman hurt you?"

Young Ann Putnam glowered at the old woman, whose back was to her. "Yes, she beat me this morning!" the girl cried out.

"And I, too!" Abigail Williams added. At that, Rebecca turned toward the children and looked upon them with a strange mixture of pity, kindness and disappointment. As she did so, the girls started screaming, picking at their skirts as if shooing away an attacker. Ann's mother started screaming as well, shouting that Rebecca was even at that moment attempting to bite her. The crowd gasped at the sight.

"Goody Nurse!" Judge Hathorne said. "Here are two – Ann Putnam Jr. and Abigail Williams – who complain of you hurting them. What do you say to it?"

"I can say before my eternal father that I am innocent, and God will clear my innocency," Rebecca answered, more calm than Sarah felt, as if the Lord himself was holding her in His hands.

"Everyone in this assembly does desire it," the judge said. "But if you be guilty, pray God discover you! Here are not only these, but here is the wife of Thomas Putnam who accuses you by credible information, that you are tempting her to iniquity, and greatly hurting her."

"She did!" Goody Putnam shouted. "She comes to me at night, carrying my poor babe in winding sheets, saying that she took him for the Devil himself!"

Wails went up from the girls, and the rest of the crowd gaped in awe. In the back, Samuel Sewall was gripped with a cold fear that prickled at the back of his neck. To him it was clear that these girls were being tortured. The old woman in the front of the room certainly did appear kindly, yet if she were not indeed sending her specter to hurt these girls, why then would they cry out so?

"I am innocent and clear and have not been able to get out of doors these eight or nine days," Rebecca was saying. "I never afflicted no child, never in my life!"

"But you see these accuse you, is it true?"

"No!"

"Are you an innocent person relating to this witchcraft?"

But Rebecca was prevented from answering by Goody Putnam, who screamed out once more. "Did you not bring the black man with you?" she demanded. "Did you not bid me tempt God and die? How often have you eat and drunk your own damnation, Goody Nurse?"

Judge Hathorne, his eyes stormy, pointed toward Goody Putnam, and asked: "What do you say to them, Goody Nurse?"

"Oh Lord, help me!" Rebecca cried out, raising her eyes to the heavens and holding up her arms in supplication. To Sarah she looked like a saint of God, her face, despite its fatigue and age, shining as the sun. But the next moment a larger clamor went up from the girls and from Goody Putnam, who lifted their own arms in the same manner, yet seeming pained to do so. "See how she moves my limbs!" the woman wailed, and the other girls followed. "I cannot control their movement! Can you not see she is bewitching me?"

Rebecca seemed not to hear the accusation, but looked toward the judges to see what they had to say next. As she lowered her arms, so too did Ann Putnam and the girls with her. Judge Corwin nudged his partner, and they both regarded the scene with amazement.

As did Samuel Sewall, from his place at the back of the room.

"Can you not see what a solemn condition these are in?" Judge Corwin demanded. "When your hands are loose, the people are afflicted!"

Rebecca shook her head, but in her face was only sadness, not anger. "Can we not do something, Peter?" Sarah whispered loudly to her husband. Peter gave her a hard look. "I beg of you, Sarah, for all of our sakes," he said. "I have seen the last examinations in this place. It will do no good to speak up for Rebecca. Not here. Later we can petition the court with an affidavit of support."

"The Lord knows I have not hurt them. I am an innocent person!" Rebecca was saying. Detained by Peter, Sarah clutched the bench in front of her, her knuckles white with exertion, willing her love to fly through the air and reach her sister. If the ghostly spectres that these girls described were true, why then could Sarah not herself send her spirit to comfort her poor sister, standing there so tiny and helpless in front of people who were once her friends? Sarah shook her head to rid herself of such thoughts.

"It is very awful to all to see these agonies, Goody Nurse," Judge Corwin said, shaking his head in disappointment. "And you an old professor of the word, thus charged with contracting with the devil. Yet to see you now stand with dry eyes when these sufferings are so many!"

Hearing this man remind the crowd of her good standing in the church, Rebecca seemed to finally gather some resistance in her soul. She stood more straight and looked right into the judge's eyes. "You do not know my heart," she stated with a dignity that momentarily quieted the shouts of the afflicted. It silenced the rest of the room as well. Sarah hoped all of these people who had for decades been helped by the charity and devotion of her dear sister, who had accepted her ministrations of food and healing herbs when there was sickness in the family, who were comforted after bad crops and death from the Indian wars, in the face of loneliness and woe – Sarah wished with all of her heart that they see the evil of what they were doing. Shame on them. Shame on them all.

But the silence was interrupted by Judge Hathorne, who continued the questioning. "You would do well if you are guilty to confess and give glory to the Lord," he chastened Rebecca.

With the same quiet strength, Rebecca looked at him and replied, "I am as clear as the child unborn."

"You are at this very present charged with familiar spirits, that they speak to your bodily person. Now what do you say to that?"

"I have none sir," Rebecca replied, and the judge looked confused, as it seems that she was answering a different question. "If you have confessed and give glory to God," he tried again, "I pray God clear you if you be innocent, and if you are guilty discover you. And therefore give me an upright answer: have you any familiarity with these spirits?"

"No, I have none but with God alone."

At that, Abigail Williams and Ann Putnam Jr. screamed again, this time joined by Mary Warren, Mercy Lewis and Elizabeth Hubbard. "There is a black man whispering in Goody Nurse's ear!" Abigail shrieked. "Do you not see it? He is telling her what words to say!"

"And the yellow birds!" her friend Ann added, covering her ears in visible fright. "They do fly about her head, and she tells them to bite me!"

Rebecca looked around her, addled, looking for the man and the birds that these girls described. The onlookers strained forward to do the same thing, yet they all saw nothing.

Nothing, Samuel Sewall thought to himself as he looked on. He could see nothing. Yet the girls were obviously in pain. He had heard before that the devil can indeed use human specters to do his evil, and it was clear that this was what was happening today. Already his keen mind started working: how to wage war against what was clearly being unleashed on Salem Village?

"Now you see that these girls testify of a black man whispering in your ear, and birds about you," Judge Corwin said. "What do you say to it?"

"It is all false," Rebecca stayed stalwart. "I am clear!"

"Possibly you may appreciate you are no witch, but have you not been led aside by temptations that way?"

"I have not."

"What a sad thing is it," the two judges looked at each other in woe, "that a church member here and now be thus accused and charged."

"What?" Sarah lamented from her seat, and Peter held her back. "Do not restrain me, husband!" she scolded. "They have already decided her fate, despite the fact that she continues to profess her innocence with the dignity that is so characteristic of her goodness!"

"I know, I know," Peter said, her sister Mary looking on, terror in her face. "It is a fiasco to be sure."

Rebecca stumbled from where she stood, and it appeared as if she might faint. Judge Corwin motioned to George Herrick who brought her a straight-backed wooden chair to sit in. Goody Putnam, who had been standing up until that moment, fell back on her bench and started flinching. "Can you not see that she bids me sit as well?" she screamed. "And now I cannot raise my body from this place. Thomas, do try to lift me!"

Her husband dutifully pulled on her arms to bring her to standing, yet he could not do it. He was a large, strong man and his wife a tiny, frail thing, so it was an amazing sight to behold. John

Gould, who was sitting next to Thomas, jumped up from his seat to try to help, but this, too, was to no avail. Thomas cried out in agony to see his wife so tortured.

"Do you think these suffer voluntarily or involuntarily?" Judge Hathorne demanded of Rebecca.

"I cannot tell."

"This is surely strange, as everyone in this room can tell it is so!"

"I cannot tell what to think of it," Rebecca said, and the judges stood together, angry at her response. It was obvious to them that Goody Putnam and the girls were being hurt and could not control what was being done to them, and they thought Rebecca was defying a reality that everyone else saw. But Sarah could see that the noise in the room was too loud for her sister, who had had difficulty hearing for years now. "She cannot hear!" she yelled, finally unable to resist. "She is saying she does not understand your question!"

The judges sighed and sat back down. Hathorne held up his hand, calling for quiet in the room. The crowd went silent, but the afflicted continued to whimper, holding onto each other for comfort.

"Well then give an answer now," Judge Corwin commanded. "Do you think these suffer against their wills or not?"

Everyone looked at Rebecca, waiting with anxiety for her answer.

"I do not think these suffer against their wills," she said, and a clamor of wails began once again from the girls and Goody Putnam. "I have got nobody to look to but God!" Rebecca cried, and lifted her arms again. As before, the girls lifted their own arms, and it appeared that they were being pulled up by an invisible string. "It hurts! It hurts!" Ann Putnam Jr. bellowed, as did the other girls.

"Do you believe these afflicted persons are bewitched?" Judge Hathorne yelled above the noise. Rebecca nodded her head, lowering her arms as the girls did, too. "I do think they are," she said, sadly.

"When this witchcraft came upon the stage, Tituba professed much love to the child Betty Parris. But it was her apparition that did the mischief. Why should you not also be guilty, for your apparition does also hurt these girls?" Corwin asked.

Rebecca once again gathered up her strength, growing taller in her chair, making Sarah wonder how much more of this she could take. "Would you have me belie myself?" Rebecca asked, tilting her head in challenge. Sarah silently applauded for her sister, who was handling this mockery of a trial much better than the four accused women who had come before her.

"Make her head straight, I beg of you!" Abigail Williams roared, pointing to Elizabeth Hubbard who sat next to her. Elizabeth's head was twisted in a painful-looking imitation of Rebecca's stance, and the girl's eyes were widening, seeming to pop out of her head. "The maid's head will be broke should you not!"

George Herrick rushed to Rebecca's side and forcefully pulled her head up straight, shocking Rebecca into crying out in pain. Sarah started sobbing, as did Mary beside her. Now they were manhandling an innocent old woman. What was happening here?

That was enough for the magistrates. They announced that the accusations against her were true, and signed a warrant for George Herrick to take her to the Salem Town jail. After placing shackles on Rebecca's fragile wrists, he had to protect her from the surging crowd, putting his large body between hers and the raised fists of her brothers and sisters in Christ. The last thing Sarah saw of her sister was her shock of white hair, poking out in all directions as her cap was wrested from her head from the jostling crowd.

Sarah crumpled to the floor in front of the bench, covering her eyes with her hands, wracked with sobs that seemed to come from a deep, primal place deep inside of her soul.

Samuel Sewall had already departed the meeting house, having seen enough. He was at that moment riding back to Boston in his carriage, his thoughts racing. Something had to be done about this malevolence. With everything on the line – the very survival of the colony, the charter negotiations Mr. Mather was having with the king and queen, continued massacres in the Indian wars – the devil could not be allowed to run loose in Massachusetts Bay Colony.

~ ~ ~

On Sunday, the day of services and the Lord's Supper, a row was brewing at the Cloyce homestead. After laying out the morning meal for her family, Sarah went out into the yard in front of the barn, pumping water into a large wooden cask. "What are you doing, Sarah?" her husband asked, following her as she proceeded with her chore. "We need to leave for the meeting house."

Sarah clucked her tongue, pumping the water with unnecessary vigor, droplets flying from the bucket onto her skirts. "I am not attending, Peter. Nor will the girls."

Peter gently pulled her away from her work, her body rigid beneath his touch, her face red with rage. She hadn't spoken much since Rebecca had been taken to the Salem Town jail with little Dorothy Good after their examinations. Peter had warned the children to leave her alone, as he knew that when she was angry, it was best to let her stew. He, too, was heartbroken, unable to sleep with images running through his head of his sister-in-law slowly wasting away in a dank and dirty jail cell. Yet he knew that his own visions were nothing compared to the agony Sarah was experiencing.

"Sarah," he said, soothingly. "I know you do not want to go back to that place. But we must be careful, especially now. The accusations continue to fly in the village. You cannot become a target. Think of the children. Hepzibah is but four years old."

Sarah stared up at him, her eyes blazing. "That place is no longer my home," she spat. "Those people are no longer my congregation."

"I know that. But we still live here. We must protect ourselves."

Eventually he convinced her to climb into the wagon seat next to him, the children riding in the back. She hadn't changed into her clean Sunday skirts, nor had she bothered to tuck her unruly hair – now almost totally gray – into her cap. The family rode in stony silence, bumping along the road that led to the meeting house.

Once inside the building, as the children scrambled up the ladder to the balcony above, Sarah rushed to her usual bench, where Mary was sitting, pale as a ghost. Sarah had no interest in talking with any of her neighbors as she usually did. She felt extreme gratitude to see her sister there, and wanted to talk with her alone.

"Oh, Mary," Sarah said as Mary put her bony arm around her shoulders, her anger finally giving way to sadness. "I cannot bear to think of Rebecca. I just cannot bear it."

Mary made comforting noises, patting Sarah's head in a maternal, caring way. There was nothing more to say. They were both bereft.

The air in the meeting house seemed electrified, as it seemed that everyone was keenly aware of what had happened the last time they gathered there. The adults sent furtive glances up to the rafters, where the afflicted girls sat together, back in their traditional places. Abigail, Ann and the rest of them gazed steadily back at them, not looking down in deference to their elders as they did before the hysteria started. The girls were docile, not afflicted, yet the congregation knew by then that the fits could start at any moment.

They had disturbed the last two Sunday sermons. What stood in wait for them all now?

Reverend Parris walked into the room from the side door, alone this time, without any of his minister colleagues. He looked stormy, resolved, almost as if ready for battle, although there were dark circles in the hollows beneath his blazing eyes. The congregation was silent as his heavy boots stomped up the narrow stairs to the pulpit and he opened the huge bible in front of him. He leaned on both his hands, looking hard into the faces of the people who sat, waiting, beneath him.

Sarah did not look up in response, although she knew Mary did as was expected and gazed upward. Mary's hand continued its soothing, steady tattoo on her sister's shoulder. The rhythmic tapping seemed the only thing that was holding Sarah together. Thank God for Mary, Sarah thought. If she had to go through this alone she thought she would go mad.

After the opening prayer, Parris announced that he was taking his text from the sixth chapter of the Book of John. He had the habit of reading the entire passage at the beginning of his sermons, discussing the implications afterward. Today was no different, as he read from the bible in front of him in slow, deliberate, loud sentences:

"Then Jesus said unto them, Verily, verily, I say unto you, Except ye eat the flesh of the Son of man, and drink his blood, ye have no life in you. Whoso eateth my flesh, and drinketh my blood, hath eternal life; and I will raise him up at the last day. Many therefore of his disciples, when they had heard this, said, This is a hard saying; who can hear it? When Jesus knew in himself that his disciples murmured at it, he said unto them, Doth this offend you? But there are some of you that believe not. For Jesus knew from the beginning who they were that believed not, and who should betray him. And he said, Therefore said I unto you, that no man can come unto me, except it were given unto him of my Father. Then Simon Peter answered him, Lord, to whom shall we go? Thou hast the words of eternal life. And we believe and are sure that thou art that Christ, the Son of the living God. Jesus answered them, Have not I chosen you twelve, and one of you is a devil?"

At the last word, Sarah felt her chest constrict, and it was all she could do to not scream out loud.

"There were twelve that stayed with Christ," Parris began his investigation of the text. "One out of twelve. How many members are in our church? How many devils?"

He pointed across the room, indiscriminately. The people shrank in fear.

"Christ's church consists of good and bad," he continued. "As a garden that has weeds as well as flowers. Here we have not only true saints, but hypocrites who profess their love of God. These hypocrites are the heirs of the Devil, the freeholders of Hell!"

The congregation gasped together, in unison. Many looked upward at the girls, expecting them at any minute to start writhing in pain. Sarah was surprised that, at least for now, they remained quiet. She started rocking back and forth herself, wrapping her arms around her body, trying hard to keep herself in check. She knew Parris was referring to Rebecca, who was not even there to defend herself. And even if she was, Sarah knew that it would do no good, no more than it had during Rebecca's examination. Her sister had done nothing wrong. Everyone in that room knew how righteous she was – at least they used to. Now the people who had been her lifelong friends were turning on her, and they were being led by this man, this newcomer who never really did know Rebecca. The injustice of it was almost too much to bear. How could such evil be celebrated while her sister's goodness was trampled into the mud? How could this be happening?

"I choose this text on the occasion of the dreadful witchcraft that has overtaken our village," Parris intoned, his voice growing louder. "One of the accused is a member of this church. I cannot adequately divulge to you how much this pains me. But Christ Himself reminds us that such devils can survive in our midst. He Himself knew that the devil in his flock was Judas Iscariot, many months before Judas was to betray Him. We are either saints or devils, in reality. The horrifying hypocrisy of devils taking communion with us can only subject us to Satan's power and the hottest of God's wrath!"

That was it for Sarah. She could take it no longer. She broke away from Mary's embrace, standing almost without her own volition, her anger and frustration rushing through her limbs like fire. Mary tried to pull her back down to the bench, but Sarah would have none of it. She clenched her fists and stared up at the minister, so tall and threatening above her. She narrowed her eyes, wishing she knew a curse to mutter. Instead, without words, she turned on her heel and moved to the center aisle, showing her back to Mr.

Parris, and walking toward the door. It was so heavy that she had to use two hands to pull at the iron latch. Once the door was open, she finally turned and glared once more at the minister, who stood there, mouth open in astonishment. At that moment Sarah felt like the whole scene focused only on the two of them, as the congregation fell away from sight. He was the devil, she thought. HE was the devil.

With one long heave, she slammed the door shut behind her, and the heavy planks shook in their frame. The sound was like the loud crack of gunfire in a silent forest.

As Sarah stomped away, her mind a tangle of thoughts. The sound of her blood pumping in her ears, she could hear the girls start up their fits back inside the meeting house. She couldn't mistake what they were shouting, even from outdoors.

It was her name.

CHAPTER NINE

April 1692
Boston, Salem Village

When Judge Samuel Sewall returned to Boston after observing Rebecca Nurse's examination in Salem Village, he went immediately to his friend Thomas Danforth's home in Cambridge. It was a Tuesday in the middle of the afternoon, and the judge discovered that Thomas was not at his house; rather, his wife Mary informed Samuel, he was meeting with Governor Bradstreet in Boston. Politely refusing Mary's offer of sustenance, Samuel jumped back up into his carriage, bidding his coachman to take him across the Charles River to the governor's abode on School Street.

It was an unseasonably warm day for early spring after the cold snap they had been having, and Samuel found the governor and his lieutenant governor sitting together at the edge of the apple orchard behind Bradstreet's home. The governor, almost ninety years old, was very frail and sat with an embroidered quilt over his knees, despite the warmth of the day. To Samuel he looked withered and small, his weak appearance contradicting the power that the great man had had in leading the colony since he sailed with Governor Winthrop on the ship Arbella over sixty years before. Thomas, too, was aging, now closing in on seventy years old, but he still had the energy of a much younger man. As he walked toward them, Samuel was struck, as he often was, with a feeling of gratitude, to be in the presence of such fine men, so dedicated as they were to this holy experiment in the Massachusetts wilderness.

After exchanging greetings, Samuel accepted the bench brought to him by one of the governor's maidservants, and the three men set to their conversation.

"You look concerned, Samuel," Thomas commented, peering with worry into his friend's face. Having lost all of his boys as infants or in battle, the lieutenant governor had come to consider Samuel almost like his son, someone to be respected, yes, but also protected.

"Aye, I come with news from the north, from Salem Village," Samuel said. He noticed that the good governor was starting to doze off, his head slowly lowering to his chest, but didn't worry about it.

Thomas was the one who was the real leader of the colony these days, taking over all of the duties that Bradstreet once had. The old man had dedicated his whole life to the success of the colony; he was more than due his rest. "I am most disquieted."

Thomas looked away, out toward the apple trees on the hill that sloped gently down toward the bay below. In the distance he could see the beehive activity of the wharves, with several ships docked along the piers and men running to and fro, busy with their work. From his standpoint he could not hear the shouts and calls of the men, and the house behind screened them from the street noise. Here it felt warm and calm, with a slight breeze blowing through the trees with their buds just starting their spring burst. For a moment he wanted to preserve this moment of serenity, because he knew what Samuel was talking about. And it wasn't a pleasant thing at all.

Samuel went on to relay the troubling scenes he had just witnessed in Salem Village while Thomas listened intently and the old governor napped in his seat. "Tis truly an abomination, Thomas," Samuel said, running his hand through his hair as he thought of the images he had seen. "It brings terror to my soul, to see these girls so attacked. This Goody Nurse seemed confused and did profess her innocency several times over, yet it was clear that the girls were telling the truth. They say this woman was as near to a saint as anyone could be. Yet I also know that Satan chooses his minions with nefarious skill. Who else to poison the souls of our people than the one least suspected?"

Thomas leant over to pull up the quilt over the governor's lap, as it had slipped close to the ground during their conversation. He gazed at Bradstreet's sleeping face, and remembered what the man had had to endure as a leader of the colony for so long. The early days when the colonists had to carve a sustenance out of pure wilderness. The massive influx of newcomers during King James' rule, and then the exodus of many of the same families when King Charles was beheaded. Years when crops failed and many died. Two Indian wars. The loss of the charter. Governor Andros' tyranny. Thomas felt grateful that at least this pillar of the community might be too old and sick to have to deal with this most recent travesty. One that might destroy them all, for good.

"Then, Samuel," he said, returning to his seat. "If there are to be more accusations, I will declare it right now. You and I will serve as the judges for the next examination. If this is a war, I want to be on the front lines for God."

~ ~ ~

The jail in Salem Town was like any other in the colony: dark and dank, just one big room for all the prisoners. No beds, no windows, except for a small one carved into the stone up toward the ceiling. As soon as the constable shoved Sarah into the shadowy interior, an acrid stench filled her nose, and at first she couldn't make out any shapes inside. The iron and wooden door slammed behind her, the crash echoing against the walls.

"Sarah!" a weak voice cried out in the gloom. The room around Sarah became more in focus as her eyes adjusted to the dim light around her. She took in the whole scene at once, recognizing those who had been accused of witchcraft, sitting in huddles with other people – men and women both – who were strangers to her. Horror overcame her as she saw the dirt on these poor people's faces and clothes, their ragged hair, the odors emanating from their bodies and the large chamber pot in the corner. For a moment Sarah felt dizzy, about to faint.

"Sarah!" she heard again, and she slowly walked to where the voice was coming from. As they approached, Sarah could see that it wasn't a pile of rags at all, but the muddled mass of her sister Rebecca.

Sarah fell to her knees in front of her, finally letting loose the sobs of rage and anguish she had kept inside throughout her whole ordeal so far. She laid her head onto her sister's lap, letting relief come over her, even though she was shocked at the fetid smell of Rebecca's skirts. Since Sarah was a child she always associated her sister with a comforting combination of lavender, freshly-milled wheat flour and sweet milk. Gone now were those comforting scents, and Sarah was overwhelmed with a new sense of loss. She clutched Rebecca's arms and hands, soaking her skirts with her tears, feeling like a young girl again, desperately needing her sister's motherly care.

"My dear, dear one," Rebecca was murmuring, one arm wrapped tightly around Sarah, the other smoothing her unruly hair. "It grieves me so to see you here."

For a long time Sarah lay there like that, wondering if her weeping would ever stop, feeling guilty: shouldn't she be the one to comfort Rebecca, who had suffered in this horrid jail for three weeks now? Yet she could only give in to her sorrow and fear. Despite the older woman's frailty, her presence seemed to give Sarah some kind of permission to finally let go of her feelings. Since that day ten days ago – had it really only been that short a time? – when she had stormed out of the church in a rage, it was as if she covered her body with a hard, protective armor. The invisible layer not only insulated her from the injustice and shame that plagued her in the days that followed; it also kept her from falling apart. Which she was doing now, wrenchingly, wholeheartedly.

The events of the past week flooded Sarah's mind as her tears flowed. George Herrick at her door, a surreal repetition of the scene just weeks before that, when he came for Rebecca. This time Sarah knew that it would do no good to fight. She remained stalwart, and immediately went about making preparations to be taken away from her home. Hepzibah squalled in terror, clutching onto her mother's skirts as she tried to make her away around the house, putting various little things to rights, calling Alice to fetch more potatoes from the cellar so she could make sure the big pot over the fire was filled with enough for her family to eat for the next few days. Alice helped her mother stuff a large muslin bag with an extra shift, a blanket and food – apples, a loaf of bread, several chunks of cheese – the girl's chin quivering, trying not to cry. Now as Sarah thought of the desolate faces of her children and also her husband Peter's – especially the red, wet face of Hepzibah, calling out "Mia! Mia! Don't go!" – her own tears came on harder than before.

It seemed an eternity before Sarah's tears ebbed. But now that she had let go of all of the pain she had been holding so tightly to her chest, she felt empty, spent, as if she were recovering from a grave illness. Throughout her emotional storm, her sister remained indomitable, allowing Sarah her fit, holding tight so that Sarah felt contained, safe, even in such squalor.

It was only after the sobbing quit entirely that Sarah was able to lift her head and look about her, clearly this time. Her sister seemed to have shrunk several sizes, although she had always been tiny to begin with. The skin around her face hung in hollows, reminding Sarah of a corpse. Her shift was filthy. Yet Rebecca's sea-blue eyes were as shining as always, her smile as warm and comforting. Cuddled next to her was a very young child, around four years of age, peering out at Sarah from under her dirty cap with enormous brown eyes that held terror and confusion and innocence all at once. Sarah remembered her as Dorothy Good, the girl who went with Rebecca in the wagon when the constable had come for her. She wondered why the child was hanging on to Rebecca and not her own mother, who was one of the first to be jailed.

Sarah rose to a sitting position, blinking several times. Rebecca lifted a hand to her sister's face, wiping away the tears from her cheek. "Dear Sarah," she said, smiling sadly. "How did you come to be here?"

Sarah sighed and told her sister the whole story. How mortified she was to be taken into a back room, told to disrobe completely, and give herself over to a humiliating examination of her entire body. The women who poked and prodded her were her own neighbors and fellow church members, people with whom she had worked side-by-side for years, people she had helped in times of sickness. Now their eyes were cold, and some appeared downright afraid of her as they proceeded with their inspection. "What are you seeking?" Sarah had demanded over and over, confused, trying to cover her nakedness with her hands, although no one answered her. Finally one of them cried out: "Tis here, I have found it! Look, women: the witch's tit sits most obviously on her hip!" The women all took turns pushing their faces to within two inches of Sarah's bare hip, each nodding gravely as they moved away. Sarah herself looked down at herself, and saw the small skin protrusion that she had had since birth. She remembered showing it to her mother when she was very young, wondering about it. Joanna had chuckled and lifted her bodice to reveal the exact same mark on her own hip. "Tis nothing but a birthmark, Sarah," Joanna had reassured her. "It is how God reminds us that we are not perfect, and that we should always seek His guidance and wisdom."

Sarah's own trial was very much like the others she had seen before her own, including that of Rebecca. She was surprised, though, to see that Judges Corwin and Hathorne were not at the head table this time, replaced by two men she did not recognize. The people of Salem Village knew well Corwin and Hathorne, as they resided in Salem Town and were involved with many different aspects of the community, including the church. But the men who led her own examination were strangers. One was tall and elderly, his long hair white yet his head balding on top. He looked stern and worried, yet he exuded a sense of authority, and the people in the meeting house seemed cowed by his presence. His companion was much younger, perhaps forty-five years of age, a pudgy face with a shock of black hair and small eyeglasses perched on his prominent nose. Why were they here? Sarah wondered. Why were the Salem judges sitting at a side table instead of leading the proceedings, as before?

After Reverend Higginson gave the opening prayer, Sarah, along with everyone else in the meeting house, learned that the two presiding judges were Deputy Governor Thomas Danforth and the great Judge Samuel Sewall, from Cambridge and Boston. As soon as that fact was announced, Sarah found it difficult to breathe, and could hardly stand. Boston men? And such distinguished ones at that? News of the Salem Village witchcraft accusations had obviously spread across the colony, and now the highest leadership in Massachusetts was getting involved. What did that bode for Sarah's chances, along with those of her sister's? As Sarah turned her head to catch the eye of her husband Peter, sitting close to the front of the room with her sister Mary, Mary's husband her Issac and Francis Nurse. Peter looked encouraging, and smiled, surreptitiously pointing toward the judges. Suddenly it was as if Sarah could read his mind: perhaps this was for the best. Perhaps these men, with the wisdom and courage it took to run the entire colony, could put a stop to the hysteria.

She didn't have much time to think, though, as Mr. Danforth called the girls one by one to testify against her. Once again, as ever, the girls would swoon and sway, pointing their little fingers at Sarah, screaming as if being tortured. Sarah answered the deputy governor's questions truthfully and, she hoped, righteously. She began to feel a slight sense of optimism when she saw that he asked his questions carefully, and looked her straight in the eye when she responded. His face did not have the same degree of anger and hatred that she observed with Corwin and Hathorne – and Reverend Parris, for that matter. Yet it was also obvious that neither Danforth nor Sewall were unaffected by the girls' torments, which were as realistic and frightening as ever.

When Ann Putnam Jr. was telling the judges how the specters of Sarah and Rebecca had come to her mother with arms full of winding sheets, taking her baby brother James away to his grave, John Gould made his way to the front of the room. He looked huge in comparison to the slightness of his young niece, and the sight of him brought a new pang of fear to Sarah's heart. As the man put a big hand on Ann Jr's shoulders, looking down at her with a glance of familial love, Sarah's mind drifted to an earlier time. Time seemed to stand still as she remembered seeing Edmund Bridges go head-to-head with Gould for so many years. She recalled having to leave her home to start again in Salem Town, her children mere babes, because John Gould sued her husband. John Gould, who brought her mother to court because he thought the minister had drunk too much from his own cup at his supper. John Gould, her father's old friend who switched sides in the boundary disputes between Topsfield and Salem Village, joining the Putnams in tormenting Isaac Esty and Frances Nurse about the wood on their land.

All of these connections came flooding back to Sarah, and it was as if she could see the previous thirty years all at once. All of the feuds, the outrages between her family and this other one. Is it really coming to this, John Gould finally winning the battle by putting her into jail for witchcraft? She remembered all of the warnings she received her whole life, first from her parents, then from her sisters, and then from her husbands and her brothers-in-law to keep her mouth shut. Don't be so stubborn. Don't complain when she sees injustice at the hands of the wealthy like the Goulds and the Putnams. Accept her lot in life. She never could obey, try as she might. And she did try. She always wanted to be more like her sisters. Docile. Good. Was this the punishment she would receive for being so outspoken? But if that were true, how was it that both she and Rebecca were being accused, two sisters from the same womb, yet diametrically different?

Sarah remembered, too, how her mother used to talk about how angry the Putnams were because of the bequests they never received, because of the miscarriages that Goody Putnam suffered from – all while the fortunes of the Towne siblings seemed to flourish. She recalled the nasty looks she and her sisters would receive when they came to church on Sundays, how the anger trickled down to young Ann Putnam Jr., who teased and tormented Sarah's daughter Alice. Goodman Putnam even tried to take Isaac Esty to court for helping Reverend Burroughs, many years ago, repay Putnam's father, the elder Thomas – whereas the younger Putnam would prefer to send the reverend to debtor's prison. The animosity of that family had always seemed like a mere nuisance, nothing to really worry about. But now who was on the forefront of these accusations? It had seemed ridiculous that Rebecca had been accused. Now it seemed to make some kind of awful sense.

John Gould's own voice shocked her back into the present. He told Judges Danforth and Sewall some of the same stories the girls relayed: how Sarah's specter had supposedly tormented both Ann Jr. and Ann Sr. How she and Rebecca were at fault for killing baby James.

"Besides," Gould said, pointing his finger at Sarah with blazing eyes. "Tis fitting that Goody Cloyce is a witch, as her mother was before her."

At that, Sarah could no longer appear obedient and docile, no matter how much it might be impressing the Boston judges. "You, sir, are a grievous liar!" she screamed, pointing back at Gould, who towered over her. She went to scratch at his face as if she were a feral cat, but George Herrick held her back. The crowd went wild with shouts.

It took Danforth and Sewall several minutes to bring back order to the proceedings. They looked to Sarah quite dazed, as if they had never seen anything like what was going on before their very eyes. Sarah sank in a chair and asked for water. When it was given to her, she drank of it, and then slumped in her seat, covering her eyes with her hands.

"He lies," Sarah said again, but this time quieter. "My mother was a saint, a pillar of the church. This Goodman Gould insisted on punishing her because of her allegiance to a minister he detested. He is the one to blame for her suffering before she died. He is the one who started the witch rumor way back then."

"Do you not see?" Ann Jr. suddenly cried out. "She goes now to be with her sister the witch!"

Not one of the magistrates asked Sarah any more questions about her accusations of John Gould's bias in the case.

Rebecca now shook her head with sadness as Sarah told the tale. "But Sarah," the old woman said. "You said that the deputy governor and his fellow seemed different from the Salem Village judges. Yet still they send you to jail?"

"Aye," Sarah responded, woe in her eyes.

The little girl at Rebecca's side had fallen asleep on her lap, her dirty thumb in her mouth. Rebecca continued to stroke the girl's hair. "This is Dorothy Good," she said. "It seems the same happened to her. She couldn't even comprehend what was being said about her. Such a tiny thing. So innocent. Her mother is here, see beyond that wall? She fares poorly, and her babe does worse. She raves in the pain of sickness, yet the jailers do not come to her aid."

Sarah looked around, and could see all of them: Goody Good, Osborne, and Corey, along with Tituba, who was alert, having listened intently to Sarah's entire story. When Sarah saw her, she was filled with rage. "You, woman!" she shouted, and the others quickly came to attention, watching. "You started this whole mess, did you not? I saw you telling those judges what they wanted to hear. You spared no detail, no? So tell me, how is it that you send your miserable specter to attack those little girls? I, who have been accused of the same thing – and all of these women too – would surely like to know!"

She felt a surprisingly firm touch of Rebecca's hand on her arm, pulling her back. "Sarah," Rebecca said. "Do not blame the poor woman. She was sorely beaten to make her confess as she did."

"Aye, the woman tells the truth!" Tituba whimpered. "Mr. Parris, he beat me so bloody I could hardly stand. My husband John Indian tried to help but it was no use. If I had not confessed, surely I was to die!"

Sarah, filled with bitterness, made a noise of disgust. "Better you had died than to bring such agony to the rest of us."

"Sarah, Sarah, remember God's call for us to love!" Rebecca chided. Sarah bristled, and was about to chide her sister right back. To Sarah, God had deserted them. Yet when she turned to Rebecca, she was taken aback once again at her frailty, how pale was her skin. Her sister had always made sure to dress neatly, her hair primly pulled into a bun inside her cap, always clean. To see her now, her bodice and skirts ragged and filthy, her hands almost black with dirt, it broke Sarah's heart, and her habitual annoyance at Rebecca's goodness disappeared.

Sarah sank to her sister's side once more, and this time it was she who took Rebecca in her arms, comforting her. "I thought I would never see you again, my dear, dear one," she whispered. "What is to become of us?"

~ ~ ~

The night after Sarah's examination, Samuel Sewall and Thomas Danforth rode directly to Cotton Mather's home in Boston. Both men rode in the carriage in silence, too stunned and lost in their own thoughts to say much of anything, clasping their hands, trying to pray. They had sent word ahead that they wanted to report their experience to Mr. Mather, who was waiting back in Boston filled with great curiosity.

It was dark by the time they reached the Mather townhouse, just a block away from the Second Church in North Square. The men were ushered into the front parlor by Cotton's maidservant, but turned down any offer of food or drink, even though they had not eaten anything since before the witch examinations had begun that morning. They were both too agitated to enjoy any simple form of hospitality.

"What news from Salem Village?" Cotton asked, motioning for his friends to sit at two rocking chairs in the corner of the room. It was a chilly spring evening and the fire in the hearth was burning bright. The minister eyed the two men, who were obviously distressed.

"I can almost not speak of it," Samuel said, putting his head in his hand. "Indeed neither Thomas nor I could discuss it on our ride south."

Cotton closed his eyes and put his hands together as if in prayer. "I suspected as much," he said. "So the devil does indeed walk amongst us."

"Aye, tis true," Thomas said, his voice scratchy and rough. "We have seen his work with our own eyes."

The men went on to tell Cotton about what they had seen and heard, and about how they sent Sarah Cloyce to jail. As they relayed the story, Cotton listened carefully, his head bowed, his hands still folded in prayer.

"And this woman," he said when the men finished their tale. "She was tormenting the poor children?"

"Aye," Thomas answered. "Although she claimed over and over that she was innocent. Indeed it was difficult for me to believe that such a church-going woman could be so evil. I tried very hard to open my heart to her, yet we do know that the devil can go about in human form. And he is a trickster. What better guises would he take than the seemingly most righteous in the community? It is truly a heinous business."

"The woman did torment the children most grievously," Samuel agreed. "If she would raise a hand, the children – and some adults, too – would raise theirs as well, even though they tried to stop themselves. They had no power over the specters that taunted them. It was clear to us."

"We must stop this!" Cotton cried, standing up so quickly that he knocked over the chair he had been sitting in. The maidservant, hearing the ruckus, came back into the room and quickly righted it so that her master could sit down again. Cotton, usually a kind, gentle man, pushed her away in a fit of pique, and she ran back into the kitchen, wondering at what must be disturbing him so. "With everything that my father has accomplished in this colony, and men like the two of you as well – with all that we have suffered at the hands of the King, the heathen Indians, the Quakers, we cannot fall now. We have to fight for God's dominion!"

"I agree, Cotton. Yet when does your father arrive?" Thomas asked. "They say in Salem Village that there might be more witches to be found. But without the charter in our hands, we cannot proceed with the trials that would naturally proceed after the initial examinations."

"More witches?" Cotton asked, wary.

"Aye, more," Samuel responded. "The girls tell of witch's sabbaths, with many false congregants. They also tell of a tall man who leads them all."

Cotton wrung his hands in agony. "I must go to God in prayer, gentlemen," he said, almost in tears. "I must ask for His guidance. At times like these I wish for my dear father's wisdom. I have led his church with what I hope has been a solid command. Yet it seems that we are embarked upon a true holy war, one that perhaps needs more than I can provide."

"Cotton, you are indeed a young man," Thomas said, standing and putting a hand on the minister's shoulder. "You are young enough to be my grandson. And I have worked with your father at the College for many years now. But I tell you this: you have seen such witchcraft before. You have fought against it and have won. We on the General Court will need your pastoral guidance, believe you this."

"Before you go to your own prayer, I ask that the three of us pray together?" Samuel suggested, standing with the other two men. "We must ask for strength as we proceed into these dark days."

Later, as Thomas summoned his own carriage to take him home across the river to Cambridge, he could not shake the day's images from his mind. He knew in his heart that he had done the right thing in jailing Goody Cloyce. He knew it. Those girls, and women like Goody Putnam, they were sorely abused, that was obvious. And why would they, mere innocents and so young, contrive to say anything but the truth? Who would choose to be so tormented? And the devil was always lurking, waiting to prey upon the righteous.

Yet something in the countenances of that woman continued to prick at his conscience, and he could not stop remembering her pleading eyes. If the afflicted were not present, and he met with this Sarah Cloyce alone, he would have had a very hard time believing that she was so evil. But she became so angry at the accusations. At first so docile, her fury was like a conflagration overtaking her once the girls started pointing fingers at her. He had never seen such awful ferocity in a woman. He truly felt he was watching the very pit of hell opening up in front of him. No wonder the people of Salem Village were distraught, to have that kind of evil walking about them. Yes, he had done the right thing. Goody Cloyce was most certainly a witch.

~ ~ ~

Two days later, the huge iron and wooden door to the Salem Town jail scraped across the floor, making the ragged prisoners inside jump with fear. It was dark in the cell and the sudden brightness of the sun that exploded in the room made the people's eyes blink as they shaded them with their hands, trying to make out the scene in front of them. Sarah, who had been dozing on Rebecca's frail shoulder in the corner of the room, scrambled to her feet to see what was going on. Ten people – men and women both this time – were roughly pushed into the room, and the door closed loudly behind them. Sarah recognized the looks of bewilderment and terror that were on the newcomers' faces as they tried to adjust their own sight to the sudden dimness. She didn't recognize them, but held her hands out to them in what she hoped looked like a welcoming gesture.

It was then that the crowd parted and Sarah's face crumpled in despair as her sister Mary came forward, ashen faced. "Oh, no!" she cried as Mary stepped uncertainly toward her sister. Mary, too, was an old woman now, and not steady on her feet. Sarah's exclamation broke the waiting silence, and some of the women in the group started whimpering, the men shouting.

Sarah took Mary into her arms, and Mary gave her whole weight to her sister, almost unable to stand. Rebecca, behind them, started praying aloud. "Oh, Jesus, Lord," Sarah heard Rebecca chant. "Oh, Jesus, Lord, please protect us. Please deliver us from this misery. Please let Your face to shine upon us. Oh, my Lord above."

Looking over Mary's head – Sarah had towered over her two sisters since she became an adult – she demanded: "What has occurred? Why have you all been brought here together?"

Sarah Wildes, whom Sarah knew well from her days in Topsfield, came forward. "We have all been accused, as you have," she said, answering Sarah's earlier question. "The girls cry out against many people now. The accusations have spread to Topsfield, to Beverly, and Salem Town, too. This is Mary English. She is married to one of the wealthiest men in the Town. No one is safe."

Mrs. English, a stately woman in good dress – so unlike the more plain clothing of the goodwives around her – came forward and nodded at Sarah. The wealthy woman had a look of haughtiness about her, but her eyes were also filled with terror. Sarah stared at her. They are going after the merchants now? she thought. What is happening here?

"Sit, all of you," Sarah said, trying to sound confident, hoping her calm words would stop the new arrivals from their tears and shouting. "It does no good to protest."

She had to half-carry her troubled sister to join Rebecca, who was by now too weak to stand to welcome her. But just as Sarah had done the week before, Mary fell into Rebecca's lap and allowed herself to be comforted with her sister's soothing words and prayers. As she looked down at the two, Sarah's heart constricted once more. Has the world turned itself upside down, she thought, that she and her sisters could be here? Life had always felt tenuous in the colony. She didn't remember when she was completely without fear, of so many things – crops failing, drought, disease, Indian massacres, unjust taxation from the mother country, the perils of sin, boundary disputes, minister problems. But now it was as if all of those troubles, all of the tribulations that had pestered the colony for so long, were exploding, making the people in the colony lose their minds. It was like a terrible, killing fire, chewing up the dry tinder of Salem Village's long-festering problems. When would it stop?

"What happened, dear sister?" she asked, looking about the room, directing the question to everyone who had just arrived. Sarah Wildes came forward, looking into Sarah's face with her big, innocent eyes. "The same girls continue to accuse us," she answered. "Thomas Putnam and John Gould, along with their friends like Nathaniel Ingersoll, Joseph Hutchinson and Jonathan Walcott, all have signed the complaints on behalf of the children. It is the same group. Yet their pointing fingers are moving beyond our little village."

"But why?" Sarah demanded, clenching her fists. The last week had been hard on her, as well as the other prisoners. There was little food and water, no glimpse of the outdoors, and they were always in the dim light of the inner jail cell. The prisoners could not wash nor did they have any privacy as they used the makeshift chamber pot in the corner – a bucket that the jailer only emptied every other day. Sarah was now as filthy as Rebecca and the others who had been there before her, and fear had taken its toll. But her stubbornness had not abated, and now, with so many new prisoners, it threatened to overtake her. "What evidence do they use?"

"Tis the same with you," Sarah Wildes said. "The girls are tormented by our specters."

"Psssht!" Sarah hissed, disgusted, looking about the room. "And have you, have any of you, sent your specters to hurt these children?"

Everyone shook their heads in unison, looking down at their feet.

"Who is here?" Mrs. English asked, eyeing the women who had been in that dank hole before she arrived. "My husband Philip and I had received word of these examinations, yet never did travel to Salem Village to observe them. They tore me away from him before I could converse with him, so I know nothing."

Sarah made introductions, and Mrs. English was particularly horrified to see Sarah Good in the corner, clutching her tiny baby who had stopped her squalling two days before. A few feet away from her lay old Sarah Osborne, who, Sarah told her, hadn't moved since the night before. Tituba remained separate from the group, cowering in the opposite corner, hoping against hope not to be bothered by anyone.

"What did they say you did, Mrs. English?" Sarah asked. "The girls do not even know you, do they not? Nor some of the others here?"

"They tell the judges that I am a witch," the woman answered. "That I come to them in their sleep and bite them, urging them to sign the devil's book."

"But how do they know you?" Sarah persisted.

"They do not. My husband has business dealings with some men of the Village, like Joseph Putnam. But of Joseph Putnam's brothers, we have no experience."

Sarah nodded, as the pieces of the puzzle seemed to fall into place in her head. "Joseph Putnam! He is my own son-in-law, and a good man. He has no love for these brothers, who were borne from a different mother," she said. "There is great animosity between them. This might be the source of their distrust of you and your husband."

Mrs. English stared at Sarah. "Could this be true?" she demanded. "And the girls are truly not tormented?"

By this time the rest of the prisoners circled the two women, listening carefully, staring in wonder. Sarah shook her head. "I cannot say," she replied. "It does appear that the girls are indeed in great pain. They suffer grievously. But I can tell you that I am certain that I am clear, that I am a righteous woman. As are my two innocent sisters. We never did no witchcraft, nor did we bother with these girls, nor Goody Putnam herself. Have you?"

"Of course not!" Mrs. English bristled. The rest of the group mumbled their denials as well.

"Sarah! Sarah!" Mary cried, finally looking up from Rebecca's lap. "Do come here and talk with me. Do not rile the prisoners. I need you!"

Sarah looked around the group, sensing that they had need of her counsel, knowing their panic. She wanted desperately to help, to make some sense of what was happening. And she noticed that some of the prisoners, both the ones who just arrived and the ones who had been there for weeks, started looking to her for guidance and leadership. Even the men. They are reacting to my strength, she thought. My supposed strength. At the moment Sarah did feel a kind of small power run through her, and she recognized it. It came from extreme rage. And that extreme rage was borne out of a level of injustice that Sarah still couldn't quite fully understand.

Yet she could not stay with these poor wretches, giving them comfort while her own sisters were clamoring for her attention. She knew how she had fallen apart when she herself was in Mary's position, only days ago.

Sarah ducked her head in a quick goodbye to the others and went to Mary and Sarah. "Be with us, Sarah," Rebecca said, and even though her words were weak, Sarah could only obey, as she always did with her oldest sister. "Mary needs our love."

Mary went on to tell them her story. The young girls and also Ann Putnam Sr. had cried out against her, Goody Putnam being the most vocal. "At services several days ago she stood and started screaming, accusing me of taking her baby away in winding sheets," Mary said, her eyes wide with fright. "And that gave rise to a great clamor from the girls. And then Goodman Gould cried out that mother was a witch in her day, and that I belonged in jail just like the rest of my sisters." Mary was examined in front of Judges Corwin and Hathorne – apparently this time the judges from Boston didn't see fit to oversee the proceedings for some reason. Not much of her story differed from the experiences of the other two sisters. The meeting house had been filled with villagers, and this time people had traveled from other towns just to try to catch a glimpse of both the accused and the afflicted. The crowd had spilled out into the meeting house yard, and those outside struggled to hear through open windows. The same girls screamed from their pains, Goody Putnam joining them, and fingers were pointed at Mary. The judges peppered her with the same questions, over and over. Why did she bewitch these girls? Who else was with her in her devilish coven? Nothing Mary could say could convince them of her innocency. It was like the same horrible nightmare was being had over and over again, and the sleeper could not wake.

Rebecca and Sarah held their sister, and Rebecca prayed to God once again, rocking her wasting body back and forth, her eyes closed in deep concentration.

It won't do any good, Sarah thought. Tis certain that we are lost. All of us.

CHAPTER TEN

May 1692
Salem Village

"Where have you been, Ann?" Goody Putnam asked her daughter who had just come into the house with a basket full of spring flowers, trailed by Mercy Lewis behind her. The older woman was peeved, as she had had to spend the afternoon doing all of the household chores – catching and plucking a chicken for dinner, washing the week's clothes in the huge copper pot over the outdoor fire, peeling potatoes – by herself, without the help of her daughter or her maidservant Mercy. Now the two girls looked pleased with themselves, smiling secretly to each other, and Ann handed her mother a single sprig of a bloodroot flower, its tender white petals already drooping from lack of water.

"Here is a blossom I picked just for you, mother," Ann said sweetly, ignoring the question. Mercy giggled behind her. Ann Sr. took the flower and the basket and grimaced.

"You have left me to much work this day," she complained. "I ask again: where have you two been?"

"We were at the parsonage, mother," Ann Jr. finally replied. "Abigail, Elizabeth, Mary Walcott, and us too."

"You are shirking your duties here at home, Ann," Ann Sr. pressed. But once again her daughter did not answer her, waving away her comment with the flick of her small hand. The girl lifted the lid of the cider barrel and filled two pewter cups, handing one to her friend.

"Let us go upstairs, Mercy," she said airily. "I have need of a rest."

Ann Sr. watched them go, forlorn and frustrated. For weeks now she had not been able to control her daughter in the way that parents always treated their children in the colony. It had been that way for generations: children and servants did as they were bid to do, and had little power over their own fates, not until they grew to be adults. They were silent until asked to speak, and any stubbornness was punished, sometimes with a strop. It was especially important to discipline young girls, so that they would be ready to submit to their eventual husbands, and of course to the church.

Yet since the witch examinations had started, the village had started to treat the afflicted girls with a kind of frightened respect – and Ann Sr. and Thomas had followed suit, despite the fact that two of them lived in their own home. And despite the fact that Ann Sr. herself was tormented by the evil witches that were laying waste to the village's religious fortress. The girls could come and go as they pleased, ignoring their duties at home, taking for themselves the agency and power usually reserved for their elders. No one dared to question their actions, for fear of being accused of witchcraft, as so many already had been. The girls walked around like queens of the village, and were obviously enjoying themselves in the times between their tortured fits.

Not that Ann Sr. worried that her daughter would accuse her of witchcraft, nor any of the other girls, including her own niece Mary Walcott. Rather, she and Thomas agreed that they must let Ann and the others proceed as they would; otherwise any rift within the family might change the way the wind was blowing in the village, with so many being sent to jail based solely on the girls' – and Ann Sr.'s – reports of spectral attacks. But it was a trying time for Ann Sr., without the usual household help from Ann and Mercy. Perhaps it was a good price to pay for what they were doing: ridding the colony of these nefarious witches. Since Mary Esty was sent to jail, Ann Sr. herself had stopped seeing the witches' specters, and they no longer attacked her, and she was most grateful to be free of the pain and anguish. She still mourned the murder of her poor little babe James, and was constantly vigilant for more signs of evildoing. Despite the fact that she was no longer afflicted, she knew, through the girls' reports, that the epidemic wasn't stopping at the village boundaries, but had spread to neighboring towns as well. It may only be a matter of time that witches were found in Boston itself. A shiver of fear went through Ann as she pondered the thought.

Thomas came into the house, having finished his work in the barn, expecting the evening meal soon. He heard the loud giggling of his daughter and servant from the upstairs room, and frowned at his wife. "I gather it is a good day for them," he commented. "I am never sure what sound I'll find whenever I come into this house: laughter or screams of torment.

"Aye, their happiness seems incongruous with what is bedeviling our village," Ann agreed. "Yet I welcome these lucid moments.

Having been tormented myself, I would not wish it for my daughter, nor any of the girls. Perhaps this is the way God soothes them and allows them rest in between their suffering times."

Thomas accepted the cup of ale that his wife offered him, and sat heavily in a chair, running his hand through his thinning hair. "Jonathan and I signed new warrants today," he said. "I imagine there will be new examinations within a week."

"You are doing the Lord's work, Thomas," Ann said, raising her eyes to the ceiling and pressing her hands together as if in prayer. "Soon we will make Salem Village righteous again, as it was in your father's day. When everyone walked with God and the Putnams were the undisputed leaders of the community."

Finally Thomas smiled, and Ann was grateful for it. "You are right, Ann," he said. "We should have known what was truly happening these last years. My own cursed step brother Joseph, the way the Estys and Cloyces and Nurses have fared so well without any extra work on their part. Why did we not see that the Devil was behind all of that? We were asleep, Ann, until it was almost too late. I thank God that we have uncovered the heinous plot, although I weep that it has required such horrible sacrifice and pain to you and our dear daughter."

"Aye, and do not forget how that erstwhile minister George Burroughs held sway over our village," Ann added. "How he allowed his congregation to forego attending sabbath meetings, how he sometimes drank. And remember how you yourself had to take him to court in order to get him to pay his debts to your father? All along he had the support of your step brother, and that horrid Isaac Esty."

"Now I see that those seemingly disparate occasions are now of a piece," Thomas said. "All part of the Devil's long term plan to take over God's own family. Now I understand that our distrust of my stepbrother was warranted, even back to the time he was born."

They didn't notice that the laughter coming from above had ceased, as they continued with their conversation. Upstairs, Ann and Mercy had left the room to once again listen to the Putnams' talk from the top of the ladder. They had done so many times before, having learned weeks ago that whenever adults talked in the hall below - be it Ann's parents, or Jonathan Walcott or John Gould - they could learn a great deal about how their accusations and torments were affecting the village and beyond. They continued to eavesdrop, despite the fact that often afterward they were struck with the pinches and stabs of the specters of ever-increasing numbers of people.

Now as they heard the name of Burroughs, they looked at each other in wide-eyed surprise. They knew that the minister had left Salem Village for the District of Maine six years ago, and not much had been heard from him since. Ann still remembered how livid her father had been when Isaac Esty took up a collection from the congregation to pay Mr. Burroughs' debts to her grandfather, preventing the minister from being duly prosecuted. And how her whole family never really wanted Burroughs to lead the church in the first place. But to hear his name mentioned in her home after so many years was unexpected. And to hear it spoken in conjunction with the battle against the Devil? Interesting. Interesting indeed.

~ ~ ~

The way was slow from Cambridge to Boston, as it had just rained for two days and the paths were awash with mud. Thomas Danforth had to hold onto the seat underneath him to keep from toppling over as his carriage wheels dipped into one ditch after another. His mood was foul, and the joints in his old knees throbbed in pain, as they usually did in bad weather. He would have preferred joining his compatriots in Cambridge, and indeed suggested his Bow Street townhouse as a meeting place, but Cotton Mather wished to meet at his church in North Square instead. Thomas suspected he knew what Cotton wanted to discuss, since Samuel Sewall was invited as well, and witchcraft had become the sole subject of conversation among the three men for the past month.

But he wasn't looking forward to this meeting. News of the trials in Salem Village was now a daily occurrence, so he was aware that many people had been examined by that time. And still he was hounded with memories of the examination over which he and Samuel had recently presided. Now, worse, he had had two terrifying dreams about that woman, that Goody Cloyce – dreams that had caused his wife Mary to shake him awake, concerned with his cries of agony. The nightmares were the same both times: the woman was sobbing, sitting in a darkened room, and Thomas could see her children crying out for her as well, but they couldn't reach their mother. Goody Cloyce raised her voice in prayer to God, and a light shone above her, and at first it was beautiful, but then it became a conflagration that overtook the woman and her children both. In the dream he, too, was engulfed in the flames.

Thomas refused to tell his wife of these dreams, which worried her, because he was not someone who was often bothered by nightmares. But he could not admit the misgivings he had had since his trip north, not when he still believed that witchcraft was running rampant in Essex County.

He had always thought of himself as a kind man. A generous one. Had he not stirred up considerable ire from his fellow magistrates when he worked so hard to negotiate peace with the Abenaki to the north, when all most colonists wanted was to wipe them off the face of the earth? Had he not been more than fair in his oversight of Harvard's finances, and in his court decisions over granting land to the colony's leaders? When he himself was granted close to one hundred acres to the area south of the Sudbury River, did he not give the Wampanoags silver for them, even though he wasn't required to by law? All of this was why the colonists had voted him Lieutenant Governor under Mr. Bradstreet, and why his leadership was still so strong, even now as he was well into his seventies. Could he not be confident that he had ruled correctly in Salem Village? Why was he tormented with so many questions?

Usually a more genial man, today Thomas harrumphed at his coachman as he stepped down from the finally-stable carriage in front of the church. He looked up at the sky – which was still menacing although the rain had stopped – sighed, and went into the building. Samuel and Cotton were already there, their heads together, sitting around the communion table beneath the pulpit. As Thomas walked down the aisle toward them, his boots clicked on the wooden planks beneath him, and the sound seemed to echo throughout the huge room. He was a member of the Second Church in Cambridge and had not been inside the Mathers' church very often, but on his infrequent visits, the box pews on either side of him now were usually filled with parishioners. The room seemed empty and cold without them.

"Mr. Danforth!" Cotton cried out, beckoning him forward. "A minister is now accused in Salem Village!"

Thomas stopped in his tracks, alarmed by both the news and the incongruity of the young minister shouting so, before he even greeted his guest. He himself did not choose to be so impolite, despite the news, and waited until he reached his friends before responding.

"What minister? Mr. Parris, is it?" Thomas asked, shaking the hands of both men. "It is strange, to say the least. Yet the torments started in his own parsonage…."

"Nay, Thomas," Samuel stopped him. "Mr. Parris remains vigilant on the side of righteousness. No, the girls have accused a man named George Burroughs. He was the villagers' minister for a time, but has served in the District of Maine these several years."

"Ah, yes," Thomas said. "Now I recognize the name. He leads the church in Wells, does he not? What has he to do with Essex County?"

"The accusations have reached beyond the original borders," Cotton said, clearly agitated. "Thomas Putnam and Jonathan Walcott have signed out a warrant for his arrest. The girls say he torments them, and – dreadful, dreadful – killed his own wife when he was their minister."

"Do you remember the tall man that the girls spoke of when we led the proceedings?" Samuel asked. "We are told by the judges that such a man has been mentioned many times before. Finally we may have reached the root of the evil. The poor afflicted tell of a whole group of witches being led in an execrable black communion, with Mr. Burroughs at the helm. And on Mr. Parris' land no less! I am much saddened by this news, as I knew Mr. Burroughs when we were at Harvard together. I have always thought him a righteous man. If the Devil has won over his heart, I fear for the very soul of Massachusetts Bay Colony."

Thomas sat heavily in one of the chairs near the table. Suddenly he felt very, very tired. "This is dangerous business," he said slowly, looking up at his friends with concern in his eyes. "A man of God's church is to be accused? This seems to me to be beyond comprehension. On my many trips to Maine I have heard of this Mr. Burroughs. He sounds as if he is an upright man."

In fact, the magistrates in Boston had received many reports from Burroughs and other leaders in the Maine settlements. The Indian attacks on these areas were brutal, and many were slaughtered. At one point Burroughs had narrowly escaped with his own life and that of twenty other survivors, who took small skiffs to an island off the coast. They had huddled there, feeding themselves on fish from the ocean and mussels and clams from the rocky beaches, for several weeks before returning to the mainland.

The other two sat down with him. "What are you saying, Thomas?" Samuel asked. "Do you doubt the accusations?"

Thomas remembered the angst he had been enduring of late, repeating in his mind over and over the examination that he and Samuel had overseen. He remembered the dreams that awakened him at night. Was it doubt? Or just a review of his actions, ensuring they were done in complete lawfulness? He was always one to be careful with his speech and with his decisions. Was his recent upset merely part of that?

"I cannot say," he said haltingly. "I merely want us all to move forward thoughtfully. Once a man of God is accused…."

"Tell me again, my friends," Cotton interjected. "Tell me about the examination you witnessed. What was the evidence brought about?"

Samuel and Thomas repeated their story, trying hard to remember all of the details. As they did, Thomas felt reassured. Those poor girls, and Goody Putnam, too – their pain was so believable.

"And tell me, too," Cotton persisted. "The girls said that they were pinched and pricked by the specters of Goody Cloyce. Was there any other evidence presented? And did the accused confess?"

"Aye," Samuel answered. "A witch's mark was found on her body."

"But no, she did not confess," Thomas said. "In fact, she was quite adamant about her innocence."

"Hmm," Cotton said, getting up from his chair and pacing the floor in front of the table. Samuel and Thomas looked at each other, and Samuel shrugged, not knowing what was in the minister's thoughts. They both said nothing, leaving him to his ruminations. Gazing at his friend, Thomas realized once more how young and stalwart he looked, over twenty years younger his junior. Thomas was grateful to share the bench with such a reasonable, just man. Many of the colony's Assistants were merchants like both of them, most of them attending Harvard yet not following their fathers' footsteps into the ministry. When Samuel married Hannah Hull many years ago, he was brought into Hannah's father John's business as mint master and silversmith, making him one of the wealthiest men of Boston. Yet he also served as one of the most respected judges in the colony, even though he was still relatively young. It reassured Thomas that there were men such as Samuel overseeing the business of the colony. And it reassured him that their work was supported by ministers like the Mathers. As the three men sat in silence, the niggling doubts that had hounded Thomas abated, and he gave a long exhale, relieved that he was not alone.

"This focus on spectral evidence," Cotton finally said, "it does not bode well. The Bible tells us that the Devil can take on the shape of an innocent person, as he did when Saul called upon the Witch of Endor to raise the specter of Samuel. How can we be certain that this is not the case in Salem?"

Both Samuel and Thomas frowned, thinking about what the minister just said. They knew the story to which Cotton was referring. It was in the Book of Samuel, about a witch who supposedly brought forth Samuel, the newly-dead king, so that he could give Saul – Samuel's successor – advice on how to fight the Philistines. It was clear from the tale that it was not Samuel that the witch raised, but the Devil in disguise. If a witch in the Bible could work with the Devil to embody Samuel – who had done no wrong – could not Satan be taking on the specters of innocent people?

"Are you saying that the judges should not take this evidence into account?" Samuel asked, "Because Thomas and I did that very thing. The afflicted were most believable, and they insisted that the Devil was overtaking Goody Cloyce."

Thomas' anxiety returned, as a sickening wave came over him. What had he done?

"Nay, nay," Cotton replied. "This evidence should be strongly considered, and I commend your work, as I do Judges Corwin and Hathorne, who are equally fit for the task as the two of you are. I am merely saying that spectral evidence should not be considered as the sole symptom of witchcraft. And in the cases that you adjudicated, indeed there was other evidence submitted, as you just reported. The witch's mark is irrefutable."

"I do know that the court has always been careful about such cases," Samuel said. "From what I have learned, no court has executed an accused witch for decades, save that of the Goody Glover case with which you were so involved, Cotton."

"Aye, tis true," Cotton agreed. "And Goody Glover was hanged because she easily confessed to the crime. Everyone knows that confession should be the primary evidence of the evil."

"I would like to believe that Samuel and I conducted a just investigation," Thomas said, looking down at his hands in his lap. "But surely twas a most alarming sight, these girls and Goody Putnam, too, in such agony. I have never laid eyes on such a scene before in my life. And I must confess, Cotton, that I could feel, almost as if twas the true, cold hand of the Devil, at my neck when we walked into that room. As if I were in the presence of evil."

"And the people of the village, too," Samuel added. "These good people of God were terrified. Truly the Devil has been loosed in the colony."

"I have no doubt of that, friends," Cotton replied. "And we must do everything in our power to combat him. Especially now that a minister has been accused. We must do so, however, with caution."

All three men nodded their heads in grave agreement.

"I think I shall also write to Judges Corwin and Hathorne," Cotton said. "I want to applaud them for their judicious handling of the cases thus far. But I also think it would be prudent to remind them of the Bible's teachings about the Devil assuming the form of an innocent being."

~ ~ ~

It was a brilliant late May day when Increase Mather's ship first came into sight in Boston Harbor. The harbormaster rang the gong as soon as he spied the glorious flapping white sails on the horizon, casting a dazzling contrast with the azure blue above and below. The ringing was heard through the bustle of the wharves all the way up to the Trimountain. Magistrates, ministers, merchants, indentured servants – they all knew what the tolling foretold, and everyone who was able left their work at hand to make their way down to the docks. By the time the ship dropped anchor, the wharves were lined with Boston residents and even those who had traveled to the city to welcome the arrival of the colony's new charter. Handkerchiefs waved in the breeze, creating a flying sea of white amidst shouts of joy and relief. It was a day to celebrate in the capital.

The first to greet Increase Mather at the bottom of the gang plank was his own son, Cotton, who embraced his father with great gusto. The younger man could be seen with a look of reverence and elation on his face, replicating the feelings of so many in the crowd. By contrast, the great Reverend Mather seemed serious and flinty, adding an element of gravitas to the merrymaking about him. He turned to lend a hand to a second man following him down the gangplank. Everyone knew by now that this was William Phips, the wealthy ship merchant who had worked with Mr. Mather to negotiate the new charter with King William and Queen Mary. When the royals allowed the minister to appoint the new governor of the newly-named Province of Massachusetts Bay, Mr. Mather tapped Mr. Phips for the position. Old Mr. Bradstreet would be out, as well as Mr. Danforth as his lieutenant. Mr. Bradstreet, having reached his 90s by then, was more than happy to retire from public life. Mr. Danforth was not so pleased, especially when he heard that Governor Phips appointed William Stoughton as his lieutenant.

"Stoughton!" he cried, pounding the table at the Anchor Tavern, several blocks up the hill from where he and Samuel Sewall had welcomed the elder Mr. Mather and Mr. Phips. "The man is more a traitor than a lieutenant governor!"

"I know you are disappointed, Thomas," Samuel said, trying to soothe his friend. "I am, too. But the man has gained great favor with the elder Reverend Mather during their long journey to and from England. And I do trust Mr. Mather's judgment."

"My loyalty lies with his son," Thomas spat back. "I would imagine that I was also loved by his father, after all the years I spent serving him at the College. I know not why he turns his back on me at this crucial time in the life of the colony. Have I not steered the ship in seas that have been rife with turmoil? Have I not husbanded Harvard's finances wisely for all these years?"

"Of course you have, my friend. But you have also been controversial at times."

"Why, because I remained true to my convictions that we must negotiate with the Abenaki and the other tribes to the north?" Thomas demanded, but then let out a heavy sigh. "I know as well as you that most people down here in the city would prefer that we destroy all the savages. Do you think that is the reason behind Stoughton's appointment?"

"I know not," Samuel answered. "Mr. Mather was a long time in England with Mr. Phips. His ear might have been bent by the new governor. I worry about his appointment as well. There are many other Boston and Cambridge men who are much more seasoned at governing the colony. Phips' central skill is in growing wealthy with his ships, after such humble beginnings as a farmer's son up in Maine. There is so much strife in Massachusetts, and I do not mention only the witchcraft in Salem Village. I do pray that our two new leaders can manage us well."

~ ~ ~

It took just a week for the General Court to vote in Phips and Stoughton, and for the magistrates to report to them on the issues of the day, including the massacres in the District of Maine and the great number of men and women sitting in both the Salem and Boston jails, accused of witchcraft. Every day more were accused and more imprisoned. The hysteria was taking on a new dimension now that Reverend Burroughs had been accused, examined and jailed. The normal schedule of open trial courts could not handle the sheer numbers of cases that needed to be heard right away. Phips addressed the problem by creating, as one of his first orders, a Court of Oyer and Terminer, a special tribunal that could focus solely on the witchcraft cases outside the normal sitting of the General Court. And then he assigned William Stoughton as the new court's Chief Justice. It wasn't long after that Phips left Boston, traveling to his native Maine to fight the Indians and to oversee the building of a stone fort at Pemaquid, retaking the District of Maine settlement after the French and their Indian allies destroyed the original fortress. Stoughton was left to choose the magistrates for the special court.

Among others, he appointed Samuel Sewall. Thomas Danforth was not selected. The aging judge was much displeased.

CHAPTER ELEVEN

June - July 1692

Salem Village

Sarah Cloyce wanted to curl up in a fetal position but there was no room on the jail floor to lie down. There were too many prisoners' bodies crushed up against hers. And even if she could recline it would have been a nasty business, since the dirt floor had become muddy with sweat and other bodily fluids, combined with the damp the constable brought in on his boots every time he pushed new prisoners into the crowded room. So Sarah put her head in her hands and tried hard to keep her wits about her. She could feel her husband's hand on one of her shoulders, Rebecca's on the other one, but they seemed very far away. Her ears were still ringing with Peter's news: they had just hanged Bridget Bishop for witchcraft.

And more trials were scheduled in the coming weeks. There would be no more waiting, now that the new governor had established the new Court of Oyer and Terminer.

"Sarah, dear Sarah," Peter was whispering in her ear. "The Lord will save us, I am sure of it. Do not fret. Please, dear Sarah. I assure you that you and your sisters are clear. It is well known that Goody Bishop has been accused of witchcraft before, and she often pestered her neighbors in Salem Town. Mr. Noyes testified that she did not attend his church. The difference between you and your sisters and Goody Bishop is like night is to day. You will not suffer the same fate."

But his words of comfort hit deaf ears. A wail went up from the sea of prisoners around her, once the word spread from person to person. Just yesterday the constable had come for Goody Bridget Bishop, but he would not tell anyone what was happening. Sarah and her sisters – and the rest of the prisoners – thought it was just one more routine pre-trial examination. But when night fell and Bridget did not return, a terror came over those within the jail's walls. Many other relatives came to the jail to see their loved ones every day, but often they were not admitted. It was Peter who had been given permission by the constable to visit and to spread the word.

He told them all about what he had observed two days before, which was very much like the previous examinations. The difference was that this time Bridget was questioned in front of more judges besides Mr. Corwin and Hathorne – Mr. Stoughton was now the chief justice, and was accompanied by several others – and also in front of a jury. Besides these discrepancies, the questions were the same. The girls' hysterics were the same. The accused woman's protests of innocency were the same. At this trial, a guilty verdict meant hanging, as everyone knew that witchcraft was a capital crime in Massachusetts. They took Bridget away in a rattling cart and hanged her on Gallows Hill the next day.

Rebecca started to pray out loud, begging God for His guidance and protection. By now her voice was hoarse and barely audible, as water and food were scarce and the prisoners' throats were parched. Peter quickly pulled out a leather flask from beneath his coat and gave it to Rebecca to drink. The old woman pushed it away and pointed to her sisters. Sarah wasn't as generous as her sister, and quickly drank of the sweet cider within. It seemed she couldn't get enough. Already the outside world had dimmed in her mind, along with the normal blessings of life like simple food and drink. Her children's faces faded in front of her, but Hepzibah in particular came to her in fevered dreams, crying out for her Mia. The dark damp around her, the overwhelming stench of the place, the almost-starvation was what she now knew. She and her sisters had tried to hold each other up with the telling of stories from their childhood, memories of better days, and the singing of hymns. But with each passing day, the prospect of hope seemed to gradually evaporate, like water spilled on a stone on a hot summer afternoon. And now, with this news from Peter, Sarah felt true despair. She did not believe that she and her sisters would survive this.

Peter was urging her to have faith. He told her of Hepzibah's warm greeting and of how the farm was faring. Of Hannah's new babe and her continued happiness with Joseph. He neglected to relay how all of Sarah's two younger daughters cried through the night and day, worried so for their mother and aunts. Peter also had news for Sarah's sisters from their husbands as well, trying to cheer them up with tales from the outside as he slid packets of food to each of them. Rebecca continued to pray. Mary sat in abject silence.

"What of the accusers, Peter?" Sarah asked, feeling some sense of agency return to her. "Are any of the Putnams yet accused?"

"Nay," her husband replied. "Hannah's Joseph has made no progress in convincing his half-brothers to cease with their warrants. Both Ann Jr. and her mother continue to cry out against others, as do the maid Mercy Lewis and the Walcott girl. No one dares to rebuke them."

"What of Joseph and Hannah and the babe?" Sarah asked, another fear entering her tortured mind. "Could Joseph's half-brothers turn on him? I certainly wouldn't be surprised if they did. So my dear Hannah is in danger as well!"

Peter tried hard to calm down his wife, to no avail. "Joseph has made preparations to steal off into the night if need be," he assured Sarah. "And now that the new court has been established, the trials can start in earnest."

"The court, the court," Sarah seethed. "The magistrates seem to have lost their senses. Tell me of this new court."

"The new charter has finally arrived with Mr. Mather and the new governor William Phips, after so long waiting. Mr. Phips has appointed Mr. Stoughton as his lieutenant, and the chief justice of the special court. Justices Hathorne and Corwin were certainly aggressive in their dealings with the examinations, but this Mr. Stoughton overtakes them in a new vigor that we have not seen before. He seems a veritable minister on a high pulpit, or a soldier at a most terrible war. The other judges follow his lead."

"And who is to go next, Peter? Which of us here in this hellish jail? Do they not say?"

Peter shook his head, forlorn. "We know not what is to come. The order of trial is uncertain to us who come to observe. Goody Bishop was not the first to be accused, so I do not know why she was tried before the rest. It may be that the magistrates need time to gather witnesses for each trial, and some come easily, some not so much."

Sarah put her head in her hands again, unable to provide any succor to her sisters, nor any of the other prisoners. Suddenly she was overwhelmed by a memory of being a child, and being rocked to sleep by Rebecca. She remembered snuggling under the warm quilts, the soft murmur of her parents' voices below, her sister Mary lying next to her in the loft. She wanted desperately to go back to that time when all seemed right and safe.

"Is there nothing to be done, Goody Cloyce?" Sarah Wildes, one of the other prisoners, shyly approaching the Towne sisters.

Her flaming red hair was now more of a dirty brown, and Sarah could make out the tracks of the younger woman's tears, dragging a swath of white through almost-black cheeks.

"To be done?" Sarah replied, bitterness tasting like poison in her mouth. "Do you think I know any more than you, nay, any of these poor souls? I am not someone who can help any of you."

Peter stared at his wife, totally unaccustomed to her expressing any bit of weakness to anyone. He was terrified that despair would overtake her and she would go down under, unable to do anything to change her fate. This was not the Sarah he knew and fell in love with. His Sarah was fierce, she stood up against injustice, she spoke her mind, even when it hurt her. Who was this woman she was becoming?

For Sarah's part, she no longer cared that she was sinning.

She wished Thomas Putnam and his family dreadful harm.

~ ~ ~

Now that the Court of Oyer and Terminer had been established and an accused witch had been hanged so shortly thereafter, news flew through the colony that this was only the beginning. Abigail Williams, Ann Putnam and their friends continued to point fingers at women and men both. Many times the girls had never before met the ones they accused. There were so many imprisoned that some had to be transferred to the Boston jail because the one in Salem Town became way too overcrowded. While the magistrates in Boston, including Thomas Danforth in his diminished capacity, worked hard to get the colony running again now that they had the new charter from England, most of the settlers themselves were preoccupied with the news from Essex County.

The new Governor Phips was concerned. When he had signed on with Increase Mather, he knew it would take a great deal of effort to lead the colony through the transition ahead. The Indian wars to the north raged on, and the General Court had not met to determine necessary laws while they were waiting for Mr. Mather to return. But he had had no idea that he would be thrown into such a nest of complications that the witchcraft outbreak brought with it. He was hoping that he could just deputize William Stoughton to run the colony while he himself could return to his native Maine to do what he did best: fight the Indians and try to continue his shipbuilding business.

But the Boston magistrates weren't happy with Phips' heading off to the north so quickly after his arrival, and as that word reached him, he knew he had to return. As soon as he arrived back in Boston he summoned Mr. Mather's son Cotton to meet with him at his townhouse in School Street. He had heard that while he – Phips – was overseas with Cotton's father, the younger minister had become interested in the witchcraft cases, having written about a similar situation with the Goodwin children the year before. Increase's influence in the colony was still powerful, and he was enjoying the well-deserved praise he was receiving from the magistrates in Boston for successfully negotiating the new charter. But Phips was more interested in getting advice from Cotton, who had been tracking the progress of the examinations back home and was therefore better placed to know how best to proceed.

"The man strikes me as a strong leader," Cotton reported to Thomas Danforth and Samuel Sewall as he joined them at the Sewall home the day after his meeting with the governor. "He is truly concerned with the situation in Essex, especially now that a soul has been hanged for witchcraft."

Thomas sneered, still harboring resentment at the appointments of the new governor and lieutenant governor, ousting Bradstreet and himself. "He's a pirate," he sniffed. "He gives no attention to the colony's business. He up and left during one of our most distressed crises."

The two men gave him an understanding smile but weren't willing to indulge him any further. "He has asked me for advice on how to handle the trials," Cotton continued.

"In what way?" Samuel asked. He was particularly curious as he was one of the ten men who had been tapped as justices of the new court. The appointment was an auspicious one, reserved for the most respected magistrates in the colony. Samuel was proud to have been chosen, yet he did not relish the many trips to Salem Village that would be required to discharge his duty. At least he didn't have to attend every trial, and in fact he hadn't been in attendance when Bridget Bishop was sentenced to death. The special court required that William Stoughton, as Chief Justice, oversee every trial, and at least one of the other appointed judges, but not all of them were required to be in attendance.

"He has asked me to convene a synod of ministers to create a document outlining our words of wisdom to the court's justices,"

Cotton replied. "And I am humbled to be enlisted in this way."

"What will you say?" Thomas asked, still sore from the talk of Governor Phips.

"It depends, I imagine, on the consensus of the ministers. I have already discussed the case with several of them, and much of our opinions are similar to the ones the three of us have shared, but others are adamant that we remain vigilant against evil, with complete support of the trials and what they believe will be more hangings. For my part, I support the work of Mr. Stoughton and the Salem judges, first and foremost. And I am most heartened to hear that you, Samuel, are joining that group."

Samuel smiled, yet gave a worried look in Thomas' direction. He knew that his friend had felt rebuffed when he hadn't been chosen to serve on the special court. Indeed Samuel himself had watched as Thomas' good work on behalf of the colony over these many decades seemed to have been disregarded completely by the new guard. It was unfair, to say the least, yet Samuel did not know how it might be changed.

"Thank you, Cotton," Samuel said. "I, too, am grateful for God's foot soldiers in this battle against Satan. The gates of Hell hath been opened in Massachusetts, and we must do everything we can to combat the forces of evil."

Thomas' countenance remained dark and stormy. "What of the use of spectral evidence? Didn't you discount that when last we met?" he demanded. The other two men stared at him with surprise. It was unusual for the old judge to act so peevishly.

But in fact, Thomas had already come fully round to the conclusion that these trials were an abomination.

He had doubt before, especially after witnessing first-hand the torments of the afflicted girls and women. And he knew that he himself had ordered Sarah Cloyce to the Salem Town jail. But the fact that that pretender, that William Stoughton, had so enthusiastically embraced the opinion that witchcraft was afoot swayed Thomas to regret his part in the entire thing. If Stoughton was such a believer, Thomas chose to take the opposite stance. Now his dreams continued to hound him, but lately they brought images of himself standing in front of the Court of Heaven, and the Good Lord in all of His shining light pointing a long finger at him. "Shame, shame," God thundered, and Thomas was filled with the heat of a thousand suns, burning his flesh as he fell down, down, down into the pits of Hell.

He desperately wanted to go back in time to reverse his decision about sending Goody Cloyce to jail. He wanted to do anything he could to stop the trials. But his authority had been stripped of him by the elder Mr. Mather, and now he was but a member of the General Court, nothing more, nothing less. Just as he had been when he was in his twenties, before making so many sacrifices for the colony. So many people in Boston and the surrounding towns were clamoring for more hangings. This was not like when Thomas chose to negotiate with the Indians in Maine, much to some colonists' chagrin. At least then he had a strong contingent supporting him, including Mr. Eliot and Thomas' own brother Samuel out in Natick. Now it seemed no one was thinking clearly. Thomas had hoped that his two friends sitting here with him were more level-headed than most of the people around him, especially when Cotton had decided to write to the Salem judges, urging them caution in the sole use of spectral evidence. But now here they were, praising those very judges.

"Spectral evidence must be considered as well," Cotton replied. "But I do remain cautious of the <u>sole</u> use of such evidence in making convictions."

"And I, too," Samuel agreed.

Thomas stood up and paced the floor, clearly perturbed. "How can you support Stoughton, Corwin and Hathorne on the one hand, yet excoriate their methods? This is murky territory, to be sure!"

Cotton winced. He stood up and put a calming hand on the much older man's arm, pulling on his own white collar in a move to subtly remind Thomas of his role as religious leader. "I only advise them to take other evidence into account as well, Thomas," he said, soothingly. "Truly you cannot believe that they do not do God's work?"

"I think this is a complicated time, and in fact we may be dealing with the invisible world," Thomas said, not willing to be pacified by the younger man, no matter how powerful he was in the colony. "And the girls in Salem Village do rile up great emotions. But if I had been appointed to the court, I would be sure to bring utmost care to the proceedings. No one benefits from the tactics of a mob."

Before Cotton or Samuel were able to answer, Thomas picked up his hat and stormed out of the room.

~ ~ ~

"NO!" Sarah screamed, sounding even to herself like a wild banshee. "You shall not take her! She shall not go!"

Others in the jail joined her in her wailing, but Sarah's voice, much louder than the others, sounded as if it were coming from the very gates of hell. It terrified everyone around her. The cacophony that ensued was ear-splitting.

Yet it did nothing to stop George Herrick from wresting Rebecca's worn body away from the clutches of her sisters, dragging her to the door. The job didn't take much effort, as Rebecca was now as small and weak as a child.

Sarah clung to her sister Mary as the heavy iron door slammed behind Rebecca and Herrick. Sarah felt like she couldn't breathe. They had come for Rebecca. Rebecca, of all people. After Peter's visit, she allowed herself the slight glimmer of hope that he was right: that hanging Bridget Bishop, while reprehensible, was also understandable, given the woman's propensity for misbehavior. That they wouldn't dare go forward with trying cases against visible saints like her sisters. But it had only been a week and now one more was being taken. One who, Sarah knew, didn't have a sinful bone in her body. Why her, when there were so many in prison? Why not Sarah, who had angered Mr. Parris so when she stalked out of the meeting house that day that now seemed like a lifetime ago? Wasn't she herself the sister who was always stubborn, misbehaving? Her parents and family had been telling her for years to keep quiet about things. She never listened to them, and always got into trouble because of it. Meanwhile Rebecca and Mary remained devout, loyal wives who never had a single bad thing to say about anyone else.

Why hadn't they taken Sarah in her sister's place?

"All will be well, sister," Mary was saying. "Goody Bishop was found guilty, but surely Rebecca will be set free. Perhaps this will be a most happy day. I trust God that He will protect her. We must pray, Sarah. We must pray!"

But Sarah wasn't listening. She was done with praying. Any loving God would not torment such a saintly woman, nor would He allow this contagion of witchcraft accusations to continue. She looked about her, taking stock once more of her fellow prisoners. As a group they had nothing in common with each other. They hailed from many different towns in Essex County. They were farmers, or they were wealthy merchants. They were men and women both. There were known thieves among them, along with covenanted church members who had been considered among the elect before the accusations started to fly. The only thing that they shared was the fact that for whatever reason, each of them had been deemed evil by a group of young girls who were even now holding the entire region hostage with their little pointing fingers.

Meanwhile, Rebecca was rudely thrown into Goodman Herrick's rickety cart. Her body ached with pain and she could hardly stand, but she was preoccupied with the dazzling sunlight of the morning. She hadn't laid her eyes on such beauty in a very long time. She looked around at the trees with their new early summer leaves and the flowering Sweet William, wild ginger and Culver's Root growing on the ground along the road to Salem Village.

"I am soothed, dear Lord," Rebecca said, clasping her withered, dirty hands to her chest. "I see Your righteousness in everything about me. You will protect me. I am certain of it."

~ ~ ~

Rebecca Nurse had to be given a chair when her trial began, as she was too weak to stand by herself. She had sat in this meeting house countless times before, but now the place was transformed into a sea of angry people. Her eyes were failing and her hearing too so it was difficult to discern the edges of each face. She became very confused. She couldn't know that her dear Francis was there, not six feet away from her, nor could she see all of the people who loved her: her sons and daughters, Joseph Putnam and her niece Hannah, her sisters' husbands. They were sitting to her back, and her weary body did not allow her to turn easily. She could only feel anger around her. Why such anger? she silently asked God. Why do they hate me so?

In front of her, Judge Sewall noticed that the accused seemed baffled and not quite with them. He knew that this was the woman thought to be the godliest in the Village, and that the court had received several petitions on her behalf. He himself had urged his fellow judges to consider these petitions, yet William Stoughton refused to take them into account, reminding his compatriots how a witch could fool a great many people.

"Why would these souls risk being accused themselves?" Samuel had asked, trying hard to act appropriately deferential to the lieutenant governor and chief justice. "It seems to me that they did that very thing by affixing their signature to these entreaties. That in and of itself lends credence to their pleas, does it not?"

Samuel had already seen how Stoughton was dealing with these trials, so he wasn't surprised that he still remained adamant about not considering the petitions on behalf of Goody Nurse. While Samuel remained certain that they were making the right choices in the court's several decisions to execute witches, he was also growing slightly uncomfortable with Stoughton's obvious belief that they were on a crusade. It seemed to cloud the man's judgment. In turn, he could tell that Stoughton was getting tired of Samuel's questioning of his tactics, and Samuel knew he had to be careful. The colony had entered a new chapter with the arrival of the charter from England, and Samuel had a lot riding on his being a success on this special court. He had always been considered a fair judge, and he was committed to being so; indeed he believed that none other than God Himself had called him to that role. He just wished the evidence presented at these trials was more straightforward. And he wished his friend Thomas Danforth had been appointed to the special court so that the two could discuss the merits together as they occurred. Yet didn't Thomas seem way too adamant on the other side, that these trials were becoming a travesty, the last time they met?

Ann Putnam Sr. was testifying against Goody Nurse, telling the judges of how her poor son withered and died soon after Rebecca visited. She was interrupted by her own daughter, who cried out: "I can see my baby brother in winding sheets, can you not as well? Goody Nurse pricks him and he does not wail! Oh Goody Nurse, Goody Nurse, do be gone!"

Abigail stood up right on the bench she was sitting on, pulling up the sleeve of her shift, showing the court red blotches from what seemed pin pricks on her pale skin. "Goody Nurse does attack me as well! Oh, it does pain me! Oh the pain!"

At that point Mary Tarbell, Rebecca's grown daughter, stood up and pointed a finger at the girl. "You do but dissemble, young Abigail! I did see you prick your own arm with a needle not five minutes before. Shame, shame! How dare you accuse my mother, who is as close to God as anyone else living or dead!"

Samuel watched as Stoughton roared his bid to quiet the

crowd. He lifted his black-robed arms and did seem to be a dark angel, so much that the girls indeed quit for a time.

"Goody Nurse, how do you answer these charges?" Stoughton demanded, ignoring her daughter's claim that Abigail was injuring herself. Why did he discount such things? Samuel wondered. Again the old woman in front of him did not answer. He imagined that she might not have heard any of what had just happened.

"She is a witch, as her mother before her was," Goody Putnam said, calmly and clearly. "My uncle John Gould can attest to that, as he saw first-hand how evil was the mother. Here Goody Nurse appears to be a godly woman, yet the Devil is most clever, is he not? What other to choose as his leader than one of the supposedly covenanted?"

The girls' screaming and accusing went on and on, but Samuel was relieved to see that Stoughton eventually agreed to listen to testimonies on behalf of the accused. The magistrates took depositions from Joseph Putnam and other friends to the Nurses. Samuel knew of these men, especially Joseph Putnam ,who was making a name for himself in Salem Town, so he understood that their support should weigh heavily on the court's decision. They painted a picture of a woman most good and kind, akin to a saint herself. Samuel was impressed. Surely this was no witch.

Finally, after a full two hours of testimonies, accusations, tortures of the young girls – but with very little input from Rebecca herself, besides her repeated pleas of innocence – the judges set the jury to consider what they had just heard.

While the jurists adjourned to Ingersoll's ordinary to discuss the case, the constable, with Mr. Stoughton's permission, allowed Rebecca's family and friends to come to her side. At first the old woman seemed startled and frightened to see people come so close, but as her loved ones came into focus, she smiled a rapturous smile and allowed her frail body to be embraced by everyone. Rebecca Preston, her eldest child, pulled out a white linen cloth from her apron and ran it gently over her mother's face, trying hard to clear it of the grit and filth of the Salem Town jail. The fabric came away more black than white. Francis Nurse took his wife's hand and kissed it, not caring that this kind of display was frowned upon by the church. Meanwhile, Joseph Putnam spoke fast, knowing that they might not have a lot of time, but wanting to coach Rebecca in case the questioning started over again.

"My dear Aunt," he said, taking Rebecca's other hand and urging her to look him in the eye. "I know it has been a most noisome trial, and you have not heard most of it. Should you be in the position to do so, please do tell the judges that your hearing is delinquent and you request a member of the court to repeat what is being said. There are many here, testifying on your behalf, and I do believe we made a strong case against the girls' accusations. This has been a most different trial than the one that came before, and it is a most fortuitous thing. This may be the time when hardened hearts are softened and we can put an end to these trials. We know these accusations are false. I know you are weak, and your days in jail have taken their terrible toll. And your pure countenance is helping to a very significant extent. I have been watching the judges' faces, and not all of them are closed – "

"Yes, dear Rebecca," Hannah urged, embracing her old aunt. "Do as my husband advises. Please do."

But Hannah was interrupted by George Herrick, who announced that the chief justice had just bid him put a halt to the group assembled around the prisoner. And besides, the jury was returning and the trial was to resume. Quickly the meeting house filled once again, and Rebecca's family was wrested from her loving arms. Her daughters and niece began to cry, weeping huge tears that stained their faces. Rebecca was left alone on her chair, and her shackles were replaced, but this time Goodman Herrick took better care to do it gently.

"Jurists, how do you decide?" William Stoughton intoned, once everyone had taken their seats. A young woman coughed into her handkerchief somewhere in the crowd, but this was the only sound to be heard as everyone held their breaths, waiting. Samuel gazed upon the prisoner, who seemed to emanate a calmness that was out of place in such a scene. He wasn't sure whether she was hearing the chief justice's words.

"Ignoramus," one of the men of the jury said, his voice quavering.

It took a moment for this word to sink into the people's consciousness: "We don't know." The girls were open-mouthed and couldn't manage to speak. Rebecca's children's eyes were wide, not quite comprehending what they thought they had heard. Hannah gripped Joseph's hand in hope.

Then suddenly another burst of screams and shouts erupted from the crowd. Now the accusing voices were almost overrun by cheers of happiness. Peter Cloyce helped his brother-in-law Francis Nurse to his feet so he could go to Rebecca's side, hugging her, kissing her head. Rebecca remained dazed, but could tell from her husband's face that the news was good.

"Silence!" William Stoughton bellowed, pounding his gavel on the table in front of him. The sheer power of his voice echoed through the cavernous room, and the people quieted immediately.

"You, the members of the jury," Stoughton said sternly, staring at the men gathered before him, one at a time. "Are you certain of your decision?"

The men shuffled their feet and looked warily at each other. They seemed cowed by the lieutenant governor before them. "Aye?" said the leader of the group, but his answer came out as more of a question than a statement.

"I do beseech you to reconsider," Stoughton demanded. Samuel Sewall whipped his head around to stare at his fellow judge. Judges Corwin and Hathorne were nodding their heads in agreement with the chief justice. What was going on here? It was highly unusual for a judge not to accept a jury's decision. "I ask you to think again of the accusers' words. And again, Goody Nurse, what do you have to say for yourself?"

Rebecca sat in silence, looking at the judge towering above her, but not aware that he had posed a question of her. To her eyes he was a hulking figure without detail, and to her ears the room was quiet.

"She cannot hear!" Joseph Putnam cried out, and his half brother Thomas Jr. shot him a look of disgust. "Can you not see that!?"

"Nay, that is not the case," Stoughton replied. "She has nothing to say because she is guilty. Should that not be true, God would stand by her, but anyone can see that He does not."

"Witch! Witch! Witch!" roared the crowd, and the girls began their twitching again.

The jury was sent away once more, and this time their decision was unequivocal.

Goody Nurse was guilty of witchcraft, and would be hanged.

~ ~ ~

The terror was gone, and in its place rage flooded Sarah's body. She no longer much noticed the dank, stinking, crowded room she was sharing with way too many people. Instead, she used what space she had – no more than a small worn-out circle on the dirt floor roughly the circumference of her own body – to at once sit, then stand, then pace in place, pounding her fist into her other palm. Anything to expend the racing energy that pulsed through her veins. She felt like a caged rat, and it took every ounce of will not to start screaming. Because if she started, she feared she would never stop.

She didn't know what else to do with her anger. It blossomed out of tears that sprung from her eyes when she heard from Peter the unthinkable: that Rebecca was gone. That they had murdered her beloved sister. It gained momentum as Peter went on with his story, how the constable had taken Rebecca with four other women who had been convicted earlier along with her. How the crowd jeered and cheered from the side of the path up to a place they called Gallows' Hill. Some of them even threw overripe tomatoes at the prisoners, and one hit Rebecca smack on the cheek. Peter said that she was not moved to cry out, however; in fact her face radiated a strange kind of calm that seemed to emanate from God's own grace. Sarah's sister remained silent and brave throughout the entire horrible scene, and every one of her relatives were there to hold her up in spirit: her eight children, their spouses, and their own children; about thirty nieces and nephews and grandchildren; her sisters' husbands; and of course Francis. Francis was hardly able to stay upright, but he wanted to stand firm, watching as his wife of fifty years was kicked off the platform and went to her death. That was the only thing he could do for her in the end.

"And what of her body, Peter?" Sarah asked through clenched teeth. The image of her beautiful sister dangling miserably from the noose was almost more than she could bear. Mary stood next to her, her mouth open in horror, not able to say a word. "They did not leave her there, did they?"

"Nay, nay," her husband answered, wringing his hands and hating every word that came out of his own mouth. "Isaac and I went with John Tarbell and Thomas Preston that night, after everyone had gone home. They told us we were not allowed to touch the bodies, but Francis could not manage to sleep knowing that his dear wife was out there, unprotected and alone. He pushed us out the door with a strength we didn't know he had, and we put away our fear of being jailed ourselves so we could retrieve our sister. We took a knife to the rope and pulled her down, taking her back to the Nurse Farm to take her final rest."

"And did you pray over her body?" Sarah pressed, unwilling to accept that by then Rebecca had been excommunicated when she had been accused, and so would never be blessed with a Christian burial.

"Aye, we did. We were all there. I do believe we numbered over fifty souls, all connected by blood or marriage to her. We prayed and prayed and Francis read her favorite psalm and we bid her soul to God. Francis did not allow a marker, however, as he was unwilling to draw the attention of the ministers or the magistrates. We will always know where she rests, however, I assure you that, Sarah."

Mary started to wail with sobs, which startled Sarah: Mary was usually so quiescent, even in the midst of terror. The other prisoners stood by as close as they could, listening intently to Peter's tale. When Mary started to cry, the others did, too. Little four-year-old Dorothy Good, who was such a sweet companion to Rebecca as they both wasted away in the jail, came up to take Sarah's hand, although her eyes were dry. Dorothy's mother Sarah Good was one of the accused who had perished that day, and the child had already lost her baby sister to starvation several weeks ago. Sarah looked down at Dorothy, who had a blank look to her, as if her soul had already died. She thought of Hepzibah, and her older daughters. She wondered if she would ever lay eyes on them again.

Since hearing the news of Rebecca's death, Sarah could not rest. Her rage kept her awake, even at night. She just couldn't get her mind to comprehend what was happening. The injustice of it was like a giant boulder she was expected to swallow, but she could not. She believed in the Devil, and remembered how as a young child she asked her mother if the Indians she spied in the forest were his minions. She had read Cotton Mather's book about the Goodwin children and how Goody Glover admitted to witchcraft. That was a clear-cut case. There were some in the jail with Sarah whom she imagined could indeed be witches, although not many of them confessed to it. Tituba still rotted in prison with the rest of them, but she was shunned by the rest of the crowd, and she had taken to talking gibberish to herself, picking at her hair and teeth, clearly out of her head. But the others? People like Mary English, and Sarah's own dear sisters? It made no sense. Those girls were surely counterfeit. But why? Was it really to right old wrongs thought up by their parents? How could that be? How were the girls benefiting from the situation?

The more Sarah tried to apply reason to what was going on, the more her mind spun and spun into a downward spiral. It was as if the world had turned upside down, where the righteous were accused of evil, and hateful people were uplifted. But who let this happen? How was it that she – and the rest of the accused – had no power over their own fate? Peter had told her that the people of Essex County were walking around in stark terror, unwilling to venture far from their own farms for fear of running into the girls' accusations, or somehow angering their neighbors. And now that several women have been hanged, the collective panic had grown worse.

Sarah found that most of her fellow prisoners, including Mary, had fallen to despair and praying. Whenever she tried to share her feelings with her sister, Mary would shake her head and start crying. She had taken over Rebecca's role as surrogate mother to little Dorothy Good, and the two spent their days cuddling and dozing on the filthy floor. Indeed most people slept most of the time, as there was little else to do. Without sufficient food, their bodies went into a kind of hibernation, which made the hunger easier to take.

But Sarah could not sleep. She was too angry.

CHAPTER TWELVE

Cambridge Town and Essex County
August 1692

The first of August dawned already hot, and by the time the black-robed ministers made their way down the path to the First Harvard Hall at the college, sweat was trickling down their collared necks. None were looking forward to the meeting to which they had been summoned by the president, but when one of the most esteemed church leaders in the colony called upon them for help, help would not be denied him. One by one the ministers arrived to take his seat at a long polished table in the middle of the college's largest lecture rooms, looking around to welcome his colleagues. As a group they represented the core of the colony's ministerial power, the next generation of leaders walking in the boots of founding reverends such as John Cotton in Boston and Thomas Shepard in Cambridge. Those earlier ministers presided over congregations filled with those who had traveled to Massachusetts during the Great Migration of the 1630s: people whose devotion to God and His word was steadfast and unambiguous. This new crop, some in their twenties, some like James Allen who was as old as sixty, had had a more difficult time ensuring that the second and third generation of colonists adhered to the strict tenets of their faith. They had to deal with men and women who were more apt than their forebears to skip church services, to engage in wantonness and sloth, to value financial profit over righteousness.

Yet the trepidation felt by all of these men was palpable in the room. They were not all of the same mind about the witch trials in Salem Village and beyond. The subject was the only thing people in the streets of Boston and Cambridge could talk about, and the ministers were trying to control the hysteria from their respective pulpits. Yet their approaches were vastly different, as some spent the hours railing against the accused witches and the need to destroy them, while others were beginning to express doubts. It seemed no one could agree on what was truly God's will.

The last to arrive was Increase Mather himself, trailed by his son Cotton. It had been almost two months since Mr. Mather re-

turned from England with the colony's new charter, and since then
he had been very busy. Governor Phips was almost totally absent
from colonial affairs, and the Lieutenant Governor Stoughton was
spending most of his time in Salem Village. That left Mr. Mather to
work with the General Court to reestablish legal practices according
to the new rules from England. He continued to give sermons at the
Second Church in Boston, as well as run Harvard as its president.
This morning he looked exhausted, with heavy circles under his
eyes. He seemed older than his fifty-three years, emanating a sense
of concern and frustration.

"Thank you all for coming," he started, bidding them all to
sit after they rose in greeting. "At this woeful time, God has directed me to summon your guidance as I wrestle with doubts that do
unsettle my soul."

"We are all here in Christian love, Mr. Mather," Samuel Willard of the Third Church in Boston replied, and the rest of the men
nodded with an austere solemnity.

They all bowed their heads as their leader intoned a prayer
that lasted for twenty minutes. It was only after that vital ritual was
completed that the meeting could start in earnest.

"I wish to speak today of the Court of Oyer and Terminer in
Salem Village," the elder Mather announced, pulling at his graying
beard in a worrying gesture. "There have now been five women
hanged for the capital crime of witchcraft, and I hear from our good
Mr. Stoughton that there are close to one hundred souls accused
and jailed for the same reason."

The minister stood up and started pacing the room, seeming
to almost talk to himself, while his colleagues remained silent and
waiting.

"One of the hanged was a church member who was a well-respected woman in the community," he continued. "From what
I gather, until these accusations, Goody Nurse was untarnished
in her devotion to God. Mr. Stoughton assures me that the judg-
ments of witchcraft have been accurate. And I do not doubt the
power of the Devil to recruit seemingly righteous people into his
devious plans. We have all seen the devastation he has caused in
this very colony over the years. Tis imperative that we remain vigilant in all of our efforts to seek him out and destroy him. Indeed
tis now more important than ever, as we all strive to keep our
flocks pure of heart."

The other men looked askance at each other, wondering if any of them should say anything. It seemed that Mr. Mather was merely voicing his stream of consciousness, not asking for any intervention from the very group from which he had just said he wanted advice. Cotton Mather, well-used to this habit of his father to wax on like this, discreetly put his hand up, sending the message that they should remain silent until the older man had finished his ruminations.

"Aye, vigilance is imperative, to keep up the fight against evil. Yet something about these cases does trouble me; indeed sometimes my disordered mind wakens me at night and deprives me of much-needed rest. There are so many souls being accused. We have not seen anything like it in the colony. Could it be true that this Goody Nurse was leading an entire dark congregation of the Devil's minions? That this good woman has shared leadership of the coven with none other than Mr. Burroughs, himself a man of the cloth – and an alumnus of this very institution, no less? That their unholy sabbaths took place right on Reverend Parris' property? Tis a strange thing indeed."

Mr. Mather walked to the tall diamond-paneled window and gazed out at the yard in front of the Hall. The sun beat down mercilessly, making the room sweltering and close, but he didn't seem to notice.

"My son has already written to the special court with his objections to the sole use of spectral evidence in these cases," he went on. "Yet Mr. Stoughton does not feel the need to take his report into consideration. Does that not indicate a mind that may be closed to the entire picture? When we point our bow toward a deer in the forest, our eye trains on the beast in our sight; yet do we then not spy the wolf behind us?"

This time the minister looked at the men gathered at the table, seeming to come out of his reverie. The ministers shook themselves out of their listening stance but were not sure that the question posed was a rhetorical one or not.

It was Mr. Mather's son who spoke, hoping to facilitate a dialogue now that his father had voiced his worries. "What would you have us do, Father?" he asked.

"I seek this synod's thoughts about two biblical issues I see at play here. The first is found in the Book of Samuel, in the story of the Witch of Endor. In this story does not God tell us that the Devil can take on an innocent's shape?"

All of the ministers knew the story, and they pondered the elements in silence. The Bible taught that even though the new king Saul had banished all of the mediums and magicians from the land, Saul was desperate. The Philistine enemies were at the village gate, and Saul's people were about to be slaughtered. Despite his hatred of witches, he called upon a local woman living in the town of Endor and asked her to conjure Samuel so he could get his predecessors' advice. The witch did so, but as her power resided with the Devil, it was he whom she raised in the appearance of the prophet Saul. Samuel was dead and innocent, yet it was his face that Saul countenanced.

"Aye, I do believe it does," said Samuel Willard from the Third Church in Boston. "Tis certain it does."

"Yet the judges in Salem Village – not only Mr. Stoughton but Mr. Sewall and the others – say that the Devil, in this case, speaks and acts through those accused. The evidence is clear in the young girls' suffering and whom they say torments them," added Nehemiah Walter, the youngest of them, of Roxbury. His face was twisted in confusion.

"And I do believe what they report," the elder Mather was quick to reply. "There is no reason for the afflicted to lie. And it is certain that they are steadily injured."

Reverend Walker was agitated, rifling through his well-worn Bible with a thick, black leather cover. The noise of the thin pages turning caught the attention of the other ministers, who waited anxiously to hear what he was seeking. "'For such are false apostles,'" the young man read, his voice shaking slightly, "'deceitful workers, transforming themselves into the apostles of Christ. And no marvel, for Satan himself is transformed into an angel of light. Therefore it is no great thing if his ministers also be transformed as the ministers of righteousness; whose end shall be according to their works.' We need to smite these devils, Mr. Mather. By any means necessary."

Mr. Walker's voice rose as he spoke, until he was almost shouting. The other ministers shifted nervously in their seats.

"To be sure, there are many instances in the Bible, besides this one in First Corinthians, that do describe the Devil as the false

Angel of Light," agreed Cotton Mather, anxious to build consensus. He watched his father carefully, hoping desperately that his comment did not anger the elder minister. While Increase had spent two years in England, his son had taken his place at the pulpit at Second Church, and by now had become used to being the authority on ecclesiastical matters, despite his young age. Now he was having a difficult time giving the reins back to his father, who was clearly the elder and wiser of the two.

But Increase was in a thoughtful, receptive mood, and seemed to welcome the differences of opinion. He continued to pull at his beard as he listened to his colleagues, including the very young ones.

"So God in His wisdom has given us examples of two different circumstances, telling us that each can be true in its own right. The Devil can take on the shape of an innocent on the one hand, and on the other he can recruit seemingly righteous – but actually evil – beings to his dark strategies," he mused.

The men around the table nodded their heads, comprehending the disquieting ambiguity of the situation at hand. Mr. Walker's face turned increasingly red.

"So how does this affect the workings of the Court of Oyer and Terminer?" asked James Allen, the eldest of the group.

"Methinks it means that we cannot be certain!" Cotton cried out, standing up and rapping the table with his right hand. "It means that the Devil is assuredly at work in Salem Village. This we cannot deny. Yet those he impersonates to injure the innocent girls – they may or may not be complicit."

"Yes!" Cotton's father pointed at his son with fire in his eyes. "That is what vexes me! Do you not see the conundrum?"

The ministers all opened their own well-used bibles, seeking the wisdom that was sorely needed at this moment.

"Are we saying that we do not trust the judgment of those men of the special court, those who have demonstrated their wisdom and devotion to the colony for so many years?" piped up Nathaniel Gookin, who led the Cambridge church. As he spoke, the reverend stood up and moved closer to the still-apoplectic Mr. Walker. "Are we to deny the reality that they are reporting to us, after taking on such a formidable task with which we have assigned them? And how will the colony respond to such questioning?"

"I will tell you how they will respond," Reverend Walker said, obviously trying to contain himself. "They will turn on us. They will no longer trust us. We cannot bring such nuance to our congregations. They will not understand, and I fear it will cause a veritable war within the colony. Besides, with apologies, dear Mr. Mather, I believe that God is calling upon us to be steadfast in this matter. God Himself. He is testing us, don't you see? Remember, will you, what He says in Ephesians: "be strong in the Lord and in His mighty power. Put on the full armor of God, so that you can take your stand against the devil's schemes!'"

As Mr. Walker made his case through gritted teeth, he jabbed his fingers loudly on each word in his worn Bible.

Increase Mather came to the table and bent over it, hands on the surface, and glared at Mr. Gookin and Mr. Walker. "Are we to worry at this critical moment about how we might appear to our congregations?" he demanded, bordering on angry. "Or should we not, as men of God, be more interested in ensuring justice?"

The two younger ministers held Mr. Mather's gaze, but only for a moment. Cowed, they looked down again, seeming to be preoccupied with finding another Bible verse.

"Mr. Mather," the reverend James Allen said quietly, "surely you cannot deny that the Devil stands at the ready, waiting for the weak to fall?"

Cotton watched guardedly as his father responded. He wished prodigiously that the elder Mather could continue to accept differences of opinion. He had always been good at that. Yet Cotton knew that the stakes were high, and his father could easily give up his composure when it came to something that was important to him and the colony.

But Cotton needn't have worried. Increase smiled indulgently at Mr. Allen and said, "to be sure, my friend. And indeed our vulnerability to evil is more significant than ever, what with so many of our people moving away from the embrace of our dear Father."

The room was silent for several moments, all lost in thought.

"Here I wish to introduce my second ecclesiastical question that involves the trials," Increase said, opening his bible on the table, sitting heavily in the seat in front of him. When some of the men in the room groaned audibly, the old minister looked up, annoyed. Looking down at his Bible, he read: "'Then the Lord said, 'The outcry against

Sodom and Gomorrah is so great and their sin so grievous that I will go down and see if what they have done is as bad as the outcry that has reached me. If not, I will know.' The men turned away and went toward Sodom, but Abraham remained standing before the Lord. Then Abraham approached him and said: 'Will you sweep away the righteous with the wicked? What if there are fifty righteous people in the city? Will you really sweep it away and not spare the place for the sake of the fifty righteous people in it? Far be it from you to do such a thing—to kill the righteous with the wicked, treating the righteous and the wicked alike. Far be it from you! Will not the Judge of all the earth do right?' The Lord said, 'If I find fifty righteous people in the city of Sodom, I will spare the whole place for their sake.' Then Abraham spoke up again: 'Now that I have been so bold as to speak to the Lord, though I am nothing but dust and ashes, what if the number of the righteous is five less than fifty? Will you destroy the whole city for lack of five people?' 'If I find forty-five there,' he said, 'I will not destroy it.' Once again he spoke to him, 'What if only forty are found there?' He said, 'For the sake of forty, I will not do it.' Then he said, 'May the Lord not be angry, but let me speak. What if only thirty can be found there?' He answered, 'I will not do it if I find thirty there.' Abraham said, 'Now that I have been so bold as to speak to the Lord, what if only twenty can be found there?' He said, 'For the sake of twenty, I will not destroy it.' Then he said, 'May the Lord not be angry, but let me speak just once more. What if only ten can be found there?' He answered, 'For the sake of ten, I will not destroy it.' When the Lord had finished speaking with Abraham, he left, and Abraham returned home."

The room was silent.

"Ten people," Mr. Mather said. "That is how God leaves us with those verses in Genesis. Yet it is not beyond reason to suppose that his conversation with Abraham might have continued in the same manner, bringing the number down to five innocent beings, to three – to even a single soul. Canst thou imagine that we can rightfully say that God would not destroy one hundred beings should He believe that one of those might be righteous?"

"But Mr. Mather," Nathaniel Gookin of Cambridge spoke up. "God did go on to destroy Sodom, even after he spoke with Abraham."

"But only after he saved Lot and his family, Mr. Gookin, you should know that," Cotton Mather chastised. "After that, the Lord was certain that no single righteous person remained in Sodom."

"How does this apply to the special court, Mr. Mather?" James Allen asked the elder minister, trying to bring the conversation back to the business at hand.

"I do believe that we have biblical proof that tis better to allow a witch to live if there is single doubt that an innocent person might be mistakenly condemned. And there was indeed a doubt about this Goody Nurse woman. The jury initially acquitted her. It was only after Mr. Stoughton criticized their decision that they reversed their judgment. But the first acquittal is proof that there was some doubt."

"And my letter to the court questioned their sole use of spectral evidence to convict," the younger Mather pointed out. "Methinks that practice brings about a case of doubt as well."

"Yet your letter was not accepted," Mr. Walker muttered, almost to himself. "As well it shouldn't have been."

"I still harbor reservations about this line of reasoning," Mr. Gookin said, pointing his finger at a page toward the front of his bible. "In Exodus the Lord saith, 'thou shalt not suffer a witch to live.' Is this not the word of God as well?"

"I do not deny that witches do exist," the elder Mr. Mather said, suddenly sounding very tired. "We have tried and convicted them in the past. Last year Goody Glover was hanged on Boston Common for such a crime. Yet she readily confessed, which should be the primary evidence against such a criminal. Many men have written that a confession should be considered over all other evidence. Yet the people who have confessed in Salem Village have been saved from the noose! Every woman who has gone to the gallows has died with outcries of innocence loosening from their lips. How can this be?"

The men grew silent again, considering the minister's arguments. Even young Mr. Walker seemed to be softening to his rationale. Mr. Mather stood once more, pacing the large room.

"I do agree with you, Father," Cotton Mather said. "Methinks we should bring such musings to the attention of the court."

One by one – some speaking slowly, some fast – the other ministers gave their approval as well. By the end of the meeting it was decided that the elder Mr. Mather would explore more of his texts and create a document outlining their ecclesiastical concerns. The research and writing would take some time, which the minister and president of the College did not have. Yet the situation was dire enough that it should take precedence over most of his other duties.

The matter was settled, and Cotton looked forward to telling the news to his friends Thomas Danforth and Samuel Sewall.

~ ~ ~

In Salem Village, Thomas Putnam was not pleased. After watching so many of those closest to him – his wife, daughter, maid and niece – suffer so terribly at the hands of the specters of witches around them, he thought that now more than ever the villagers should be sorely worried for their souls. Yet attendance at services on Sundays and Wednesdays was steadily declining, and it irked him. Were he and his family not on the forefront of the war against evil in the colony? Had they not been horribly tortured in the service of bringing the people back to God? Yet they turn away even further, making all of the Putnams' torments come to naught.

As these thoughts rushed through his head, Thomas stomped heavily up the hill to the parsonage. For once Reverend Parris was alone, telling his visitor that his wife and niece had walked down to the Ipswich River where the lowbush blueberries were at the peak of their harvest. The minister's face, too, was dark like Thomas'.

"It sometimes feels as if we cannot win this fight against evil!" Thomas complained after the initial pleasantries were exchanged. "The more people are hanged, the more our dear girls are attacked. And now the villagers stay home in their comfortable beds rather than come out to serve God in church."

Samuel nodded, banging his fist against the board. "I know, my friend," he said. "And many of them continue to refuse to pay my wages. There is no wood to be burned! We live on the raw vegetables and fruits we can harvest out of the ground. I do not know what we shall do once the winter arrives."

"How does young Abigail fare? My wife and Ann continue to be tormented, although my wife does better now that Goody Nurse has been sent to her death."

"Abigail's fits continue. The constable takes her and the other girls to towns far afield in order to identify those who attack their innocent souls. Yet at other times Abigail is undisturbed. And young Betty has recovered completely with Mr. Sewall in town."

Thomas paused for a moment, remembering the minister's decision several weeks ago to send his daughter from Salem Village, away from all of the tumult, to stay temporarily with Steven Sewall, the brother of the Boston judge. After a mere week Betty was talking and walking and taking food. Perhaps Thomas should send his own daughter to stay with relatives in Boston. What might happen then?

Shaking off his thoughts, Thomas said "As I just mentioned the accursed Goody Nurse, it reminds me to bring to you the fact that her extended family are most noticeably among those absent from the meeting house come Sundays and Wednesdays. You would think that they would be the first to arrive and to ask God to bless them, given that Goody Esty and Goody Cloyce are in jail awaiting their own trials."

"Aye, the family does comprise a large portion of our congregation, and so I have indeed noticed their empty seats come a Sunday morning," the minister agreed.

"Should they not, of all people, worry for their souls?"

"They remain adamant that their wives and mothers are not witches, even as evidence against them is solid. And they continue to have the support of your half-brother."

Annoyance flooded anew through Thomas' body, and he could not help his face turning bright red. "Do not speak to me, please, of my so-called brother. He is dead to me, given his flagrant support of the accused witches," he stewed, teeth clenched. "Those Towne women have been our bane from the days when we were all children. My dear father would tell me of the battles over land that he had with their father many years back. He was always filled with trepidation since some thought old Joanna Towne was a witch herself. We never trusted that family. And now my father's favorite, that young Joseph, has aligned himself with them, marrying Hannah Bridges. Tis truly an abomination."

"The special court sits again, two days hence," Samuel said, removing for a moment to his study where he retrieved a twine-bound bundle of thin parchment. "Mr. Stoughton has asked me once again to transcribe the proceedings. My supply of paper runs low, as does everything else in this house."

"I have heard that news. I understand Reverend Burroughs will be called, and for good reason, too." Thomas scowled, remembering his own arguments with the minister from Maine. Although it always pained him to see his daughter in such distress, he was secretly glad when she pointed her finger at Mr. Burroughs. He had never gotten over his anger at that man's loathsome unwillingness to pay his debts, and how his supporters in the village – led by Isaac Esty – swooped in to save him by coming up with the necessary money. When a man goes into debt, it is only proper that he pay it himself, or go to jail for it. The Putnams were in the right when they demanded retribution, yet so many villagers flocked to the minister's side, deriding Thomas' family in the meantime. Why should a failed minister deserve such respect when so many of his neighbors criticized the Putnams? Why should so many move up in the world while Thomas and Ann lost the bequests that were rightfully theirs? Things were off in Salem Village, and they had been for a very long time. Finally now Thomas was in the position to bring justice to the whole community. The Lord was on his side, he knew it.

"Aye, my predecessor comes before the judges," the minister was saying. "The evidence against him is strong. The girls say that his poor dead wife comes to them in winding sheets, warning them against the man who killed her in her own bed."

"The very woman whose funeral put him into debt to my father," Thomas commented wryly. "God does work in mysterious ways. He has set us all on the path of righteousness, and we should be grateful for our part in cleansing Essex County of evil."

"Grateful I am," Samuel agreed, his mouth twisting in anguish. "Yet I would be much more content if I did not have to worry about my family going hungry. Or if those in my flock were loyal to their leader."

"It does seem that up continues to seem down, and light dark," Thomas said. "But we are working diligently to bring God's order to Salem Village once more. We must remain vigilant."

~ ~ ~

Cotton Mather stayed at an inn in Salem Town the night before the next set of executions so that he could awaken early the next morning to attend the hangings. He wanted to observe the proceedings himself after hearing so much about the trials and attempting – but failing – to encourage the judges to be more thoughtful in their oversight.

Leaving his father's meeting two weeks before, Cotton was filled with a strong conviction that the judges should alter their practices at the Court of Oyer and Terminer. Up until then he had felt overwhelming ambivalence about the whole matter: one day he would be certain that witches were running rampant to the north, while the next day he would think the judges were making mistakes. But his father's reliance on the word of God to make a strong case against the trials assured him that he should work to put a stop to them.

But when he met with Thomas and Samuel after the Harvard meeting, the light of his doubt was ignited once again. Upon hearing Cotton's news, Thomas was obviously in agreement with the elder Mather, and urged Cotton to do whatever he could to help his father draft his letter to the judges. Since being overlooked for Lieutenant Governor and not being chosen to sit at the special court, Thomas was clearly against the process that he himself had been a party to back in June. He had spoken with Cotton many times about his regret that he was so quick to put that woman, Goody Cloyce, in jail after the examination that he led. Thomas had hoped that once her formal trial was held, the judges and jury would let her go free. He had watched in despair as now six women had been accused and hanged, and William Stoughton's zealotry showed no signs of abating. How could Thomas be certain that Goody Cloyce would escape Stoughton's wrath?

On the other hand, Samuel Sewall had joined Stoughton as he ruled that all six women were guilty, and this was causing a rift in his friendship with Thomas, his old mentor. Cotton could see it with his own eyes, and he was sorry for it. Sewall was not as confident as Stoughton was that these women were evil and must hang, yet he believed he had made the right decision. Cotton knew that Samuel's heart was filled with doubt himself, to the extent that he had made excuses for not being able to attend the recent trials of Mr. Burroughs and the rest. There were plenty of other men assigned to the special court, and Samuel had already presided over two, so no one questioned his absence. But the fact that Samuel was not outright renouncing the trials bothered Thomas, who had already made up his mind that the colony was mishandling the whole thing.

So when Samuel looked doubtful when he heard Cotton's news of the ministers' meeting, Thomas grew heated and almost stalked out of the room. It was Cotton himself who had to step in front of the much older man to prevent his exit, pleading with him for patience and understanding. But when presented with Thomas' unambiguous beliefs, Samuel sunk deeper into his own resolve that the courts were acting appropriately, rather than share his own doubts about it. The embroiled argument that ensued only rekindled Cotton's own misgivings, and he left Thomas' house dejected and uncertain once again. This was why he decided to take the journey to Salem Town to see for himself what was happening.

This time there were four men and only one woman to be hanged. The minister George Burroughs was in the group, and this was another reason why Cotton wanted so desperately to observe the execution. Like with Goody Nurse, there had been some opposition to such a man being accused of witchcraft. No other man of God had been cried out upon, and his case was more talked about than the others. Some colonists believed that his involvement with the witches meant that the infiltration by the devil was even more virulent than they had previously thought. Others – especially those who had supported the man's ministry in Salem Village – started to consider that the judges might be going too far. Cotton still did not know what he himself believed.

It was a warm August day but he could hardly stop to enjoy the sun on his face as he rode atop his horse on the path to Gallows Hill. Suddenly he wished he had any place to go but there. He prayed to God to give him the strength and wisdom to be a true witness to what he was about to encounter.

By the time he arrived, there were many people huddled together in groups, whispering. Some seemed downtrodden and morose, while others had a celebratory air about them, clapping their hands in excitement. Still others bowed their heads in prayer, the white caps of the women gleaming in the sunshine. Cotton decided to stay on his horse, preferring the view of the hanging platform from above.

As Constable Herrick's cart rattled slowly up the hill, the crowd started to cheer and boo at the same time. The faces of the five accused were filthy with dirt, as were the tattered clothes they wore. Bony, shackled hands clutched the sides of the cart so tightly that Cotton could see the white of their knuckles. There was only one woman among the group, and she was much shorter than the four men: her head hardly came up above the edge of the wood of the cart. Cotton tried to peer into their eyes, hoping to find some shred of good or evil inherent in them, but their faces were all downcast. All looked utterly miserable.

John Proctor was the first to hang. He was a big man and the constable would have a difficult time climbing the ladder with him on his back as he had with the last six prisoners. Herrick stiffly made his way up to the platform, rung by rung, and as he did the crowd quieted, seeming almost mesmerized by the action in front of them. Cotton could feel his hands grip the horse's reins so tightly that the rope began to chafe the skin of his palms. He watched as Proctor glared at those assembled below him and they stared back. The constable asked him if he had any last words, and the man growled a single syllable – "no" – and as he did, he looked directly into Cotton Mather's eyes as if he were seeking him out. Cotton gasped and put a hand up to his mouth, as his heart filled with fear at the sheer fury in the other man's face. Was Goodman Proctor cursing him? He had never seen the man before in his life; why would he be staring at him right before his soul left his body? The moment seemed to hover in the air, suspended, for many minutes as Cotton struggled for breath himself, as if he were the one about to be hanged. Surely this was witchcraft that was being cast upon him by this total stranger. Surely it was!

But the moment passed with a vengeance as the constable pushed the man off the platform, arousing the crowd to start howling. Cotton couldn't be sure whether the cries were of anger or despair, but the sound was deafening to his ears. As the man's body twitched on its rope for several seconds and then became unmoving, it was difficult for Cotton himself not to cry out, or to put his hands over his eyes in terror. He could not demonstrate such weakness in front of all of the people gathered on the ground. Still, his own body shook with the bewilderment of what had just been cast upon him.

The second to come to the platform was the minister. As Mr. Burroughs climbed the ladder by himself as well – gruffly pushing away the constable's open arms, summoning him to be carried – Cotton swallowed several times and tried to take in the scene. Yet his mind was reeling, recalling over and over the look he had just received from Goodman Proctor. He felt his mind slip away from the hanging that was about to occur, as if he were in some kind of strange fog.

"Constable, constable!" a man in the crowd called out. "We hear that a witch cannot recite the Lord's Prayer without making a mistake! Make this Mr. Burroughs say the prayer before he gives us his soul to the Devil, once and for all!"

The others sent up words of agreement, urging the minister on. The old man looked down at those gathered with a look of a fathomless sadness, and nodded to the constable, who had asked him for last words. Once again the crowd became silent, so that all that was heard was the song of the birds in the trees across the field and an occasional snort from the horses. As Mr. Burroughs folded his hands together, the iron shackles on his wrists clanged together, making a noise that echoed across the grass and wildflowers blooming all about them. He started to speak in a booming, assured voice – the voice of men of God throughout the ages, well-used to delivering Sunday sermons and prayers for their parishioners. Slowly, slowly he enunciated every word, his eyes closed:

"Our Father, who art in heaven,
Hallowed be thy name.
Thy kingdom come, thy will be done
On earth as it is in heaven.
Give us this day our daily bread,
And forgive us our debts, as we forgive us our debtors.
And lead us not into temptation,
But deliver us from evil
For thine is the kingdom, the power, and the glory forever.
Amen."

The last word rang out, slowly and clearly, causing the crowd to gasp and clutch their chests with the solemnity of what had just happened. Even the constable was dumbstruck. When Mr. Burroughs opened his eyes and looked toward the heavens, a great light seemed to emanate from his face, which had the look of unearthly peace about it.

"He did it!" many people started to shout. "He did not make a mistake! Could he be a witch?"

Everyone knew that a true witch would not be able to recite the Lord's Prayer. The Devil would trip his or her tongue so that the words could not be uttered.

A man recognized Cotton atop his horse, and he pointed his finger at the minister. "Mr. Mather! You, Mr. Mather!" the man cried. "Surely you saw what he did! What say you to these accusations? Are they not false?"

The sound of his name caught Cotton's attention, and he

shook himself free of the waking sleep he seemed to have fallen into. He looked down into the pleading faces of countless villagers below him, and had no idea why they were asking him these questions. Then he realized that Reverend Burroughs had already climbed to the platform and he, too, was looking anxiously at Cotton. What kind of bewitchment had befallen on him, that he had lost time since that man Proctor had swung? And what were they asking of him? It was as if the last few moments had not existed.

"Is Reverend Burroughs a witch?" another villager demanded. Cotton did not say anything for several moments, but it was clear that nothing would happen until the people heard his thoughts.

"Why, why," Cotton stuttered. He continued, slowly: "Why, yes of course he is a witch."

Why would they ask him such a thing, when the prisoner had been tried and convicted? Why had they not posed the same question about John Proctor? Wasn't the truth already clear? It certainly was to him at that moment, now that he had experienced firsthand the power of witchcraft.

Because he had not heard the Lord's Prayer recital. He had not heard it at all.

"Yes, he is a witch!" he now announced, more confident now. "He must hang!"

With that, the constable pushed Mr. Burroughs off the platform, and the minister sank to his twitching death.

The people turned back to the gallows, forgetting Cotton now that he had made his proclamation. This time, though, there were no cheers as Reverend Burroughs' feet stopped their trembling.

Cotton had had enough. As quietly as he could, he pulled on the reins to steer the horse away from the crowd and down the narrow path that led to the town below. He had come here looking for resolution for his garbled thoughts, but now he was as confounded as ever. Too much had just happened in the span of a short twenty minutes, and he needed time and space to comprehend it all.

CHAPTER THIRTEEN

Essex County
September 1692

"We have to do something, Mary," Sarah Cloyce said through gritted teeth. Her sister sat next to her on the floor of the Salem Town jail, looking befuddled, like someone whose mind was not all there. Mary could hardly focus her eyes, and instead gazed into the distance as if watching some invisible scene happening before her. Since they took Rebecca away, Mary spent her days in this kind of trance, and Sarah fought hard to bring her back into the real world. Her fellow accused people existed in the dank, putrid jail in a similar state as Mary was: hardly living at all. Every week or so the constable would call for yet another group of people to be tried, and those poor prisoners never returned. Not a single one. Yet the jail was as crowded as ever, as the afflicted girls continued their sojourn across Essex County, accusing an ever-growing number of men and women both. These days when the constable came, the desperate inmates no longer ever cowered, covering their heads in fierce hope that their names would not be called. It seemed that all hope was truly lost, and those stinking bodies in the jail were no longer even quite human.

Sarah had watched as the same thing happened to Rebecca – but she herself would not give in. Her sleep was invaded by dreams, some horrid, as when she saw Rebecca dangle from the hangman's rope with countless people below her, screaming their curses upon her. Yet in others she saw a land of hope, where the hearts of the trial judges were broken open by a wave of light coursing through them, and the jail doors were thrown open, their weary guests blinking in the sunshine of their freedom. What could she do to reverse the perversion of what was happening to these poor souls? Who would help <u>her</u>?

Food continued to be scarce, but at least the oppressive heat of the high summer was giving way to the cooler breezes of autumn. The air inside the jail walls remained stale and putrid, but at least it was not so hot. George Herrick was beginning to allow more visitors inside, and Sarah kept her sanity by Peter's and Isaac's reports of the goings-on of the special court. The last time Isaac arrived, he was as disheartened as ever to see his beloved wife's dazed existence. Tears came to Sarah's eyes as she watched him take Mary – always tiny in stature but now weighing almost nothing – into his arms, telling her tales of their children and grandchildren, sharing memories of better days. The ministrations did little good. When her own husband visited, he found a resolute and angry wife in Sarah, one who paced back and forth in the small corner where she had taken up residence with her sister, one who looked at him with fierce, blazing eyes. Peter always came away from those visits slightly encouraged. At least Sarah was not letting this nightmare break her. Even when she demanded real news from the outside, not allowing him to give him a watered-down version of the truth. Even when he had to tell her of terrible events, like how their friend old Giles Corey had been sent to his death on accusation of witchcraft. Because Goodman Corey refused to enter a plea of innocence or guilt in the court, the judges sent the constable and his lieutenant to slowly pile rocks upon his prostrate body until the old man either complied with the courts or died. When she heard that he had perished, instead of expressing sorrow, Sarah had stifled a small smirk. Good old Corey. He had found a way to prevent them from hanging him for witchcraft. A resistor to the end. Just like her.

"The judges, Peter," Sarah said to her husband after digesting the news about Goodman Corey. "It is well-known that the judges in such trials should defend the accused as well as hear the testimony of the afflicted, is it not true?"

She had been pondering this for many days. She was familiar with court proceedings from the days when she was Edmund Bridges' wife. Edmund was always an ambitious man with opinions that were as strong as her own. His constant attempts at bringing his family and himself up in the world often ended up in court, and he also often served as witness for others. He would tell Sarah about what was said and done in the local courts, so she knew that judges were expected to support both the accused and the accusers. She had seen little of this during her own examination – that awful Thomas Danforth hardly seemed her savior – and had heard of the same bias when Peter told her of the other trials. Should this injustice not be brought to the Court's attention now?

"Aye, tis true, here and in England as well," Peter agreed.

"Then should we not ask the judges to help us – Mary and me both – in our defense?"

Peter looked about the room, feeling once again the shock of seeing his friends and neighbors in such low states. The ragged creatures around him hardly even resembled the people he had known for so many years. "Are you saying you want to enlist the help of men such as William Stoughton? Men who have shown quite clearly that they wish to rid the entire colony of these so-called witches? Do you expect that his heart holds love for you, or for your sister? After what he did to poor Rebecca?"

"This is not about love," Sarah insisted, pounding one fist against her other opened hand. "It is about the law. And the lieutenant governor is not the only magistrate on the special court. You yourself have reported that you note a softening in some of the others. Like Mr. Sewall? And has not one of the judges resigned from the court in protest to its decisions?"

Sarah was right. One of the judges appointed to the Court of Oyer and Terminer, Nathaniel Saltonstall, had walked away from his appointment, voicing grave concern over the sole use of spectral evidence in condemning so many people to die for witchcraft. Even though she had never seen Mr. Saltonstall, she often thought of him in her countless hours of reverie in the jail, feeling gratitude that there was such a brave, principled man among the magistrates of the court. At least there was one. And if one, why not more?

"Aye, tis so," Peter agreed. "And we do hear of rumblings from Boston that some important ministers – even the great Increase Mather – are questioning the special court."

"I shall petition the court, then," Sarah said, resolute. "I shall speak on behalf of Mary and myself. I shall ask the magistrates for their guidance in our case."

Peter looked at his wife with awe and a respect that always seemed to grow every time he had any kind of conversation with her. He had been happy with his first wife, Eleanor, and that dear woman had given him children and a long life of contentment. Yet it was only when he met and married Sarah that he felt truly understood, that he experienced a partnership that was much more equal and rewarding than even the Bible recommended. This woman had been put down so many times, and now she was losing so much. Peter knew how she adored Rebecca, and how Rebecca's death had rent an astonishing gash in Sarah's life, one that most likely would never heal. But here she was, fighting for her own life, and that of her sister Mary. She alone among the downcast was coming up with ways to resist what was befalling them. Peter knew that his wife's strength and her stubbornness had dogged her throughout her whole life, making her think that she was ungodly or somehow wrong. But by God, that obstinacy just might save her now. That afternoon he drove his cart the many miles between the jail and their farm in Salem Village, filled with a hope that he had not felt for many months. He could not wait to tell Alice and Hepzibah about what a warrior their mother was.

~ ~ ~

Petition to the Court of Oyer and Terminer by Sarah Cloyce and Mary Esty, dated September 9, 1692:

"The humble request of Mary Esty and Sarah Cloyce to the Honoured Court: that whereas we two sisters stand now before you, charged with the suspicion of witchcraft, our humble request is firstly: that seeing we are neither able to plead our own cause, nor is council allowed to those in our condition, that you who are our Judges, would please to be of council to us, to direct us wherein we may stand in need. Secondly that whereas we are not conscious to ourselves of any guilt in the least degree of that crime, whereof we are now accused, nor of any other scandalous evil, or miscarrying inconsistent with Christianity, we ask that those who have had the longest and best knowledge of us, being persons of good report, may be suffered to testify upon oath what they know concerning each of us. Thirdly that the testimony of the Afflicted may not be improved to condemn us, without other legal evidence concurring. We hope the Honoured Court and jury will be so tender of the lives of such as we are who have for many years lived under the unblemished reputation of Christianity as not to condemn us without a fair and equal hearing of what may be said for us, as well as against us."

~ ~ ~

The heavy oak door, inlaid with iron bars, crashed open, breaking the silence of the jail's interior. These days when the constable opened the door he had to cover his nose with a worn strip of flax linen soaked in witch hazel, as the stink from the room was intolerable. This afternoon he pushed inside all eight of the prisoners whom he had called away just that morning. They all looked about the room, dazed.

Sarah Cloyce, who had not uttered a word since they took away Mary that morning, looked up and at first thought she must have fallen into a kind of dream state. When George Herrick took away other prisoners in the recent past, they were never to be seen again, as after their sentencing they all went immediately to be hanged. Yet here they all were – not only Mary, but Alice Parker and Samuel Wardwell and Dorcas Hoar and all the rest. They were back. They were saved!

"Mary!" Sarah screamed, jumping up and crawling over the people sprawled over the filthy floor. "Mary, you survive! Have they deemed you innocent?"

But her sister stood in front of her, mute, her eyes wide in confusion. She shook her head.

"We have not been reprieved, not a one of us," Samuel Wardwell, Mary's fellow prisoner, announced to the entire jail room. "We have all been condemned to die. We know not why they wait to schedule the day of our execution."

With that, Mary Esty collapsed into the arms of her sturdy sister. She was so frail that Sarah felt as if she could crush her bones if she held too tight. It was surreal, to be actually touching her sister who, in Sarah's mind, had already gone to God. When Mary was so roughly pulled out of the jail just hours before, Sarah felt empty, devoid of any feeling. She had been imprisoned for months now, with little to occupy her but her thoughts. When Rebecca had been torn from them, it was as if the grief was never-ending, a gigantic maw from which she could never escape – but still she had Mary with her. Mary had fallen into a despair that would not let her go, but still Sarah could hold her, talk to her, tell her stories. And her anger had kept her hope alive. But her petition to the court had obviously no effect, since the guilty decisions just kept coming down from on high. When the jail door had closed behind Mary that morning, everything just stopped for Sarah. But now, here she was, back again. In the flesh. With Mary's return, Sarah's soul revived and her thoughts started swirling once again.

"But I am to die, sister," Mary whispered, her throat dry and parched. "Those girls. Goody Putnam. All of them. They pointed their fingers at me. Their faces – so rageful, so mean. Young Ann Putnam told of my specter threatening her with a knife should she not sign the devil's book. Where do these things come from? What have I done, Sarah, what did Rebecca do, but serve God and our brothers in Christ? I have hardly laid eyes on these accusing girls. Why such hate? Oh, Sarah, I have such fear in my heart. They are to put a rope about my neck! Will I perish immediately? Will there be pain? Oh my dear Lord where are You? Where is Rebecca? What will happen to Isaac without me? Oh my children, my children!"

Sarah knew that her sister was rambling, filled with the insanity that stark terror brings with it, but she let her go on, as these were the first words she had uttered in weeks. The two women stood there, clutching each other, and Sarah heard similar greetings take place among other family members. She did her best to smooth Mary's hair, pat her back, whisper soothing sounds as her sister continued to rave. She was afraid that Mary was going mad, but could not stop her.

"Tis an unforgivable thing," Sarah heard an old woman say loudly across the room, "to leave us here, not knowing the hour of our death, yet knowing it is imminent. I would rather go to the gallows today. They have taken my husband already. Let them take me, those hounds!"

A number of ragged souls around her nodded their heads in sad agreement.

"Take me! Take me!" Mary cried out, and now Sarah shushed her, pulling at her to sit on the floor with her. "Mary, Mary," she pleaded, looking directly into her sister's clouded blue eyes, trying to reach a rational place inside her heart. "We have time, dear one. It may be a single hour, it may be a day, it may be longer than that. But let us not lose one moment of it. We are together, you and I. Look – I can touch your hand! And you can touch mine!"

As Sarah took her sister's shaking hand, Mary stopped her wailing and squeezed back with a strength Sarah thought was gone from her. She smiled.

"Aye, that's right," she encouraged. "Find me here, dear sister. Our hearts beat as one, even if it be for a moment. What would Rebecca bid us do?"

Mary's cracked lips moved just a tiny bit into a hint of a smile. "Rebecca," she said, her breath still rasping. "Rebecca. She would tell us that God is with us, even now."

Sarah's heart contracted. While she knew Mary was right that Rebecca would most likely respond that way, she also chafed at the notion. God is not with us, she thought. He has forsaken his disciples. Yet she would not contradict Mary, not when she was in this newly-lucid state.

"Aye, she would," Sarah agreed, pushing down her annoyance for her sister's sake. "And perhaps she would tell us a story. Remember how well she spun a tale? I used to hate it when she would tell me how I behaved as a child – because I was usually the naughty one!"

Was that a chuckle that she heard come from her dear sister? Yes, she was coming out of her stupor indeed.

"And you and I," Sarah continued. "Remember how we would hide under the covers in the upstairs loft, right before you went to marry Isaac? Remember how you were so worried that father would not like him because of his shyness?"

"And mother would tell us to be silent," Mary said slowly, enunciating every word as if it were difficult to summon it up, looking up at Sarah for approval. At this moment Sarah, so many years younger, felt like an ancient mother to her suffering sister. So be it, Sarah thought. Let me be the strong one. Just let me give my beloved a few moments of happiness before she is taken from this world.

"Aye, you are right!" Sarah cried out, laughing. The other prisoners looked their way in surprise. Laughter was not a sound that was often heard in such depths.

"And remember how you confounded her?" Mary said, this time a bit more strongly. "You with your cap askew and your hands on your hips and your pointing fingers. Always challenging her. You used to stomp your tiny foot when you were but two years of age. Mother would complain, but often I saw her smiling as she turned from you. She could not help herself."

The two went on like that for the hours that followed, not noticing when it grew dark outside. There was so little food that they had stopped feeling hunger a long time ago. All that existed was the two of them, clutching hands together, foreheads touching, coming up with story after story of how it used to be. About their parents William and Joanna, about all the backbreaking work of settling the land, but always suffused with great joy and love among the Towne family members. Sarah was filled with memories that she had long forgotten, and for now she allowed herself to feel cheered, reliving such precious moments with her big sister.

~~~
~~~

"Have you brought the documents?" Cotton Mather asked Samuel Sewall as the judge entered the Mathers' Second Church in Boston. Sitting at the table in front of the room was Thomas Danforth, looking sour. He had not wanted to accept Cotton's invitation to yet another meeting with these two men, as he continued to suspect Samuel of enthusiastic support of his fellow judges at the Court of Oyer and Terminer. And he was most displeased with the news that Cotton himself urged the execution of a fellow minister, even in the face of growing questions by the people. Since they last met, Thomas' guilt and shame for his own part in the trials had only grown as he read reports from Essex County. How now a full eight people waited to hang, and they had even pressed to death an old man who refused to enter a plea at his trial. What had seemed God's own work was now barbarous in Thomas' mind, and he wished he had never agreed to participate. Meanwhile, the detested William Stoughton – that usurper of Thomas' own position in the colony – continued to be as zealous as ever, ignoring the somber recommendations to expand his search for evidence beyond the spectral. Thomas could brook no endorsement of the proceedings, not even a hint of one.

"Aye, I have them here," Samuel was saying, handing a large leather-bound stack of papers to Cotton and doffing his hat. "They are not complete, yet it is what I could copy with my own hand with the short time I had to do it."

At that, Thomas' curiosity was piqued. Cotton had not told him the agenda for their meeting – only calling for his wisdom and grace, hinting at news, to get him here – so he had no idea to what the others were referring.

"Here, Thomas," Cotton said, handing him the portfolio. "Samuel has brought us some transcripts of the special court. Since none of us attend the proceedings any longer, I thought it good that we review the notes ourselves."

Thomas' rheumy eyes brightened, and he reached for the papers with more enthusiasm than he expected to have.

"The transcripts aside, Cotton," Samuel said, reaching out to stop Thomas from his reach. "I have just had more news from the north. The hanging date has been set for the morrow, and eight are to be executed."

Both Cotton and Thomas shook their heads in consternation.

"And more, I have made a copy of a petition that was sent to the court by one of the accused," Samuel said, holding up a single piece of parchment with a single paragraph written upon it. "You must read this most heartfelt and powerful plea for justice. This Goody Esty repeats and reinforces our own arguments in a convincing way. Yet Mr. Stoughton and the others have chosen to ignore it. I cannot sit on the fence any longer. This is surely an abomination that must be stopped."

Thomas grabbed the thin paper from Samuel, his hand shaking in anger. It only took him a moment to read what was on it. When he passed it to Cotton, Thomas had tears in his eyes.

"I cannot, I cannot," Thomas started, emotion overtaking him. "Cotton, how can you stand there, shaking your head in woe, when you yourself condemned Mr. Burroughs to die? I understand that the crowd suggested innocency after the man quoted the Lord's Prayer in its totality. It was you, young man. You were the one who killed him."

Cotton's face turned bright white, while Samuel jumped up to stand between them. "Thomas, please," he urged. "Cotton has already told us of how he felt befuddled at the scene."

"Bewitched is a better word for it," Cotton said, cowering slightly from Thomas' attack. "Aye, I did believe witchcraft was afoot. I did not hear the minister's words, I assure you. It was as if a full ten minutes were taken away from my ken. I only knew of the judges' decision, which was hanging. Tis the only thing I could attest to."

"Bah!" Thomas spat, walking away from the two men. "These times require steadfastness, not fainting spells."

"Mr. Mather is as concerned as we are that proper procedure is carried out," Samuel said, wringing his hands, hoping desperately for his friend and mentor to come back to them. "He believes in witchcraft as we do. But he also believes that justice is not necessarily being served."

"Not necessarily?" Thomas echoed. "Tis surely not! Again, tis time for true leaders to take a stand!"

"And that is what this meeting is for, I assure you," Samuel soothed, holding out his hand to Thomas. "I said myself that I no longer sit on the fence. And I do believe Cotton is in agreement."

"Aye, tis true," Cotton agreed. "Especially now."

The three men stood in the middle of the room, staring into each other's faces, challenging, questioning, certain and uncertain at the same time.

"Is the author not Goody Esty who is sister to Rebecca Nurse?" Thomas asked quietly, his anger now replaced with sadness. "Who is herself sister to the one I ruled guilty?"

Samuel did not answer until Cotton finished reading the document in front of him. "And you say that the judges were not moved by this missive?" he asked Samuel.

"To be sure they were not," Samuel replied. "They are so certain of their judgment that their eyes are clouded."

"'And why beholdest thou the mote that is in they brother's eye, but considerest not the beam that is in thine own eye?'" Cotton murmured, almost to himself, quoting the Book of Matthew.

"And yes, Thomas, these accused are indeed sisters," Samuel added.

"And eight are to die on the morrow?" Thomas asked. "And Goody Esty and Goody Cloyce are among them?"

He had always known what Goody Cloyce's fate would be, ever since he saw that every single person being tried for witchcraft had been hanged since the beginning of this hysteria. But now that it seemed a reality, he found he could hardly speak. The goodwife had invaded his nightmares for months. Now, he feared, she would come to haunt him for the rest of his days.

"Nay, not Goody Cloyce, but her sister Esty is among the group. The time is set for dawn," Samuel said. "There is nothing to be done, I fear."

Thomas felt a deep sense of relief, even while realizing it was only a matter of time for that poor woman that he himself as good as sent her to her death.

The three men sat in dismayed silence, each lost in his own thoughts.

"How comes your father's missive to the court, Cotton?" Thomas asked, calmer now, convinced that they were all of the same mind. He was grateful for it. Until then he felt like he was the only person seeing with a clear eye, as if everyone about him – even learned, righteous men – were suddenly overcome with some kind of disease that robbed them of their sanity. His conversion to the truth had come months ago, and even his wife Mary argued against him. It was a lonely existence. He had been most angry with these two compatriots, but at least they were now finally coming around.

"He is close to finished with it," Cotton answered him. "The last we spoke, he told me that he means to publish it as a booklet entitled <u>Cases of Conscience</u>. In this way the people can read the recommendations of those gathered at the College last month. The audience will be much wider than merely that of the court."

"Tis a wise strategy," Thomas commented. "And the people may indeed be swayed by the arguments, making them more potent by far. But I fear that by formally publishing the work, it is taking more time to complete than if it had been a mere letter to the court. This madman Stoughton is killing people by the week."

Cotton stared at the older man, not having thought of this conundrum before. It had not occurred to Samuel, either. They were all struck with the same thought: the work of the ministers, and their own part in it, would do nothing to save the souls who were set to hang on the morrow. Whether they were indeed witches or not.

~ ~ ~

As Mary Esty was thrown over George Herrick's shoulder to be carried aloft, her hands and feet bound, she appeared to the crowd below as a mere sack of hops flowers, no heavier than what a child might carry. While the sight was shocking to some, others sent up cries of "Woe! Woe!" that by now had become common amongst them. Thomas Putnam and John Gould stood at one edge of the crowd, both with heads high, hats remaining on their heads. Others were not so haughty, including Mary's husband Isaac, her grown children gathered about him, their own children told to stay home on this awful morning. The Esty women were sobbing. So were their Cloyce and Nurse cousins.

When Mary was helped to her feet on the hangman's platform, she looked down on those gathered below her but seemed not to comprehend their presence. Instead, her eyes rested on her beloved Isaac, her sons and daughters around him. As soon as Isaac met her gaze, she smiled as if he alone existed. The last time he had seen her, she had seemed lost, almost mad – yet today she stood erect, diminutive as she was, and at a strange peace. Isaac, despite the grief that had threatened to knock him down, couldn't help smiling himself, as scenes from their happy past flooded his memory as if they were all happening at once. He loved this woman. She had brought him a joy that was unbound.

As if reading his thoughts, Mary continued to look upon Isaac and her family and began to speak. At first the shouts of anger were so loud and her voice so low that her words could not be heard. But the crowd immediately quieted down, as the people were always eager to hear the last words of these heinous witches as they fell to their deserved deaths.

"…..love to my family, I do send you all of my prayers and look to that great day when we meet each other in Heaven, when we shall all sit at the feast prepared for us by our glorious God. And ye shall remain happy in this life, I beg this of you, and do not mourn for my soul, as today is my Welcome Day, and God awaits with His loving arms open to me - "

But she was stopped short by George Herrick's kick to her legs, and the snapping of the noose, and the swishing of the rope. Back and forth, back and forth.

At that moment, some who had cried "woe!" now found that they had to wipe away tears from their wet cheeks.

CHAPTER FOURTEEN

Essex County
October - November 1692

By now nineteen women and men were hanged and Giles Corey was pressed to death, all convicted of witchcraft. There were still over one hundred people languishing in the Salem Town and Boston prisons, all there for the same reason.

But to Sarah Cloyce, she did not care any longer. She had lost hope, and now she was merely waiting for her own death. She had also lost her faith, not even being certain that there existed a heaven where she would meet her sisters again.

Everything was dark; not only on the inside of the jail, but in Sarah's heart as well.

She wondered why her heart continued to beat at all.

Rebecca and Mary were both gone. Ever since she was born, her sisters were the ones who kept her going when she suffered. They came to her side when she was struggling with Edmund and running the Salem Town ordinary. When Edmund died, her sisters were there to pick her up and help her heal. They all mourned the deaths of their parents together. They shared everything they owned.

Vaguely, through the dense fog of Sarah's despair, she caught glimpses of images in her mind of those who were still alive and who still loved her. Her three daughters, of course, and Peter too. All of Rebecca's and Mary's extended families.

But these murky reminders could not cut through the knife-edge sharp pain of losing her sisters.

No more did she try to rally together her fellow prisoners, nor was she the first person to gobble up news when it came in from the outside through various visitors and from her husband Peter. Her petition to the court had done as much good as the ones entered into evidence at Rebecca's trial. They had all made no difference, no difference at all. There was nothing Sarah could do to reverse the terrible tide that was sweeping over the colony. More people would be cried out upon, and more people would die. Perhaps it was like a scourge from God – or from the Devil? – like the pestilence and war in the Bible stories where whole communities were wiped out.

But the Bible meant nothing any longer to Sarah, nor did God
or the Devil or anything else she had been taught her entire life.
Her two sisters – hearts as pure as the white sand beaches north of
Salem Town – were dead. She would die, too, she was certain of it.

How many motherless children would be left after this whole
thing was over?

Hannah was already grown and married, but what of young
Hepzibah, and Alice? What would happen to them, without Sarah?

Would it ever be over?

Would the colony eventually destroy itself with this hateful
rampage?

It no longer mattered to Sarah. It was only a matter of time
until they came for her, and she would be killed like her sisters.
They should have come for her first. Why didn't they come for
her first, when it was so well-known in the village that she was the
unwifely one, the one who was too strong and loud and contrary?
Perhaps she was being punished for such sins. But if she no longer
believed in God, then shouldn't she no longer believe in sin? Or
righteousness?

Or common sense?

She wished they would come for her because her thoughts
and despair and hopelessness and grief hounded her every hour of
every cursed day until she felt she might scream.

She was screaming in her head.

Without Mary or Rebecca to soothe and guide her, to hold
her in their warm, strong arms, she was untethered.

Injustice. Unfairness. The killing of innocents by ignorant,
frightened people with a grudge. There was no making sense of it
all. She had tried to find reason to it, but had now given up.

As the weeks wore on, rules about visitors to the jail slack-
ened, as now the constable was allowing in two and three from a
single family at the same time. These friends and family brought
with them baskets of food and drink, and sometimes new clothing.
At least there was that. It immensely cheered some of the prisoners,
but Sarah was beyond cheer.

One afternoon in early October her husband Peter came to
the jail, hoping against hope to see some of the fire in his wife's eyes
that came from her fighting for her sisters.

But his hopes were unfounded.

Sarah hardly lifted her head as Peter approached her. She spent her days crouched on the floor, in a twilight sleep throughout the day and night, her appetite gone. Her shift and skirts hung on her body that had always been well-cushioned but was now riddled with bones jutting out beneath paper-like skin. The eyes that gazed into his were lackluster, as if a shade had been drawn over them. Gone was the light that always shone through, sometimes with happiness, often with stubbornness.

"Sarah, I bring you greetings from the girls," Peter said. "Hannah. She has a fine, healthy young baby, and she and Joseph have named her Rebecca. And Alice. And young Hepzibah."

In truth, Hepzibah had fallen into her own depression. When Sarah was first taken, the child screamed and screamed through the night, calling out for her mother. After weeks of this – weeks where Peter, old enough to be Hepzibah's grandfather, could only cover his head with one of the duck feather and ticking striped pillows, hoping that the cacophony would stop – she just ceased, realizing her fits were not bringing Sarah to her. Since then, she walked about in a sad daze, not willing to be cheered no matter how hard Peter tried. And no matter how Hepzibah's grown sister, Hannah, would try to cheer up the little girl by giving her baby Rebecca to hold, to take her out of the house for summer walks, or visits to her own home, Hepzibah would not be roused. Hannah would bring news to her stepfather Peter from her husband Joseph, who reported to her daily about the trials. Recently Joseph had received word from Boston was that Governor Phips had returned from the District of Maine and was not happy with all of the executions. Perhaps the tyranny was coming to a close?

But how would Sarah react to this news? Peter thought. In her state, she didn't seem worried about dying. Would she be relieved that she might be saved, or would she rave because Rebecca and Mary had already been executed, never to be helped by any change of opinion by the magistrates?

Before that, Peter had been relieved to see his wife hopeful; indeed, it was he who had carried her petition to Judge Hathorne. Before Mary's death he had spied in Sarah a bit of her old obstinacy, her refusal to be cowed. The first time he had met his wife, so many years ago, he saw the same beautiful courage in her, showing no signs of the depression she had just recovered from. Indeed there were some occasions when he felt she was stronger than he, that she was the one to lead the family. He relied on her fortitude. They all did.

So seeing Sarah in her current state brought dread into Peter's heart.

Sarah did not respond to Peter's greetings from her children, nor about her first grandchild. She merely stared straight ahead, as if Peter was not talking to her at all. He wanted to sob. He no longer prayed.

Were they all, in fact, truly lost?

~ ~ ~

"Governor Phips is not pleased, Cotton," Thomas Danforth announced. He was sitting with the two Mathers and Samuel Sewall in the same Harvard class hall where the group of ministers developed their argument against the witch trials back in early August. Now the sun was as brightly shining through the tall windows, but the trees out in the yard were blazing the gold and oranges that were so prevalent at this time of year. Thomas had been excited when he received word that Phips was perturbed when he heard that there had been so many executions.

"Aye, tis true," Samuel said. "He thought that when he established the Court of Oyer and Terminer last spring we would have been done with the situation by now. But word is that he thought that meant that many people would be tried and acquitted so that the jails could be thinned out. But he came home to them being as crowded as ever – "

"And we hear that he is angry that so many people have been hanged!" Thomas added.

"Aye," Samuel agreed. "All of us on the court received word. The governor is particularly frustrated with his lieutenant."

"Tis not a surprise!" Thomas cried out, so achingly relieved that all of his work behind the scenes might be coming to fruition. "Stoughton has lost all perspective. You should read the heart-felt petitions being submitted to the court, Increase – missives that are systematically ignored. Mr. Sewall here no longer has the stomach to travel to Salem Village on behalf of the court. And Mr. Saltonstall resigned long ago!"

"Yet Mr. Hathorne and Mr. Corwin are as rabid as ever," Samuel said. Both he and Thomas watched the father and son ministers closely as they took in the news. Cotton looked more dubious than Increase, though the elder appeared resolute.

"Tis good that my book will be published this week," Increase said slowly, pulling on his beard as he was wont to do. "I will take an advance copy to Mr. Phips myself. I will do it this day."

"Tis excellent timing," Thomas said. "We cannot waste another moment. There are trials already scheduled for next week."

Thomas exhaled heavily as he left the hall, relieved beyond measure. While at first, when he was called to oversee that early examination up in Salem Village, he felt certain that he was doing God's work. For his entire life he thought himself a good man, a godly man, and it seemed that the Lord had rewarded him with earthly goods. Indeed over the past several decades Thomas had grown his holdings to the west of Boston from the initial grants he received from the colonial government, purchasing plots from settlers who braved the wilderness only to return to Boston, chastened by the difficulty of clearing the huge boulders from the ground for farming and the danger of the Indian tribes moving up from Narragansett. They were only too happy to sell their fledgling farms to the Deputy Governor. Thomas expanded his holdings, too, by negotiating with the Wampanoag who gladly sold their own acres for bits of wampum, blankets and beaver skins. By now Danforth's Farms covered a full two hundred acres, by the grace of God himself. This was not to mention the family townhouse he owned in Cambridge, and other holdings to the north. He had no interest in settling his Farms himself, but continued to offer long-term leases to colonists willing to break farms into the vast wilderness that spread out for so many miles. He was getting old – now in his seventies – and he knew that such arrangements could provide for him and his family for many generations.

So God had been good. And Thomas did not ever give up the chance to do His work on earth. But since his first inklings of doubt that arose in him when that Goody Cloyce looked at him so clearly during her examination, to hearing about her two sisters' demise, to watching that dreaded William Stoughton wreak havoc over the law, he became more and more convinced that the whole business was a complete travesty of justice.

For months now Thomas had been talking with the judges from Boston who had been assigned to the special court – men like John Richards, Peter Sargent and Wait Winthrop, not to mention

Mr. Sewall – trying hard to persuade them to disagree with the Salem judges and Mr. Stoughton. He had grown frustrated with them, including his friend Samuel, because they would not outright rebel; rather, they just stopped presiding over the trials. Since the law only required four judges to sit at any one time – and Chief Justice Stoughton and Salem judges Hathorne, Corwin and Jonathan Gedney were more than happy to lead all of the proceedings – the others could bow out with little cause or consequence. No one was willing to take a stand against the hangings, and Stoughton would not listen to Thomas himself, as he knew Thomas was his rival who was upset that he hadn't been chosen to participate in the Court of Oyer and Terminer. It was truly maddening to be in such an inferior position, no longer being able to affect change in the colony as he used to, under the old charter.

It was particularly disheartening to see Samuel and Cotton waver so in their convictions. At one moment they were railing against the trials and the next, Cotton himself was on his horse, urging the execution of a fellow minister. And Samuel appeared to be constantly struggling with his own conscience, believing now that the colony was truly in the devil's snare, and then that at least some of the victims had been innocent. To Thomas, the situation was clear.

He was glad when Samuel and Cotton finally did come down off the fence of uncertainty and agree that the witchcraft judges were misusing their authority. And now the elder Mather was also convinced that the judges should show more restraint. Thomas had seen the first draft of his <u>Cases of Conscience</u> manuscript, and to him it was brilliant. Mr. Mather had laid out quite clearly his arguments, using specific examples from the past, when similar mistakes were made. He examined the Witch of Endor and the Book of Samuel, where it could be proven that the Devil personified an innocent man. And he reiterated that it was better for ten witches to go free than a single pure soul be executed. Finally, as a coda to the whole work, Mr. Mather added Cotton's arguments presented in the ministers' earlier letter which the court rejected, including the recommendation that the court not rely solely on the use of spectral evidence to convict. If the judges continued to ignore such rationales against what they were doing, then Thomas hoped Governor Phips would consider it. He had no love for Phips, either, but at least there was hope that he could be persuaded, especially now when it seemed that the governor might think the entire thing would make him look bad to the colony.

Thomas walked the short two blocks to his townhouse on Bow Street, and tonight he greeted his wife Mary with open arms and smiles. It was an unusual scene for them both, after such long evenings of despair, sadness and often bitter arguments about what was happening in Essex County.

~ ~ ~

Several days later, a cold autumn rain swept over Boston, turning the streets into paths of mud that covered men's boots and splattered the bottoms of women's petticoats. The weather did not deter Increase Mather, though, as he made his way down Prison Lane, past the first meeting house, to the Boston Town House where the governor was waiting for him. The day before the minister had sent to Mr. Phips via courier an advance copy of his new book, with a note requesting that the governor pay it immediate attention. That morning a messenger knocked on the door of the Second Church, bidding the minister to an urgent meeting scheduled a few hours later. As Mr. Mather walked down the lane he pushed his bible and several texts further inside his cloak, protecting them from the wet. He wanted to be prepared to answer any of the governor's questions.

It was dark before the minister left the Town House to return to his church. Even though he knew his wife Anne would most likely have dinner ready for him by then, he wanted to be alone to digest his discussion with the governor. Ducking into the Anchor Tavern on School House Lane, the minister sought out a corner table and welcomed a large wooden cup of ale. As he stared into the fire, his mind wandered to what had just happened.

Mr. Danforth and Mr. Sewall were right: the governor was gravely displeased with the proceedings of the special court in Salem Village. For months now people had been hinting to Increase that he had made the wrong decision in tapping Mr. Phips to be the head of the colony. He had done so because Mr. Phips had been instrumental in convincing the King and Queen to grant them a new charter; and besides, the younger man had spent a full year in England, convincing the minister that he was the one for the job. Now in retrospect, Increase saw that Phips was a man more inclined toward war making, shipbuilding and even pirating than handling the quotidian responsibilities of running the colony. It was clear that he was hoping that his lieutenant governor would be the statesman he was not. He did not expect Mr. Stoughton to focus all of his attention on the outbreak in Salem Village at the expense of the rest of the colony's business. Indeed he had done nothing to help the General Court get through their normal cases, and he continued to withhold much-needed financial and military assistance to the poor English settlers still being attacked by the Abenaki in Maine. Already the crown was demanding increased taxes for products like sugar and coffee from the Caribbean and Spain, and nothing was being done about that, either. Since his return from the north, seemingly countless magistrates and ministers accosted him with questions about the twenty people – twenty! – being executed in Salem Village. Just that morning he heard that the good Reverend Hale in Beverly – the very man who was first called to Mr. Parris' parsonage to examine the afflicted girls – reported that his own wife had been cried out upon. Surely something must be done.

Mr. Phips told Increase that he had read every word of his manuscript with great interest, staying awake late into the night to finish it. The minister was surprised that the governor would have such careful questions of the book's arguments, as Phips had not attended the College and was not known to be a learned man. He wanted to know how Increase could on the one hand support the work of the judges of the Court of Oyer and Terminer and on the other criticize their methods to such a degree. He outright asked the minister if he believed innocent people were being hanged. After hours of discussion, he wanted Increase's advice: should he disband the special court?

Increase pulled on his beard absently as he took another quaff from his cup, thankful for the comfort the drink brought him as he contemplated the end of his meeting with Phips. He was used to being a counselor to great men in the colony. He knew the people and the magistrates both looked to him for wisdom and strength. Increase could always rely on the word of God and His grace to lead him. But the governor's question had daunted him, he couldn't deny it. The trials had taken up the hearts and minds of the colonists for six months now, and people were genuinely frightened that the Devil had been loosed upon the colony. And the Bible taught that witchcraft was indeed real and something to be affronted at every turn by righteous men.

At the end of his meeting with the governor, Increase had opened his well-worn bible with the pages so used that the corners felt like the soft underside of a lamb's ear. He opened it to one of the earlier sections and read aloud Exodus 23:7: "Thou shalt keep thee far from a false matter, thou shalt not slay the innocent and the righteous: for I will not justify a wicked man." The governor stared hard at him. Increase turned the book toward the governor and pointed to the notes inscribed to the side of the verse, as was common with the Geneva Bible that all the colonists used. "The notes tell us," he intoned, "'Whether thou be magistrate or art commanded by the magistrate.' Tis almost as if God is pointing his all-knowing finger toward us, Mr. Phips, knowing our situation as if it had happened during Jesus' own time. I must believe in Him at this crucial juncture."

"And so?" Phips had asked again, his eyes blazing as he stared at the minister.

Increase Mather had spoken each word carefully, deliberately, feeling an immense relief at finally making a decision. "My advice, dear sir, is to halt the proceedings."

CHAPTER FIFTEEN

Essex County
December 1692 - January 1693

Peter Cloyce sat at his small writing table in the corner of the best parlor of his home, struggling to determine which words he should put on the parchment in front of him. He gazed outside to the snow-covered scene beyond the diamond-paned windows, feeling the cold that crept into the house. His hand hovered over the inkwell, suspended there as he remembered the last time he had seen his wife.

Still bereft and almost totally unresponsive, Sarah had not even fluttered an eye when he told her the amazing news that Governor Phips had disbanded the Court of Oyer and Terminer. He expected that she would have shown some relief – her long ordeal may be soon over – but was disappointed in this. All of the fight seemed to have gone completely out of her, and Peter barely recognized his wife.

So now it's time for me to take the lead, he thought to himself. I will not let my beloved wife die from heartbreak. And the first thing he needed to do was to get her out of that hell that they called a jail. He needed to petition Boston to allow her to go free on bail until her trial. Because trials would have to continue, once Phips and Stoughton created a new General Court under the new charter. All of that had been put off until the witch trials could be done with. But now the special court was disbanded, and there was news that Governor Phips was not happy with the practice of the sole use of spectral evidence to convict prisoners. Rebecca's son-in-law John Tarbell had ridden his horse all the way into Boston to procure as many copies of Increase Mather's <u>Crises of Conscience</u> as he could get his hands on, to deliver to the people of Salem Village. Peter himself had purchased a copy as soon as John returned with two sacks on either side of the horse filled with the small pamphlets. Even though Peter felt great anger at God for what He had loosed upon the colony, he couldn't help thanking Him for giving the good Mr. Mather the courage to bring sanity back to Massachusetts. Now he prayed that the new court would heed the minister's warnings, and justice could be served.

Little Hepzibah and her older sister Alice interrupted their father's thoughts by clambering down the narrow, steep steps leading up to the loft upstairs. Hepzibah came to Peter and rested her little curly-haired head on his shoulders and he instinctively wrapped one arm around her tiny waist. Alice stood by, sticking her thumb into her mouth – a habit she had long ago eschewed but which she had recently taken up again – the light in her eyes dull and lifeless.

"What are you writing, papa?" Hepzibah asked plaintively.

"Oh my dear, I am writing an important letter."

"Why is it important?"

Should he tell them, and give them hope that might not come to fruition? he thought. It probably wasn't prudent to do so. But he was heartsick to see both his daughters' despair, and wanted to do everything to bring them out of it. Lately Hepzibah had been asking him to tell her what Sarah looked like, as her mother was becoming a mere faint memory in her very young mind. At least the girl was talking about Sarah. She had stopped asking about her Aunts Rebecca and Mary months ago. Peter supposed it would be better if his daughter forgot about them entirely. He didn't think such a young child could truly handle such a devastating loss. And poor Alice had become almost mute in the last weeks, refusing to eat, listless.

"I am asking important men in Boston to let your mother go free," Peter said to Hepzibah, making his decision. Hepzibah looked up at him in wonder, her sky blue eyes shining with the hope that had been gone from them for so long.

"Mia is to come home?" she asked, her voice almost a whisper.

"Mama?" Alice muttered, pulling her thumb out of her mouth.

"That is my hope, little ones," Peter answered. "I cannot be certain that my letter will work. But you can help by sending a special prayer up to God to save her. Oh, she misses you both so very much."

Hepzibah did not reply; she only pushed on him so she could sit on his lap, wrapping her arms around his neck. Peter was surprised to see that Alice, now way too big for laps, clambered up as well, so that he could hardly breathe from the tight embraces. This was best, he thought. He was glad that the children weren't demanding a guarantee. In the last year they had become quiet, introspective girls, their big eyes taking in everything around them, seeming almost otherworldly in their aspect. Peter hoped against hope that their young beauty and grace could help Sarah out of her own pit of misery.

The three sat like that for a very long time, both embracing, even after Peter's old bones started to grow pained from staying in the position. Finally, Hepzibah wordlessly let him go, moving toward the kitchen behind the parlor. Alice followed. Their father suspected they had grown hungry. Though only four and nine respectively, they had grown used to cooking and cleaning for the family.

They are growing up too fast, Peter thought. Please, God, bring their mother home. Soon.

Eventually he was able to write the petition, using some of the rationale he had heard that other villagers were arguing: now that winter was upon them, there was great doubt that their loved ones would survive the horrid conditions of the jail. He had also learned that the constable was demanding that the families of the prisoners pay for the meager food they had eaten, their portion of Herrick's salary, and other costs that the colony had taken on in order to jail them. Goodman Herrick was even requiring payment for the shackles that he had placed on the poor innocents. Peter couldn't help feeling deep resentment for such demands, thinking of the great suffering that Sarah – and the others – had endured. So unfairly. Yet he swallowed his anger and added a sentence to the petition that he was willing and able to pay what was necessary to gain his wife's release on bail. He had heard that other families weren't able to do this. There was hope for Sarah, but there was no hope for these others. Would the injustice never stop?

~ ~ ~

By now, Thomas Danforth was no longer enraged when he was told that Governor Phips appointed William Stoughton as the Chief Justice of the new Judicial Superior Court. He had no faith at all in the colonial government that Phips was leading. Yes, it was a very good thing that the governor had disbanded the Court of Oyer and Terminer, and thank God that he had been open to Increase Mather's recommendations against it. At the same time, he was rewarding Stoughton – the very man who had rejected Cotton Mather's similar warnings earlier in the year, the man who ran roughshod over established legal practices. The man who most likely sent at least one innocent to her grave, which was a sin against God and man. It was just one more instance when the powers that be could not, in the end, take a real stand against the villainy that had overtaken the colony.

"But Mr. Stoughton wants you to join the new Superior Court!" Samuel Sewall protested when he heard of his friend and mentor's decision to reject membership in the court. "I beg of you, Thomas: join me in this. You and I can ensure that these prisoners will see a fair trial!"

"Pffft," Thomas said, noticing that what he felt was more relief than anger. "You do not need me. Mr. Stoughton may want to continue in his hunt. But Mr. Winthrop, Mr. Richards – and you as well – will keep him in line, I am sure of it. And besides, Mr. Phips has ruled that the sole use of spectral evidence is forbidden. The pendulum has swung, Samuel."

The two men were sitting in rocking chairs under quilts in front of the huge fireplace in Thomas' front parlor, sipping hot rum from pewter cups that his wife Mary had poured for them. It was a bitterly cold winter night outside, and Thomas was pleased to sit at leisure in his home, away from politics and the courts and heinous men like Mr. Stoughton.

"But Thomas, what will you do if you walk away from public life?" Samuel asked. "How can you be happy in such a situation? You, who have devoted your entire career to the good of the colony!"

Thomas took another sip of rum, enjoying the warmth as it trickled down his throat. "I am an old man, Samuel. Not like you, who has his whole career in front of him. I believe I have done what I could for Massachusetts, and the District of Maine as well. But my active support of this witch trial hysteria in its early days has shaken me to the core. It has shown me how my mind can be addled by the power I used to have over the fates of men. I cannot, in good faith, return to such a position."

"But does that mean that a political life is inherently evil?" Samuel asked, with worry on his face. "Does that mean that I should feel the same as you, and quit the court?"

"Nay, nay, my friend," Thomas said, waving his hand in dismissal. "Not inherently evil. Much good has been done in this colony for many decades. And I am certain it can continue. Yet it requires younger men than I."

"It will be unusual, serving the people without your good guidance and wisdom."

"I am sure you will be fine. However Samuel, you yourself did sway in your convictions throughout these trials. Pardon my impertinence, but again I am an old man and you say that you think of me as a mentor. Throughout these months, you walked away from the trials. Yet you never took a stand against them."

Samuel was quiet for many moments, gazing into the roaring fire. A large log hissed and fell to the side, giving out red and yellow sparks that bounced against the copper pots hanging from the crane. Thomas did not worry that his friend might be angered by his comment. It needed to be said.

"Aye, you are right, my friend," Samuel finally agreed. "It is difficult to question the likes of unwavering men like Mr. Stoughton. He was indeed certain that he was doing God's work. He still does. I do hear that he is not pleased with Mr. Phips' restriction of his methods."

"'Tis true that Mr. Stoughton seems most assured. In my experience, such zealous men should always be questioned. I prefer a more nuanced intelligence. One that doubts. One that regards situations with open eyes. That was my sin, last spring. I walked a straight line of seeming truth. But it was not the truth, Mr. Sewall. Indeed it was not."

Samuel was quiet once again.

"I advise questioning at every turn, Mr. Sewall," Thomas added. "I advise apologizing when one is wrong. I advise standing for the truth, even when everyone around you is sitting."

The only thing that could be heard was the cracking of the fire, and the distant sounds of pots clattering together, as Mary was washing the evening meal's dishes in the kitchen at the back of the house. Thomas took another quaff of his drink and snuck a glance over at Samuel. He was pleased to see that the younger man was clearly struggling with his conscience. It reassured Thomas that Samuel would indeed serve the colony with reasoned justice.

"I take your advice, Thomas," Samuel finally said. "It is my solemn vow."

"Then all is well," Thomas said, with good humor.

"But what will you do now?"

"I intend to continue my work on behalf of the College. And I have come up with a plan that I hope will help me regain God's mercy."

Samuel shook his head slightly, now most curious. "And what is this plan?"

Thomas placed his cup on the small table that sat between the two men and leaned forward, ignoring the pain that shot up his spine. "Tis impossible to adequately atone for my part in these trials," he said. "And tis impossible to restore the happiness of those who have lost their innocent family members in an unjust and revolting cause. Yet I do wish to make some kind of reparation to those I have harmed."

"That woman you have spoken of so many times before? Goody Cloyce?"

"Aye. I was the one who sent her to jail."

"But she survives, Thomas. It is everyone's hope that she will be found ignoramus – her guilt couldn't be determined one way or the other – when she comes to the new court. I for one will vote that way."

"She survives, but to what life? She has lost her two sisters. I have made many inquiries around Salem Village. I understand that these three sisters were very close."

"And what will you offer her?"

"I will give her property on Danforth's Farms."

Samuel's eyes widened with wonder. "You mean to take her away from Salem Village?"

"Aye. I have little to give, but I have property. Significant acres, as you well know. Several settlers are there now, renting whole swaths of land from me, carving small farms out of the untamed earth. The Sudbury River runs through the Farms, and the land is rich. So far – praise be to God – Indian insurrections are few. I myself am not interested in farming there, as I am old and content to sit in front of this hearth for my remaining years. But the existing rents are lucrative and will continue to be after I go to my heavenly home. I have more than enough to grant these poor families a new life after what they have suffered. At no further cost to them."

Thomas smiled at the thought of this idea, and his friend had not seen such satisfaction on his face in a long time.

"T'would not excuse the harm I have wrought upon her, mind you," he added. "Yet perhaps in one small way it can bring some comfort to those so unjustly treated."

<center>~~~</center>

Indictment of Sarah Cloyce, for afflicting Mary Walcott

The jurors for our Lord and Lady the King and Queen do present that Sarah Cloyce, wife of Peter Cloyce of Salem Village in the County of Essex in or upon the eleventh day of Januarry 1692 and diverse other days and times as well committed certain detestable arts called Witchcrafts and Sorceries against one Mary Walcott of Salem. Mary Walcott was tortured, afflicted, consumed, wasted, pined and tormented by the said Sarah Cloyce.

January 4, 1693 court decision: Ignoramus.

~ ~ ~

As Peter Cloyce drove his wagon over the snow-covered road home from the Salem Town jail, he made sure to go very slowly. He was worried that his wife, sitting in a bundled pile of blankets on the seat next to him, would feel great pain at every bump and dip. When he had lifted her up to the wagon, she felt no heavier than a small bag of corn; he had been shocked at how tiny she was in his arms. Her eyes were hollowed-out dark holes in the midst of sagging pale skin, all light having gone out of them. The fire and energy that had made her the strong woman she was had completely vanished, leaving an empty shell, like that of a rattling milkweed pod after giving off its silky seeds to the autumn winds. He couldn't wait to get her home, where she could, he desperately hoped, start to heal.

He had sent young Hepzibah and Alice to stay with their sister Hannah's family in Salem Town, concerned that the children would be frightened at the sight of their mother. Hepzibah was forgetting Sarah already; her father did not want her to be traumatized at what she might think as a ragged old crone. Hannah had also kindly agreed to try to explain the situation to her baby sisters – although how she would do that, Peter had no idea.

Peter nickered at the horses, pulling on their reins to veer off the main road, sneaking a glimpse at his wife to see if she noticed that he was taking them on a circuitous route home. The main road ran directly in front of Rebecca's farm, and he did not want her to have to take in such a sight, at least not on this first day. Now that most of the prisoners were being freed with decisions of "ignoramus" – "we are ignorant," indicating that the jury could not find enough evidence to convict – Francis Nurse and many of his kinsmen have already started to loudly complain of the court's injustice.

They could do nothing to gain recompense from the government in Boston, but they could certainly protest Mr. Parris' part in it. Peter agreed with his brothers-in-law: without the minister's encouragement of the afflicted girls' woes, Rebecca, Mary and all the others would probably still be alive. Once he got Sarah settled at home and he was certain that she would recover, he planned to join Francis and the others in their fight.

Finally, after what seemed like hours, Peter pulled up the wagon in front of their farmhouse. He had made sure to build up the fire before he left, and hoped that the front hall would seem warm and cheery. But as they entered the front door, he could tell that Sarah didn't notice. She had spent three-fourths of a year becoming inured to the squalor and stink of the Salem Town jail; he hoped she could eventually open her heart and mind to her surroundings one again. He would not give up on her.

CHAPTER SIXTEEN

Essex County
February 1693

Sarah had been home for close to a month, but Peter's hopes
for her recovery were slowly fading. She still sat in the rocking chair
in front of the hearth that he and the girls kept lit, wrapped in thick
woolen rugs, staring into the flames without saying much of anything at all. By now Hepzibah and Alice had grown accustomed to
this new mother, although when they first saw Sarah they ran into
the next room, fearful, despite how Hannah had tried to prepare
them. Since then, though, Hepzibah seemed to have matured
beyond her years, taking on the role of parent to her own mother,
dutifully cooking and cleaning and fetching water and firewood.
She would heat cider over the fire and present Sarah with a fresh
cup several times a day, even though Sarah drank little of it. The
other day Peter walked in from feeding the animals in the barn to
see his little daughter brushing out her mother's long, curly tresses
that had faded from bright flax to a dull gray. Hepzibah was humming a nursery rhyme, lost in her task, and she had a faraway, wise
look in her eyes. I am afraid for her, Peter thought. I am afraid that
she is growing up too fast.

Alice had been slower to embrace this new mother, preferring
to stay in bed up in the loft, feigning illness. She had tried to understand it when both Hannah and then her father explained that
the trials were over and that her mother was home for good. She
couldn't believe that those terrible girls had stopped their accusations. Alice remembered how they would torture her in the meeting
house yard, and how Hannah would have to rescue her. Everyone
had said it was all in fun. But look what that Abigail and her little
minions had done to the Cloyce family. To Alice's dear aunts. To
her own mother.

Peter himself tried hard to remain strong as he vowed that
he would bring Sarah, somehow, out of her darkness. But it was
difficult to hope, when he saw no improvement at all. At night he
would carry Sarah to their bed on the second floor, her body still
thin and very easy to bear, and after he tucked her in he slid under
the heavy blankets with her, moving his feet this way and that,

warming the cold sheets with the friction. He whispered words of love to her, words of hope, memories of brighter days, reports from her various nieces' and nephews' families. He carefully avoided any word about her brothers-in-law Isaac and Francis, as they, too, were grieving for the loss of Mary and Rebecca. Every so often Sarah would clasp Peter's hand tightly, as if she were falling and needed something to hold onto. But more often she just lay there, unmoving, unresponsive.

As Peter held his wife close, he wished he could send hope and joy to her, just through his touch. Inevitably she would fall asleep, leaving him wide awake, filled with worry. How could they exist like this? How could they remain in this village, after what their neighbors had done to them? Since last summer most of the extended Towne family refused to attend Mr. Parris' services, including Peter, despite the fact that the minister tried to visit their homesteads several times, attempting to impress upon them the sin of their absence. Every time he was met with a loud slam of the door and resounding imprecations. But how could this continue? How could the Village move on from this hysteria, now that most of the accused had been let free by the new Judicial Court? Those hated Putnams, the Goulds, the Walcotts, the Ingersolls – their families had been untouched by death and injustice, and still held powerful positions in the church and the local government. Peter had heard that the afflicted girls had by now stopped their fits, after realizing that their pointing fingers had no more power. But they were alive, and unpunished. It was almost too much for Peter to bear.

One very cold February afternoon a knock came to the door of the Cloyce homestead. Sarah was in her usual position in front of the fire, Hepzibah was cutting up turnips for the evening meal's stew, and Peter was at the large table, recaning a chair whose slats had weathered away in the last year. Though it was frigid outside, Alice had offered to feed the cow and the horse in the barn, preferring to be anywhere but in the house.

Peter bid Hepzibah to answer the door.

As Peter jumped up to greet the visitor, he immediately recognized him. The man was dressed in well-tailored finery and his hat was made of the best leather. His hair was white and his face mottled with age.

It was the magistrate who had sent his dear Sarah to jail. Mr. Thomas Danforth.

Peter instinctively held out his hand in greeting, but upon seeing who the visitor was, he pulled it back. Young Hepzibah looked up at her father, surprised at his lack of courtesy.

"Hepzibah," Peter said, gravely. "Do go upstairs to your room. You can finish your dinner preparations later."

The child dutifully walked away, bending down to kiss her mother's worn cheek as she went. The old man's eyes followed her, and as they alighted on the bundled mass in front of the fire, Peter could see him wince.

"I imagine, sir, that you are not pleased to see me," he said to Peter. "But I beg your patience and just a small bit of your time."

Peter raised his eyebrows at such a great man addressing him as "sir," but this did nothing to assuage the great anger that was flooding through his body. This man. This judge. He was to blame for the torture that befell his wife. What could he possibly want?

Thomas did not wait for a response; he merely shed his cloak and hat and hung them on one of the empty pegs near the door. Peter remained speechless, dumbfounded. Enraged. He should throw the man out of his house right that second. Why wasn't he moving?

"In truth," Thomas was saying. "I wish to speak with your wife."

At that, Peter sprung to life. "You cannot, sir," he said sternly, pulling the judge back from approaching Sarah. "She is ill and barely breathing. And grieving for the murders of her two dear sisters. She is entertaining no visitors. Especially you, Mr. Danforth."

In all other circumstances, a farmer would never think to address a magistrate in such a way, but Peter did not care. What could Danforth do to him now?

"I understand your acrimony, Goodman Cloyce," Thomas said, looking deep into Peter's eyes. "I deserve all of it, and more. I am here not to antagonize you or your wife. I come instead with true and faithful sorrow for my part in her incarceration."

His words struck Peter, who was not expecting this apology. Indeed many of the families of the witchcraft trials victims had already started petitioning the Boston government for restitution, but were meeting with rejection, even refusal of an audience. And he knew his brothers-in-law Francis and Isaac had been trying to meet with Mr. Parris to urge him to renounce his part in the trials, but the minister only castigated them for not attending services. They had been trying to get Peter to join them, but so far he was too busy trying to help Sarah. He never expected a man like Mr. Danforth – until recently Lieutenant Governor, and one of the leaders of the colony – to be here at Peter's modest farm, asking for forgiveness.

His surprise was enough for Peter to allow the judge to approach the hearth once more.

The man sat wearily in the rocking chair next to Sarah, and then pulled it closer to her so he could look her in her heavily-lidded eyes. The woman in front of him hardly resembled the outspoken, tenacious person he remembered from her examination last spring. He remembered when she yelled out at her accuser – "You, sir, are a grievous liar!" – challenging the whole proceedings where other prisoners were cowed by it. Her courage and determination were what made him start to question his own position in the first place. But here she was, appearing as if she were barely alive. Tiny. Spent. Destroyed.

By him.

Peter stared, astonished, as tears glistened in the magistrate's eyes, reflecting the light of the fire in front of him.

Thomas took Sarah's withered hands in his own bigger ones, hoping she would look at him. She, however, continued to stare blankly into the fire.

"Goody Cloyce," Thomas said, his words muffled because he had bowed his head. "I am Thomas Danforth, the Lieutenant Governor who oversaw your examination for witchcraft last June. I, along with my colleague Mr. Sewall and the other Salem Village judges, heard testimony from the afflicted girls who cried out against you. At the time I was moved by this testimony, and the girls' terrible fits. It was my opinion that witchcraft had been cast, and that you were at fault for it."

Thomas' words were slow, and choked by his own tears. Peter stood by, taking in the whole scene, amazed. He let out a small gasp when he saw Sarah move, turning her body toward the judge. She had not responded to anyone before this, nor had she shown any sign that she was comprehending anything that had been said to her. But now she opened her eyes and in their depths Peter saw that well-known light come into them once again. She was listening to Mr. Danforth.

And she was angry.

Thomas saw it, too, and moved back slightly, as he found it painful to be the target of such a forceful look. Sarah's eyes pierced his own, and in hers he saw an ocean of rage which seemed to flood his soul. Suddenly he felt relief that she was such a small woman, and obviously devoid of physical strength; otherwise he would fear for his own safety.

But he forced himself to maintain eye contact, despite how terrible it was. Did he expect nothing less than such anger? This woman had lost those dearest to her. And she herself had suffered so – at his hands. He must remain, even though every ounce of him wished to run away from the terrible scene. He deserved everything that this woman had to say to him.

"I come asking for forgiveness for that mistake, Goody Cloyce," he said in a strangled voice. "I know now that I was terribly wrong. Not a week after you were sent to jail, I began to have doubts, as did Mr. Sewall and others. But we could do nothing about it, since Governor Phips had established the special court and formal trials began. It was my sincere hope that justice would be served during these proceedings, and I was much distressed to see that so many convictions were being decided. I worked with Mr. Mather and his father and others to develop a case against the trials, and Mr. Sewall stopped his participation in them. Throughout I never forgot your pleading face."

There was a long, uncomfortable silence that Thomas forced himself to let remain as his words slowly sunk into Sarah's mind. He steeled himself for anything that might come next. A diatribe. Stinging accusations. Let it all rain down on his head, he thought. He deserved everything she could do to him.

Sarah's eyes flashed with indignation, but they seemed to be the only thing alive in her: her body remained still and unmoving. It was as if she were being kept hostage inside a dead prison, her eyes the only thing showing life inside.

"And yet," Sarah said, in an almost inaudible whisper, the words sounding hollow and rattling like seeds inside an old dry gourd. "I remained shackled. My sisters murdered."

Peter had to hold himself back from running to his wife and embracing her with joy, as these were the first words he had heard from her in over a month. But he knew that this was her moment with the judge. It was her confrontation to make, not his.

Thomas bowed his head again in anguish. "Aye, tis true," he admitted. "I was ousted from my position by the new government. I had no more power to change anything."

"Mr. Sewall….." Sarah said, with much effort. Thomas winced once more.

"Aye, he was on the bench of the special court, you are right," he said. "I could have done more to convince him. I did wrong there, too."

Sarah lifted her worn eyes to gaze at her husband who was standing in awe just a few feet behind the judge. Tears came to his own eyes as he saw that his wife recognized him. She was awake! She had come back to him! She lifted her other hand to him, and now he couldn't help going to her to take it in his own.

Sarah looked back at Thomas. The rage that emanated like fire from her eyes seemed to dissipate, just a tiny bit. Thomas breathed a sigh of relief.

"What…..what do you believe now?" she rasped, long pauses between her words. Thomas seemed uncomfortable with the question, and thought to himself for many minutes.

"Goody Cloyce, I am a Christian and believe that witches do exist, as it says in the Bible," he said slowly. "And there may have been a witch among those who were accused. But I cannot say for certain. I do know that most of them were convicted through problematic rules of evidence, and that was wrong."

Sarah gazed back into the fire in the hearth. Peter held tightly to her hand, and the judge clasped the other. Were the two men somehow bringing her to life through the connection they were making?

"And my sisters?" Sarah asked, turning back to Thomas. "And me?"

"I have heard many stories about them both, about how good they were, and your petition moved my heart. Yes, Goody Cloyce, they were wrongfully hanged. And you were wrongfully jailed. That is my solemn belief. And I am grievously sorry."

A sound started in the base of Sarah's throat, like that of the dull roar of an ocean wave crashing upon the rocks, and the two men stared at her in trepidation. The sound rose up in her, blooming into a wretched sob that shook her entire body. It led to a torrent of crying, tears streaming down her pale twisted face. It was a truly horrible sight to behold, but Peter stood firmly, bearing witness to his wife's gaping grief. And Mr. Danforth did as well. For a full year now, ever since the whole tragedy started, Sarah had cried out for justice, for someone – anyone – to acknowledge the truth of what was going on. It had been unbearable, being swept up in the proceedings, being so unfairly accused, being robbed of a voice or any control whatsoever. Seeing so many people – many whom she used to consider friends – turn their back on her sisters and her. And losing so very, very much.

But here was the very judge who put her in prison, saying the words that she herself knew to be true. All at once she felt the ground grow solid beneath her feet, the foundation which had been destroyed up until then. As her sobs continued and then slowly abated, she could feel her body again. She could feel her mind moving again.

Thomas and Peter let Sarah cry and wail for as long as she needed, both holding her hands steadily, keeping her from drowning in her grief and sorrow. When the sobs finally let up and Sarah sat there, spent but alive, Thomas spoke again.

"I know I could never provide the restitution that you and your family truly deserve," he said. "Nothing can replace the lives of your sisters. But I humbly offer a token as a sign of my grief at how I have hurt you. I invite you and your extended family to settle lands on Danforth's Farms to the west of Boston. You can have as many acres as you can handle. And you need not pay me a shilling."

Peter's heart leapt at his words. Sarah, her eyes still shining from her tears, gazed at the judge with a steady look that held rage, yes, but also acceptance. Thomas wanted to look away from the intensity of it.

Slowly, Sarah nodded, and then let her chin fall to her chest, falling immediately into a deep sleep.

~ ~ ~

And so Peter packed up everything in their farm – the farm on which he had lived and worked for decades – so that he, Sarah and the girls could make their way down the Ipswich Road and then to the Boston Road, traveling the twenty-five miles southwest from Salem Village to their new home on Danforth's Farms. It took them several weeks to prepare for the move, and during that time Peter watched as his wife slowly climbed out of the darkness. Soon she was moving about the house, taking over the chores that Hepzibah and Alice had assumed, even though she was still weak and in physical pain. The girls in turn became more cheerful, happy that their mother was returning their embraces, even though sadness emanated from Sarah's face. This mother was not the strong and competent mother Hepzibah and Alice now remembered, but at least she was less scary than the walking corpse she had been.

Sarah's other daughter, Hannah, was not pleased to see her mother leave Salem Village, especially after being wrested away from her so unfairly for so long.

"Oh, mama!" Hannah cried, dropping to her knees in front of Sarah, who was sitting in her rocking chair in front of the fire. "Whatever am I going to do without you?"

Hannah had rushed to Sarah's home as soon as she heard the news that the Cloyces were to go to Danforth's Farms.

Sarah was now smiling wanly – smiling, she was! – and Hannah was cheered.

"Now, now, young Hannah," Sarah cooed, patting her daughter on the head, running her rough hand across the smoothness of Hannah's cheek. "'Tis best for us. I must be away from this place. And you could come, too, with Joseph and the baby."

Hannah sat in the settle next to Sarah's chair and took her mother's hand in hers. Both women already knew that the Joseph Putnams would not be making the trip to Danforth's Farms. Joseph had invested in yet a third frigate sailing out of Salem Harbor, and the little family spent the majority of their time in Salem Town now. Joseph had brought his aging mother Mary to live with them, and Hannah was grateful for her help with the baby. They were all content to be away from Salem Village and Joseph's half-siblings' killing looks. Both Hannah and Joseph were ashamed of their surname, and did not want anyone to believe that they had anything to do with the Putnams' terrorism.

"I wish we could," Hannah said to Sarah, sniffling, rising to sit next to her mother in the nearby settle. She looked about the room, nearly empty now of furnishings as most of them were tied up in ropes in the carriage outside, awaiting their journey southward. It all just seemed wrong somehow. "But Joseph's dealings are in the Town. He can't leave them."

"And what of his holdings here in the Village?" asked Sarah.

"He and Mary have decided to divest of them," Hannah answered. "There are plenty of families who would like to purchase our acres, even though we can't stand most of those men. We are done with Salem Village."

"As are we all," Sarah muttered, looking off in the distance, the dark mood overcoming her once more.

"I am so, so sorry, mama," Hannah said, hating the sadness that shaded her mother's face like a cloud suddenly covering the sun. "I would do anything to make things different for you."

Sarah chuckled bitterly. "You always were my savior, my dear one. But this time you have your own life to lead, you don't have to take care of your old mother any longer."

Hannah gazed into the fire. It had almost died down but a slight breeze coming down the chimney fanned the embers so that one of the logs erupted into flame. "I wish we were back there," she said quietly, almost to herself. "Those days before you met Peter. When you had risen from your bed to rejoin the family after papa died. We were so happy then."

"Aye, there were happy times, to be sure," Sarah agreed. "I am uncertain about my future, although I know in my heart that yours is bright. Joseph does love you so, and I am glad for Mary Veren who can be your mother now. And the baby. Rebecca...."

"And you?" Hannah asked, tears starting to flow again, the flames of the fire reflecting off her cheeks. "What will become of you? And my dear sisters?"

Sarah smiled weakly and reached for her oldest daughter for an embrace. "We will have an adventure. We will see what it is like to run our own lives, without depending on our community or this God that people believe in. And we will be together, even in spirit. And we shall be safe, all of us. I am glad you and Joseph will be clear of Salem Village. It is a most hateful place."

~~~

Now that his wife had received such acknowledgment from Mr. Danforth, Peter urged her to join the family's confrontation with Mr. Parris – and also with the Putnams themselves. More and more people of Salem Village were expressing regret at how they cheered on the executions, and many were moving away. The Putnams and their ilk remained unscathed, yet there may soon be no more village to hold sway over. It was time that Sarah confront them, especially Goody Putnam who was so vociferously against Rebecca and Mary.

But Sarah would have nothing of it. She was done with Salem Village, and refused to set foot outside the bounds of their farm. The Putnams had won their control over the community, while the
~~~

Towne family had been devastated. There was nothing Sarah could do about that outcome, and doubted that the likes of Mr. Parris and the Putnams would ever accept the fact that they had taken part in such a miscarriage of justice. Mr. Danforth had, yes. But he obviously had more integrity and courage than she had ever seen in her neighbors. She even begged her husband to change the spelling of their surname so that they could distance themselves even further from Salem Village once they arrived at Danforth's Farms.

Once the whole family heard of Mr. Danforth's offer, many of them jumped at the chance to move. Several of Rebecca's grown children started to dismantle their own farms so that they could join Sarah, while the others decided to stay to continue pressing Mr. Parris for a public apology for his influence over the trials. Isaac Esty stayed as well, not willing to leave his wife's grave, and adding his own signature to the petitions against Mr. Parris.

Initially Peter had wanted to stay in Salem Village until the warm months of spring, so that they could begin building new homes immediately upon their arrival. Sarah vociferously disagreed, wanting to be gone as soon as possible. Peter could hardly argue; he was just elated that some of his wife's stubbornness was returning after he had almost lost hope. Leaving in late February meant they would have to somehow find shelter in the woods; perhaps he could build one of the wigwam-style abodes that the original English settlers had learned from the local tribes. Or they might find temporary shelter in the caves that heavy granite outcroppings sometimes made in the earth. It would not be easy. But at least the Cloyces – now going by Clayes – could escape the pit of hell that Salem Village had become.

~ ~ ~

The night before the family's sojourn to Danforth's Farms, Sarah stayed up late, sending an exhausted Peter and the girls to their beds before her. It was a freezing night and Sarah made sure that her daughters took with her two large rocks warmed by the fire and bundled in soft cloth so they could fall asleep cradled by heat rather than the chill that even several wool rugs could not stave off.

The work required to prepare them for the move had been torturous, and Sarah's body was wracked with pain from it – but she was too keyed up to sleep. She walked the wide pine floors of the house, each creaking as her feet passed, and she lightly dragged her fingertips along the mantle above the stone hearth, the well-worn boards of the table that would be carried to the wagon the next morning. All the time remembering all of the activity that had gone on within those walls. The laughter of her children. The quiet nights with Peter. Her family.

Her sisters.

Though the night was cold, the dark sky outside the front window was lit with stars and a shining full moon. Sarah felt drawn to the window, wrapping her indoor cloak more closely around her and gazing up to the light above. She no longer prayed, having turned her back on a God whose words and lessons were used as ammunition against the devastation wrought upon her family. But she felt compelled to speak out loud, not understanding why. For some reason the moon seemed to be beckoning her to speak, so she did. Her voice still came in dry bursts, rasping through her throat, which hurt her. Still, she had to speak. She liked to think that she was talking to her sisters.

"My body is frail, and when I stand up from a chair my back throbs with pain. Can you believe that, my dear sisters? You always called me Young Sarah. What happened to that girl? My hands can hardly hold a tray, and my newly-gray hair continues to fall from my head. I am fifty years old but I feel twice that. My strength has been twisted out of me, but still I hope that it may return.

"Hope. Do I hope? Rebecca, you always said we had much to hope for. Did you still believe that as the hangman kicked the stool from beneath your beautiful feet and you fell down into darkness? That darkness is still with me, the black of that accursed jail, the gloom of my dreams. I still find it difficult when I realize I will never see you both ever again. And the fury of the injustice of it all can threaten to overpower me at times.

"But I was truly lost, and am now saved, despite the fact that I may never truly experience joy again. And it wasn't God who saved me. No, I have no more use for Mr. Parris' God. For the God who keeps ignorant people like the Putnams in power while the innocent are brutally murdered. I am sorry, Rebecca and Mary, I know you kept your faith until the very end. But for me it was the love of my husband and the integrity of Mr. Danforth that proved to me that there is still good in the world. I so needed someone to say what he could say: we have been unjustly hurt. Why did I need so much for the truth to be voiced by someone else? I will never know. But this small glimmer seems very tiny in comparison with the forces of fear and anger that run rampant over the colony. Yet I must hold onto it, cherish it, protect it.

"And we are moving away from the place that turned on us. There will be twelve families forming our little outpost in the wilderness. Our mother and father's blood flows through all of us, and with it comes love and trust. My own family. The purest of us have been taken away, and with you goes my heart. But your children remain, as mine do. I need no one beyond my own kin, nor will I venture outside of our safe little circle ever again.

"Rebecca. Mary. My sisters. My otherwise mothers.

"I love you so.

"I am so sorry I could not save you."

APPENDICES

APPENDIX A: Inspiration

I was inspired to write this story when I heard, around 2004, that there was a "witch house" in the town of Framingham, MA, located on a street called "Salem End Road." I had just purchased a home in Ashland, MA – on land that was once in Framingham – that abutted 800 acres of conservation forest and trails. My new neighbors pointed out on the trail map for the forest that "witch caves" were clearly marked not a half mile from my home. I was told: "Oh yes, that's where the witches hid out when they escaped from Salem."

Thinking this an urban legend, I did some exploring with the Ashland and Framingham Historical Societies, and I discovered that in fact there was some truth in the story. It is true that Framingham started out as "Danforth's Farms," with acres granted to then-Deputy Governor Thomas Danforth, and that Sarah Towne Bridges Cloyce – known as Clayes in Framingham (although they still refer to her as "Cloyce" in today's Salem) – settled there with her husband and extended family in 1693, the year after the last witch trial ended.

Not much else could be proven. What was the relationship between Danforth and Sarah Cloyce, I wondered? How could the magistrate who oversaw her examination (another historical fact) own land that she eventually settled on, after being released from jail?

While I was exploring this question, I also began a fifteen year journey to save the house that Sarah and Peter supposedly built in 1693 in Framingham – the name they gave to the town when they were some of the signatories of the town's incorporation papers in the year 1700. Thomas Danforth's ancestral home was in Framlingham, in England's Suffolk county; the name somehow morphed into "Framingham." I found out that Sarah's and Peter's home was still standing, at 693 Salem End Road, but it was in danger of demolition by neglect, having gone through a divorce, liens for back taxes and a problematic foreclosure process. By this time it was 2008 and the housing crisis was in full effect. I discovered that the mortgage had been bundled along with other failed mortgages into securities that passed from one large bank to another, making it impossible to even determine who owned the house.

The process of saving the house is a long and complicated story, and might even make for a sequel to this novel. As a professional fundraiser I led two different groups of concerned citizens and neighbors to help me not only garner a donation of the property from whatever bank owned it, but also to raise money to restore the house and make it into a public resource. During the process we were successful in raising close to $50,000 from 200 people who were connected to Sarah's story in one way or the other.

Unfortunately once we did receive the house as a donation from the bank in 2016, the board of trustees I had put together decided on a different strategy: to fix up the house themselves and flip it to a private buyer. This was heartbreaking, as I had been the one to put in most of the work in the project, and had always been inspired by the vision of bringing Sarah's story to the public consciousness.

I left Ashland and Framingham to move to Harpswell, Maine in 2017, in large part to escape the failure of this "labor of love" that I had worked on for so many years, and lost – to a set of people I considered my closest friends and colleagues.

If you google "Janice Thompson" and "Sarah Clayes," you can find many more details, images and stories about the house preservation project. It was written about in the Boston Globe, the Metrowest Daily News and many other publications.

Grieving over the loss of preserving this historic house for the public good, I decided that there was another way of saving the story of Sarah and her sisters: write a novel about it.

To be clear: I am profoundly grateful that Sarah's house in Framingham was saved from destruction, and I applaud my colleagues' efforts in making that happen. Having the house in private hands is better than it being destroyed – and I understand that the new owners are sensitive to the history of their house, which is a bonus. That said, I am also profoundly disappointed that the people of Framingham and beyond have lost a tangible learning experience. In the end, expediency won out over the long, hard work it would have taken to raise the money to make the place into a house museum.

APPENDIX B: **Historical Fact vs. Fiction**

While all of these characters are based on actual people, I have changed some relationships and names for the narrative's sake.

For example, Hannah Bridges did not marry Joseph Putnam in real life; rather she married Samuel Barton. I fabricated this marriage in order to emphasize the deep animosity between the Townes and the Putnams. In addition, the scene where Cotton Mather falls into a muddled fog while watching the execution of John Proctor from his horse is made up.

Also, all three Towne sisters had many children, but I took most of them out of my story, as they would make the narrative too complicated. In true history, the various relationships among the accused and the accusers have many layers: for example, someone from the accused side might have married the second cousin on the accusers side. The "sides" were often not clearly defined – as in the case of my story, when John Gould, in the boundary disputes over the Ipswich River, started out joining the Topsfield farmers against the Putnams – Gould's cousins – but later joined the other side.

Some of the narrative, especially that of the proceedings of the examinations and trials (these have all been meticulously catalogued by Bernard Rosenthal and Margo Burns in *Records of the Salem Witch-Hunt* (Cambridge University Press, 2009), are taken directly from court records. For example, the affadavit that Sarah Cloyce and Mary Esty write to the judges in the witch trials is taken verbatim from trial records. But once again I do take liberties in some of these testimonies. For example, Sarah Cloyce is recorded as saying "you, sir, are a grievous liar!" during her examination overseen by Thomas Danforth; however, in my story she says this to John Gould and not John Indian. In truth it was John Indian who was the subject of her comment.

It is historically accurate to say that Samuel Sewall and Thomas Danforth were friends, as Sewall describes some of their actual conversations in his diary. It is also true that Thomas Danforth worked directly for Harvard President Increase Mather, as the College's Treasurer. The rest of the personal relationship among Sewall, Danforth and the two Mathers (Cotton and Increase) is a fabrication.

The map of Salem Village that accompanies the book (and was created by my sister Kathy Martin) is a combination of truth and fiction. The general boundaries of Salem Village, Topsfield, Salem Town and the disputed territory are generally correct. However, the three sisters' homesteads – as well as the Putnams' – are not in the exact location as they were in real life.

At the outset of this project, I didn't want to write just another fictionalized story about the witch trials themselves. These have been depicted by hundreds of novelists and scholars, movies and books in the past. These stories are usually quite black-and-white – the accusing girls are evil for no apparent reason, the accused are just poor saps who didn't know any better – and sometimes even advance the fallacy that witchcraft was actually being practiced in Salem Village. They also describe a situation that seemed an anomaly, just something weird that happened without context. In my opinion, none of this is true. In my book I try to describe the trials within the broader context of generations-old boundary disputes, anxieties vis-à-vis England (colonial autonomy vs. being ruled from afar), how the colonists approached their Christian faith, Indian wars, etc. In this view, the witch trials weren't an anomaly; like dry tinder to a carelessly lit match, the conflagration that followed should not be a surprise.

The actual trials took place in Salem Village, an inland farming village which is now known as Danvers, MA. Salem Town was roughly 10 miles to the southeast; Salem Town is what we now know of as Salem. Salem is known worldwide as "Witch City," complete with crystal and tarot shops and a month-long celebration of Halloween in October of every year. This "witchy-kitschy" element of the Salem experience has no basis in truth, in my opinion (and many others'), as none of the accused "witches" actually practiced witchcraft. It is solely the function of tourism, which is great fun – I've participated in the events and visited many of the wonderful shops for years now – but not based on fact.

Another misconception of the witch trials comes from Arthur Miller's fabulous play, *The Crucible*. While this is a brilliant work of fiction, many have believed many of its tenets – for example, that Abigail Williams had an affair with John Proctor, and that it was Thomas Danforth who was the "hanging judge" (rather than William Stoughton). Both of these elements are untrue, but make for wonderful drama and dialogue – just as I have changed some of the facts of the story to fit my own narrative.

Most information on the actual birth and death dates of the Towne family comes from *Towne Family: William and Joanna Blessing, Salem, Massachusetts, 1635: Five Generations of Descendants* (Lois Payne Hoover, editor, Baltimore, MD: Otter Bay Books, 2015). I am deeply indebted to the Towne Family descendants and the support that the Towne Family Association has granted me during the writing of this book and my attempts at saving Sarah Clayes' home in Framingham, MA.

Originally my book had several chapters on the boundary dispute between Salem Village and Topsfield, as that had started many decades before the witch trials began, and I also believe it was central to the "dry tinder" that caused the hysteria. The swath of acres directly south of the Ipswich River was thought by the Topsfield farmers to be theirs, while the Salem Village claimed the same thing. The General Court of the colony ruled the disputed territory as Salem Village's in 1639, and then reversed its decision eleven years later, saying it belonged to Topsfield. For years both sides made new petitions to the court, and the Court continued to rule in Topsfield's favor. The Putnams, who led the Salem Village contingent, had to pay fees for the meeting houses in both Topsfield and Salem, and they weren't happy about it.

APPENDIX C: **Characters**

All of this book's characters are based on real people.

THE TOWNES

Joanne Blessing Towne (baptized 1595 in Caister-on-Sea, Norfolk, England) and William Towne (baptized 1599 in Great Yarmouth, Norfolk, England)– William died in my book in 1669 (in truth it was 1673). Married in 1620 in Great Yarmouth, sailed to Massachusetts Bay Colony in 1635 with their children Rebecca, John, Susan, Edmund, Jacob and Mary. They had two children – Joseph and Sarah – after moving to the new world. In my book their only three children were Rebecca (Nurse), Mary (Esty) and Sarah (Bridges Cloyce). In my book William has just died the year before the narrative starts, but Joanna is living in Topsfield.

Rebecca Towne Nurse (b. 1620 in Great Yarmouth, Norfolk, England) + Francis Nurse (born 1618 in England) – at the beginning of my narrative the couple are living in Salem Town, but move to Salem Village in 1678. The couple had eight children, but in my book there only two are named: Rebecca, who married Thomas Preston, Mary, who married John Tarbell.

Mary Towne (baptized 1628 in Great Yarmouth, Norfolk, England) + Isaac Esty (baptized 1628 in Freston, Suffolk, England) — at the outset of my book they are living in Topsfield, but move to Salem Village in 1678. Mary and Isaac had ten children. In my book they have only three, and they are not named.

Sarah Towne (born circa 1642 in Salem Town) + Edmund Bridges (born circa 1637 in Topsfield). At the outset of my novel they are living in Topsfield. In real life they had five children: Edmund, Benjamin, Hannah, Caleb and Alice. In my book Sarah and Edmund only have two:

Hannah (b. 1669 in Salem Village). In my book, Hannah marries Joseph Putnam in 1688, but this is a complete fabrication, in order to support the narrative. In reality, Hannah married Samuel Barton in about 1690. Hannah is the 3x great grandmother to Clara Barton, born 1821 and the founder of the American Red Cross.

<u>Alice</u> (b. 1680 in Salem Village).

<u>Sarah Towne Bridges</u> + <u>Peter Cloyce</u> (b. 1639 in Watertown, Massachusetts). This was both Sarah's and Peter's second marriage. In real life Sarah and Peter had two children, Benoni and Hepzibah. In my book there is only one:

<u>Hepzibah</u> (b. 1685 in Salem Village). In my book she is born in 1688.

THE GOULDS/PUTNAMS

<u>John Gould</u> (born 1635 in Great Missenden, Buckinghamshire, England). In real life he married Sarah Baker in Charlestown, Massachusetts Bay Colony, in 1660, but in my book there is only passing reference to Sarah, in the scene at Reverend Gilbert's home where he drank too much. John's father was Zaccheus Gould (b. 1589 in Hemel Hempstead, Hertfordshire, England). Zaccheus' sister was Priscilla Gould, who married John Putnam Sr. (born 1580). Priscilla was mother to Thomas Sr. (see below), who was father to Thomas Jr. (see below). Therefore John Gould was was a great-uncle to Thomas Jr.

The Goulds have another connection with the Salem Witch Trials that I couldn't include due to lack of space. In real life, John Gould had a daughter with Sarah Baker Gould; the daughter's name was Priscilla (born 1628). Priscilla was married to John Wildes in Topsfield. Priscilla died in 1663, and Wildes married a Sarah (Averill) Wildes. According to Familypedia.com, "It appears that the Gould family feathers were ruffled when John Wildes remarried so soon after Priscilla's death. But the serious nature of the problems between John Wildes and the siblings of his first wife, Priscilla, - Lt. John Gould & Mary (Gould) Redington - began in the mid-1680s." John Gould's sister Mary (Gould) Redington started to spread rumors about Sarah (Averill) Wildes. Redington died in 1990.

Sarah Wildes was one of the accused women during the witch trials. John Gould testified against her, saying that Mary had "at one time been pulled off a horse by Sarah Wildes 'in spirit form.' He also stated that hens that Sarah had gifted to Mary had 'moped around until they died.'

Interestingly, after Sarah Wildes was hanged for witchcraft in 1692, John Wildes married a third time, to Mary Jacobs, the widow of George Jacobs, who had also been hanged in the same year.

In my original story, Sarah Wildes was a primary character, but in this published version, she is a minor player, being one of the jailed people who speaks with Sarah Cloyce when Sarah is arrested. Mary Redington is also a minor character, attending the fateful dinner with Joanna Towne and Reverend Gilbert with her brother John.

I add this background information to demonstrate even more clearly how the relationships among the people of Topsfield, Salem Village and Salem Town were complicated, and provided the "dry tinder" of the entire hysteria.

Thomas Putnam Sr. (b. 1614, Aston Abbotts, Buckinghamshire, England), married first to Ann Putnam (b. 1621, d. 1665). In real life Thomas and Ann had ten children, but in my book they only had two:

Thomas Putnam Jr. (b. 1651 in Salem Village), who married Ann Carr Putnam (b. 1661). In real life they had 13 children, and I reference a few of them in my book, but the only central character is one daughter:

Ann Putnam Jr. (b. 1679). This daughter was referred to as "Ann Jr." to distinguish her from her mother, who was commonly called "Ann Sr." Ann Jr. is one of the accusing girls.

Deliverance Putnam Wolcott (b. 1656 in Salem Village). Deliverance married Jonathan Walcott (b. 1639 in Salem Village). In real life this was Jonathan's second marriage; he was first married to a woman named Mary. Jonathan and Mary gave birth to a daughter, Mary Walcott, who was one of the accusing girls. However in my book I make Jonathan younger – more the age of Thomas Putnam Jr. – and Mary Walcott is the birth daughter of Deliverance, so that Ann Putnam Jr. and Mary Walcott are first cousins.

    <u>Ann Putnam Sr and Deliverance Wolcott together</u>: They are
sisters-in-law. Ann is married to Thomas Putnam Jr. and Deliverance is Thomas Jr. Putnam's sister.

    <u>Ann Putnam Jr. and Mary Wolcott together:</u> They are part of
the accusing girls' group. They are also cousins: Ann's mother Ann
is Mary Walcott's sister-in-law (see above).

    <u>Mercy Lewis</u>: Thomas Jr. and Ann Putnam's serving girl.
Friends to Ann Putnam Jr. and Mary Walcott, and part of the larger
group of accusing girls. Born 1683 in Falmouth, District of Maine.
Her family was attacked by Indians in King Philip's War, and everyone died except for Mercy. George Burroughs was in the same attack.
In real life Mercy became a servant in Burroughs' home when he
came to Salem Village, and then later in the Putnams' home. In my
book I left out the part about the Burroughs (I substituted a fictitious
family, the Johnsons, who took her in instead).. I also have her born
in 1674, so that she would be 14 or 15 by the time the trials started.

    <u>Thomas Putnam Sr.</u> married Mary Veren (b. 1626 in Salem
Village) after his first wife, Mary, died. In real life Thomas and
Mary had two children, but in my book they only had one:

    <u>Joseph Putnam</u> (b. 1669 in Salem Village). In real life Joseph
married Elizabeth Porter, the daughter of Israel Porter, one of the
wealthiest families in Salem Town and Salem Village, and reputed to
be a rival to the Putnam family (Boyer and Nissenbaum discuss this
rivalry in their book <u>Salem Possessed: The Social Origins of Witch-
craft</u>, (Cambridge, MA: Harvard University Press, 1974).. Israel was
one of my central characters whom I had to cut for brevity. Instead
in my book I have Joseph marrying Hannah Bridges Cloyce for
the sake of the narrative. See above. I create a significant rivalry
between Joseph and his three half-siblings, Thomas Jr., Edward and
Deliverance. This is based on historical fact: Boyer and Nissenbaum
write: "Perhaps Mary Veren had acquired some of the business
acumen of the Salem circles in which she had moved, or perhaps her
new husband had decided on hius own to shift his deepest loyalties
from the connections of his first marriage to those of his second.
In any case, one or both of them began to promote the interests of
their son Joseph at the expense of Thomas Putnams other children,

including Thomas Jr., now on the threshold of manhood." (*Salem Possessed: The Social Origins of Witchcraft*, page 136).

THE PARRIS HOUSEHOLD

<u>Reverend Samuel Parris</u> (b. 1653, London, England) married Elizabeth Eldred Parris (b. 1648, Boston). Parris was the fourth ordained minister to lead the congregation of Salem Village in 1689. He resigned his post in 1696. In real life Samuel and Elizabeth had five children; in my book they only have one:

<u>Elizabeth "Betty" Parris</u> (b. 1682, Concord, Middlesex County), one of the child accusers.

<u>Abigail Williams</u> (b. 1680), niece to Samuel Parris. She moved to Salem Village after her parents were killed by Native Americans in the District of Maine. She is one of the accusing girls.

<u>Tituba</u> and <u>John Indian</u>. Slaves in the Parris household. It is thought that they were purchased in Barbados by Samuel Parris, who ran a plantation there before he lost his riches (I make up the fact that there was a hurricane that sent him back to New England). Some historians say that the two were of Carribean descent, although others believe that they were Native American.

THE MINISTERS

<u>Reverend Thomas Gilbert</u> – Topsfield's first ordained minister, starting his ministry in 1663. Joanna Towne was a supporter, while John Gould and his family accused him of drinking too much. Gilbert was ousted in 1671, much to the chagrin of Goody Towne. According to Paul Boyer and Stephen Nissenbaum in <u>The Salem Witchcraft Papers</u> (Boyer and Nissenbaum, New York: Da Capo Press, 1977), John Putnam reported in a deposition that "it is no wonder they (Rebecca, Mary and Sarah) were witches for their mother was so before them." These are historical facts, although I do not believe that there is any documented evidence of anyone formally accusing Joanna Towne of witchcraft when she was alive. The connection between her support of Reverend Gilbert and this accusation is a fabricated one. I quote the accusation of Joanna Towne's being a witch in my depiction of John Gould's testimony in my book.

James Bayley – A native of Newbury, Massachusetts and Salem Village's first minister, arriving in 1672 after being graduated from Harvard in 1669 and marrying Mary Carr of Salisbury earlier in 1672. Mary Carr was the sister of Ann Carr, who traveled with James and her sister Mary to Salem Village. Ann Carr would later become Ann Carr Putnam, married to Thomas Putnam Jr. Reverend Bayley resigned in 1679, after the different factions of Salem Village couldn't come together to support him. He and his wife Mary left for Connecticut.

George Burroughs - Salem Village's second minister, starting in 1680. He was a native of Roxbury, Massachusetts, and was graduated from Harvard in 1670, just a year after Bayley. After graduation he was a minister in Wells, on Casco Bay in the District of Maine. During King Philip's War, the Falmouth settlement was attacked by Indians. Burroughs returned to the Massachusetts Bay Colony, first in Salisbury, then in Salem Village. Burroughs was one of the eighteen people who were hanged for witchcraft.

Deodat Lawson – The third minister in Salem Village, starting in 1684. He, like his two predecessors, could not unite the Village congregation and only lasted for three years. He went on to settle in Boston and became an itinerant preacher.

Samuel Parris - Salem Village's fourth minister, arriving in 1689. He was in power when the witch hysteria erupted.

Cotton Mather – son to Increase Mather, and Increase's assistant minister at Boston's North Church from 1685–1728 (now the First and Second Unitarian Church in Boston, not to be confused with Old North Church).

Increase Mather - Boston clergyman and president of Harvard (1681-1701). He was the second minister to lead Boston's North Church from 1664-1723 (now the First and Second Unitarian Church in Boston, not to be confused with Old North Church).

John Higginson - Salem Town minister at the time of the witch trials. He lived where the current Salem Witch Museum resides, at 19 ½ Washington Square North.

John Hale - minister for Beverly at the time of the witch trials. His home, called the John Hale Farm, still exists at 39 Hale Street in Beverly, is a nonprofit museum, run by Historic Beverly.

Nicholas Noyes – assistant minister to John Higginson in Salem Town at the time of the witch trials. In reality Higginson was elderly – 76 years old – and was giving more work to Noyes, who was much younger (45 years old). However in my book Higginson is the more active minister, and Noyes is only mentioned in passing, as one of the ministers overseeing some of the examinations.

THE OTHER ACCUSING GIRLS

Elizabeth Hubbard. At age 17, Elizabeth is the second-oldest of the accusing girls. Elizabeth is an orphan – in my book she loses her parents to smallpox in 1690 (although this isn't a historical fact) – and is taken in by her great-aunt Rachel Hubbard Griggs, the wife of Dr. Griggs, in Salem Village.

Mary Warren. She is the oldest accuser, at age 18. She is known to be an orphan, and is an indentured servant to John and Elizabeth Proctor. In my book I have her suffer from Indian massacres to the north, like Mercy Lewis and Abigail Wiliams.

THE MAGISTRATES

Thomas Danforth, born 1623 in Framlingham, England to Nicholas and Elizabeth Symmes Danforth. A politician, landowner and magistrate in the Massachusetts Bay Colony. Treasurer of Harvard College and President of the District of Maine. Deputy Governor under Simon Bradstreet. The Danforths sail to the new world in 1634. In reality Thomas has four siblings, but in my book he has just two brothers: Samuel and Richard. In both my book and in real life, Samuel is ordained in the First Church in Cambridge and goes on to work with John Eliot to convert the "praying Indians" in an area now known as Natick, MA. Thomas marries Mary Withinton in 1664. They go on to have 12 children, half of these dying before the age of 3. In my book he only has daughters Mary and Elizabeth; he is also mourning the recent death of his namesake son, Thomas, who fights and dies in the Indian wars at Narragansett.

I understand from David Dearinger, a colleague of mine when I was working at the Boston Athenaeum (he was then the Susan Morse Hilles Curator of Painting and Sculpture), that there does not exist a formal portrait of Danforth. According to David, this is unusual for governors and lieutenant governors in the colony.

Samuel Sewall, born 1652 in England to Henry and Jane Dummer Sewall. A judge and merchant in the Massachusetts Bay Colony. He is well-known for his journal, The Diary of Samuel Sewall (1674–1729), one of the only first-person accounts of life in the colony that exists today. He is the only magistrate involved with the Salem witch trials to publicly apologize for his role in the hysteria. In 1697 he attended his church – the Third Church in Boston – when the minister read his public apology. In 1942 the artist Albert Herter painted a full-sized mural entitled 1697 - Dawn of Tolerance in Massachusetts: Public Repentance of Judge Samuel Sewall for His Actions in the Witchcraft Trials. The mural now is hung in the House Chamber in the Massachusetts State House in Boston, MA.

John Hathorne, born 1641 in Massachusetts Bay Colony, a merchant and magistrate in Boston and Salem Town. A member of the court that oversaw the witch examinations and trials. An interesting tidbit: Hathorne's great-great-grandson was the novelist Nathaniel Hawthorne, who was thought to have added the "w" to his last name in order to distance himself from his ancestor, of whom he was ashamed to be associated.

Jonathan Corwin, born 1640 in Salem Town, a merchant and magistrate in Salem Town. A member of the court that oversaw the witch examinations and trials.

William Stoughton, born 1631 in Massachusetts Bay Colony, a magistrate in Boston. He was appointed by Sir William Phips, the new governor of the colony, to head the special Court of Oyer and Terminer to try accused witches.

Sir William Phips, born 1651 in the District of Maine, a man of humble origins who became wealthy as a shipbuilding merchant. He was one of the agents who traveled with Increase Mather to negotiate the new charter for the colony. King William and Queen Mary appointed Phips as new governor of the colony, overthrowing Simon Bradstreet. One of his first orders was to establish the Court of Oyer and Terminer to oversee the witch trials.

APPENDIX D: **Towne Family Tree**

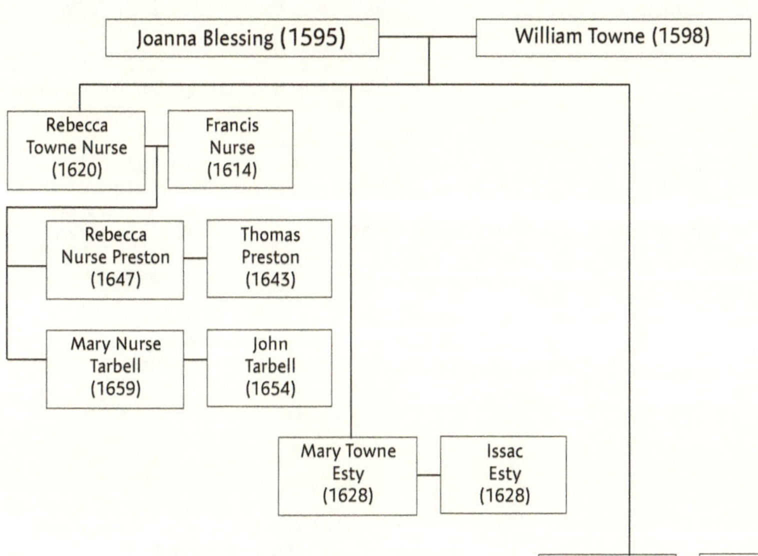

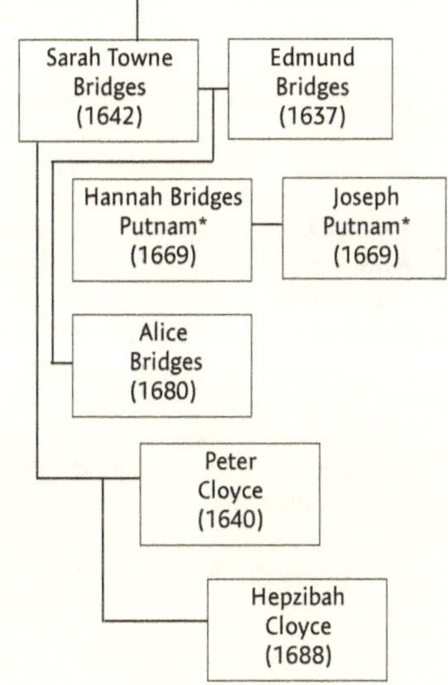

All of these characters had many children — the three Towne sisters, for example, actually had five other siblings — but for narrative's sake (and in the pursuit of not confusing my readers) I have focused on a limited number of family members.

* Hannah Bridges actually married Samuel Barton. I have taken dramatic liberty in making her wife to Joseph Putnam, the detested half-brother of Thomas Putnam, Jr. and Deliverance Walcott.

Peter Cloyce's last name was either Cloyce or Cloyse in Salem Village. Peter and Sarah were referred to as Clayes once the moved to Danforth's Farms / Framingham, Massachusetts. Some historians believe this was an attempt at separating themselves from the tragedy of the witch hysteria, although this has not been proven.

APPENDIX E: Putnam Family Tree

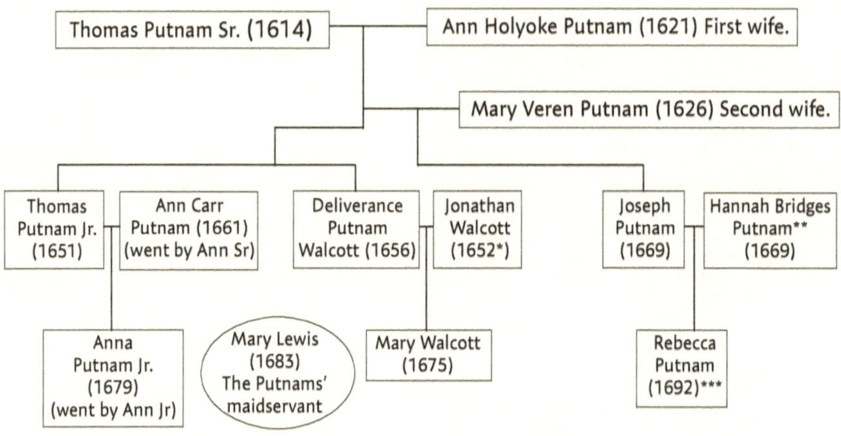

All of these characters had many children but for narrative's sake (and in the pursuit of not confusing my readers) I have focused on a limited number of family members.

About John Gould: John's father was Zaccheus Gould (1589). Zaccheus' sister was Priscilla Gould, who married John Putnam Sr. (1580) Priscilla was mother to Thoma Putnam Sr., who was father to Thomas Putnam Jr. Therefore John Gould was a great-uncle to Thomas Putnam Jr.

* In real life this was Jonathan Walcott's second marriage; he was first married to a woman named Mary. Jonathan and Mary gave birth to a daughter, Mary Walcott, who was one of the accusing girls. Howver in my book I make Jonathan younger – more the age of Thomas Putnam Jr – and Mary Walcott is the birth daughter of Deliverance, so that Ann Putnam Jr. and Mary Walcott are first cousins.

** Hannah Bridges actually married Samuel Barton. I have taken dramatic liberty in making her wife to Joseph Putnam, the detested half-brother of Thomas Putnam Jr. and Deliverance Putnam Walcott.

*** Rebecca Putnam (baby to Hannah and Joseph Putnam) is a made-up character.

APPENDIX F: **Timeline**

1620: Rebecca Town Nurse is born.

1623: Thomas Danforth is born.

1625: Charles I is crowned in England. Charles was born into the House of Stuart, second son of James VI of Scotland, who ruled England until his death in 1625. Charles I believes in the divine right of kings and argues with Parliament over issues of taxation, war and the kings' power. He also marries a Catholic, Henrietta Maria, daughter of Henry IV of France, causing the Puritans in England to consider him an unwelcome "papist." Note: the title "Puritan" was actually not used in the 17th century; rather, they called themselves "the people of God." For purposes of this appendix, I will refer to them as Puritans for ease of reference.

Puritans are unhappy with the practices of the Church of England, because they were thought of to be too similar to Catholicism. They do not like the Church's use of vestments, church decorations, the authority of priests and other "papist" rituals. They believe in the elect - that God preordains who would go to heaven and who does not, regardless of their works during their lifetimes. Congregants who could prove a "conversion experience" – could prove that they are among the elect. Only those whose conversion experiences are accepted by the congregation can vote in church matters.

1620 - 1640: "The Great Migration:" many Puritans sail to the New World from England, to escape the rules of the Church of England. In 1630 the Arbella sails to the New World from England, carrying John Winthrop and the charter that establishes the Massachusetts Bay Colony.

1628: Mary Towne Esty is born.

1634: John Putnam, Thomas Jr's grandfather, and his wife Priscilla Gould Putnam, sail from England, to Salem Town, eventually settling in Salem Village.

1634: Nicholas Danforth sails from England to Boston, eventually settling in Cambridge with his children, including Thomas Danforth. Nicholas becomes a prominent figure and a member of the General Court. He works as a surveyor and sets boundaris for Concord, Roxbury, Dedham and Dorchester.

1636: William Towne, with his wife Joanna and children, sail from Great Yarmouth, England, to settle in the Northfields section of Salem Town. They later move to a farm in Topsfield, directly north of the Ipswich River.

1638: Nicholas Danforth dies, leaving Thomas Danforth to head the family at age 15.

1639: The Massachusetts Bay Colony General Court issues an order: "whereas the inhabitants of Salem have agreed to plant a village near the (Ipswich River), it is ordered that all the land near their bounds between Salem and (Ipswich River) not belonging to any other town or person by any former grant, shall belong to the said village." This allows farmers in Salem Town to settle the area north of the town, called Salem Village. The farmers in Topsfield, living on the north side of the Ipswich River, consider this area theirs, and are unhappy with the verdict. William Towne, Edmund Bridges and Isaac Esty are part of the contingent that fight against it. Thomas Putnam Sr. leads the Salem Village against them.

1640: The Massachusetts Bay Colony General Court reverses their 1639 decision, and order that the land south of the Ipswich River belongs to Topsfield.

1642: England's first Civil War between Parliamentarians and Charles I. The Great Migration stops, as many Puritans return to England, hoping that the Parliamentarins would win, resulting in a reformed Church of England.
   - Sarah Towne Bridges Cloyce/Clayes is born.

1643: Thomas Putnam Sr. marries Ann Holyoke and they go on to have 14 children. In my book they only have two: Thomas Putnam Jr. and Deliverance Putnam Walcott.

1645: Parliament creates the New Model Army to defend them-
selves. Many Puritans join the New Model Army.
- Rebecca Towne marries Francis Nurse and they settle in
Salem Town.

1646: Charles I surrenders but escapes confinement to go to Scotland, where he wins support.

1648: England's second Civil War is initiated, as the New Model
Army defeats Charles I.
- Thomas Danforth is appointed Treasurer of Harvard Col-
lege. His brother Samuel, a minister of the Roxbury church, works
with John Eliot, a missionary to the local Indian tribes (the "praying
Indians"), attempting to convert them to Christianity.

1649: Charles I is beheaded. His son, Charles II, escapes to France,
and then to Scotland. He becomes the King of Scotland.

1650: Oliver Cromwell, a leader in the New Model Army and instrumental in the beheading of Charles I, is promoted by Parliament
to Lord General and the Commonwealth of England, Scotland and
Ireland is established.

1651: Cromwell and his army defeat Charles II and his Scottish
army, and Charles II flees to Europe in exile.

1652: Samuel Sewall is born in England.

1653: Cromwell is promoted to Lord Protector, the king in everything but name.

1655: Mary Towne marries Isaac Esty, a farmer and cooper in Salem
Village.

1658: Cromwell dies, and his son Richard succeeds him. Richard is
a weak leader.

1659: Sarah Towne marries Edmund Bridges.

1660: the Stuart Restoration: Charles II is brought back to England and becomes king. Another wave of Puritans flee to the New World.

1661: Charles II rules that in the Massachusetts Bay Colony, voting should not be restricted to church members only, and allowed Anglicans (of the Church of England) to vote. This rule is ignored by the colonists.
    - Samuel Sewall, along with his parents, sail to Massachusetts Bay Colony.

1662: A congregational synod in Boston establishes the Half Way Covenant, allowing those who had not had the conversion experience to participate in church affairs.
    - Thomas Danforth is commissioner who negotiates treaties with the Indians. He holds this position until 1679.

1664: The Massachusetts Bay General Court divides up the 500 acres south of the Ipswich River among Topsfield farmers, including William Towne, Edmund Bridges, Isaac Esty and John Gould.

1665: Thomas Danforth is appointed to the commission that oversees the colony's expansion to what is now southern Maine.

1668: Joseph Putnam is born to Thomas Putnam Sr. and Mary Veren Putnam. Thomas Jr. and Deliverance Putnam are stepsiblings to Joseph.

1669: There is a ministerial battle in Topsfield, where Reverend Gilbert is accused of drinking too much. Joanna Towne testifies for Reverend Gilbert. It is thought by many historians that this situation is the basis for some of the accusing girls during the trials of 1692 to testify that Sarah Towne Bridges Cloyce, Rebecca Nurse and Mary Esty are obviously witches because Joanna Towne had been a witch before them.
    - William Towne dies.

    - Hannah Bridges is born to Sarah and Edmund Bridges.

    - James Bayley is asked to be Salem Village's first minister. He is from Salisbury and brings his wife, Mary Carr Bayley, and her sister Ann Carr with him as he travels to Salem Village. Mary and Ann Carr are daughters of one of the richest men in Salisbury. Interesting note: the present-day Carr Island State Reservation, located between Merrimack and Salisbury, MA, is where the Carrs were from.

1670: Edmund Bridges is in debt to John Gould in Topsfield. Since the Bridges' do not have the money to pay him back, Edmund goes to jail, loses eight acres, their house and barn. Eventually he is able to pay off the debt (it is uncertain how) and is released from jail. He and Sarah move to Salem Town and run a waterfront tavern ("ordinary").

1672: Salem Town magistrates agree to let Salem Village build its own meetinghouse and hire a minister.

1675: King Philip's war in the Massachusetts Bay Colony and the District of Maine between indigenous people and the colonists: heavy damages are suffered on both sides, especially to the north of the colony where settlements are small and sparse.

During King Philip's War, Thomas Danforth, along with his brother Samuel and the missionary John Eliot, support the "praying Indians."

1678: Thomas Putnam Jr. marries Ann Carr.

- Salem Town's minister John Higginson rails again un-licensed innkeepers ("ordinaries"), especiall Edmund and Sarah Bridges. Edmund has to continually go to court, where William Hathorne (father of the witch trials' judge) is magistrate. Edmund also goes to court for wearing a periwig.

- Francis Nurse buys Bishop Farm in Salem Village from Rev. James Allen, minister of the first church in Boston, and Rebecca and Francis move there from Salem Town. It is uncertain how Goodman Nurse, a poor traymaker, could gather the price for the farm: 400 pounds. In my book I answer that question fictiously by having Francis and Rebecca's grown children purchase the farm and grant part of it to their parents.

- Mary and Isaac Esty move from Topsfield to Salem Village.

1679: Thomas Danforth elected Deputy Governor of the Colony, under Governor Bradstreet.

1680: James Bayley leaves Salem Village with his wife and children amongst contentions in the church; leaves Ann Carr Putnam behind.

- George Burroughs from the District of Maine is hired to be the second minister of the Salem Village church.

- General Court grants the disputed acres south of the Ipswich River to the Topsfield contingent, taking it away from Salem Village.

- Thomas Danforth is appointed the President of the District of Maine, makes land grants and helps rebuild settlements demolished by the Indians.

- Alice Bridges is born to Edmund and Sarah Bridges.

1682: Ann Carr Putnam's father George dies, and gives his entire estate to his sons, which angers Ann and Thomas Putnam Jr.

- Edmund Bridges dies in Salem Town, insolvent. The true history is this: Edmund and Sarah had another child, Edmund III; whatever he had was inherited by the son. Edmund III died a few months later, and left his paltry inheritance to his widow. Sarah and her other children were penniless, and moved back to Topsfield. The Topsfield constable ordered her out of the settlement, which sometimes occurred when a community didn't want to be burdened by poor people in their community. It is unknown why relatives didn't take her in. She almost immediately married Peter Cloyce of Salem Village. In my book I take out all of these details to streamline the narrative.

- Joanna Blessing Towne dies.

1683: George Burroughs leaves Salem Village amongst contentions within the church.

1684: Charles II revokes the Massachusetts Bay Colony charter and establishes the "Dominion of New England."
- Deodat Lawson becomes third minister of the Salem Village church.

1685: Charles II dies, his brother James II succeeds him. James is a visible Catholic and is not liked by the colonists.

1686: Sir Edmund Andros in office to rule the colony. Rules of self-governance that had been established and practiced for decades are taken away, including rights of property. Colonists are angry that Andros establishes a Church of England in Boston, and he is anti-Puritan.

- Sarah Bridges marries Peter Cloyce.

1687: Deodat Lawson leaves the Salem Village church.

1688: "The Glorious Revolution:" The unpopular James II is unseated by William of Orange and his wife Mary, who is James II's daughter. William and Mary vow to protect Protestant rights, and are popular with the Puritans in Massachusetts Bay Colony.

- Increase Mather, the president of Harvard College and a respected minister in the colony, travels to England to present William and Mary a set of grievances of the colonists toward Sir Andros.

- Cotton Mather, another respected colonial minister and Increase's son, learns about a case of witchcraft in Boston and writes about it in his book Witchcraft and Possessions.

- Hepzibah is born to Peter and Sarah Cloyce (in real life her actual year of birth was 1685).

- Hannah Cloyce marries Joseph Putnam.

1689: Rebellion in Boston topples Sir Andros' government, and he is sent back to England. William Bradstreet is brought back in as governor of the colony.

- Reverend Parris is invited to the Salem Village church.

1690: French and Indian wars. France and England are fighting back in Europe, and the war is brought to the New World, as France provides guns and financing to the indigenous people to fight against the colonists.

1691: Increase Mather and William Phips return to the colony with
a new charter from William and Mary. Phips is named Governor,
ousting Bradstreet, and William Stoughton is named Deputy Governor, unseating Thomas Danforth.

1692: the beginning of the witch hysteria in Salem Village.

1693: the witch hysteria is brought to a close by Governor Phips.
Sarah Towne Bridges Cloyce, her husband Peter and members of
their extended family move to Danforth's Farms, twenty-five miles
to the west of Boston. In real life there is no documented evidence
that this was by invitation of Thomas Danforth, who had been
granted those acres by the colony many years before; in my book
the interaction between Sarah Cloyce and Thomas Danforth is a
fabrication, based on a reasonable assumption that there was an
invitation extended. Peter Cloyce was one of the signatories of the
papers that incorporated his new home as Framingham in 1700.
The word Framingham is a paean to Thomas Danforth, whose family seat was in Framlingham, England. Peter Cloyce signed his name
as "Peter Clayes." It is assumed that the family changed its name in
order to distance itself from Salem Village.

APPENDIX G: **Bibliography**

This is a partial list of the books and other reference materials that I used in my research for Dry Tinder. The publications marked in bold were especially helpful.

Bailyn, B. (2012). *Barbarous Years*. Vintage.

Bailyn, B. (2013). *The New England Merchants in the Seventeenth Century*. Porter Press.

Baker, E. W. (2016). *A Storm of Witchcraft: The Salem Trials and the American Experience*. Oxford University Press.

Boyer, P. (Ed.). (1993). *Salem Village Witchcraft: A Documentary Record of Local Conflict in Colonial New England*. Northeastern University Press.

Boyer, P., & Nissenbaum, S. (1976). *Salem Possessed: Social Origins of Witchcraft*. Harvard University Press.

Bremer, F. J. (2022). *The Puritan Experiment: New England Society from Bradford to Edwards*. University Press of New England.

Brown, D. C. (1984). *A Guide to the Salem Witchcraft Hysteria of 1692*. David C Brown.

Coffey, J., & Lim, P. C. H. (Eds.). (2012). *The Cambridge Companion to Puritanism*. Cambridge University Press.

Conde, M. (2000). *I, Tituba*. Faber & Faber.

Demos, J. (2000). *A Little Commonwealth: Family Life in Plymouth Colony (2nd ed.)*. Oxford University Press.

Dimancescu, K. (2013). *The Forgotten Chapters: My Journey into the Past*. Katherine Dimancescu.

Dow, G. F. (1988). *Everyday Life in the Massachusetts Bay Colony*. Dover Publications.

Dow, G. F. (2022). *History of Topsfield Massachusetts* (classic reprint). Forgotten Books.

Foulds, D. (2013). *Death in Salem: The Private Lives Behind the 1692 Witch Hunt.* Globe Pequot Press.

Fowler, S. P. (2013). *Salem Witchcaft; Comprising More Wonders of the invisible World,* collected by Robert Calef, and *Wonders of the Invisible World,* by Cotton Mather: Rarebooksclub.com.

Francis, R. (2005). *Biography of Samuel Sewall.* Fourth Estate.

Gozzaldi, M. I. (1986). *History of Cambridge, Massachusetts: Supplement & Index.* Heritage Books.

Graham, E., Hobby, E., Hind, H., & Wilcox, H. (Eds.). (1989). *Her Own Life: Autobiographical Writings by Seventeenth-Century Englishwomen.* Routledge.

Herring, S. W. (2000). *Framingham: An American Town.*

Hill, C. (1974). *Century of Revolution, 1603-1714.* Cardinal Books.

Hill, F. (2000). *The Salem Witch Trials Reader.* Da Capo Press.

Hill, F. (2002). *Hunting for Witches.* Commonwealth Editions.

Hoover, Lois Payne. (2010). Towne Family: William Towne and Joanna Blessing of Salem Massachusetts: Five Generations of Descendants. Otter Bay Books.

Hosmer, J. K., & Winthrop, J. (2018). *Winthrop's Journal: History of New England, 1630-1649.* Franklin Classics.

Koehler, L. (1980). *Search for Power: Weaker Sex in Seventeenth Century New England.* University of Illinois Press.

Laplante, E. (2009). *Salem Witch Judge: The Life and Repentance of Samuel Sewall.* HarperSanFrancisco.

Mather, C. (1991). *Cotton Mather on Witchcraft*. Dorset Press.

Mather, C. (1999). *Memorable Providences: Relating to Witchrafts & Possessions*. Reprint Services Corporation.

Mather, I. (2014). *Tales of Conscience Concerning Evil Spirits*. Literary Licensing.

McMillen, P. W. (1990). Currents of Malice: Mary Towne Esty and her Family in Salem Witchcraft. Peter E. Randall.

Norton, M. B. (2007). *In the devil's snare: The Salem Witchcraft Crisis of 1692*. Vintage.

Paige, L. R. (1986). *History of Cambridge, Massachusetts, 1630-1877*. Heritage Books.

Parr, J. L., & Swope, K. A. (2009). *Framingham Legends & Lore*. History Press.

Peachey, S. (Ed.). (2014). *Clothes of the Common People in Elizabethan and Early Stuart England*. Stuart Press.

Powell, S. C. (2019). *Puritan Village: The Formation of a New England Town*. Wesleyan University Press.

Roach, M. K. (2002). The Salem Witch Trials: A Day-by-Day Chronicle of a Community Under Siege. Cooper Square.

Roach, M. K. (2021). *Six Women of Salem: The Untold Story of the Accused and Their Accusers in the Salem Witch Trials*. Tantor Audio.

Robinson, E. A. (1991). *The Devil Discovered: Salem Witchcraft, 1692*. Hippocrene Books.

Rosenthal, B. (1995). *Salem Story: Reading the Witch Trials of 1692*. Cambridge University Press.

**Rosenthal, B. and Burns, M. (2013). *Records of the Salem Witch-Hunt.*
Cambridge University Press.**

Ryan, M. P. (1975). *Womanhood in America, From Colonial Times to the Present.* Franklin Watts.

Sammarco, A. M. (1999). *Cambridge.* Arcadia Publishing.

Schama, S. (2000). *A History of Britain - volume 1 - 3.* Hyperion Books.

Scheller, B. (2019). *Colonial New England on 5 Shillings a Day.* Thames & Hudson.

Schiff, S. (2016). *The Witches: Salem, 1692.* Weidenfeld & Nicolson.

Schultz, E. B., & Tougias, M. J. (1999). *King Philip's War: The History and Legacy of America's Forgotten Conflict.* Countryman Press.

Sewall, S. (2015). *Diary of Samuel Sewall: 1674-1729,* Arkose Press.

Temple, J. H. (2010). *History of Framingham, Massachusetts.* General Books.

The Geneva Bible: The Bible of the Protestant Reformation. (2007). Hendrickson.

Thompson, R. (2005). *Cambridge Cameos: Stories of Life in Seventeenth-Century New England.*

Trask, R. B. (1992). *"the devil hath been raised": A Documentary History of the Salem Village Witchcraft Outbreak of March 1692.* Self published.

Upham, C. W. (1959). *Salem Witchcraft.* Continuum.

Whitehill, W. M. (1990). *Boston: A Topographical History* (2nd ed.). Harvard University Press.

APPENDIX H: **Acknowledgments**

I am indebted to many people who guided, supported and encouraged me throughout the past twenty years, as I have lived with Sarah's story, tried to save her home in Framingham, Massachusettts,
and finally completed this novel.

My friends in the Towne Family Association (TFA): a group
composed of descendants of Joanna Blessing Towne and William
Towne, especially Gail Garda, Elizabeth Hanahan and Virginia
Towne. The TFA has not only a wealth of information about Sarah
and her sisters; they were also instrumental in my early efforts to
save the Clayes House in Framingham.

My early readers, including Margo Burns, Kathy Martin, Mari-
lynne Roach, Allen Thompson, Jeremy Jones, Nancy Thompson,
Don "Cliff" Clifford and many members of the Towne Cousins'
Facebook page.

Kathy Martin, my brilliant artist sister who created the map of
Salem Village.

Jeremy Jones, my beloved husband, who painstakingly read through
the final draft of this book, catching discrepancies and typos that I
hadn't found before.

My friend Chris Tomasino, who gave me great advice on how to
edit down my original manuscript. It was close to 800 pages at the
time. Chris said "Janice, this book doesn't need a trim here or there.
It needs an entirely new haircut." She was right. She also put me in
touch with Leslie Wells, who edited my manuscript.

Tim McCreight, a fellow Harpswell resident and wonderful artist,
who designed this book for me.

The entire team at the Harpswell Anchor newspaper, all of whom
give me daily reminders of what it means to write well, make editori-
al decisions, work hard and always strive for excellence.

The baristas at the Starbucks in Framingham, Natick and Wayland (MA), and in Brunswick and Topsham (ME) who kept me company and well-caffeinated while I worked for up to six hours a day, researching and writing in their cafes.

All of the authors and scholars who wrote the books and periodicals listed in my bibliography, who provided important information about 17th century history (in both England and the Massachusetts Bay Colony).

Even though most people think of Salem as "The Witch City," with all of its touristy attractions that have nothing to do with the real story of the trials, the city (and beyond it) is home to many serious scholars who have provided knowledge and information about the subject: Emerson "Tad" Baker, Margo Burns, John Goff, Marilynne Roach, Bernie Rosenthal, Richard Trask and employees at the Salem Witch House (Jonathan Corwin's home), the Rebecca Nurse Homestead, and the Education Department of the Salem Witch Museum.

Steve Herring, the Town Historian of Framingham, MA, who gave me his copy of Samuel Sewall's diary as he was retiring and moving to Florida, around 2007. At the time I was still trying to find historical evidence of the relationship between Thomas Danforth and Sarah Cloyce. He had underlined this passage in the book:

"Satterday, October 15th. Went to Cambridge and visited Mr. Danforth, and discoursed with Him about the Witchcraft; thinks there cannot be a procedure in the Court except there be some better consent of Ministers and People. Told me of the woman's coming into his house last Sabbath-day sennight at Even." (sic)

While "the woman" is not identified, the passage inspired me to find out more. Was "the woman" Sarah Cloyce? Had he helped her escape and now was coming to his house? Since then I know that this couldn't be true, since Sarah is on record as being determined "ignoramus" by the special court in early 1693, so she wasn't released until then. However, that one little paragraph started me on a long, interesting quest.

The actress Vanessa Redgrave, who played Sarah in the PBS miniseries "Three Sovereigns for Sarah," (1984) and who agreed to help with my early fundraising efforts to save the Clayes House in Framingham.

And of course my family, especially my husband, Jeremy, and son, Xander, my father Allen, and my sisters Nancy, Kathy, Barbara and Wendi, who served as my cheerleaders throughout this whole process.

Finally, I would like to acknowledge the fact that in my novel I depict Native Americans as "red devils" and through the lens of other stereotypes. I do so because this was how they were regarded by my characters in the late 17th century. However, I want to emphasize here that tribes such as the Abenaki, Pequot, Narragansett and the Wampanoag were native to the area and had lived there for thousands of years at the time, and it was unjust and cruel for the European settlers to try to destroy their cultures. Despite many attempts at genocide on the part of the colonists, native peoples survived, and continue to thrive to this day.

Peace.